The Collected Supernatural and Weird Fiction of May Sinclair

The Collected Supernatural and Weird Fiction of May Sinclair

Eight Short Stories and Four Novellas of the Strange and Unusual Including 'The Token', 'The Victim', 'The Mahatma's Story', 'The Flaw in the Crystal' and 'The Intercessor'

May Sinclair

LEONAUR

The Collected
Supernatural and Weird
Fiction of
May Sinclair
Eight Short Stories and Four Novellas of the Strange and Unusual Including 'The
Token', 'The Victim', 'The Mahatma's Story', 'The Flaw in the Crystal' and 'The
Intercessor'
by May Sinclair

FIRST EDITION

Leonaur is an imprint of Oakpast Ltd

Copyright in this form © 2022 Oakpast Ltd

ISBN: 978-1-915234-38-4 (hardcover)
ISBN: 978-1-915234-39-1 (softcover)

http://www.leonaur.com

Publisher's Notes

Contents

Where Their Fire is Not Quenched   7

The Token   27

The Flaw in the Crystal   39

The Nature of the Evidence   93

If the Dead Knew   103

The Victim   121

The Finding of the Absolute   141

The Mahatma's Story   157

Jones's Karma   169

Heaven   181

The Intercessor   205

The Villa Désirée   245

Where Their Fire is Not Quenched

There was nobody in the orchard. Harriott Leigh went out, carefully, through the iron gate into the field. She had made the latch slip into its notch without a sound.

The path slanted widely up the field from the orchard gate to the stile under the elder tree. George Waring waited for her there.

Years afterwards, when she thought of George Waring, she smelt the sweet, hot, wine-scent of the elder flowers. Years afterwards, when she smelt elder flowers, she saw George Waring, with his beautiful, gentle face, like a poet's or a musician's, his black-blue eyes, and sleek, olive-brown hair. He was a naval lieutenant.

Yesterday he had asked her to marry him and she had consented. But her father hadn't, and she had come to tell him that and say goodbye before he left her. His ship was to sail the next day.

He was eager and excited. He couldn't believe that anything could stop their happiness, that anything he didn't want to happen could happen.

"Well?" he said.

"He's a perfect beast, George. He won't let us. He says we're too young."

"I was twenty last August," he said, aggrieved.

"And I shall be seventeen in September."

"And this is June. We're quite old, really. How long does he mean us to wait?"

"Three years."

"Three years before we can be engaged even—Why, we might be dead."

She put her arms round him to make him feel safe. They kissed; and the sweet, hot, wine-scent of the elder flowers mixed with their kisses. They stood, pressed close together, under the elder tree.

Across the yellow fields of charlock, they heard the village clock strike seven. Up in the house a gong clanged.

"Darling, I must go," she said.

"Oh stay—Stay *five* minutes."

He pressed her close. It lasted five minutes, and five more. Then he was running fast down the road to the station, while Harriott went along the field-path, slowly, struggling with her tears.

"He'll be back in three months," she said. "I can live through three months."

But he never came back. There was something wrong with the engines of his ship, the *Alexandra*. Three weeks later she went down in the Mediterranean, and George with her.

Harriott said she didn't care how soon she died now. She was quite sure it would be soon, because she couldn't live without him.

The two lines of beech trees stretched on and on, the whole length of the park, a broad green drive between. When you came to the middle, they branched off right and left in the form of a cross, and at the end of the right arm there was a white *stucco* pavilion with pillars and a three-cornered pediment like a Greek temple. At the end of the left arm, the west entrance to the park, double gates and a side door.

Harriott, on her stone seat at the back of the pavilion, could see Stephen Philpotts the very minute he came through the side door.

He had asked her to wait for him there. It was the place he always chose to read his poems aloud in. The poems were a pretext. She knew what he was going to say. And she knew what she would answer.

There were elder bushes in flower at the back of the pavilion, and Harriott thought of George Waring. She told herself that George was nearer to her now than he could ever have been, living. If she married Stephen, she would not be unfaithful, because she loved him with another part of herself. It was not as though Stephen were taking George's place. She loved Stephen with her soul, in an unearthly way.

But her body quivered like a stretched wire when the door opened and the young man came towards her down the drive under the beech trees.

She loved him; she loved his slenderness, his darkness and sallow whiteness, his black eyes lighting up with the intellectual flame, the way his black hair swept back from his forehead, the way he walked, tiptoe, as if his feet were lifted with wings.

He sat down beside her. She could see his hands tremble. She felt that her moment was coming; it had come.

"I wanted to see you alone because there's something I must say to you. I don't quite know how to begin. . . ."

Her lips parted. She panted lightly.

"You've heard me speak of Sybill Foster?"

Her voice came stammering, "N-no, Stephen. Did you?"

"Well, I didn't mean to, till I knew it was all right. I only heard yesterday."

"Heard what?"

"Why, that she'll have me. Oh, Harriott—do you know what it's like to be terribly happy?"

She knew. She had known just now, the moment before he told her. She sat there, stone-cold and stiff, listening to his raptures; listening to her own voice saying she was glad.

Ten years passed.

Harriott Leigh sat waiting in the drawing-room of a small house in Maida Vale. She had lived there ever since her father's death two years before.

She was restless. She kept on looking at the clock to see if it was four, the hour that Oscar Wade had appointed. She was not sure that he would come, after she had sent him away yesterday.

She now asked herself, why, when she had sent him away yesterday, she had let him come today. Her motives were not altogether clear. If she really meant what she had said then, she oughtn't to let him come to her again. Never again.

She had shown him plainly what she meant. She could see herself, sitting very straight in her chair, uplifted by a passionate integrity, while he stood before her, hanging his head, ashamed and beaten; she could feel again the throb in her voice as she kept on saying that she couldn't, she couldn't; he must see that she couldn't; that no, nothing would make her change her mind; she couldn't forget he had a wife; that he must think of Muriel.

To which he had answered savagely: "I needn't. That's all over. We only live together for the look of the thing."

And she, serenely, with great dignity: "And for the look of the thing, Oscar, we must leave off seeing each other. Please go."

"Do you mean it?"

"Yes. We must never see each other again."

And he had gone then, ashamed and beaten.

She could see him, squaring his broad shoulders to meet the blow. And she was sorry for him. She told herself she had been unnecessarily hard. Why shouldn't they see each other again, now he understood where they must draw the line? Until yesterday the line had never been very clearly drawn. Today she meant to ask him to forget what he had said to her. Once it was forgotten, they could go on being friends as if nothing had happened.

It was four o'clock. Half-past. Five. She had finished tea and given him up when, between the half-hour and six o'clock, he came.

He came as he had come a dozen times, with his measured, deliberate, thoughtful tread, carrying himself well braced, with a sort of held-in arrogance, his great shoulders heaving. He was a man of about forty, broad and tall, lean-flanked and short-necked, his straight, handsome features showing small and even in the big square face and in the flush that swamped it. The close-clipped, reddish-brown moustache bristled forwards from the pushed-out upper lip. His small, flat eyes shone, reddish-brown, eager and animal.

She liked to think of him when he was not there, but always at the first sight of him she felt a slight shock. Physically, he was very far from her admired ideal. So different from George Waring and Stephen Philpotts.

He sat down, facing her.

There was an embarrassed silence, broken by Oscar Wade.

"Well, Harriott, you said I could come. He seemed to be throwing the responsibility on her.

"So, I suppose you've forgiven me," he said.

"Oh, yes, Oscar, I've forgiven you."

He said she'd better show it by coming to dine with him somewhere that evening.

She could give no reason to herself for going. She simply went.

He took her to a restaurant in Soho. Oscar Wade dined well, even extravagantly, giving each dish its importance. She liked his extravagance. He had none of the mean virtues.

It was over. His flushed, embarrassed silence told her what he was thinking. But when he had seen her home, he left her at her garden gate. He had thought better of it.

She was not sure whether she were glad or sorry. She had had her moment of righteous exaltation and she had enjoyed it. But there was no joy in the weeks that followed it. She had given up Oscar Wade because she didn't want him very much; and now she wanted him furiously, perversely, because she had given him up. Though he had no resemblance to her ideal, she couldn't live without him.

She dined with him again and again, till she knew Schnebler's Restaurant by heart, the white panelled walls picked out with gold; the white pillars, and the curling gold fronds of their capitals; the Turkey carpets, blue and crimson, soft under her feet; the thick crimson velvet cushions, that clung to her skirts; the glitter of silver and glass on the innumerable white circles of the tables. And the faces of the diners, red, white, pink, brown, grey and sallow, distorted and excited; the curled mouths that twisted as they ate; the convoluted electric bulbs pointing, pointing down at them, under the red, crinkled shades. All shimmering in a thick air that the red light stained as wine stains water.

And Oscar's face, flushed with his dinner. Always, when he leaned back from the table and brooded in silence, she knew what he was thinking. His heavy eyelids would lift; she would find his eyes fixed on hers, wondering, considering.

She knew now what the end would be. She thought of George Waring, and Stephen Philpotts, and of her life, cheated. She hadn't chosen Oscar, she hadn't really wanted him; but now he had forced himself on her she couldn't afford to let him go. Since George died no man had loved her, no other man ever would. And she was sorry for him when she thought of him going from her, beaten and ashamed.

She was certain, before he was, of the end. Only she didn't know when and where and how it would come. That was what Oscar knew.

It came at the close of one of their evenings when they had dined in a private sitting-room. He said he couldn't stand the heat and noise of the public restaurant.

She went before him, up a steep, red-carpeted stair to a white door on the second landing.

From time to time, they repeated the furtive, hidden adventure. Sometimes she met him in the room above Schnebler's. Sometimes, when her maid was out, she received him at her house in Maida Vale. But that was dangerous, not to be risked too often.

Oscar declared himself unspeakably happy. Harriott was not quite sure. This was love, the thing she had never had, that she had dreamed of, hungered and thirsted for; but now she had it she was not satisfied. Always she looked for something just beyond it, some mystic, heavenly rapture, always beginning to come, that never came. There was something about Oscar that repelled her. But because she had taken him for her lover, she couldn't bring herself to admit that it was a certain coarseness. She looked another way and pretended it wasn't there. To justify herself, she fixed her mind on his good qualities, his generosity, his strength, the way he had built up his engineering business. She made him take her over his works and show her his great dynamos. She made him lend her the books he read. But always, when she tried to talk to him, he let her see that, *that* wasn't what she was there for.

"My dear girl, we haven't time," he said. "It's waste of our priceless moments."

She persisted. "There's something wrong about it all if we can't talk to each other."

He was irritated. "Women never seem to consider that a man can get all the talk he wants from other men. What's wrong is our meeting in this unsatisfactory way. We ought to live together. It's the only sane thing. I would, only I don't want to break up Muriel's home and make her miserable."

"I thought you said she wouldn't care."

"My dear, she cares for her home and her position and the children. You forget the children."

Yes. She had forgotten the children. She had forgotten Muriel. She had left off thinking of Oscar as a man with a wife and children and a home.

He had a plan. His mother-in-law was coming to stay with Muriel in October and he would get away. He would go to Paris, and Harriott should come to him there. He could say he went on business. No need to lie about it; he *had* business in Paris.

He engaged rooms in an hotel in the rue de Rivoli. They spent two weeks there.

For three days Oscar was madly in love with Harriott and Harriott with him. As she lay awake, she would turn on the light and look at him as he slept at her side. Sleep made him beautiful and innocent; it laid a fine, smooth tissue over his coarseness; it made his mouth gentle; it entirely hid his eyes.

In six days, reaction had set in. At the end of the tenth day, Harriott, returning with Oscar from Montmartre, burst into a fit of crying. When questioned, she answered wildly that the Hotel Saint Pierre was too hideously ugly; it was getting on her nerves. Mercifully Oscar explained her state as fatigue following excitement. She tried hard to believe that she was miserable because her love was purer and more spiritual than Oscar's; but all the time she knew perfectly well she had cried from pure boredom. She was in love with Oscar, and Oscar bored her. Oscar was in love with her, and she bored him. At close

12

quarters, day in and day out, each was revealed to the other as an incredible bore.

At the end of the second week, she began to doubt whether she had ever been really in love with him.

✶✶✶✶✶✶✶✶✶✶

Her passion returned for a little while after they got back to London. Freed from the unnatural strain which Paris had put on them, they persuaded themselves that their romantic temperaments were better fitted to the old life of casual adventure.

Then, gradually, the sense of danger began to wake in them. They lived in perpetual fear, face to face with all the chances of discovery. They tormented themselves and each other by imagining possibilities that they would never have considered in their first fine moments. It was as though they were beginning to ask themselves if it were, after all, worthwhile running such awful risks, for all they got out of it. Oscar still swore that if he had been free, he would have married her. He pointed out that his intentions at any rate were regular. But she asked herself: Would I marry *him?* Marriage would be the Hotel Saint Pierre all over again, without any possibility of escape. But, if she wouldn't marry him, was she in love with him? That was the test. Perhaps it was a good thing he wasn't free. Then she told herself that these doubts were morbid, and that the question wouldn't arise.

One evening Oscar called to see her. He had come to tell her that Muriel was ill.

"Seriously ill?"

"I'm afraid so. It's pleurisy. May turn to pneumonia. We shall know one way or another in the next few days."

A terrible fear seized upon Harriott. Muriel might die of her pleurisy; and if Muriel died, she would have to marry Oscar. He was looking at her queerly, as if he knew what she was thinking, and she could see that the same thought had occurred to him and that he was frightened too.

Muriel got well again; but their danger had enlightened them. Muriel's life was now inconceivably precious to them both; she stood between them and that permanent union, which they dreaded and yet would not have the courage to refuse.

After enlightenment the rupture.

It came from Oscar, one evening when he sat with her in her drawing-room.

"Harriott," he said, "do you know I'm thinking seriously of settling down?"

"How do you mean, settling down?"

"Patching it up with Muriel, poor girl.... Has it never occurred to you that this little affair of ours can't go on for ever?"

"You don't want it to go on?"

"I don't want to have any humbug about it. For God's sake, let's be straight. If it's done, it's done. Let's end it decently."

"I see. You want to get rid of me."

"That's a beastly way of putting it."

"Is there any way that isn't beastly? The whole thing's beastly. I should have thought you'd have stuck to it now you've made it what you wanted. When I haven't an ideal, I haven't a single illusion, when you've destroyed everything you didn't want."

"What didn't I want?"

"The clean, beautiful part of it. The part *I* wanted."

"My part at least was real. It was cleaner and more beautiful than all that putrid stuff you wrapped it up in. You were a hypocrite, Harriott, and I wasn't. You're a hypocrite now if you say you weren't happy with me."

"I was never really happy. Never for one moment. There was always something I missed. Something you didn't give me. Perhaps you couldn't."

"No. I wasn't spiritual enough," he sneered.

"You were not. And you made me what you were."

"Oh, I noticed that you were always very spiritual *after* you'd got what you wanted."

"What I wanted?" she cried. "Oh, my God—"

"If you ever knew what you wanted."

"What—I—wanted," she repeated, drawing out her bitterness.

"Come," he said, "why not be honest? Face facts. I was awfully gone on you. You were awfully gone on me—once. We got tired of each other and it's over. But at least you might own we had a good time while it lasted."

"A good time?"

"Good enough for me."

"For you, because for you love only means one thing. Everything that's high and noble in it you dragged down to that, till there's nothing left for us but that. That's what you made of love."

Twenty years passed.

★★★★★★★★★★

14

It was Oscar who died first, three years after the rupture. He did it suddenly one evening, falling down in a fit of apoplexy.

His death was an immense relief to Harriott. Perfect security had been impossible as long as he was alive. But now there wasn't a living soul who knew her secret.

Still, in the first moment of shock Harriott told herself that Oscar dead would be nearer to her than ever. She forgot how little she had wanted him to be near her, alive. And long before the twenty years had passed, she had contrived to persuade herself that he had never been near to her at all. It was incredible that she had ever known such a person as Oscar Wade. As for their affair, she couldn't think of Harriott Leigh as the sort of woman to whom such a thing could happen. Schnebler's and the Hotel Saint Pierre ceased to figure among prominent images of her past. Her memories, if she had allowed herself to remember, would have clashed disagreeably with the reputation for sanctity which she had now acquired.

For Harriott at fifty-two was the friend and helper of the Reverend Clement Farmer, Vicar of St. Mary the Virgin's, Maida Vale. She worked as a deaconess in his parish, wearing the uniform of a deaconess, the semireligious gown, the cloak, the bonnet and veil, the cross and rosary, the holy smile. She was also secretary to the Maida Vale and Kilburn Home for Fallen Girls.

Her moments of excitement came when Clement Farmer, the lean, austere likeness of Stephen Philpotts, in his cassock and lace-bordered surplice, issued from the vestry, when he mounted the pulpit, when he stood before the altar rails and lifted up his arms in the Benediction; her moments of ecstasy when she received the Sacrament from his hands. And she had moments of calm happiness when his study door closed on their communion. All these moments were saturated with a solemn holiness.

And they were insignificant compared with the moment of her dying.

She lay dozing in her white bed under the black crucifix with the ivory Christ. The basins and medicine bottles had been cleared from the table by her pillow; it was spread for the last rites. The priest moved quietly about the room, arranging the candles, the *Prayer Book* and the *Holy Sacrament*. Then he drew a chair to her bedside and watched with her, waiting for her to come up out of her doze.

She woke suddenly. Her eyes were fixed upon him. She had a flash of lucidity. She was dying, and her dying made her supremely important to Clement Farmer.

"Are you ready?" he asked.

"Not yet. I think I'm afraid. Make me not afraid."

He rose and lit the two candles on the altar. He took down the crucifix from the wall and stood it against the foot-rail of the bed.

She sighed. That was not what she had wanted.

"You will not be afraid now," he said.

"I'm not afraid of the hereafter. I suppose you get used to it. Only it may be terrible just at first."

"Our first state will depend very much on what we are thinking of at our last hour."

"There'll be my—confession," she said.

"And after it you will receive the Sacrament. Then you will have your mind fixed firmly upon God and your Redeemer. . ... Do you feel able to make your confession now, Sister? Everything is ready."

Her mind went back over her past and found Oscar Wade there. She wondered: Should she confess to him about Oscar Wade? One moment she thought it was possible; the next she knew that she couldn't. She could not. It wasn't necessary. For twenty years he had not been part of her life. No. She wouldn't confess about Oscar Wade. She had been guilty of other sins.

She made a careful selection.

"I have cared too much for the beauty of this world. . . . I have failed in charity to my poor girls. Because of my intense repugnance to their sin. . . . I have thought, often, about—people I love, when I should have been thinking about God."

After that she received the Sacrament.

"Now," he said, "there is nothing to be afraid of."

"I won't be afraid if—if you would hold my hand."

He held it. And she lay still a long time, with her eyes shut. Then he heard her murmuring something. He stooped close.

"This—is—dying. I thought it would be horrible. And it's bliss. . . . . . .Bliss."

The priest's hand slackened, as if at the bidding of some wonder. She gave a weak cry.

"Oh—don't let me go."

His grasp tightened.

"Try," he said, "to think about God. Keep on looking at the crucifix."

"If I look," she whispered, "you won't let go my hand?"

16

"I will not let you go."

He held it till it was wrenched from him in the last agony.

★★★★★★★★★★

She lingered for some hours in the room where these things had happened.

Its aspect was familiar and yet unfamiliar, and slightly repugnant to her. The altar, the crucifix, the lighted candles, suggested some tremendous and awful experience the details of which she was not able to recall. She seemed to remember that they had been connected in some way with the sheeted body on the bed; but the nature of the connection was not clear; and she did not associate the dead body with herself. When the nurse came in and laid it out, she saw that it was the body of a middle-aged woman. Her own living body was that of a young woman of about thirty-two.

Her mind had no past and no future, no sharp-edged, coherent memories, and no idea of anything to be done next.

Then, suddenly, the room began to come apart before her eyes, to split into shafts of floor and furniture and ceiling that shifted and were thrown by their commotion into different planes. They leaned slanting at every possible angle; they crossed and overlaid each other with a transparent mingling of dislocated perspectives, like reflections fallen on an interior seen behind glass.

The bed and the sheeted body slid away somewhere out of sight. She was standing by the door that still remained in position.

She opened it and found herself in the street, outside a building of yellowish-grey brick and freestone, with a tall slated spire. Her mind came together with a palpable click of recognition. This object was the Church of St. Mary the Virgin, Maida Vale. She could hear the droning of the organ. She opened the door and slipped in.

She had gone back into a definite space and time, and recovered a certain limited section of coherent memory. She remembered the rows of pitch-pine benches, with their Gothic peaks and mouldings; the stone-coloured walls and pillars with their chocolate stencilling; the hanging rings of lights along the aisles of the nave; the high altar with its lighted candles, and the polished brass cross, twinkling. These things were somehow permanent and real, adjusted to the image that now took possession of her.

She knew what she had come there for. The service was over. The choir had gone from the chancel; the sacristan moved before the altar, putting out the candles. She walked up the middle aisle to a seat that she knew under the pulpit. She knelt down and covered her face with her hands. Peeping sideways through her fingers, she could see the door of the vestry on her left at the end of the north aisle. She watched it steadily.

Up in the organ loft the organist drew out the Recessional, slowly and softly, to its end in the two solemn, vibrating chords.

The vestry door opened and Clement Farmer came out, dressed in his black cassock. He passed before her, close, close outside the bench where she knelt. He paused at the opening. He was waiting for her. There was something he had to say.

She stood up and went towards him. He still waited. He didn't move to make way for her. She came close, closer than she had ever come to him, so close that his features grew indistinct. She bent her head back, peering, short-sightedly, and found herself looking into Oscar Wade's face.

He stood still, horribly still, and close, barring her passage.

She drew back; his heaving shoulders followed her. He leaned forward, covering her with his eyes. She opened her mouth to scream and no sound came.

She was afraid to move lest he should move with her. The heaving of his shoulders terrified her.

One by one the lights in the side aisles were going out. The lights in the middle aisle would go next. They had gone. If she didn't get away, she would be shut up with him there, in the appalling darkness.

She turned and moved towards the north aisle, groping, steadying herself by the book ledge.

When she looked back, Oscar Wade was not there.

Then she remembered that Oscar Wade was dead. Therefore, what she had seen was not Oscar; it was his ghost. He was dead; dead seventeen years ago. She was safe from him for ever.

★★★★★★★★★★

When she came out on to the steps of the church, she saw that the road it stood in had changed. It was not the road she remembered. The pavement on this side was raised slightly and covered in. It ran under a succession of arches. It was a long gallery walled with glittering shop windows on one side; on the other a line of tall grey columns divided it from the street.

She was going along the arcades of the rue de Rivoli. Ahead of her she could see the edge of an immense grey pillar jutting out. That was the porch of the Hotel Saint Pierre. The revolving glass doors swung forward to receive her; she crossed the grey, sultry vestibule under the pillared arches. She knew it. She knew the porter's shining, wine-coloured mahogany pen on her left, and the shining wine-coloured mahogany barrier of the clerk's bureau on her right; she made straight for the great grey carpeted staircase; she climbed the endless flights that turned round and round the caged-in shaft of the well, past the latticed doors of the lift, and came up on to a landing that she knew, and into the long, ash-grey, foreign corridor lit by a dull window at one end.

It was there that the horror of the place came on her. She had no longer any memory of St. Mary's Church, so that she was unaware of her backward course through time. All space and time were here.

She remembered she had to go to the left, the left. But there was something there; where the corridor turned by the window; at the end of all the corridors. If she went the other way, she would escape it.

The corridor stopped there. A blank wall. She was driven back past the stairhead to the left.

At the corner, by the window, she turned down another long ash-grey corridor on her right, and to the right again where the night-light sputtered on the table-flap at the turn.

This third corridor was dark and secret and depraved. She knew the soiled walls and the warped door at the end. There was a sharp-pointed streak of light at the top. She could see the number on it now, 107.

Something had happened there. If she went in it would happen again.

Oscar Wade was in the room waiting for her behind the closed door. She felt him moving about in there. She leaned forward, her ear to the key-hole, and listened. She could hear the measured, deliberate, thoughtful footsteps. They were coming from the bed to the door.

She turned and ran; her knees gave way under her she sank and ran on, down the long grey corridors and the stairs, quick and blind, a hunted beast seeking for cover, hearing his feet coming after her.

The revolving doors caught her and pushed her out into the street.

★★★★★★★★★★

The strange quality of her state was this, that it had no time. She remembered dimly that there had once been a thing called time; but she had forgotten altogether what it was like. She was aware of things happening and about to happen; she fixed them by the place they occupied, and measured their duration by the space she went through.

So now she thought: If I could only go back and get to the place where it hadn't happened.

To get back farther—

She was walking now on a white road that went between broad grass borders. To the right and left were the long raking lines of the hills, curve after curve, shimmering in a thin mist.

The road dropped to the green valley. It mounted the humped bridge over the river. Beyond it she saw the twin gables of the grey house pricked up over the high, grey garden wall. The tall iron gate stood in front of it between the ball-topped stone pillars.

And now she was in a large, low-ceilinged room with drawn blinds. She was standing before the wide double bed. It was her father's bed. The dead body, stretched out in the middle under the drawn white sheet, was her father's body.

The outline of the sheet sank from the peak of the upturned toes to the shin bone, and from the high bridge of the nose to the chin.

She lifted the sheet and folded it back across the breast of the dead man. The face she saw then was Oscar Wade's face, stilled and smoothed in the innocence of sleep, the supreme innocence of death. She stared at it, fascinated, in a cold, pitiless joy.

Oscar was dead.

She remembered how he used to lie like that beside her in the room in the Hotel Saint Pierre, on his back with his hands folded on his waist, his mouth half open, his big chest rising and falling. If he was dead, it would never happen again. She would be safe.

The dead face frightened her, and she was about to cover it up again when she was aware of a light heaving, a rhythmical rise and fall. As she drew the sheet up tighter, the hands under it began to struggle convulsively, the broad ends of the fingers appeared above the edge, clutching it to keep it down. The mouth opened; the eyes opened; the whole face stared back at her in a look of agony and horror.

Then the body drew itself forwards from the hips and sat up, its eyes peering into her eyes; he and she remained for an instant motion-less, each held there by the other's fear.

Suddenly she broke away, turned and ran, out of the room, out of the house.

She stood at the gate, looking up and down the road, not know-ing by which way she must go to escape Oscar. To the right, over the bridge and up the hill and across the downs she would come to the arcades of the rue de Rivoli and the dreadful grey corridors of the hotel. To the left the road went through the village.

If she could get further back, she would be safe, out of Oscar's reach. Standing by her father's death-bed she had been young, but not young enough. She must get back to the place where she was younger still, to the Park and the green drive under the beech trees and the white pavilion at the cross. She knew how to find it. At the end of the village the high road ran right and left, east and west, under the Park walls; the south gate stood there at the top, looking down the narrow street.

She ran towards it through the village, past the long grey barns of Goodyer's farm, past the grocer's shop, past the yellow front and blue sign of the "Queen's Head," past the post office, with its one black window blinking under its vine, past the church and the yew-trees in the churchyard, to where the south gate made a delicate black pattern on the green grass.

These things appeared insubstantial, drawn back behind a sheet of air that shimmered over them like thin glass. They opened out, floated past and away from her; and instead of the high road and park walls she saw a London street of dingy white *façades*, and instead of the south gate the swinging glass doors of Schnebler's Restaurant.

★★★★★★★★★★

The glass doors swung open and she passed into the restaurant. The scene beat on her with the hard impact of reality: the white and gold panels, the white pillars and their curling gold capitals, the white circles of the tables, glittering, the flushed faces of the diners, moving mechanically.

She was driven forward by some irresistible compulsion to a table in the corner, where a man sat alone. The table napkin he was using hid his mouth, and jaw, and chest; and she was not sure of the upper part of the face above the straight, drawn edge. It dropped; and she saw Oscar Wade's face. She came to him, dragged, without power to resist; she sat down beside him, and he leaned to her over the table; she could feel the warmth of his red, congested face; the smell of wine floated towards her on his thick whisper.

"I knew you would come."

She ate and drank with him in silence, nibbling and sipping slowly, staving off the abominable moment it would end in.

At last, they got up and faced each other. His long bulk stood before her, above her; she could almost feel the vibration of its power.

"Come," he said. "Come."

And she went before him, slowly, slipping out through the maze of

21

the tables, hearing behind her Oscar's measured, deliberate, thoughtful tread. The steep, red-carpeted staircase rose up before her.

She swerved from it, but he turned her back.

"You know the way," he said.

At the top of the flight, she found the white door of the room she knew. She knew the long windows guarded by drawn muslin blinds; the gilt looking-glass over the chimney-piece that reflected Oscar's head and shoulders grotesquely between two white porcelain babies with bulbous limbs and garlanded loins, she knew the sprawling stain on the drab carpet by the table, the shabby, infamous couch behind the screen.

They moved about the room, turning and turning in it like beasts in a cage, uneasy, inimical, avoiding each other.

At last, they stood still, he at the window, she at the door, the length of the room between.

"It's no good your getting away like that," he said. "There couldn't be any other end to it—to what we did."

"But that *was* ended."

"Ended there, but not here."

"Ended forever. We've done with it forever."

"We haven't. We've got to begin again. And go on. And go on."

"Oh, no. No. Anything but that."

"There isn't anything else."

"We can't. We can't. Don't you remember how it bored us?"

"Remember? Do you suppose I'd touch you if I could help it?... That's what we're here for. We must. We must."

"No. No. I shall get away—now."

She turned to the door to open it.

"You can't," he said. "The door's locked,"

"Oscar—what did you do that for?"

"We always did it. Don't you remember?"

She turned to the door again and shook it; she beat on it with her hands.

"It's no use, Harriott. If you got out now, you'd only have to come back again. You might stave it off for an hour or so, but what's that in an immortality?"

"Immortality?"

"That's what we're in for."

"Time enough to talk about immortality when we're dead.... Ah—"

22

They were being drawn towards each other across the room, moving slowly, like figures in some monstrous and appalling dance, their heads thrown back over their shoulders, their faces turned from the horrible approach. Their arms rose slowly, heavy with intolerable reluctance; they stretched them out towards each other, aching, as if they held up an overpowering weight. Their feet dragged and were drawn.

Suddenly her knees sank under her; she shut her eyes; all her being went down before him in darkness and terror.

★★★★★★★★★★

It was over. She had got away, she was going back, back, to the green drive of the Park, between the beech trees, where Oscar had never been, where he would never find her. When she passed through the south gate her memory became suddenly young and clean. She forgot the rue de Rivoli and the Hotel Saint Pierre; she forgot Schnebler's Restaurant and the room at the top of the stairs. She was back in her youth. She was Harriott Leigh going to wait for Stephen Philpotts in the pavilion opposite the west gate. She could feel herself, a slender figure moving fast over the grass between the lines of the great beech trees. The freshness of her youth was upon her.

She came to the heart of the drive where it branched right and left in the form of a cross. At the end of the right arm the white Greek temple, with its pediment and pillars, gleamed against the wood.

She was sitting on their seat at the back of the pavilion, watching the side door that Stephen would come in by.

The door was pushed open; he came towards her, light and young, skimming between the beech trees with his eager, tiptoeing stride. She rose up to meet him. She gave a cry.

"Stephen!"

It had been Stephen. She had seen him coming. But the man who stood before her between the pillars of the pavilion was Oscar Wade.

And now she was walking along the field-path that slanted from the orchard door to the stile; further and further back, to where young George Waring waited for her under the elder tree. The smell of the elder flowers came to her over the field. She could feel on her lips and in all her body the sweet, innocent excitement of her youth.

"George, oh, George!"

As she went along the field-path she had seen him. But the man who stood waiting for her under the elder tree was Oscar Wade.

"I told you it's no use getting away, Harriott. Every path brings you back to me. You'll find me at every turn."

"But how did you get *here?*"

"As I got into the pavilion. As I got into your father's room, on to his death bed. Because I *was* there. I am in all your memories."

"My memories are innocent. How could you take my father's place, and Stephen's, and George Waring's? You?"

"Because I did take them."

"Never. My love for *them* was innocent."

"Your love for me was part of it. You think the past affects the future. Has it never struck you that the future may affect the past? In your innocence there was the beginning of your sin. You *were* what you *were to be*."

"I shall get away," she said.

"And, this time, I shall go with you."

The stile, the elder tree, and the field floated away from her. She was going under the beech trees down the Park drive towards the south gate and the village, slinking close to the right-hand row of trees. She was aware that Oscar Wade was going with her under the left-hand row, keeping even with her, step by step, and tree by tree. And presently there was grey pavement under her feet and a row of grey pillars on her right hand. They were walking side by side down the rue de Rivoli towards the hotel.

They were sitting together now on the edge of the dingy white bed. Their arms hung by their sides, heavy and limp, their heads drooped, averted. Their passion weighed on them with the unbearable, unescapable boredom of immortality.

"Oscar—how long will it last?"

"I can't tell you. I don't know whether this is one moment of eternity, or the eternity of one moment."

"It must end some time," she said. "Life doesn't go on for ever. We shall die."

"Die? We *have* died. Don't you know what this is? Don't you know where you are? This is death. We're dead, Harriott. We're in hell."

"Yes. There can't be anything worse than this."

"This isn't the worst. We're not quite dead yet, as long as we've life in us to turn and run and get away from each other; as long as we can escape into our memories. But when you've got back to the farthest memory of all and there's nothing beyond it—When there's no memory but this—

"In the last hell we shall not run away any longer; we shall find no more roads, no more passages, no more open doors. We shall have no

24

need to look for each other.

"In the last death we shall be shut up in this room, behind that locked door, together. We shall lie here together, for ever and ever, joined so fast that even God can't put us asunder. We shall be one flesh and one spirit, one sin repeated for ever, and ever; spirit loathing flesh, flesh loathing spirit; you and I loathing each other."

"Why? Why?" she cried.

"Because that's all that's left us. That's what you made of love."

****

The darkness came down swamping, it blotted out the room. She was walking along a garden path between high borders of phlox and larkspur and lupin. They were taller than she was, their flowers swayed and nodded above her head. She tugged at the tall stems and had no strength to break them. She was a little thing.

She said to herself then that she was safe. She had gone back so far that she was a child again; she had the blank innocence of childhood. To be a child, to go small under the heads of the lupins, to be blank and innocent, without memory, was to be safe.

The walk led her out through a yew hedge on to a bright green lawn. In the middle of the lawn there was a shallow round pond in a ring of rockery cushioned with small flowers, yellow and white and purple. Goldfish swam in the olive brown water. She would be safe when she saw the goldfish swimming towards her. The old one with the white scales would come up first, pushing up his nose, making bubbles in the water.

At the bottom of the lawn there was a privet hedge cut by a broad path that went through the orchard. She knew what she would find there; her mother was in the orchard. She would lift her up in her arms to play with the hard red balls of the apples that hung from the tree. She had got back to the farthest memory of all; there was nothing beyond it.

There would be an iron gate in the wall of the orchard. It would lead into a field.

Something was different here, something that frightened her. An ash-grey door instead of an iron gate.

She pushed it open and came into the last corridor of the Hotel Saint Pierre.

The Token

I have only known one absolutely adorable woman, and that was my brother's wife, Cicely Dunbar. Sisters-in-law do not, I think, invariably adore each other, and I am aware that my chief merit in Cicely's eyes was that I am Donald's sister; but for me there was no question of extraneous quality—it was all pure Cicely.

And how Donald—— But then, like all the Dunbars, Donald suffers from being Scottish, so that, if he has a feeling, he makes it a point of honour to pretend he hasn't it. I daresay he let himself go a bit during his courtship, when he was not, strictly speaking, himself; but after he had once married her, I think he would have died rather than have told Cicely in so many words that he loved her. And Cicely wanted to be told. You say she ought to have known without telling? You don't know Donald. You can't conceive the perverse ingenuity he could put into hiding his affection. He has that peculiar temper—I think it's Scottish—that delights in snubbing and fault-finding and defeating expectation. If he knows you want him to do a thing, that alone is reason enough with Donald for not doing it. And my sister, who was as transparent as white crystal, was never able to conceal a want. So that Donald could, as we said, "have" her at every turn.

And, then, I don't think my brother really knew how ill she was. He didn't want to know. Besides, he was so wrapt up in trying to finish his *Development of Social Economics* (which, by the way, he hasn't finished yet) that he had no eyes to see what we all saw: that, the way her poor little heart was going, Cicely couldn't have very long to live.

Of course, he understood that this was why, in those last months, they had to have separate rooms. And this in the first year of their marriage when he was still violently in love with her. I keep those two facts firmly in my mind when I try to excuse Donald; for it was the main cause of that unkindness and perversity which I find it so hard to forgive. Even now, when I think how he used to discharge it on the poor little thing, as if it had been her fault, I have to remind myself that the lamb's innocence made her a little trying.

She couldn't understand why Donald didn't want to have her with him in his library any more while he read or wrote. It seemed to her sheer cruelty to shut her out now when she was ill, seeing that, before she was ill, she had always had her chair by the fireplace, where she would sit over her book or her embroidery for hours without speaking, hardly daring to breathe lest she should interrupt him. Now was the time, she thought, when she might expect a little indulgence.

Do you suppose that Donald would give his feelings as an explanation? Not he. They were his feelings, and he wouldn't talk about them; and he never explained anything you didn't understand.

That—her wanting to sit with him in the library—was what they had the awful quarrel about, the day before she died: that and the paperweight, the precious paperweight that he wouldn't let anybody touch because George Meredith had given it him. It was a brass block, surmounted by a white alabaster Buddha painted and gilt. And it had an inscription: *To Donald Dunbar, from George Meredith. In Affectionate Regard.*

My brother was extremely attached to this paperweight, partly, I'm afraid, because it proclaimed his intimacy with the great man. For this reason, it was known in the family ironically as the Token.

It stood on Donald's writing-table at his elbow, so near the ink-pot that the white Buddha had received a splash or two. And this evening Cicely had come in to us in the library, and had annoyed Donald by staying in it when he wanted her to go. She had taken up the Token, and was cleaning it to give herself a pretext. She died after the quarrel they had then.

It began by Donald shouting at her.

"What are you doing with that paperweight?"

"Only getting the ink off."

I can see her now, the darling. She had wetted the corner of her handkerchief with her little pink tongue and was rubbing the Buddha. Her hands had begun to tremble when he shouted.

"Put it down, can't you? I've told you not to touch my things."

"*You* inked him," she said. She was giving one last rub as he rose, threatening.

"Put—it—down."

28

And, poor child, she did put it down. Indeed, she dropped it at his feet.

"Oh!" she cried out, and stooped quickly and picked it up. Her large tear-glassed eyes glanced at him, frightened.

"He isn't broken."

"No thanks to you," he growled.

"You beast! You know I'd die rather than break anything you care about."

"It'll be broken someday, if you *will* come meddling."

I couldn't bear it. I said, "You mustn't yell at her like that. You know she can't stand it. You'll make her ill again."

That sobered him for a moment.

"I'm sorry," he said; but he made it sound as if he wasn't.

"If you're sorry," she persisted, "you might let me stay with you. I'll be as quiet as a mouse."

"No; I don't want you—I can't work with you in the room."

"You can work with Helen."

"You're not Helen."

"He only means he's not in love with *me*, dear."

"He means I'm no use to him. I know I'm not. I can't even sit on his manuscripts and keep them down. He cares more for that damned paperweight than he does for me."

"Well—George Meredith gave it me."

"And nobody gave you me. I gave myself."

That worked up his devil again. He *had* to torment her.

"It can't have cost you much," he said. "And I may remind you that the paperweight has *some* intrinsic value."

With that he left her.

"What's he gone out for?" she asked me.

"Because he's ashamed of himself, I suppose," I said. "Oh, Cicely, why *will* you answer him? You know what he is."

"No!" she said passionately—"that's what I don't know. I never have known."

"At least you know he's in love with you."

"He has a queer way of showing it, then. He never does anything but stamp and shout and find fault with me—all about an old paperweight!"

She was caressing it as she spoke, stroking the alabaster Buddha as if it had been a live thing.

"His poor Buddha. Do you think it'll break if I stroke it? Better not. . . . Honestly, Helen, I'd rather die than hurt anything he really cared for. Yet look how he hurts me."

"Some men *must* hurt the things they care for."

"I wouldn't mind his hurting, if only I knew he cared. Helen—I'd give anything to know."

"I think you might know."

"I don't! I don't!"

"Well, you'll know some day."

"Never! He won't tell me."

"He's Scotch, my dear. It would kill him to tell you."

"Then how'm I to know! If I died tomorrow I should die not knowing."

And that night, not knowing, she died.

She died because she had never really known.

2

We never talked about her. It was not my brother's way. Words hurt him, to speak or to hear them.

He had become more morose than ever, but less irritable, the source of his irritation being gone. Though he plunged into work as another man might have plunged into dissipation, to drown the thought of her, you could see that he had no longer any interest in it; he no longer loved it. He attacked it with a fury that had more hate in it than love. He would spend the greater part of the day and the long evenings shut up in his library, only going out for a short walk an hour before dinner. You could see that soon all spontaneous impulses would be checked in him and he would become the creature of habit and routine.

I tried to rouse him, to shake him up out of his deadly groove; but it was no use. The first effort—for he did make efforts—exhausted him, and he sank back into it again.

But he liked to have me with him; and all the time that I could spare from my housekeeping and gardening I spent in the library. I think he didn't like to be left alone there in the place where they had the quarrel that killed her; and I noticed that the cause of it, the Token, had disappeared from his table.

And all her things, everything that could remind him of her, had been put away. It was the dead burying its dead.

Only the chair she had loved remained in its place by the side of the hearth—*her* chair, if you could call it hers when she wasn't allowed to sit in it. It was always empty, for by tacit consent we both avoided it.

We would sit there for hours at a time without speaking, while he worked and I read or sewed. I never dared to ask him whether he sometimes had, as I had, the sense of Cicely's presence there, in that room which she had so longed to enter, from which she had been so cruelly shut out. You couldn't tell what he felt or didn't feel. My brother's face was a heavy, sombre mask; his back, bent over the writing-table, a wall behind which he hid himself.

You must know that twice in my life I have more than *felt* these presences; I have seen them. This may be because I am on both sides a Highland Celt, and my mother had the same uncanny gift. I had never spoken of these appearances to Donald because he would have put it all down to what he calls my hysterical fancy. And I am sure that if he ever felt or saw anything himself, he would never own it.

I ought to explain that each time the vision was premonitory of a death (in Cicely's case I had no such warning), and each time it only lasted for a second; also, that, though I am certain I was wide awake each time, it is open to anybody to say I was asleep and dreamed it. The queer thing was that I was neither frightened nor surprised.

And so, I was neither surprised nor frightened now, the first evening that I saw her.

It was in the early autumn twilight, about six o'clock. I was sitting in my place in front of the fireplace; Donald was in his armchair on my left, smoking a pipe, as usual, before the lamplight drove him out of doors into the dark.

I had had so strong a sense of Cicely's being there in the room that I felt nothing but a sudden sacred pang that was half joy when I looked up and saw her sitting in her chair on my right.

The phantasm was perfect and vivid, as if it had been flesh and blood. I should have thought that it was Cicely herself if I hadn't known that she was dead. She wasn't looking at me; her face was turned to Donald with that longing, wondering look it used to have, searching his face for the secret that he kept from her.

I looked at Donald. His chin was sunk a little, the pipe drooping from the corner of his mouth. He was heavy, absorbed in his smoking. It was clear that he did not see what I saw.

And whereas those other phantasms that I told you about disappeared at once, *this* lasted some little time, and always with its eyes fixed on Donald. It even lasted while Donald stirred, while he stooped forward, knocking the ashes out of his pipe against the hob, while he sighed, stretched himself, turned, and left the room. Then, as the door shut behind him, the whole figure went out suddenly—not flickering, but like a light you switch off.

I saw it again the next evening and the next, at the same time and in the same place, and with the same look turned towards Donald. And again, I was sure that he did not see it. But I thought, from his uneasy sighing and stretching, that he had some sense of something there.

No; I was not frightened. I was glad. You see, I loved Cicely. I remember thinking, "At last, at last, you poor darling, you've got in. And you can stay as long as you like now. He can't turn you away."

The first few times I saw her just as I have said. I would look up and find the phantasm there, sitting in her chair. And it would disappear suddenly when Donald left the room. Then I knew I was alone.

But as I grew used to its presence, or perhaps as it grew used to mine and found out that I was not afraid of it, that indeed I loved to have it there, it came, I think, to trust me, so that I was made aware of all its movements. I would see it coming across the room from the doorway, making straight for its desired place, and settling in a little curled-up posture of satisfaction, appeased, as if it had expected opposition that it no longer found. Yet that it was not happy, I could still see by its look at Donald. *That* never changed. It was as uncertain of him now as she had been in her lifetime.

Up till now, the sixth or seventh time I had seen it, I had no clue to the secret of its appearance; and its movements seemed to me mysterious and without purpose. Only two things were clear: it was Donald that it came for—the instant he went it disappeared; and I never once saw it when I was alone. And always it chose this room and this hour before the lights came, when he sat doing nothing. It was clear also that he never saw it.

But that it was there with him sometimes when I was not, I knew; for, more than once, things on Donald's writing-table, books or papers, would be moved out of their places, though never beyond reach; and he would ask me whether I had touched them.

"Either you lie," he would say, "or I'm mistaken. I could have sworn I put those notes on the *left*-hand side; and they aren't there now."

And once—that was wonderful—I *saw*, yes, I saw her come and push the lost thing under his hand. And all he said was, "Well, I'm—I could have sworn—"

For whether it had gained a sense of security, or whether its purpose was now finally fixed, it began to move regularly about the room, and its movements had evidently a reason and an aim.

It was looking for something.

One evening we were all there in our places, Donald silent in his chair and I in mine, and it seated in its attitude of wonder and of waiting, when suddenly I saw Donald looking at me.

"Helen," he said, "what are you staring for like that?"

I started. I had forgotten that the direction of my eyes would be bound, sooner or later, to betray me.

I heard myself stammer, "W—w—was I staring?"

"Yes. I wish you wouldn't."

I knew what he meant. He didn't want me to keep on looking at that chair; he didn't want to know that I was thinking of her. I bent my head closer over my sewing, so that I no longer had the phantasm in sight.

It was then I was aware that it had risen and was crossing the hearthrug. It stopped at Donald's knees, and stood there, gazing at him with a look so intent and fixed that I could not doubt that this had some significance. I saw it put out its hand and touch him; and, though Donald sighed and shifted his position, I could tell that he had neither seen nor felt anything.

It turned to me then—and this was the first time it had given any sign that it was conscious of my presence—it turned on me a look of supplication, such supplication as I had seen on my sister's face in her lifetime, when she could do nothing with him and implored me to intercede. At the same time three words formed themselves in my brain with a sudden, quick impulsion, as if I had heard them cried.

"Speak to him—speak to him!"

I knew now what it wanted. It was trying to make itself seen by him, to make itself felt, and it was in anguish at finding that it could not.

It knew then that I saw it, and the idea had come to it that it could make use of me to get through to him.

I think I must have guessed even then what it had come for.

I said, "You asked me what I was staring at, and I lied. I was looking at Cicely's chair."

I saw him wince at the name.

"Because," I went on, "I don't know how you feel, but I always feel as if she were there."

He said nothing; but he got up, as though to shake off the oppression of the memory I had evoked, and stood leaning on the chimney-piece with his back to me.

The phantasm retreated to its place, where it kept its eyes fixed on him as before.

I was determined to break down his defences, to make him say something it might hear, give some sign that it would understand.

"Donald, do you think it's a good thing, a *kind* thing, never to talk about her?"

"Kind? Kind to whom?"

"To yourself, first of all."

"You can leave me out of it."

"To me, then."

"What's it got to do with you?" His voice was as hard and cutting as he could make it.

"Everything," I said. "You forget, I loved her."

He was silent. He did at least respect my love for her.

"But that wasn't what she wanted."

That hurt him. I could feel him stiffen under it.

"You see, Donald," I persisted, "*I* like thinking about her."

It was cruel of me; but I *had* to break him.

"You can think as much as you like," he said, "provided you stop talking."

"All the same, it's as bad for you," I said, "as it is for me, not talking."

"I don't care if it is bad for me. I *can't* talk about her, Helen. I don't want to."

"How do you know," I said, "it isn't bad for *her?*"

"For *her?*"

I could see I had roused him.

"Yes. If she really is there, all the time."

"How d'you mean, *there?*"

"Here—in this room. I tell you I can't get over that feeling that she's here."

"Oh, feel, feel," he said; "but don't talk to me about it!"

And he left the room, flinging himself out in anger. And instantly her flame went out.

I thought, "How he must have hurt her!" It was the old thing over again: I trying to break him down, to make him show her; he beating us both off, punishing us both. You see, I knew now what she had come back for: she had come back to find out whether he loved her. With a longing unquenched by death, she had come back for certainty. And now, as always, my clumsy interference had only made him more hard, more obstinate. I thought, "If only he could see her! But as long as he beats her off, he never will."

Still, if I could once get him to believe that she was there—

I made up my mind that the next time I saw the phantasm I would tell him.

The next evening and the next its chair was empty, and I judged that it was keeping away, hurt by what it had heard the last time.

But the third evening we were hardly seated before I saw it.

It was sitting up, alert and observant, not staring at Donald as it used, but looking round the room, as if searching for something that it missed.

"Donald," I said, "if I told you that Cicely is in the room now, I suppose you wouldn't believe me?"

"Is it likely?"

"No. All the same, I see her as plainly as I see you."

The phantasm rose and moved to his side.

"She's standing close beside you."

And now it moved and went to the writing-table. I turned and followed its movements. It slid its open hands over the table, touching everything, unmistakably feeling for something it believed to be there.

I went on. "She's at the writing-table now. She's looking for something."

It stood back, baffled and distressed. Then suddenly it began opening and shutting the drawers, without a sound, searching each one in turn.

I said, "Oh, she's trying the drawers now!"

Donald stood up. He was not looking at the place where it was. He was looking hard at me, in anxiety and a sort of fright. I supposed that was why he remained unaware of the opening and shutting of the drawers.

It continued its desperate searching.

The bottom drawer stuck fast. I saw it pull and shake it, and stand back again, baffled.

"It's locked," I said.

"What's locked?"

"That bottom drawer."

"Nonsense! It's nothing of the kind."

"It is, I tell you. Give me the key. Oh, Donald, give it me!"

He shrugged his shoulders; but all the same he felt in his pockets for the key, which he gave me with a little teasing gesture, as if he humoured a child.

I unlocked the drawer, pulled it out to its full length, and there, thrust away at the back, out of sight, I found the Token.

I had not seen it since the day of Cicely's death.

"Who put it there?" I asked.

"I did."

"Well, that's what she was looking for," I said.

I held out the Token to him on the palm of my hand, as if it were the proof that I had seen her.

"Helen," he said gravely, "I think you must be ill."

"You think so? I'm not so ill that I don't know what you put it away for," I said. "It was because she thought you cared for it more than you did for her."

"You can remind me of that? There must be something very badly wrong with you, Helen," he said.

"Perhaps. Perhaps I only want to know what she wanted. . . . You *did* care for her, Donald?"

I couldn't see the phantasm now, but I could feel it, close, close, vibrating, palpitating, as I drove him.

"Care?" he cried. "I was mad with caring for her! And she knew it."

"She didn't. She wouldn't be here now if she knew."

At that he turned from me to his station by the chimney-piece. I followed him there.

"What are you going to do about it?" I said.

"Do about it?"

"What are you going to do with this?"

I thrust the Token close towards him. He drew back, staring at it with a look of concentrated hate and loathing.

"Do with it?" he said. "The damned thing killed her! This is what I'm going to do with it—"

He snatched it from my hand and hurled it with all his force against the bars of the grate. The Buddha fell, broken to bits, among the ashes.

Then I heard him give a short, groaning cry. He stepped forward, opening his arms, and I saw the phantasm slide between them. For a second it stood there, folded to his breast; then suddenly, before our eyes, it collapsed in a shining heap, a flicker of light on the floor, at his feet.

Then that went out too.

I never saw it again.

Neither did my brother. But I didn't know this till some time afterwards; for, somehow, we hadn't cared to speak about it. And in the end, it was he who spoke first.

We were sitting together in that room, one evening in November, when he said, suddenly and irrelevantly:

"Helen—do you never see her now?"

"No," I said—"Never!"

"Do you think, then, she doesn't come?"

"Why should she?" I said. "She found what she came for. She knows what she wanted to know."

"And that—was what?"

"Why, that you loved her."

His eyes had a queer, submissive, wistful look.

"You think that was why she came back?" he said.

The Flaw in the Crystal

1

It was Friday, the day he always came, if (so she safeguarded it) he
was to come at all. They had left it that way in the beginning, that it
should be open to him to come or not to come. They had not even settled that it should be Fridays, but it always was, the week-end being the
only time when he could get away; the only time, he had explained to
Agatha Verrall, when getting away excited no remark. He had to, or he
would have broken down. Agatha called it getting away from "things;"
but she knew that there was only one thing, his wife Bella.

To be wedded to a mass of furious and malignant nerves (which
was all that poor Bella was now) simply meant destruction to a man
like Rodney Lanyon. Rodney's own nerves were not as strong as they
had been, after ten years of Bella's. It had been understood for long
enough (understood even by Bella) that if he couldn't have his week-
ends he was done for; he couldn't possibly have stood the torment and
the strain of her.

Of course, she didn't know he spent the greater part of them with
Agatha Verrall. It was not to be desired that she should know. Her
obtuseness helped them. Even in her younger and saner days she had
failed, persistently, to realise any profound and poignant thing that
touched him; so, by the mercy of heaven she had never realised Agatha
Verrall. She used to say she had never seen anything *in* Agatha, which
amounted, as he once told her, to not seeing Agatha at all. Still less
could she have compassed any vision of the tie—the extraordinary,
intangible, immaterial tie that held them.

Sometimes, at the last moment, his escape to Agatha would prove
impossible; so, they had left it further that he was to send her no forewarning; he was to come when and as he could. He could always get
a room in the village inn or at the farm nearby, and in Agatha's house

he would find his place ready for him, the place which had become his refuge, his place of peace.

There was no need to prepare her. She was never not prepared. It was as if by her preparedness, by the absence of preliminaries, of adjustments and arrangements, he was always there, lodged in the innermost chamber. She had set herself apart; she had swept herself bare and scoured herself clean for him. Clean she had to be; clean from the desire that he should come; clean, above all, from the thought, the knowledge she now had, that she could make him come.

For if she had given herself up to *that*. . . .

But she never had; never since the knowledge came to her; since she discovered, wonderfully, by a divine accident, that at any moment she could make him—that she had whatever it was, the power, the uncanny, unaccountable Gift.

She was beginning to see more and more how it worked; how inevitably, how infallibly it worked. She was even a little afraid of it, of what it might come to mean. It *did* mean that without his knowledge, separated as they were and had to be, she could always get at him.

And supposing it came to mean that she could get at him to make him do things? Why, the bare idea of it was horrible.

Nothing could well have been more horrible to Agatha. It was the secret and the essence of their remarkable relation that she had never tried to get at him; whereas Bella *had*, calamitously; and still more calamitously, because of the peculiar magic that there was (there must have been) in her, Bella had succeeded.

To have tried to get at him would have been for Agatha the last treachery, the last indecency; while for Rodney it would have been the destruction of her charm. She was the way of escape for him from Bella; but she had always left her door, even the innermost door, wide open; so that where shelter and protection faced him there faced him also the way of departure, the way of escape from *her*.

And if her thought could get at him and fasten on him, and shut him in there. . . .

It could, she knew; but it need not. She was really all right. Restraint had been the essence and the secret of the charm she had, and it was also the secret and the essence of her gift. Why, she had brought it to so fine a point that she could shut out, and by shutting out destroy, any feeling, any thought that did violence to any other. She could shut them all out, if it came to that, and make the whole place empty. So that, if this knowledge of her power did violence, she had only to close her door on it.

She closed it now on the bare thought of his coming; on the little innocent hope she had that he would come. By an ultimate refinement and subtlety of honour she refused to let even expectation cling to him.

But though it was dreadful to "work" her gift that way, to make him do things, there was another way in which she did work it, lawfully, sacredly, incorruptibly—the way it first came to her. She had worked it twenty times (without his knowledge, for how he would have scoffed at her) to make him well.

Before it had come to her, he had been, ever since she knew him, more or less ill, more or less tormented by the nerves that were wedded so indissolubly to Bella's. He was always, it seemed to her terror, on the verge. And she could say to herself: "Look at him *now!*"

His abrupt, incredible recovery had been the first open manifestation of the way it worked. Not that she had tried it on him first. Before she dared do that once she had proved it on herself twenty times, till she found it infallible.

But to ensure continuous results it had to be a continuous process; and in order to give herself up to it, to him (to his pitiful case), she had lately, as her friends said, "cut herself completely off." She had gone down into Buckinghamshire and taken a small, solitary house at Sarratt End in the valley of the Chess, three miles from the nearest station. She had shut herself up in a world half a mile long; one straight hill to the north, one to the south, two strips of flat pasture, the river and the white farm-road between.

A world closed east and west by the turn the valley takes there between the hills, and barred by a gate at each end of the farm-road. A land of pure curves, of delicate colours, delicate shadows; all winter through a land of grey woods and sallow fields, of ploughed hillsides pale with the white strain of the chalk. In April (it was April now) a land shining with silver and green. And the ways out of it led into lanes; it had neither sight nor hearing of the high roads beyond.

There were only two houses in that half-mile of valley, Agatha's house and Woodman's Farm.

Agatha's house, white as a cutting in the chalk downs, looked south-west, up the valley and across it, to where a slender beech wood went lightly up the hill and then stretched out in a straight line along the top, with the bare fawn-coloured flank of the ploughed land below. The farmhouse looked east towards Agatha's house across a field;

41

a red-brick house—dull, dark red with the grey bloom of weather on it—flat-faced and flat-eyed, two windows on each side of the door and a row of five above, all nine staring at the small white house across the field. The narrow, flat farm-road linked the two.

Except Rodney when his inn was full, nobody ever came to Woodman's Farm; and Agatha's house, set down inside its east gate, shared its isolation, its immunity. Two villages, unseen, unheard, served her, not a mile away. It was impossible to be more sheltered, more protected and more utterly cut off. And only fifteen miles, as the crow flies, between this solitude and London, so that it was easy for Rodney Lanyon to come down.

At two o'clock, the hour when he must come if he were coming, she began to listen for the click of the latch at the garden gate. She had agreed with herself that at the last moment expectancy could do no harm; it couldn't influence him; for either he had taken the twelve-thirty train at Marylebone or he had not (Agatha was so far reasonable); so, at the last moment she permitted herself that dangerous and terrible joy.

When the click came and his footsteps after it, she admitted further (now when it could do no harm) that she had had foreknowledge of him; she had been aware all the time that he would come. And she wondered, as she always wondered at his coming, whether really, she would find him well, or whether this time it had incredibly miscarried. And her almost unbearable joy became suspense, became vehement desire to see him and gather from his face whether this time also it had worked.

"How are you? How have you been?" was her question when he stood before her in her white room, holding her hand for an instant.

"Tremendously fit," he answered; "ever since I last saw you."

"Oh—seeing me—" It was as if she wanted him to know that seeing her made no difference.

She looked at him and received her certainty. She saw him clear-eyed and young, younger than he was, his clean, bronzed face set, as it used to be, in a firmness that obliterated the lines, the little agonised lines, that had made her heart ache.

"It always does me good," he said, "to see you."

"And to see you—you know what it does to me."

He thought he knew as he caught back his breath and looked at her, taking in again her fine whiteness, and her tenderness, her purity of line, and the secret of her eyes, whose colour (if they had colour) he was never sure about; taking in all of her, from her adorable feet to her hair, vividly dark, that sprang from the white parting like—was it like waves or wings?

What had once touched and moved him unspeakably in Agatha's face was the capacity it had, latent in its tragic lines, for expressing terror. Terror was what he most dreaded for her, what he had most tried to keep her from, to keep out of her face. And latterly he had not found it; or rather he had not found the unborn, lurking spirit of it there. It had gone, that little tragic droop in Agatha's face. The corners of her eyes and of her beautiful mouth were lifted, as if by—he could find no other word for the thing he meant but wings. She had a look which, if it were not of joy, was of something more vivid and positive than peace.

He put it down to their increased and undisturbed communion, made possible by her retirement to Sarratt End. Yet as he looked at her, he sighed again.

In response to his sigh, she asked suddenly: "How's Bella?"

His face lighted wonderfully. "It's extraordinary," he said; "she's better. Miles better. In fact, if it wasn't tempting Providence, I should say she was well. She's been, for the last week anyhow, a perfect angel."

His amazed, uncomprehending look gave her the clue to what had happened. It was another instance of the astounding and mysterious way it worked. She must have got at Bella somehow in getting at him. She saw now no end to the possibilities of the thing. There wasn't anything so wonderful in making him what, after all, he was; but if she, Bella, had been, even for a week, a perfect angel, it had made her what she was not and never had been.

His next utterance came to her with no irrelevance.

"You've been found out."

For a moment she wondered, had he guessed it then, her secret? He had never known anything about it, and it was not likely that he should know now. He was indeed very far from knowing when he could think that it was seeing her that did it.

There was, of course, the other secret, the fact that he did see her; but she had never allowed that it *was* a secret, or that it need be, although they guarded it so carefully. Anybody, except Bella, who wouldn't understand it, was welcome to know that he came to see her. He must mean that.

"Found out?" she repeated.

"If you haven't been, you will be."

"You mean," she said, "Sarratt End has been found out?"

"If you put it that way. I saw the Powells at the station." (She breathed freely.)

"They told me they'd taken rooms at some farm here."

"Which farm?"

He didn't remember.

"Was it Woodman's Farm?" she asked. And he said, "Yes, that was the name they'd told him. Whereabouts was it?"

"Don't you know," she said. "That's the name of *your* farm."

He had not known it, and was visibly annoyed at knowing it now. And Agatha herself felt some dismay. If it had been any other place but Woodman's Farm—it stared at them; it watched them; it knew all their goings out and their comings in; it knew Rodney; not that that had mattered in the least, but the Powells, when they came, would know too.

She tried to look as if that didn't matter either, while they faced each other in a silence, a curious, unfamiliar discomposure.

She recovered first. "After all," she said, "why shouldn't they?"

"Well—I thought you weren't going to tell people."

Her face mounted a sudden flame, a signal of resentment. She had always resented the imputation of secrecy in their relations. And now it was as if he were dragging forward the thought that she perpetually put away from her.

"Tell about what?" she asked, coldly.

"About Sarratt End. I thought we'd agreed to keep it for ourselves."

"I haven't told everybody. But I did tell Milly Powell."

"My dear girl, that wasn't very clever of you."

"I told her not to tell. She knows what I want to be alone for."

"Good God." As he stared in dismay at what he judged to be her unspeakable indiscretion, the thought rushed in on her straight from him, the naked, terrible thought, that there *should* be anything they had to hide, they had to be alone for. She saw at the same time how defenceless he was before it; he couldn't keep it back; he couldn't put it away from him. It was always with him, a danger watching on his threshold.

"Then" (he made her face it with him) "we're done for."

"No, no," she cried; "how could you think that? It was another thing. Something I'm trying to do."

"You told her," he insisted. "What did you tell her?"

"That I'm doing it. That I'm here for my health. She understands it that way."

He smiled as if he were satisfied, knowing her so well. And still his thought, his terrible, naked thought, was there. It was looking at her straight out of his eyes.

"Are you sure she understands?" he said.

"Yes. Absolutely."

He hesitated, and then put it differently.

"Are you sure she doesn't understand? That she hasn't an inkling?"

He wasn't sure whether Agatha understood, whether she realised the danger.

"About you and me," he said.

"Ah, my dear, I've kept *you* secret. She doesn't know we know each other. And if she did—"

She finished it with a wonderful look, a look of unblinking yet vaguely, pitifully uncandid candour.

She had always met him, and would always have to meet him, with the idea that there was nothing in it; for, if she once admitted that there was anything, then they *were* done for. She couldn't (how could she?) let him keep on coming with that thought in him, acknowledged by them both.

That was where she came in, and where her secret, her gift, would work now more beneficently than ever. The beauty of it was that it would make them safe, absolutely safe. She had only got to apply it to that thought of his, and the thought would not exist. Since she could get at him, she could do for him what he, poor dear, couldn't perhaps always do for himself; she could keep that dreadful possibility in him under; she could, in fact, make their communion all that she wanted it to be.

"I don't like it," he said miserably. "I don't like it."

A little line of worry was coming in his face again.

The door opened and a maid began to go in and out, laying the table for their meal. He watched the door close on her and said, "Won't that woman wonder what I come for?"

"She can see what you come for." She smiled.

"Why are you spoiling it with thinking things?"

"It's for you I think them. *I* don't mind. It doesn't matter so much for me. But I want you to be safe."

"Oh, *I'm* safe, my dear," she answered.

"You were. And you would be still, if these Powells hadn't found you out."

He meditated.

"What do you suppose *they've* come for?" he asked.

"They've come, I imagine, for his health."

"What? To a god-forsaken place like this?"

"They know what it's done for me. So, they think, poor darlings, perhaps it may do something—even yet—for him."

"What's the matter with him?"

"Something dreadful. And they say—incurable."

"It isn't—?" He paused.

"I can't tell you what it is. It isn't anything you'd think it was. It isn't anything bodily."

"I never knew it."

"You're not supposed to know. And you wouldn't, unless you *did* know. And please—you don't; you don't know anything."

He smiled. "No. You haven't told me, have you?"

"I only told you because you never tell things, and because—"

"Because?" He waited, smiling.

"Because I wanted you to see he doesn't count."

"Well—but *she's* all right, I take it?"

At first, she failed to grasp his implication that if, owing to his affliction, Harding Powell didn't count, Milly, his young wife, did. Her faculties of observation and of inference would, he took it, be unimpaired.

"She'll wonder, won't she?" he expounded.

"About us? Not she. She's too much wrapped up in him to notice anyone."

"And he?"

"Oh, my dear—he's too much wrapped up in *it*." Another anxiety then came to him.

"I say, you know, he isn't dangerous, is he?" She laughed.

"Dangerous? Oh, dear me, no! A lamb."

2

She kept on saying to herself, Why shouldn't they come? What difference did it make?

Up till now she had not admitted that anything could make a difference, that anything could touch, could alter by a shade the safe, the intangible, the unique relation between her and Rodney. It was proof against anything that anybody could think. And the Powells were not given to thinking things. Agatha's own mind had been a crystal with-

46

out a flaw, in its clearness, its sincerity.

It had to be, to ensure the blessed working of the gift; as again, it was by the blessed working of the gift that she kept it so. She could only think of that, the secret, the gift, the inexpressible thing, as itself a flawless crystal, a charmed circle; or rather, as a sphere that held all the charmed circles that you draw round things to keep them safe, to keep them holy.

She had drawn her circle round Rodney Lanyon and herself. Nobody could break it. They were supernaturally safe.

And yet the presence of the Powells had made a difference. She was forced to own that, though she remained untouched, it had made a difference in him. It was as if, in the agitation produced by them, he had brushed aside some veil and had let her see something that up till now her crystal vision had refused to see, something that was more than a lurking possibility. She discovered in him a desire, an intention that up till now he had concealed from her. It had left its hiding place; it rose on terrifying wings and fluttered before her, troubling her. She was reminded that, though there were no lurking possibilities in her, with him it might be different. For him the tie between them might come to mean something it had never meant and could not mean for her, something she had refused not only to see but to foresee and provide for.

She was aware of a certain relief when Monday came and he had left her without any further unveilings and revealings. She was even glad when, about the middle of the week, the Powells came with a cart-load of luggage and settled at the farm. She said to herself that they would take her mind off him. They had a way of seizing on her and holding her attention to the exclusion of all other objects.

She could hardly not have been seized and held by a case so pitiful, so desperate as theirs. How pitiful and desperate it had become she learned almost at once from the face of her friend, the little pale-eyed wife, whose small, flat, flower-like features were washed out and worn fine by watchings and listenings on the border, on the threshold.

Yes, he was worse. He had had to give up his business (Harding Powell was a gentle stockbroker). It wasn't any longer, Milly Powell intimated, a question of borders and of thresholds. They had passed all that. He had gone clean over; he was in the dreadful interior; and she, the resolute and vigilant little woman, had no longer any power to get him out. She was at the end of her tether.

Agatha knew what he had been for years? Well—he was worse

than that; far worse than he had been, ever. Not so bad, though, that he hadn't intervals in which he knew how bad he was, and was willing to do everything, to try anything. They were going to try Sarratt End. It was her idea. She knew how marvellously it had answered with dear Agatha (not that Agatha ever was, or could be, where *he* was, poor darling). And besides, Agatha herself was an attraction. It had occurred to Milly Powell that it might do Harding good to be near Agatha. There was something about her; Milly didn't know what it was, but she felt it, *he* felt it—an influence, or something, that made for mental peace. It was, Mrs. Powell said, as if she had some secret.

She hoped Agatha wouldn't mind. It couldn't possibly hurt her. *He* couldn't. The darling couldn't hurt a fly; he could only hurt himself. And if he got really bad, why then, of course, they would have to leave Sarratt End. He would have, she said sadly, to go away somewhere. But not yet—oh, not yet; he wasn't bad enough for that. She would keep him with her up to the last possible moment—the last possible moment. Agatha could understand, couldn't she?

Agatha did indeed.

Milly Powell smiled her desperate white smile, and went on; always with her air of appeal to Agatha. That was why she wanted to be near her. It was awful not to be near somebody who understood, who would understand him. For Agatha would understand—wouldn't she?—that to a certain extent he must be given in to? *That*—apart from Agatha—was why they had chosen Sarratt End. It was the sort of place—wasn't it?—where you would go if you didn't want people to get at you; where (Milly's very voice became furtive as she explained it) you could hide. His idea—his last—seemed to be that something was trying to get at him.

No, not people. Something worse, something terrible. It was always after him. The most piteous thing about him—piteous but adorable—was that he came to her—to *her*, imploring her to hide him.

And so, she had hidden him here.

Agatha took in her friend's high courage as she looked at the eyes where fright barely fluttered under the poised suspense. She approved of the plan. It appealed to her by its sheer audacity. She murmured that if there were anything that she could do, Milly had only to come to her.

Oh, well, Milly *had* come. What she wanted Agatha to do—if she saw him and he should say anything about it— was simply to take the line that he was safe.

Agatha said that was the line she did take. She wasn't going to let herself think, and Milly mustn't think—not for a moment—that he wasn't, that there was anything to be afraid of.

"Anything to be afraid of *here*. That's my point," said Milly.

"Mine is that here or anywhere—wherever *he* is—there mustn't be any fear. How can he get better if we keep him wrapped in it? You're *not* afraid. You're not afraid."

Persistent, invincible affirmation was part of her method, her secret.

Milly replied a little wearily (she knew nothing about the method). "I haven't time to be afraid," she said. "And as long as you're not—"

"It's you who matter," Agatha cried. "You're so near him. Don't you realise what it means to be so near?"

Milly smiled sadly, tenderly. (As if she didn't know!)

"My dear, that's all that keeps me going. I've got to make him feel that he's protected."

"He *is* protected," said Agatha.

Already she was drawing her charmed circle round him.

"As long as I hold out. If I give in, he's done for."

"You mustn't think it. You mustn't say it!"

"But—I know it. Oh, my dear! I'm all he's got."

At that she looked for a moment as if she might break down. She said the terrible part of it was that they were left so much alone. People were beginning to shrink from him, to be afraid of him.

"You know," said Agatha, "I'm not. You must bring him to see me."

The little woman had risen, as she said, "to go to him." She stood there, visibly hesitating. She couldn't bring him. He wouldn't come. Would Agatha go with her and see him?

Agatha went.

As they approached the farm, she saw to her amazement that the door was shut and the blinds, the ugly, ochreish yellow blinds, were down in all the nine windows of the front, the windows of the Powells' rooms. The house was like a house of the dead.

"Do you get the sun on this side?" she said; and as she said it, she realised the stupidity of her question; for the nine windows looked to the east, and the sun, wheeling down the west, had been in their faces as they came.

Milly answered mechanically, "No, we don't get any sun." She added with an irrelevance that was only apparent, "I've had to take all four rooms to keep other people out."

"They never come," said Agatha.

"No," said Milly, "but if they did–"

The front door was locked. Milly had the key. When they had entered Agatha saw her turn it in the lock again, slowly and without a sound.

All the doors were shut in the passage, and it was dark there. Milly opened a door on the left at the foot of the steep stairs.

"He will be in here," she said.

The large room was lit with a thick ochreish light through the squares of its drawn blinds. It ran the whole width of the house and had a third window looking west where the yellow light prevailed. A horrible light it was. It cast thin, turbid, brown shadows on the walls.

Harding Powell was sitting between the drawn blinds, alone in the black hollow of the chimney place. He crouched in his chair, and his bowed back was towards them as they stood there on the threshold.

"Harding," said Milly, "Agatha has come to see you."

He turned in his chair and rose as they entered.

His chin was sunk on his chest, and the first thing Agatha noticed was the difficult, slow, forward-thrusting movement with which he lifted it. His eyes seemed to come up last of all from the depths to meet her. With a peculiar foreign courtesy, he bowed his head again over her hand as he held it.

He apologised for the darkness in which they found him. Harding Powell's manners had always been perfect, and it struck Agatha as strange and pathetic that his malady should have left untouched the incomparable quality he had.

Milly went to the windows and drew the blinds up. The light revealed him in his exquisite perfection, his small fragile finish. He was fifty or thereabouts, but slight as a boy, and nervous, and dark as Englishmen are dark; jaw and chin shaven; his mouth hidden by the straight droop of his moustache. From the eyes downwards the outlines of his face and features were of an extreme regularity and a fineness undestroyed by the work of the strained nerves on the sallow, delicate texture. But his eyes, dark like an animal's, were the eyes of a terrified thing, a thing hunted and, on the watch, a thing that listened continually for the soft feet of the hunter. Above these eyes his brows were twisted, were tortured with his terror.

He turned to his wife.

"Did you lock the door, dear?" he said.

"I did. But you know, Harding, we needn't—here."

He shivered slightly and began to walk up and down before the hearthplace. When he had his back to Milly, Milly followed him with her eyes of anguish; when he turned and faced her, she met him with her white smile.

Presently he spoke again. He wondered whether they would object to his drawing the blinds down. He was afraid he would have to. Otherwise, he said, *he would be seen.*

Milly laid her hand on the arm that he stretched towards the window.

"Darling," she said, "you've forgotten. You can't possibly be seen—here. It's just the one place—isn't it, Agatha?—where you can't be." Her eyes signalled to Agatha to support her. (Not but what she had perfect confidence in the plan.)

It was, Agatha assented. "And Agatha knows," said Milly.

He shivered again. He had turned to Agatha.

"Forgive me if I suggest that you cannot really know. Heaven forbid that you *should* know."

Milly, intent on her "plan," persisted.

"But, dearest, you said yourself it was. The one place."

"I said that? When did I say it?"

"Yesterday."

"Yesterday? I daresay. But I didn't sleep last night. It wouldn't let me."

"Very few people do sleep," said Agatha, "for the first time in a strange place."

"The place isn't strange. That's what I complain of. That's what keeps me awake. No place ever will be strange when It's there. And it was there last night."

"Darling—" Milly murmured.

"You know what I mean," he said. "The Thing that keeps me awake. Of course, if I'd slept last night, I'd have known it wasn't there. But when I didn't sleep—"

He left it to them to draw the only possible conclusion.

They dropped the subject. They turned to other things and talked a little while, sitting with him in his room with the drawn blinds. From time to time when they appealed to him, he gave an urbane assent, a murmur, a suave motion of his hand. When the light went, they lit a lamp. Agatha stayed and dined with them, that being the best thing she could do.

At nine o'clock she rose and said goodnight to Harding Powell. He smiled a drawn smile.

"Ah—if I could sleep—," he said.

"That's the worst of it—his not sleeping," said Milly at the gate.

"He will sleep. He will sleep," said Agatha.

Milly sighed. She knew he wouldn't.

The plan, she said, was no good after all. It wouldn't work.

3

How could it? There was nothing behind it. All Milly's plans had been like that; they fell to dust; they were dust. There had been always that pitiful, desperate stirring of the dust to hide the terror; the futile throwing of the dust in the poor thing's eyes. As if he couldn't see through it. As if, with the supernatural ludicity, the invincible cunning of the insane, he didn't see through anything and provide for it. It was really only his indestructible urbanity, persisting through the wreck of him, that bore, tolerantly, temperately, with Milly and her plans. Without it he might be dangerous. With it, as long as it lasted, little Milly, plan as she would, was safe.

But they couldn't count on its lasting. Agatha had realised that from the moment when she had seen him draw down the blind again after his wife had drawn it up. That was the maddest thing he had done yet. She had shuddered at it as at an act of violence. It outraged, cruelly, his exquisite quality. It was so unlike him.

She was not sure that Milly hadn't even made things worse by her latest plan, the flight to Sarratt End. It emphasised the fact that they were flying, that they had to fly. It had brought her to the house with the drawn blinds in the closed, barred valley, to the end of the world, to the end of her tether. And when she realised that it was the end, when he realised it . . . .

Agatha couldn't leave him there. She couldn't (when she had the secret) leave him to poor Milly and her plans. That had been in her mind when she had insisted on it that he would sleep.

She knew what Milly meant by her sigh and the look she gave her. If Milly could have been impolite, she would have told her that it was all very well to say so, but how were they going to make him? And she, too, felt that something more was required of her than that irritating affirmation. She had got to make him. His case, his piteous case, cried out for an extension of the gift.

She hadn't any doubt as to its working. There were things she didn't know about it yet, but she was sure of that. She had proved it by a hundred experimental intermissions, abstentions, and recoveries.

In order to be sure, you had only to let go and see how you got on without it. She had tried in that way, with scepticism and precaution, on herself.

But not in the beginning. She could not say that she had tried it in the beginning at all, even on herself. It had simply come to her, as she put it, by a divine accident. Heaven knew she had needed it. She had been, like Rodney Lanyon, on the verge, where he, poor dear, had brought her; so impossible had it been then to bear her knowledge and, what was worse, her divination of the things he bore from Bella. It was her divination, her compassion, that had wrecked her as she stood aside, cut off from him, he on the verge and she near it, looking on, powerless to help while Bella tore at him. Talk of the verge, the wonder was they hadn't gone clean over it, both of them.

She couldn't say then from what region, what tract of unexplored, incredible mystery her help had come. It came one day, one night when she was at her worst. She remembered how, with some resurgent, ultimate instinct of surrender, she had sunk on the floor of her room, flung out her arms across the bed in the supreme gesture of supplication, and thus gone, eyes shut and with no motion of thought or sense in her, clean into the blackness where, as if it had been waiting for her, the thing had found her.

It had found her. Agatha was precise on that point. She had not found it. She had not even stumbled on it, blundered up against it in the blackness. The way it worked, the wonder of her instantaneous well-being, had been the first, the very first hint she had that it was there.

She had never quite recaptured her primal, virgin sense of it; but to set against that, she had entered more and more into possession. She had found out the secret of its working and had controlled it, reduced it to an almost intelligible method. You could think of it as a current of transcendent power, hitherto mysteriously inhibited. You made the connection, having cut off all other currents that interfered, and then you simply turned it on. In other words, if you could put it into words at all, you shut your eyes and ears, you closed up the sense of touch, you made everything dark around you and withdrew into your innermost self; you burrowed deep into the darkness there till you got beyond it; you tapped the Power, as it were, underground at any point you pleased and turned it on in any direction.

She could turn it on to Harding Powell without any loss to Rodney Lanyon; for it was immeasurable, inexhaustible.

She looked back at the farmhouse with its veiled windows. Formless and immense, the shadow of Harding Powell swayed uneasily on one of the yellow blinds. Across the field her own house showed pure and dim against the darkening slope behind it, showed a washed and watered white in the liquid, lucid twilight. Her house was open always and on every side; it flung out its casement arms to the night and to the day. And now all the lamps were lit, every doorway was a golden shaft, every window a golden square; the whiteness of its walls quivered and the blurred edges flowed into the dark of the garden. It was the fragile shell of a sacred and a burning light.

She did not go in all at once. She crossed the river and went up the hill through the beech-wood. She walked there every evening in the darkness, calling her thoughts home to sleep. The Easter moon, golden-white and holy, looked down at her, shrined under the long, sharp arch of the beech-trees; it was like going up and up towards a dim sanctuary where the holiest sat enshrined. A sense of consecration was upon her.

It came, solemn and pure and still, out of the tumult of her tenderness and pity; but it was too awful for pity and for tenderness; it aspired like a flame and lost itself in light; it grew like a wave till it was vaster than any tenderness or any pity. It was as if her heart rose on the swell of it and was carried away into a rhythm so tremendous that her own pulses of compassion were no longer felt, or felt only as the hushed and delicate vibration of the wave. She recognised her state. It was the blessed state desired as the condition of the working of the gift.

She turned when the last arch of the beech-trees broke and opened to the sky at the top of the hill, where the moon hung in immensity, free of her hill, free of the shrine that held her. She went down with slow soft footsteps as if she carried herself, her whole fragile being, as a vessel, a crystal vessel for the holy thing, and was careful lest a touch of the earth should jar and break her.

4

She went still more gently and with half-shut eyes through her illuminated house. She turned the lights out in her room and undressed herself in the darkness. She laid herself on the bed with straight lax limbs, with arms held apart a little from her body, with eyelids shut lightly on her eyes; all fleshly contacts were diminished.

It was now as if her being drank at every pore the swimming darkness; as if the rhythm of her heart and of her breath had ceased in the pulse of its invasion. She sank in it and was covered with wave upon wave of darkness. She sank and was upheld; she dissolved and was gathered together again, a flawless crystal. She was herself the heart of the charmed circle, poised in the ultimate unspeakable stillness, beyond death, beyond birth, beyond the movement, the vehemence, the agitations of the world. She drew Harding Powell into it and held him there.

To draw him to any purpose she had first to loosen and destroy the fleshly, sinister image of him that, for the moment of evocation, hung like a picture on the darkness. In a moment the fleshly image receded, it sank back into the darkness. His name, Harding Powell, was now the only earthly sign of him that she suffered to appear. In the third moment his name was blotted out. And then it was as if she drew him by intangible, super-sensible threads; she touched, with no sense of peril, his innermost essence; the walls of flesh were down between them; she had got at him.

And having got at him she held him, a bloodless spirit, a bodiless essence, in the fount of healing. She said to herself, "He will sleep now. He will sleep. He will sleep." And as she slid into her own sleep she held and drew him with her.

He would sleep; he would be all right as long as she slept. Her sleep, she had discovered, did more than carry on the amazing act of communion and redemption. It clinched it. It was the seal on the bond.

Early the next morning she went over to the farm. The blinds were up; the doors and windows were flung open. Milly met her at the garden gate. She stopped her and walked a little way with her across the field. "It's worked," she said. "It's worked after all, like magic."

For a moment Agatha wondered whether Milly had guessed anything; whether she divined the Secret and had brought him there for that, and had refused to acknowledge it before she knew.

"What has?" she asked.

"The plan. The place. He slept last night. Ten hours straight on end. I know, for I stayed awake and watched him. And this morning—oh, my dear, if you could see him! He's all right. He's all right."

"And you think," said Agatha, "it's the place?"

Milly knew nothing, guessed, divined nothing.

"Why, what else can it be?" she said.

"What does *he* think?"

"He doesn't think. He can't account for it. He says himself it's miraculous."

"Perhaps," said Agatha, "it is."

They were silent a moment over the wonder of it.

"I can't get over it," said Milly presently. "It's so odd that it should make all that difference. I could understand it if it had worked that way at first. But it didn't. Think of him yesterday. And yet—if it isn't the place, what is it? What is it?"

Agatha did not answer. She wasn't going to tell Milly what it was. If she did, Milly wouldn't believe her, and Milly's unbelief might work against it. It might prove, for all she knew, an inimical, disastrous power.

"Come and see for yourself." Milly spoke as if it had been Agatha who doubted.

They turned again towards the house. Powell had come out and was in the garden, leaning on the gate. They could see how right he was by the mere fact of his being there, presenting himself like that to the vivid light.

He opened the gate for them, raising his hat and smiling as they came. His face witnessed to the wonder worked on him. The colour showed clean, purged of his taint. His eyes were candid and pure under brows smoothed by sleep.

As they went in, he stood for a moment in the open doorway and looked at the view, admiring the river and the green valley and the bare upland fields under the wood. He had always had (it was part of his rare quality) a prodigious capacity for admiration.

"My God," he said, "how beautiful the world is!"

He looked at Milly. "And all that isn't a patch on my wife."

He looked at her with tenderness and admiration, and the look was the flower, the perfection of his sanity.

Milly drew in her breath with a little sound like a sob. Her joy was so great that it was almost unbearable.

Then he looked at Agatha and admired the green gown she wore. "You don't know," he said, "how exquisitely right you are."

She smiled. She knew how exquisitely right *he* was.

5

Night after night, she continued and without an effort. It was as easy as drawing your breath; it was indeed the breath you drew. She found that she had no longer to devote hours to Harding Powell, any more than she gave hours to Rodney; she could do his business in moments, in points of inappreciable time. It was as if from night to night the times swung together and made one enduring timeless time. For the process belonged to a region that was not of times or time.

She wasn't afraid, then, of not giving enough time to it, but she *was* afraid of omitting it altogether. She knew that every intermission would be followed by a relapse, and Harding's state did not admit of any relapses.

Of course, if time *had* counted, if the thing was measurable, she would have been afraid of losing hold of Rodney Lanyon. She held him now by a single slender thread, and the thread was Bella. She "worked" it regularly now through Bella. He was bound to be all right as long as Bella was; for his possibilities of suffering were thus cut off at their source. Besides, it was the only way to preserve the purity of her intention, the flawlessness of the crystal.

That was the blessedness of her attitude to Harding Powell. It was passionless, impersonal. She wanted nothing of Harding Powell except to help him, and to help Milly, dear little Milly. And never before had she been given so complete, so overwhelming a sense of having helped. It was nothing—unless it was a safeguard against vanity—that they didn't know it, that they persisted in thinking it was Milly's plan that worked. Not that that altogether accounted for it to Harding Powell. He said so at last to Agatha.

They were returning, he and she, by the edge of the wood at the top of the steep field after a long walk. He had asked her to go with him—it was her country—for a good stretch, further than Milly's little feet could carry her. They stood a moment up there and looked around them. April was coming on, but the ploughed land at their feet was still bare; the earth waited.

On that side of the valley she was delicately unfruitful, spent with rearing the fine, thin beauty of the woods. But, down below, the valley ran over with young grass and poured it to the river in wave after wave, till the last surge of green rounded over the water's edge. Rain had fallen in the night, and the river had risen; it rested there, poised. It was wonderful how a thing so brimming, so shining, so alive could be so still; still as marsh water, flat to the flat land.

At that moment, in a flash that came like a shifting of her eyes, the world she looked at suffered a change.

And yet it did not change. All the appearances of things, their colours, the movement and the stillness remained as if constant in their rhythm and their scale; but they were heightened, intensified; they were carried to a pitch that would have been vehement, vibrant, but that the stillness as well as the movement was intense. She was not dazzled by it or confused in any way. Her senses were exalted, adjusted to the pitch.

She would have said now that the earth at her feet had become insubstantial, but that she knew, in a flash, that what she saw was the very substance of the visible world; live and subtle as flame; solid as crystal and as clean. It was the same world, flat field for flat field and hill for hill; but radiant, vibrant, and, as it were, infinitely transparent.

Agatha in her moment saw that the whole world brimmed and shone and was alive with the joy that was its life, joy that flowed flood-high and yet was still. In every leaf, in every blade of grass, this life was manifest as a strange, a divine translucence. She was about to point it out to the man at her side when she remembered that he had eyes for the beauty of the earth, but no sense of its secret and supernatural light. Harding Powell denied, he always had denied, the supernatural. And when she turned to him her vision had passed from her.

They must have another tramp someday, he said. He wanted to see more of this wonderful place. And then he spoke of his recovery.

"It's all very well," he said, "but I can't account for it. Milly says it's the place."

"It is a wonderful place," said Agatha.

"Not so wonderful as all that. You saw how I was the day after we came. Well—it can't be the place altogether."

"I rather hope it isn't," Agatha said.

"Do you? What do you think it is, then?"

"I think it's something in you."

"Of course, of course. But what started it? That's what I want to know. Something's happened. Something queer and spontaneous and unaccountable. It's—it's uncanny. For, you know, I oughtn't to feel like this. I got bad news this morning."

"Bad news?"

"Yes. My sister's little girl is very ill. They think it's meningitis. They're in awful trouble. And I—I'm feeling like this."

"Don't let it distress you."

"It doesn't distress me. It only puzzles me. That's the odd thing. Of course, I'm sorry, and I'm anxious and all that; but I *feel* so well."

"You *are* well. Don't be morbid."

"I haven't told my wife yet. About the child, I mean. I simply daren't. It'll frighten her. She won't know how I'll take it, and she'll think it'll make me go all queer again."

He paused and turned to her.

"I say, if she *did* know how I'm taking it, she'd think *that* awfully queer, wouldn't she?" He paused.

"The worst of it is," he said, "I've got to tell her."

"Will you leave it to me?" Agatha said. "I think I can make it all right."

"How?" he queried.

"Never mind how. I can."

"Well," he assented," there's hardly anything you can't do."

That was how she came to tell Milly.

She made up her mind to tell her that evening as they sat alone in Agatha's house. "Harding," Milly said, "was happy over there with his books; just as he used to be, only more so." So much more so that she was a little disturbed about it. She was afraid it wouldn't last. And again, she said it was the place, the wonderful place.

"If you want it to last," Agatha said, "don't go on thinking it's the place."

"Why shouldn't it be? I feel that he's safe here. He's out of it. Things can't reach him."

"Bad news reached him today."

"Aggy—what?" Milly whispered in her fright.

"His sister is very anxious about her little girl."

"What's wrong?"

Agatha repeated what she had heard from Harding Powell.

"Oh—" Milly was dumb for an instant while she thought of her sister-in-law. Then she cried aloud:

"If the child dies, it'll make him ill again?"

"No, Milly, it won't."

"It will, I tell you. It's always been that sort of thing that does it."

"And supposing there was something that keeps it off?"

"What is there? What is there?"

"I believe there's something. Would you mind awfully if it wasn't the place?"

"What do you mean, Agatha?" (There was a faint resentment in Milly's agonised tone.)

It was then that Agatha told her. She made it out for her as far as she had made it out at all, with the diffidence that a decent attitude required.

Milly raised doubts which subsided in a kind of awe when Agatha faced her with the evidence of dates.

"You remember, Milly, the night when he slept?"

"I do remember. He said himself it was miraculous."

She meditated.

"And so, you think it's that?" she said presently.

"I do indeed. If I dared leave off (I daren't) you'd see for yourself."

"What do you think you've got hold of?"

"I don't know yet."

There was a long, deep silence which Milly broke.

"What do you *do?*" she said.

"I don't do anything. It isn't me."

"I see," said Milly. "I've prayed. You didn't think I hadn't?"

"It's not that—not anything *you* mean by it. And yet it is; only it's more, much more. I can't explain it. I only know it isn't me."

She was beginning to feel vaguely uncomfortable about having told her.

"And, Milly, you mustn't tell him. Promise me you won't tell him."

"No, I won't tell him."

"Because, you see, he'd think it was all rot."

"He would," said Milly. "It's the sort of thing he does think rot."

"And that might prevent its working."

Milly smiled faintly. "I haven't the ghost of an idea what 'it' is. But whatever it is, can you go on doing it?"

"Yes, I think so. You see, it depends rather—"

"It depends on what?"

"Oh, on a lot of things—on your sincerity; on your —your purity. It depends so much on that that it frightens you, lest, perhaps, you mightn't, after all be so very pure."

Milly smiled again a little differently. "Darling, if that's all, I'm not frightened. Only—supposing—supposing you gave out? You might, you know."

"*I* might. But It couldn't. You mustn't think it's me, Milly. Because if anything happened to me, if I did give out, don't you see how it would let him down? It's as bad as thinking it's the place."

"Does it matter what it is—or who it is," said Milly passionately; "as long as—" Her tears came and stopped her.

Agatha divined the source of Milly's passion.

"Then you don't mind, Milly? You'll let me go on?"

Milly rose; she turned abruptly, holding her head high, so that she might not spill her tears.

Agatha went with her over the grey field towards the farm. They paused at the gate. Milly spoke.

"Are you sure?" she said.

"Certain."

"And you won't let go?" Her eyes shone towards her friend's in the twilight. "You *will* go on?"

"*You* must go on."

"Ah—how?"

"Believing that he'll be all right."

"Oh, Aggy, he was devoted to Winny. And if the child dies—"

6

The child died three days later. Milly came over to Agatha with the news.

She said it had been an awful shock, of course. She'd been dreading something like that for him. But he'd taken it wonderfully. If he came out of it all right, she *would* believe in what she called Agatha's "thing."

He did come out of it all right. His behaviour was the crowning proof, if Milly wanted more proof, of his sanity. He went up to London and made all the arrangements for his sister. When he returned, he forestalled Milly's specious consolations with the truth. It was better, he told her, that the dear little girl should have died, for there was distinct brain trouble anyway. He took it as a sane man takes a terrible alternative.

Weeks passed. He had grown accustomed to his own sanity and no longer marvelled at it.

And still, without intermission, Agatha went on. She had been so far affected by Milly's fright (that was the worst of Milly's knowing) that she held on to Harding Powell with a slightly exaggerated intensity. She even began to give more and more time to him, she who had made out that time in this process did not matter. She was afraid of letting go, because the consequences (Milly was perpetually reminding her of the consequences) of letting go would be awful.

For Milly kept her at it. Milly urged her on. Milly, in Milly's own words, sustained her. She praised her; she praised the Secret, praised the Power. She said you could see how it worked. It was tremendous; it was inexhaustible. Milly, familiarised with its working, had become a fanatical believer in the Power. But she had her own theory. She knew, of course, that they were all, she and Agatha and poor Harding, dependent on the Power, that it was the Power that did it, and not Agatha.

But Agatha was *their* one link with it, and if the link gave way, where were they? Agatha felt that Milly watched her and waylaid her; that she was suspicious of failures and of intermissions; that she wondered; that she peered and pried. Milly would, if she could, have stuck her fingers into what she called the machinery of the thing. Its vagueness baffled and even annoyed her, for her mind was limited; it loved and was at home with limits; it desired above all things, precise ideas, names, phrases, anything that constricted and defined.

But still, with it all, she believed; and the great thing was that Milly *should* believe. She might have worked havoc if, with her temperament, she had doubted.

What did suffer was the fine poise with which she, Agatha, had held Rodney Lanyon and Harding Powell each by his own thread. Milly had compelled her to spin a stronger thread for Harding and, as it were, to multiply her threads, so as to hold him at all points. And because of this, because of giving more and more time to him, she could not always loose him from her and let him go. And she was afraid lest the pull he had on her might weaken Rodney's thread.

Up till now, the Powells' third week at Sarratt End, she had had the assurance that his thread still held. She heard from him that Bella was all right, which meant that he too was all right, for there had never been anything wrong with him *but* Bella. And she had a further glimpse of the way the gift worked its wonders.

Three Fridays had passed, and he had not come.

Well—she had meant that; she had tried (on that last Friday of his), with a crystal sincerity, to hold him back so that he should not come. And up till now, with an ease that simply amazed her, she had kept herself at the highest pitch of her sincere and beautiful intention.

Not that it was the intention that had failed her now. It had succeeded so beautifully, so perfectly, that he had no need to come at all. She had given Bella back to him. She had given him back to Bella. Only, she faced the full perfection of her work. She had brought it to so fine a point that she would never see him again; she had gone to the root of it; she had taken from him the desire to see her. And now it was as if subtly, insidiously, her relation to him had become inverted. Whereas hitherto it had been she who had been necessary to him, it seemed now that he was far more, beyond all comparison, more necessary to her.

After all, Rodney had had Bella; and she had nobody but Rodney. He was the one solitary thing she cared for. And hitherto it had not mattered so immensely, for all her caring, whether he came to her or not. Seeing him had been, perhaps, a small mortal joy; but it had not been the tremendous and essential thing. She had been contented, satisfied beyond all mortal contentments and satisfactions, with the intangible, immaterial tie. Now she longed, with an unendurable longing, for his visible, bodily presence. She had not realised her joy as long as it was with her; she had refused to acknowledge it because of its mortal quality, and it had raised no cry that troubled her abiding spiritual calm.

But now that she had put it from her, it thrust itself on her, it cried, it clung piteously to her and would not let her go. She looked back to the last year, her year of Fridays, and saw it following her, following and entreating. She looked forward and she saw Friday after Friday coming upon her, a procession of pitiless days, trampling it down, her small, piteous mortal joy, and her mortality rose in her and revolted. She had been disturbed by what she had called the "lurking possibilities "in Rodney; they were nothing to the lurking possibilities in her.

There were moments when her desire to see Rodney sickened her with its importunity. Each time she beat it back, in an instant, to its burrow below the threshold, and it hid there, it ran underground. There were ways below the threshold by which desire could get at him. Therefore, one night—Tuesday of the fourth week—she cut him off. She refused to hold him even by a thread. It was Bella and Bella only that she held now.

On Friday of that week, she heard from him. Bella was still all right. But *he* wasn't. Anything but. He didn't know what was the matter with him. He supposed it was the same old thing again. He couldn't think how poor Bella stood him, but she did. It must be awfully bad for her. It was beastly—wasn't it?—that he should have got like that, just when Bella was so well.

She might have known it. She had, in fact, known. Having once held him, and having healed him, she had no right—as long as the Power consented to work through her—she had no right to let him go.

She began again from the beginning, from the first process of purification and surrender. But what followed was different now. She had not only to recapture the crystal serenity, the holiness of that state by which she had held Rodney Lanyon and had healed him; she had to recover the poise by which she had held him and Harding Powell together. She was bound equally not to let Harding go.

It was now almost a struggle to concentrate on both Rodney and

Harding, a struggle in which Harding persisted and prevailed. Yes, there was no blinking it, he prevailed.

She had been prepared for it, but not as for a thing that could really happen. It was contrary to all that she knew of the beneficent working of the Power. She thought she knew all its ways, its silences, its reassurances, its inexplicable reservations and evasions. She couldn't be prepared for this—that it, the high and holy, the unspeakably pure thing should allow Harding to prevail, should connive (that was what it looked like) at his taking the gift into his own hands and turning it to his own advantage against Rodney Lanyon.

Not that she thought it really had connived. That was unthinkable, and Agatha did not think these things; she felt them. Hitherto she had had no misgivings as to the possible behaviour of the Power. And now she was afraid, not of It, and not, certainly not, of poor Harding (how could she be afraid of him?); she was afraid mysteriously, without knowing why or how.

It was her fear that made her write to Rodney Lanyon. She wrote in the beginning of the fifth week (she was counting the weeks now). She only wanted to know, she said, that he was better, that he was well. She begged him to write and tell her that he was well.

He did not write.

And every night of that week, in those "states" of hers, Powell predominated. He was becoming almost a visible presence impressed upon the blackness of the "state." All she could do then was to evoke the visible image of Rodney Lanyon and place it there over Harding's image, obliterating him. Now, properly speaking, the state, the perfection of it, did not admit of visible presences, and that Harding could so impress himself showed more than anything the extent to which he had prevailed.

He prevailed to such good purpose that he was now, Milly said, well enough to go back to business. They were to leave Sarratt End in about ten days, when they would have been there seven weeks.

She had come over on the Sunday to let Agatha know that; and also, she said, to make a confession.

Milly's face, as she said it, was all candour. It had filled out; it had bloomed in her happiness; it was shadowless, featureless almost, like a flower.

She had done what she said she wouldn't do; she had told Harding.

"Oh, Milly, what on earth did you do that for?" Agatha's voice was strange.

"I thought it better," Milly said, revealing the fine complacence of her character.

"Why better?"

"Because secrecy is bad. And he was beginning to wonder. He wanted to go back to business; and he wouldn't, because he thought it was the place that did it."

"I see," said Agatha. "And what does he think it is now?"

"He thinks it's *you*, dear."

"But I told you—I told you—that was what you were not to think."

"My dear, it's an immense concession that he should think it's you."

"A concession to what?"

"Well, I suppose, to the supernatural."

"Milly, you shouldn't have told him. You don't know what harm you might have done. I'm not sure even now that you haven't done it."

"Oh, have I?" said Milly triumphantly. "You've only got to look at him."

"When did you tell him, then?"

"I told him—let me see—it was a week ago last Friday."

Agatha was silent. She wondered. It had been after Friday a week ago that he had prevailed so terribly.

"Agatha," said Milly solemnly, "when we go away you won't lose sight of him? You won't let go of him?"

"You needn't be afraid. I doubt now if he will let go of me."

"How do you mean—*now?*" Milly flushed slightly as a flower might flush.

"Now that you've told him, now that he thinks it's me.

"Perhaps," said Milly, "that was why I told him. I don't want him to let go."

7

It was the sixth week, and still Rodney did not write; and Agatha was more and more afraid.

By this time, she had definitely connected her fear with Harding Powell's dominion and persistence. She was certain now that what she could only call his importunity had proved somehow disastrous to Rodney Lanyon. And with it all, unacknowledged, beaten back, her desire to see Rodney ran to and fro in the burrows underground.

He did not write, but on the Friday of that week, the sixth week, he came.

She saw him coming up the garden path, and she shrank back into her room; but the light searched her and found her, and he saw her there. He never knocked; he came straight and swiftly to her through the open doors. He shut the door of the room behind him and held her by her arms with both his hands.

"Rodney," she said, "did you mean to come, or did I make you?"

"I meant to come. You couldn't make me."

"Couldn't I? Oh, *say* I couldn't."

"You could," he said, "but you didn't. And what does it matter so long as I'm here?"

"Let me look at you."

She held him at arm's length and turned him to the light. It showed his face white, worn as it used to be, all the little lines of worry back again, and two new ones that drew down the corners of his mouth.

"You've been ill," she said. "You *are* ill."

"No. I'm all right. What's the matter with *you?*"

"With me? Nothing. Do I look as if anything was wrong?"

"You look as if you'd been frightened."

He paused, considering it.

"This place isn't good for you. You oughtn't to be here like this, all by yourself."

"Oh! Rodney, it's the dearest place. I love every inch of it. Besides, I'm not altogether by myself."

He did not seem to hear her; and what he said next arose evidently out of his own thoughts.

"I say, are those Powells still here?"

"They've been here all the time."

"Do you see much of them?"

"I see them every day. Sometimes nearly all day."

"That accounts for it."

Again, he paused.

"It's my fault, Agatha. I shouldn't have left you to them. I knew."

"What did you know?"

"Well—the state he was in, and the effect it would have on you—that it would have on anybody."

"It's all right. He's going. Besides, he isn't in a state any more. He's cured."

"Cured? What's cured him?"

She evaded him.

"He's been well ever since he came; absolutely well after the first day."

"Still, you've been frightened; you've been worrying; you've had some shock or other, or some strain. What is it?"

"Nothing. Only—just the last week—I've been a little frightened about you—when you wouldn't write to me. Why didn't you?"

"Because I couldn't."

"Then you *were* ill?"

"I'm all right. I know what's the matter with me."

"It's Bella?"

He laughed harshly.

"No, it isn't this time. I haven't that excuse."

"Excuse for what?"

"For coming. Bella's all right. Bella's a perfect angel. God knows what's happened to her. I don't. I haven't had anything to do with it."

"You had. You had everything. You were an angel too."

"I haven't been much of an angel lately, I can tell you."

"She'll understand. She does understand."

They had sat down on the couch in the corner so that they faced each other. Agatha faced him, but fear was in her eyes.

"It doesn't matter," he said, "whether she understands or not. I don't want to talk about her."

Agatha said nothing, but there was a movement in her face, a white wave of trouble, and the fear fluttered in her eyes. He saw it there.

"You needn't bother about Bella. She's all right. You see, it's not as if she cared."

"Cared?"

"About *me* much."

"But she does, she does care!"

"I suppose she did once, or she couldn't have married me. But she doesn't now. You see—you may as well know it, Agatha—there's another man."

"Oh, Rodney, no."

"Yes. It's been perfectly all right, you know; but there he is, and there he's been for years. She told me. I'm awfully sorry for her."

He paused.

"What beats me is her being so angelic now, when she doesn't care."

"Rodney, she does. It's all over, like an illness. It's you she cares for *now*."

"Think so?"

"I'm sure of it."

"I'm not."

"You will be. You'll see it. You'll see it soon."

He glanced at her under his bent brows.

"I don't know," he said, "that I want to see it. *That* isn't what's the matter with me. You don't understand the situation. It isn't all over. She's only being good about it. She doesn't care a rap about me. She *can't*. And what's more, I don't want her to."

"You—don't—want her to?"

He burst out. "My God, I want nothing in this world but *you*. And I can't have you. That's what's the matter with me."

"No, no, it isn't," she cried. "You don't know."

"I do know. It's hurting me. And"—he looked at her and his voice shook—"it's hurting you. I won't have you hurt."

He started forward suddenly as if he would have taken her in his arms. She put up her hands to keep him off.

"No, no!" she cried. "I'm all right. I'm all right. It isn't that. You mustn't think it."

"I know it. That's why I came."

He came near again. He seized her struggling hands.

"Agatha, why can't we? Why shouldn't we?"

"No, no," she moaned. "We can't. We mustn't. Not *that* way. I don't want it, Rodney, that way."

"It shall be any way you like. Only don't beat me off."

"I'm not—beating—you—off."

She stood up. Her face changed suddenly.

"Rodney—I forgot. They're coming."

"Who are they?"

"The Powells. They're coming to lunch."

"Can't you put them off?"

"I can, but it wouldn't be very wise, dear. They might think——"

"Confound them—they *would* think."

He was pulling himself visibly together.

"I'm afraid, Aggy, I ought—"

"I know—you must. You must go soon."

He looked at his watch.

"I must go *now*, dear. I daren't stay. It's dangerous."

"I know," she whispered.

"But when is the brute going?"

"Poor darling, he's going next week—next Thursday."

"Well then, I'll—I'll—"

"Please, you must go."

"I'm going."

She held out her hand.

"I daren't touch you," he whispered. "I'm going now. But I'll come again next Friday, and I'll stay."

As she saw his drawn face, there was not any strength in her to say "No."

8

He had gone. She gathered herself together and went across the field to meet the Powells as if nothing had happened.

Milly and her husband were standing at the gate of the farm. They were watching; yes, they were watching Rodney Lanyon as he crossed the river by the farm bridge. The bridge carried the field path that slanted up the hill to the farther and western end of the wood. Their attitude showed that they were interested in his brief appearance on the scene, and that they wondered what he had been doing there. And as she approached them, she was aware of something cold, ominous and inimical, that came from them, and set towards her and passed by. Her sense of it only lasted for a second, and was gone so completely that she could hardly realise that she had ever felt it.

For they were charming to her. Harding, indeed, was more perfect in his beautiful quality than ever. There was something about him that she had not been prepared for, something strange and pathetic, humble almost and appealing. She saw it in his eyes, his large, dark, wild animal eyes, chiefly. But it was a look that claimed as much as it deprecated; that assumed between them some unspoken communion and understanding. With all its pathos it was a look that frightened her. Neither he nor his wife said a word about Rodney Lanyon. She was not even sure, now, that they had recognised him.

They stayed with her all that afternoon; for their time, they said, was getting short; and when, about six o'clock, Milly got up to go she took Agatha aside and said that, if Agatha didn't mind, she would leave Harding with her for a little while. She knew he wanted to talk to her.

Agatha proposed that they should walk up the hill through the wood. They went in a curious silence and constraint; and it was not until they had got into the wood and were shut up in it together that he spoke.

"I think my wife told you I had something to say to you?"

"Yes, Harding," she said. "What is it?"

"Well, it's this—first of all, I want to thank you. I know what you're doing for me."

"I'm sorry. I didn't want you to know. I thought Milly wasn't going to tell you."

"She didn't tell me."

Agatha said nothing. She was bound to accept his statement. Of course, he must have known that Milly had broken her word, and he was trying to shield her.

"I mean," he went on, "that whether she told me or not, it's no matter; I knew."

"You—knew?"

"I knew that something was happening, and I knew it wasn't the place. Places never make any difference. I only go to 'em because Milly thinks they do. Besides, if it came to that, this place—from my peculiar point of view, mind you—was simply beastly. I couldn't have stood another night of it."

"Well."

"Well, the thing went; and I got all right. And the queer part of it is, I felt as if you were in it somehow, as if you'd done something. I half hoped you might say something, but you never did."

"One oughtn't to speak about these things, Harding. And I told you I didn't want you to know."

"I didn't know what you did. I don't know now, though Milly tried to tell me. But I felt you. I felt you all the time."

"It was not I you felt. I implore you not to think it was."

"What can I think?"

"Think as I do; think—think———" She stopped herself. She was aware of the futility of her charge to this man who denied, who always had denied, the supernatural.

"It isn't a question of thinking," she said at last.

"Of believing, then? Are you going to tell me to believe?"

"No; it isn't believing either. It's knowing. Either you know it or you don't know, though you may come to know. But whatever you think, you mustn't think it's me."

"I rather like to. Why shouldn't I?"

She turned on him her grave white face, and he noticed a curious expression there as of incipient terror.

"Because you might do some great harm either to yourself or-"

His delicate, sceptical eyebrows questioned her.

"Or me."

"You?" he murmured gently, pitifully almost.

"Yes, me. Or even—well, one doesn't quite know where the harm might end. If I could only make you take another view. I tried to make you—to work it that way—so that you might find the secret and do it for yourself."

"I can't do anything for myself. But, Agatha, I'll take any view you like of it, so long as you'll keep on at me."

"Of course, I'll keep on."

At that he stopped suddenly in his path, and faced her.

"I say, you know, it isn't hurting you, is it?"

She felt herself wince. "Hurting me? How could it hurt me?"

"Milly said it couldn't."

Agatha sighed. She said to herself, "Milly—if only Milly hadn't interfered."

"Don't you think it's cold here in the wood?" she said.

"Cold?"

"Yes. Let's go back."

As they went Milly met them at the Farm bridge. She wanted Agatha to come and stay for supper; she pressed, she pleaded, and Agatha, who had never yet withstood Milly's pleading, stayed.

It was from that evening that she really dated it, the thing that came upon her. She was aware that in staying she disobeyed an instinct that told her to go home. Otherwise, she could not say that she had any sort of premonition. Supper was laid in the long room with the yellow blinds, where she had first found Harding Powell. The blinds were drawn tonight, and the lamp on the table burnt low; the oil was giving out. The light in the room was still daylight and came level from the sunset, leaking through the yellow blinds. It struck Agatha that it was the same light, the same ochreish light that they had found in the room six weeks ago. But that was nothing.

What it was she did not know. The horrible light went when the flame of the lamp burnt clearer. Harding was talking to her cheerfully and Milly was smiling at them both, when half through the meal Agatha got up and declared that she must go. She was ill; she was tired; they must forgive her, but she must go.

The Powells rose and stood by her, close to her, in their distress. Milly brought wine and put it to her lips; but she turned her head away and whispered: "Please let me go. Let me get away."

Harding wanted to walk back with her, but she refused with a vehemence that deterred him.

"How very odd of her," said Milly, as they stood at the gate and watched her go. She was walking fast, almost running, with a furtive step, as if something pursued her.

Powell did not speak. He turned from his wife and went slowly back into the house.

9

She knew now what had happened to her. She was afraid of Harding Powell; and it was her fear that had cried to her to go, to get away from him.

The awful thing was that she knew she could not get away from him. She had only to close her eyes and she would find the visible image of him hanging before her on the wall of darkness. And tonight, when she tried to cover it with Rodney's it was no longer obliterated. Rodney's image had worn thin and Harding's showed through. She was more afraid of it than she had been of Harding; and more than anything, she was afraid of being afraid. Harding was the object of a boundless and indestructible compassion, and her fear of him was hateful to her and unholy. She knew that it would be terrible to let it follow her into that darkness where she would presently go down with him alone. "It would be all right," she said to herself, "if only I didn't keep on seeing him."

But he, his visible image, and her fear of it, persisted even while the interior darkness, the divine, beneficent darkness rose round her, wave on wave, and flooded her; even while she held him there and healed him; even while it still seemed to her that her love pierced through her fear and gathered to her, spirit to spirit, flame to pure flame, the nameless, innermost essence of Rodney and of Bella. She had known in the beginning that it was by love that she held them; but now, though she loved Rodney and had almost lost her pity for Harding in her fear of him, it was Harding rather than Rodney that she held.

In the morning she woke with a sense, which was almost a memory, of Harding having been in the room with her all night. She was tired, as if she had had some long and unrestrained communion with him.

She put away at once the fatigue that pressed on her (the gift still "worked" in a flash for the effacing of bodily sensation). She told herself that, after all, her fear had done no harm. Seldom in her experience of the Power had she had so tremendous a sense of having got through to it, of having "worked" it, of having held Harding under it and healed him. For, when all was said and done, whether she had been afraid of him or not, she had held him, she had never once let go. The proof was that he still went sane, visibly, indubitably cured.

All the same, she felt that she could not go through another day like yesterday. She could not see him. She wrote a letter to Milly. Since it concerned Milly so profoundly, it was well that Milly should be made to understand. She hoped that Milly would forgive her if they didn't see her for the next day or two. If she was to go on (she underlined it) she must be left absolutely alone. It seemed unkind when they were going so soon, but— Milly knew—it was impossible to exaggerate the importance of what she had to do.

Milly wrote back that, of course, she understood. It should be as Agatha wished. Only (so Milly "sustained" her) Agatha must not allow herself to doubt the Power. How could she, when she saw what it had done for Harding? If *she* doubted, what could she expect of Harding? But, of course, she must take care of her own dear self. If she failed—if she gave way—what on earth would the poor darling do, now that he had become dependent on her?

She wrote as if it was Agatha's fault that he had become dependent; as if Agatha had nothing, had nobody in the world to think of but Harding; as if nobody, as if nothing in the world beside Harding mattered. And Agatha found herself resenting Milly's view. As if to her anything in the world mattered beside Rodney Lanyon.

For three days she did not see the Powells.

10

The three nights passed as before, but with an increasing struggle and fear.

She knew, she knew what was happening. It was as if the walls of personality were wearing thin, and through them she felt him trying to get at her.

She put the thought from her. It was absurd. It was insane. Such things could not be. It was not in any region of such happenings that she held him, but in the place of peace, the charmed circle, the flawless crystal sphere.

Still the thought persisted; and still, in spite of it, she held him, she would not let him go. By her honour and by her love for Milly she was bound to hold him, even though she knew how terribly, how implacably he prevailed.

She was aware now that the persistence of his image on the blackness was only a sign to her of his being there in his substance; in his supreme innermost essence. It had obviously no relation to his bodily appearance, since she had not seen him for three days. It tended more and more to vanish, to give place to the shapeless, nameless, all-pervading presence. And her fear of him became pervading, nameless and shapeless too.

Somehow it was always behind her now, it followed her from room to room of her house; it drove her out of doors. It seemed to her that she went before it with quick, uncertain feet and a fluttering heart, aimless and tormented as a leaf driven by a vague light wind. Sometimes it sent her up the field towards the wood; sometimes it would compel her to go a little way towards the farm; and then it was as if it took her by the shoulders and turned her back again towards her house.

On the fourth day (which was Tuesday of the Powells' last week) she determined to fight this fear. She could not defy it to the extent of going on to the farm where she might see Harding, but certainly she would not suffer it to turn her from her hill-top. It was there that she had always gone as the night fell, calling home her thoughts to sleep; and it was there, seven weeks ago, that the moon, the golden-white and holy moon, had led her to the consecration of her gift. She had returned softly, seven weeks ago, carrying carefully her gift, as a fragile, flawless crystal. Since then, how recklessly she had held it! To what jars and risks she had exposed the exquisite and sacred thing!

She waited for her hour between sunset and twilight. It was perfect, following a perfect day. Above the wood the sky had a violet lucidity, purer than the day; below it, the pale brown earth wore a violet haze, and over that a web of green, woven of the sparse, thin blades of the young wheat. There were two ways up the hill; one over her own bridge across the river, that led her to the steep, straight path through the wood; one over the Farm bridge by the slanting path up the field. She chose the wood.

She paused on the bridge, and looked down the valley. She saw the farmhouse standing in the stillness that was its own secret and the hour's. A strange, pale lamplight, lit too soon, showed in the windows of the room she knew. The Powells would be sitting there at their supper.

She went on and came to the gate of the wood. It swung open on its hinges, a sign to her that some time or other Harding Powell had passed there. She paused and looked about her. Presently she saw Harding Powell coming down the wood-path.

He stopped. He had not yet seen her. He was looking up to the arch of the beech-trees, where the green light still came through. She could see by his attitude of quiet contemplation the sane and happy creature that he was. He was sane, she knew. And yet, no; she could not really see him as sane. It was her sanity, not his own, that he walked in. Or else what she saw was the empty shell of him. *He* was in her. Hitherto it had been in the darkness that she had felt him most, and her fear of him had been chiefly fear of the invisible Harding, and of what he might do there in the darkness. Now her fear, which had become almost hatred, was transferred to his person. In the flesh, as in the spirit, he was pursuing her.

He had seen her now. He was making straight for her. And she turned and ran round the eastern bend of the hill (a yard or so to the left of her) and hid from him. From where she crouched at the edge of the wood, she saw him descend the lower slope to the river; by standing up and advancing a little she could see him follow the river path on the nearer side and cross by the farm bridge.

She was sure of all that. She was sure that it did not take her more than twelve or fifteen minutes (for she had gone that way a hundred times) to get back to the gate, to walk up the little wood, to cut through it by a track in the undergrowth, and turn round the further and western end of it. Thence she could either take the long path that slanted across the field to the farm bridge or keep to the upper ground along a trail in the grass skirting the wood, and so reach home by the short, straight path and her own bridge.

She decided on the short, straight path as leading her farther from the farmhouse, where there could be no doubt that Harding Powell was now. At the point she had reached, the jutting corner of the wood hid from her the downward slope of the hill, and the flat land at its foot.

As she turned the corner of the wood, she was brought suddenly in sight of the valley. A hot wave swept over her brain, so strong that she staggered as it passed. It was followed by a strange sensation of physical sickness, that passed also. It was then as if what went through her had charged her nerves of sight to a pitch of insane and horrible sensibility. The green of the grass, and of the young corn, the very colour of life, was violent and frightful. Not only was it abominable in itself, it was a thing to be shuddered at, because of some still more abominable significance it had.

Agatha had known once, standing where she stood now, an exaltation of sense that was ecstasy; when every leaf and every blade of grass shone with a divine translucence; when every nerve in her thrilled, and her whole being rang with the joy which is immanent in the life of things.

What she experienced now (if she could have given any account of it) was exaltation at the other end of the scale. It was horror and fear unspeakable. Horror and fear immanent in the life of things. She saw the world in a loathsome transparency; she saw it with the eye of a soul in which no sense of the divine had ever been, of a soul that denied the supernatural. It had been Harding Powell's soul, and it had become hers.

Furiously, implacably, he was getting at her.

Out of the wood and the hedges that bordered it there came sounds that were horrible, because she knew them to be inaudible to any ear less charged with insanity; small sounds of movement, of strange shiverings, swarmings, crepitations; sounds of incessant, infinitely subtle urging, of agony and recoil. Sounds they were of the invisible things unborn, driven towards birth; sounds of the worm unborn, of things that creep and writhe towards dissolution. She knew what she heard and saw.

She heard the stirring of the corruption that Life was; the young blades of corn were frightful to her, for in them was the push, the passion of the evil which was Life; the trees, as they stretched out their arms and threatened her, were frightful with the terror which was Life. Down there, in that gross green hot-bed, the earth teemed with the abomination; and the river, livid, white, a monstrous thing, crawled, dragging with it the very slime.

All this she perceived in a flash, when she had turned the corner. It sank into stillness and grew dim; she was aware of it only as the scene, the region in which one thing, her terror, moved and hunted her. Among sounds of the rustling of leaves, and the soft crush of grass, and the whirring of little wings in fright, she heard it go; it went on the other side of the hedge, a little way behind her as she skirted the wood. She stood still to let it pass her, and she felt that it passed, and that it stopped and waited. A terrified bird flew out of the hedge, no further than a fledgling's flight in front of her. And in that place, it flew from she saw Harding Powell.

He was crouching under the hedge as she had crouched when she had hidden from him. His face was horrible, but not more horrible than the Terror that had gone behind her; and she heard herself crying out to him: "Harding! Harding" appealing to him against the implacable, unseen Pursuer.

He had risen (she saw him rise), but as she called his name, he became insubstantial, and she saw a Thing, a nameless, unnameable, shapeless Thing, proceeding from him. A brown, blurred Thing, transparent as dusk is, that drifted on the air. It was torn and tormented, a fragment parted and flung off from some immense and as yet invisible cloud of horror. It drifted from her; it dissolved like smoke on the hillside; and the Thing that had born and begotten it pursued her.

She bowed under it, and turned from the edge of the wood, the horrible place it had been born in; she ran before it, headlong down the field, trampling the young corn under her feet. As she ran, she heard a voice in the valley, a voice of amazement and entreaty, calling to her in a sort of song.

"What—are—you—running for—Aggy—Aggy?"

It was Milly's voice that called.

Then as she came, still headlong, to the river, she heard Harding's voice saying something, she did not know what. She couldn't stop to listen to him, or to consider how he came to be there in the valley, when a minute ago she had seen him by the edge of the wood, up on the very top of the hill.

He was on the bridge—the farm bridge—now. He held out his hand to steady her as she came on over the swinging plank.

She knew that he had led her to the other side, and that he was standing there, still saying something, and that she answered.

"Have you no pity on me? Can't you let me go?" And then she broke from him and ran.

11

She was awake all that night. Harding Powell and the horror begotten of him had no pity; he would not let her go. Her gift, her secret, was powerless now against the pursuer.

She had a light burning in her room till morning, for she was afraid of sleep. Those unlit roads down which, if she slept, the Thing would surely hunt her, were ten times more terrible than the white-washed, familiar room where it merely watched and waited.

In the morning she found a letter on her breakfast-table, which she said Mrs. Powell had left late last evening, after Agatha had gone to bed. Milly wrote:

Dearest Agatha,—Of course I understand. But are we *never* going to see you again? What was the matter with you last night?

You terrified poor Harding.—Yours ever, M. P.

Without knowing why, Agatha tore the letter into bits and burned them in the flame of a candle. She watched them burn.

"Of course," she said to herself, "that isn't sane of me."

And when she had gone round her house and shut all the doors and locked them, and drawn down the blinds in every closed window, and found herself cowering over her fireless hearth, shuddering with fear, she knew that, whether she were mad or not, there was madness in her. She knew that her face in the glass (she had the courage to look at it) was the face of an insane terror let loose.

That she did know it, that there were moments—flashes—in which she could contemplate her state and recognise it for what it was, showed that there was still a trace of sanity in her. It was not her own madness that possessed her. It was, or rather, it had been, Harding Powell's; she had taken it from him. That was what it meant—to take away madness.

There could be no doubt as to what had happened, nor as to the way of its happening. The danger of it, utterly unforeseen, was part of the very operation of the gift. In the process of getting at Harding to heal him she had had to destroy, not only the barriers of flesh and blood, but those innermost walls of personality that divide and protect, mercifully, one spirit from another. With the first thinning of the walls Harding's insanity had leaked through to her, with the first breach it had broken in.

It had been transferred to her complete with all its details, with its very gestures, in all the phases that it ran through; Harding's premonitory fears and tremblings; Harding's exalted sensibility; Harding's abominable vision of the world, that vision from which the resplendent divinity had perished; Harding's flight before the pursuing Terror. She was sitting now as Harding had sat when she found him crouching over the hearth in that horrible room with the drawn blinds. It seemed to her that to have a madness of your own would not be so very horrible. It would be, after all, your own. It could not possibly be one-half so horrible as this, to have somebody else's madness put into you.

The one thing by which she knew herself was the desire that no longer ran underground, but emerged and appeared before her, lit by her lucid flashes, naked and unshamed.

She still knew her own. And there was something in her still that was greater than the thing that inhabited her, the pursuer, the pursued, who had rushed into her as his refuge, his sanctuary; and that was her fear of him and of what he might do there. If her doors stood open to him, they stood open to Bella and to Rodney Lanyon too.

What else had she been trying for, if it were not to break down in all three of them the barriers of flesh and blood, and to transmit the Power? In the unthinkable sacrament to which she called them they had all three partaken. And since the holy thing could suffer her to be thus permeated, saturated with Harding Powell, was it to be supposed that she could keep him to herself, that she would not pass him on to Rodney Lanyon?

It was not, after all, incredible. If he could get at her, of course he could get, through her, at Rodney.

That was the Terror of terrors, and it was her own. That it could subsist together with that alien horror, that it remained supreme beside it, proved that there was still some tract in her where the invader had not yet penetrated. In her love for Rodney and her fear for him she entrenched herself against the destroyer. There at least she knew herself impregnable.

It was in such a luminous flash that she saw the thing still in her own hands, and resolved that it should cease.

She would have to break her word to Milly. She would have to let Harding go, to loosen deliberately his hold on her and cut him off. It could be done. She had held him through her gift, and it would be still possible, through the gift, to let him go. Of course, she knew it would be hard.

It *was* hard. It was terrible; for he clung. She had not counted on his clinging. It was as if, in their undivided substance, he had had knowledge of her purpose and had prepared himself to fight it. He hung on desperately; he refused to yield an inch of the ground he had taken from her. He was no longer a passive thing in that world where she had brought him. And he had certain advantages. He had possessed her for three nights and for three days. She had made herself porous to him; and her sleep had always been his opportunity.

It took her three nights and three days to cast him out. In the first night she struggled with him. She lay with all her senses hushed, and brought the divine darkness round her, but in the darkness, she was aware that she struggled. She could build up the walls between them, but she knew that as fast as she built them, he tore at them and pulled them down.

She bore herself humbly towards the Power that permitted him.

She conceived of it as holiness—estranged and offended; she pleaded with it. She could no longer trust her knowledge of its working, but she tried to come to terms with it. She offered herself as a propitiation, as a substitute for Rodney Lanyon, if there was no other way by which he might be saved.

Apparently, that was not the way it worked. Harding seemed to gain. But, as he kept her awake all night, he had no chance to establish himself, as he would otherwise have done, in her sleep. The odds between her and her adversary were even.

The second night *she* gained. She felt that she had built up her walls again; that she had cut Harding off. With spiritual pain, with the tearing of the bonds of compassion, with a supreme agony of rupture, he parted from her.

Possibly the Power was neutral; for in the dawn after the second night she slept. That sleep left her uncertain of the event. There was no telling into what unguarded depths it might have carried her. She knew that she had been free of her adversary before she slept, but the chances were that he had got at her in her sleep. Since the Power held the balance even between her and the invader, it would no doubt permit him to enter by any loophole that he could seize.

On the third night, as it were in the last watch, she surrendered, but not to Harding Powell.

She could not say how it came to her; she was lying in her bed with her eyes shut and her arms held apart from her body, diminishing all contacts, stripping for her long slide into the cleansing darkness, when she found herself recalling some forgotten, yet inalienable knowledge that she had.

Something said to her: "Do you not remember? There is no striving and no crying in the world which you would enter. There is no more appeasing where peace is. You cannot make your own terms with the high and holy Power. It is not enough to give yourself for Rodney Lanyon, for he is more to you than you are yourself. Besides, any substitution of self for self would be useless, for there is no more self there. That is why the Power cannot work that way. But if it should require you, here on this side the threshold, to give him up, to give up your desire of him, what then? Would you loose your hold on him and let him go?"

"Would you?" the voice insisted.

She heard herself answer from the pure threshold of the darkness: "I would."

Sleep came on her there; a divine sleep from beyond the threshold; sacred, inviolate sleep.

It was the seal upon the bond.

12

She woke on Friday morning to a vivid and indestructible certainty of escape.

But there had been a condition attached to her deliverance; and it was borne in on her that instead of waiting for the Power to force its terms on her, she would do well to be beforehand with it. Friday was Rodney's day, and this time she knew that he would come. His coming, of course, was nothing, but he had told her plainly that he would not go. She must, therefore, wire to him not to come.

In order to do this, she had to get up early and walk about a mile to the nearest village. She took the shortest way, which was by the farm bridge, and up the slanting path to the far end of the wood. She knew vaguely that once, as she turned the corner of the wood, there had been horrors, and that the divine beauty of green pastures and still waters had appeared to her as a valley of the shadow of evil, but she had no more memory of what she had seen than of a foul dream, three nights dead. She went at first uplifted in the joy of her deliverance, drawing into her the light and fragrance of the young morning. Then she remembered Harding Powell.

She had noticed as she passed the farmhouse that the blinds were drawn again in all the windows. That was because Harding and Milly were gone. She thought of Harding, of Milly, with an immense tenderness and compassion, but also with lucidity, with sanity. They had gone—yesterday—and she had not seen them. That could not be helped. She had done all that was possible. She could not have seen them as long as the least taint of Harding's remained with her. And how could she have faced Milly after having broken her word to her?

Not that she regretted even that, the breaking of her word, so sane was she. She could conceive that, if it had not been for Rodney Lanyon, she might have had the courage to have gone on. She might have considered that she was bound to save Harding, even at the price of her own sanity, since there *was* her word to Milly. But it might be questioned whether by holding on to him she would have kept it, whether she really could have saved him that way. She was no more than a vehicle, a crystal vessel for the inscrutable and secret Power, and in destroying her utterly, Harding would have destroyed himself. You could not transmit the Power through a broken crystal —why, not even through one that had a flaw.

There had been a flaw somewhere; so much was certain. And as she searched now for the flaw, with her luminous sanity, she found it in her fear. She knew, she had always known, the danger of taking fear, and the thought of fear with her into that world where to think was to will, and to will was to create. But for the rest, she had tried to make herself clear as crystal. And what could she do more than give up Rodney?

As she set her face towards the village, she was sustained by a sacred ardour, a sacrificial exaltation. But as she turned homewards across the solitary fields, she realised the sadness, the desolation of the thing she had accomplished. He would not come. Her message would reach him two hours before the starting of the train he always came by.

Across the village she saw her white house shining, and the windows of his room (her study, which was always his room when he came); its lattices were flung open as if it welcomed him.

Something had happened there.

Her maid was standing by the garden gate, looking for her. As she approached, the girl came over the field to meet her. She had an air of warning her, of preparing her for something.

It was Mrs. Powell, the maid said. She had come again. She was in there, waiting for Miss Agatha. She wouldn't go away; she had gone straight in. She was in an awful state. The maid thought it was something to do with Mr. Powell.

They had not gone, then.

"If I were you, miss," the maid was saying, "I wouldn't see her."

"Of course, I shall see her."

She went at once into the room where Rodney might have been, where Milly was. Milly rose from the corner where she sat averted.

"Agatha," she said, "I had to come."

Agatha kissed the white, suppliant face that Milly lifted.

"I thought," she said, "you'd gone—yesterday."

"We couldn't go. He—he's ill again."

"Ill?"

"Yes. Didn't you see the blinds down as you passed?"

"I thought it was because you'd gone."

"It's because that *thing's* come back again."

"When did it come, Milly?"

"It's been coming for three days."

Agatha drew in her breath with a pang. It was just three days since she began to let him go.

Milly went on. "And now he won't come out of the house. He says he's being hunted. He's afraid of being seen, being found. He's in there—in that room. He made me lock him in."

They stared at each other and at the horror that their faces took and gave back each to each.

"Oh, Aggy—" Milly cried it out in her anguish.

"You *will* help him?"

"I can't." Agatha heard her voice go dry in her throat.

"You *can't?*"

Agatha shook her head.

"You mean you haven't, then?"

"I haven't. I couldn't."

"But you told me—you told me you were giving yourself up to it. You said that was why you couldn't see us."

"It *was* why. Do sit down, Milly."

They sat down, still staring at each other. Agatha faced the window, so that the light ravaged her.

Milly went on. "That was why I left you alone. I thought you were going on. You said you wouldn't let him go; you promised me you'd keep on-"

"I did keep on, till—"

But Milly had only paused to hold down a sob. Her voice broke out again, clear, harsh, accusing.

"What were you doing all that time?"

"Of course," said Agatha, "you're bound to think I let you down."

"What am I to think?"

"Milly—I asked you not to think it was me."

"Of course, I knew it was the Power, not you. But you had hold of it. You did something. Something that other people can't do. You did it for one night, and that night he was well. You kept on for six weeks, and he was well all that time. You leave off for three days—I know when you left off—and he's ill again. And then you tell me it isn't you. It *is* you; and if it's you, you can't give him up. You can't stand by, Aggy, and refuse to help him. You know what it was. How can you bear to let him suffer? How can you?"

"I can, because I must."

"And why must you?"

Milly raised her head more in defiance than in supplication.

83

"Because—I told you—I might give out. Well—I *have* given out."

"You told me the Power can't give out—that you've only got to hold on to it—that it's no effort. I'm only asking you, Aggy, to hold on."

"You don't know what you're asking."

"I'm asking you only to do what you have done, to give five minutes in the day to him. You said it was enough. Only five minutes. It isn't much to ask."

Agatha sighed.

"What difference could it make to you—five minutes?"

"You don't understand," said Agatha.

"I do. I don't ask you to see him, or to bother with him; only to go on as you were doing."

"You don't understand. It isn't possible to explain it. I can't go on."

"I see. You're tired, Aggy. Well—not now, not today. But later, when you're rested, won't you?"

"Oh, Milly, dear Milly, if I could—"

"You can. You will. I know you will-"

"No. You must understand it. Never again. Never again."

"Never?"

"Never."

There was a long silence. At last Milly's voice crept through, strained and thin, feebly argumentative, the voice of a thing defeated and yet unconvinced.

"I don't understand you, Agatha. You say it isn't you; you say you're only a connecting link; that you do nothing; that the Power that does it is inexhaustible; that there's nothing it can't do, nothing it won't do for us, and yet you go and cut yourself off from it—deliberately, from the thing you believe to be divine."

"I haven't cut myself off from it."

"You've cut Harding off," said Milly. "If you refuse to hold him."

"That wouldn't cut him off—from It. But, Milly, holding him was bad; it wasn't safe."

"It saved him."

"All the same, Milly, it wasn't safe. The thing itself isn't."

"The Power? The divine thing?"

"Yes. It's divine and it's—it's terrible. It does terrible things to us."

"How could it? If it's divine, wouldn't it be compassionate? Do you suppose it's less compassionate than—*you* are? Why, Agatha, when it's goodness and purity itself—?"

"Goodness and purity are terrible. We don't understand it. It's got its own laws. What you call prayer's all right—it would be safe, I mean—I suppose it might get answered anyway, however we fell short. But *this*—this is different. It's the highest, Milly; and if you rush in and make for the highest, can't you see, oh, can't you *see* how it might break you? Can't you see what it requires of *you*? Absolute purity. I told you, Milly. You have to be crystal to it—crystal without a flaw."

"And—if there were a flaw?"

"The whole thing, don't you see, would break down; it would be no good. In fact, it would be awfully dangerous."

"To whom?"

"To you—to them, the people you're helping. You make a connection; you smash down all the walls so that you—you get through to each other; and supposing there was something wrong with *you*, and it doesn't work any longer (the Power, I mean), don't you see you might do harm where you were trying to help?"

"But—Agatha—there was nothing wrong with you."

"How do I know? Can anybody be sure there's nothing wrong with them?"

"You think," said Milly, "there was a flaw somewhere?"

"There must have been—somewhere-"

"What was it? Can't you find out? Can't you think? Think."

"Sometimes—I've thought it may have been my fear."

"Fear?"

"Yes, it's the worst thing. Don't you remember, I told you not to be afraid?"

"But, Agatha, you were *not* afraid."

"I was—afterwards. I got frightened."

"*You?* And you told *me* not to be afraid," said Milly.

"I had to tell you."

"And I wasn't afraid—afterwards. I believed in you. He believed in you."

"You shouldn't have. You shouldn't. That was just it."

"That was it? I suppose you'll say next it was I who frightened you?"

As they faced each other there, Agatha, with the terrible, the almost supernatural lucidity she had, saw what was making Milly say that. Milly had been frightened; she felt that she had probably communicated her fright; she knew that was dangerous, and she knew that if it had done harm to Harding, she, and not Agatha, would be responsible.

And because she couldn't face her responsibility, she was trying to fasten upon Agatha some other fault than fear.

"No, Milly, I don't say you frightened me; it was my own fear."

"What was there for *you* to be afraid of?"

Agatha was silent. That was what she must never tell her, not even to make her understand. She did not know what Milly was trying to think of her; Milly might think what she liked; but she should never know what her terror had been and her danger.

Agatha's silence helped Milly.

"Nothing," she said, "will make me believe it was your fear that did it. That would never have made you give Harding up. Besides, you were not afraid at first, though you may have been afterwards."

"Afterwards?"

It was her own word, but it had as yet no significance for her.

"After—whatever it was you gave him up for. You gave him up for something."

"I did not. I never gave him up until I was afraid."

"You gave It up. You wouldn't have done that if there had not been something. Something that stood between."

"If," said Agatha, "you could only tell me what it was."

"I can't tell you. I don't know what came to you. I only know that if I'd had a gift like that, I would not have given it up for anything. I wouldn't have let anything come between. I'd have kept myself—"

"I did keep myself—for it. I couldn't keep myself entirely for Harding; there were other things, other people. I couldn't give them up for Harding or for anybody."

"Are you quite sure you kept yourself what you were, Aggy?"

"What *was* I?"

"My dear—you were absolutely pure. You said *that* was the condition."

"Yes. And, don't you see, who is absolutely? If you thought I was, you didn't know me."

As she spoke, she heard the sharp click of the latch as the garden gate fell to; she had her back to the window so that she saw nothing, but she heard footsteps that she knew, resolute and energetic footsteps that hurried to their end. She felt the red blood surge into her face, and saw that Milly's face was white with another passion, and that Milly's eyes were fixed on the figure of the man who came up the garden path. And without looking at her Milly answered:

"I don't know now; but I think I see, my dear—"

In Milly's pause the doorbell rang violently. Milly rose and let her have it. "What the flaw in the crystal was."

13

Rodney entered the room, and it was then that Milly looked at her. Milly's face was no longer the face of passion, but of sadness and reproach, almost of recovered incredulity. It questioned rather than accused her. It said unmistakably, "You gave him up for *that?*"

Agatha's voice recalled her. "Milly, I think you know Mr. Lanyon."

Rodney, in acknowledging Milly's presence, did not look at her. He saw nothing there but Agatha's face, which showed him at last the expression that to his eyes had always been latent in it, the look of the tragic, hidden soul of terror that he had divined in her. He saw her at last as he had known he should someday see her. Terror was no longer there, but it had possessed her; it had passed through her and destroyed that other look she had from her lifted mouth and hair, the look of a thing borne on wings. Now, with her wings beaten, with her white face and haggard eyes, he saw her as a flying thing tracked down and trampled under the feet of the pursuer. He saw it in one flash as he stood there holding Milly's hand.

Milly's face had no significance for him. He didn't see it. When at last he looked at her his eyes questioned her; they demanded an account from her of what he saw.

For Agatha, Milly's face, prepared as it was for leave-taking, remained charged with meaning; it refused to divest itself of reproach and of the incredulity that challenged her. Agatha rose to it.

"You're not going, Milly, just because he's come? You needn't."

Milly *was* going.

He rose to it also.

If Mrs. Powell *would* go like that—in that distressing way—she must at least let him walk back with her. Agatha wouldn't mind. He hadn't seen Mrs. Powell for ages.

He had risen to such a height that Milly was bewildered by him. She let him walk back with her to the farm and a little way beyond it. Agatha said goodbye to Milly at the garden gate and watched them go. Then she went up into her own room.

He was gone so long that she thought he was never coming back again. She didn't want him to come back just yet, but she knew she was not afraid to see him. It didn't occur to her to wonder why, in spite of her message, he had come, nor why he had come by an earlier train than usual; she supposed he must have started before her message could have reached him. All that, his coming or his not coming, mattered so little now.

For now, the whole marvellous thing was clear to her. She knew the secret of the gift. She saw luminously, almost transparently, the way it worked. Milly had shown her. Milly knew; Milly had seen; she had put her finger on the flaw.

It was not fear; Milly had been right there too. Until the moment when Harding Powell had begun to get at her Agatha had never known what fear felt like. It was the strain of mortality in her love for Rodney; the hidden thing, unforeseen and unacknowledged, working its work in the darkness. It had been there all the time, undermining her secret, sacred places. It had made the first breach through which the fear that was *not* her fear had entered. She could tell the very moment when it happened.

She had blamed poor little Milly; but it was the flaw, the flaw that had given their deadly point to Milly's interference and Harding's importunity. But for the flaw they could not have penetrated her profound serenity. Her gift might have been trusted to dispose of them.

For before that moment the gift had worked indubitably; it had never missed once. She looked back on its wonders; on the healing of herself; the first healing of Rodney and Harding Powell; the healing of Bella. It had worked with a peculiar rhythm of its own, and always in a strict, a measurable proportion to the purity of her intention. To Harding's case she had brought nothing but innocent love and clean compassion; to Bella's nothing but a selfless and beneficent desire to help. And because in Bella's case at least she had been flawless, of the three, Bella's was the only cure that had lasted. It had most marvellously endured. And because of the flaw in her she had left Harding worse than she had found him. No wonder that poor Milly had reproached her.

It mattered nothing that Milly's reproaches went too far, that in Milly's eyes she stood suspected of material sin (anything short of the tangible had never been enough for Milly); it mattered nothing that (though Milly mightn't believe it) she had sinned only in her thought; for Agatha, who knew, that was enough; more than enough; it counted more.

For thought went wider and deeper than any deed; it was of the very order of the Powers intangible wherewith she had worked. Why, thoughts unborn and shapeless, that run under the threshold and hide there, counted more in that world where It, the Unuttered, the Hidden and the Secret, reigned.

She knew now that her surrender of last night had been the ultimate deliverance. She was not afraid any more to meet Rodney; for she had been made pure from desire; she was safeguarded forever.

He had been gone about an hour when she heard him at the gate again and in the room below.

She went down to him. He came forward to meet her as she entered; he closed the door behind them; but her eyes held them apart.

"Did you not get my wire?" she said.

"Yes. I got it."

"Then why—?"

"Why did I come? Because I knew what was happening. I wasn't going to leave you here for Powell to terrify you out of your life."

"Surely—you thought they'd gone?"

"I knew they hadn't or you wouldn't have wired."

"But I would. I'd have wired in any case."

"To put me off?"

"To—put—you—off."

"Why?"

He questioned without divination or forewarning. The veil of flesh was as yet over his eyes, so that he could not see.

"Because I didn't mean that you should come, that you should ever come again, Rodney."

He smiled.

"So, you went back on me, did you?"

"If you call it going back."

She longed for him to see.

"That was only because you were frightened," he said.

He turned from her and paced the room uneasily, as if he saw. Presently he drew up by the hearth and stood there for a moment, puzzling it out; and she thought he had seen.

He hadn't. He faced her with a smile again.

"But it was no good, dear, was it? As if I wouldn't know what it meant. You wouldn't have done it if you hadn't been ill. You lost your nerve. No wonder, with those Powells preying on you, body and soul, for weeks."

"No, Rodney, no. I *didn't* want you to come back. And I think—now—it would be better if you didn't stay."

It seemed to her now that perhaps he had seen and was fighting

89

what he saw.

"I'm not going to stay," he said, "I am going—in another hour—to take Powell away somewhere."

He took it up where she had made him leave it. "Then, Agatha, I shall come back again. I shall come back—let me see—on Sunday."

She swept that aside.

"Where are you going to take him?"

"To a man I know who'll look after him."

"Oh, Rodney, it'll break Milly's heart."

She had come, in her agitation, to where he stood. She sat on the couch by the corner of the hearth, and he looked down at her there.

"No," he said, "it won't. It'll give him a chance to get all right. I've convinced her it's the only thing to do. He can't be left here for you to look after."

"Did she tell you?"

"She wouldn't have told me a thing if I hadn't made her. I dragged it out of her, bit by bit."

"Rodney, that was cruel of you."

"Was it? I don't care. I'd have done it if she'd bled."

"What did she tell you?"

"Pretty nearly everything, I imagine. Quite enough for me to see what, between them, they've been doing to you."

"Did she tell you how *he got well?*"

He did not answer all at once. It was as if he drew back before the question, alien and disturbed, shirking the discerned, yet unintelligible issue.

"Did she tell you, Rodney?" Agatha repeated.

"Well, yes. She *told* me."

He seemed to be making, reluctantly, some admission. He sat down beside her, and his movement had the air of ending the discussion. But he did not look at her.

"What do you make of it?" she said.

This time he winced visibly.

"I don't make anything. If it happened—if it happened like *that*, Agatha—"

"It did happen."

"Well, I admit it was uncommonly queer."

He left it there and reverted to his theme.

"But it's no wonder—if you sat down to that for six weeks—it's no wonder you got scared. It's inconceivable to me how that woman could have let you in for him. She knew what he was."

"She didn't know what I was doing till it was done."

"She'd no business to let you go on with it when she did know."

"Ah, but she knew—then—it was all right."

"All right?"

"Absolutely right. Rodney——" She called to him as if she would compel him to see it as it was. "I did no more for him than I did for you and Bella."

He started. "Bella?" he repeated.

He stared at her. He had seen something.

"You wondered how she got all right, didn't you?"

He said nothing.

"That was how."

And still, he did not speak. He sat there, leaning forward, staring now at his own clasped hands. He looked as if he bowed himself before the irrefutable.

"And there was you, too, before that."

"I know," he said then; "I can understand *that*. But—why Bella?"

"Because Bella was the only way."

She had not followed his thoughts, nor he hers.

"The only way?" he said.

"To work it. To keep the thing pure. I had to be certain of my motive, and I knew that if I could give Bella back to you that would prove—to me, I mean—that it was pure."

"But Bella," he said softly—"Bella. Powell I can understand—and me."

It was clear that he could get over all the rest. But he could not get over Bella. Bella's case convinced him. Bella's case could not be explained away or set aside. Before Bella's case he was baffled, utterly defeated. He faced it with a certain awe.

"You were right, after all, about Bella," he said at last. "And so was I. She didn't care for me, as I told you. But she does care now."

She knew it.

"That was what I was trying for," she said. "That was what I meant."

"You meant it?"

"It was the only way. That's why I didn't want you to come back."

He sat silent, taking that in.

"Don't you see now how it works? You have to be pure crystal. That's why I didn't want you to come back."

Obscurely, through the veil of flesh, he saw.

"And I am never to come back?" he said.

"You will not need to come."

"You mean you won't want me?"

"No. I shall not want you. Because, when I did want you, it broke down."

He smiled.

"I see. When you want me, it breaks down."

He rallied for a moment. He made his one last pitiful stand against the supernatural thing that was conquering him.

He had risen to go.

"And when *I* want to come, when I long for you, what then?"

"*Your* longing will make no difference."

She smiled also, as if she foresaw how it would work, and that soon, very soon, he would cease to long for her.

His hand was on the door. He smiled back at her.

"I don't want to shake your faith in it," he said.

"You can't shake my faith in It."

"Still—it breaks down. It breaks down," he cried.

"Never. You don't understand," she said. "It was the flaw in the crystal."

Soon, very soon he would know it. Already he had shown submission.

She had no doubt of the working of the Power. Bella remained as a sign that it had once been, and that, given the flawless crystal, it should be again.

The Nature of the Evidence

This is the story Marston told me. He didn't want to tell it. I had to tear it from him bit by bit. I've pieced the bits together in their time order, and explained things here and there, but the facts are the facts he gave me. There's nothing that I didn't get out of him somehow.

Out of him—you'll admit my source is unimpeachable. Edward Marston, the great K.C., and the author of an admirable work on *The Logic of Evidence.* You should have read the chapters on "What Evidence Is and What It Is Not." You may say he lied; but if you knew Marston, you'd know he wouldn't lie, for the simple reason that he's incapable of inventing anything. So that, if you ask me whether I believe this tale, all I can say is, I believe the things happened, because he said they happened and because they happened to him. As for what they *were*—well, I don't pretend to explain it, neither would he.

You know he was married twice. He adored his first wife, Rosamund, and Rosamund adored him. I suppose they were completely happy. She was fifteen years younger than he, and beautiful. I wish I could make you see how beautiful. Her eyes and mouth had the same sort of bow, full and wide-sweeping, and they stared out of her face with the same grave, contemplative innocence.

Her mouth was finished off at each corner with the loveliest little moulding, rounded like the pistil of a flower. She wore her hair in a solid gold fringe over her forehead, like a child's, and a big coil at the back. When it was let down it hung in a heavy cable to her waist. Marston used to tease her about it. She had a trick of tossing back the rope in the night when it was hot under her, and it would fall smack across his face and hurt him.

There was a pathos about her that I can't describe—a curious, pure, sweet beauty, like a child's; perfect, and perfectly immature; so immature that you couldn't conceive its lasting—like that—any more than childhood lasts. Marston used to say it made him nervous. He was afraid of waking up in the morning and finding that it had changed in the night. And her beauty was so much a part of herself that you couldn't think of her without it. Somehow you felt that if it went, she must go too.

Well, she went first.

For a year afterwards Marston existed dangerously, always on the edge of a break-down. If he didn't go over altogether it was because his work saved him. He had no consoling theories. He was one of those bigoted materialists of the nineteenth century type who believe that consciousness is a purely physiological function, and that when your body's dead, *you're* dead. He saw no reason to suppose the contrary. "When you consider," he used to say, "the nature of the evidence!"

It's as well to bear this in mind, so as to realise that he hadn't any bias or anticipation. Rosamund survived for him only in his memory. And in his memory, he was still in love with her. At the same time, he used to discuss quite cynically the chances of his marrying again.

It seems that in their honeymoon they had gone into that. Rosamund said she hated to think of his being lonely and miserable, supposing she died before he did. She would like him to marry again. If, she stipulated, he married the right woman.

He had put it to her: "And if I marry the wrong one?"

And she had said, that would be different. She couldn't bear that.

He remembered all this afterwards; but there was nothing in it to make him suppose, at the time, that she would take action.

We talked it over, he and I, one night.

"I suppose," he said, "I shall have to marry again. It's a physical necessity. But it won't be anything more. I shan't marry the sort of woman who'll expect anything more. I won't put another woman in Rosamund's place. There'll be no unfaithfulness about it."

And there wasn't. Soon after that first year he married Pauline Silver.

She was a daughter of old Justice Parker, who was a friend of Marston's people. He hadn't seen the girl till she came home from India after her divorce.

Yes, there'd been a divorce. Silver had behaved very decently. He'd let her bring it against *him*, to save her. But there were some queer stories going about. They didn't get round to Marston, because he was so mixed up with her people; and if they had he wouldn't have believed them. He'd made up his mind he'd marry Pauline the first minute he'd seen her. She was handsome; the hard, black, white and vermilion kind, with a little aristocratic nose and a lascivious mouth.

It was, as he had meant it to be, nothing but physical infatuation on both sides. No question of Pauline's taking Rosamund's place.

Marston had a big case on at the time.

They were in such a hurry that they couldn't wait till it was over; and as it kept him in London, they agreed to put off their honeymoon till the autumn, and he took her straight to his own house in Curzon Street.

This, he admitted afterwards, was the part he hated. The Curzon Street house was associated with Rosamund; especially their bed-room—Rosamund's bedroom—and his library. The library was the room Rosamund liked best, because it was his room. She had her place in the corner by the hearth, and they were always alone there together in the evenings when his work was done, and when it wasn't done, she would still sit with him, keeping quiet in her corner with a book.

Luckily for Marston, at the first sight of the library Pauline took a dislike to it.

I can hear her. "*Br-rr-rh!* There's something beastly about this room, Edward. I can't think how you can sit in it."

And Edward, a little caustic:

"You needn't, if you don't like it."

"I certainly shan't."

She stood there—I can see her—on the hearthrug by Rosamund's chair, looking uncommonly handsome and lascivious. He was going to take her in his arms and kiss her vermilion mouth, when, he said, something stopped him. Stopped him clean, as if it had risen up and stepped between them. He supposed it was the memory of Rosam-und, vivid in the place that had been hers.

You see it was just that place, of silent, intimate communion, that Pauline would never take. And the rich, coarse, contented creature didn't even want to take it. He saw that he would be left alone there, all right, with his memory.

But the bedroom was another matter. That, Pauline had made it understood from the beginning, she would have to have. Indeed, there was no other he could well have offered her. The drawing-room cov-ered the whole of the first floor. The bedrooms above were cramped, and this one had been formed by throwing the two front rooms into one. It looked south, and the bathroom opened out of it at the back.

Marston's small northern room had a door on the narrow landing at right angles to his wife's door. He could hardly expect her to sleep there, still less in any of the tight boxes on the top floor. He said he wished he had sold the Curzon Street house.

But Pauline was enchanted with the wide, three-windowed piece that was to be hers. It had been exquisitely furnished for poor little Rosamund; all seventeenth century walnut wood, Bokhara rugs, thick silk curtains, deep blue with purple linings, and a big, rich bed covered with a purple counterpane embroidered in blue.

One thing Marston insisted on: that *he* should sleep on Rosamund's side of the bed, and Pauline in his own old place. He didn't want to see Pauline's body where Rosamund's had been. Of course, he had to lie about it and pretend he had always slept on the side next the window.

I can see Pauline going about in that room, looking at everything; looking at herself, her black, white and vermilion, in the glass that had held Rosamund's pure rose and gold; opening the wardrobe where Rosamund's dresses used to hang, sniffing up the delicate, flower scent of Rosamund, not caring, covering it with her own thick trail.

And Marston (who cared abominably)—I can see him getting more miserable and at the same time more excited as the wedding evening went on. He took her to the play to fill up the time, or perhaps to get her out of Rosamund's rooms; God knows. I can see them sitting in the stalls, bored and restless, starting up and going out before the thing was half over, and coming back to that house in Curzon Street before eleven o'clock.

It wasn't much past eleven when he went to her room.

I told you her door was at right angles to his, and the landing was narrow, so that anybody standing by Pauline's door must have been seen the minute he opened his. He hadn't even to cross the landing to get to her.

Well, Marston swears that there was nothing there when he opened his own door; but when he came to Pauline's he saw Rosamund standing up before it; and, he said, "*She wouldn't let me in.*"

Her arms were stretched out, barring the passage. Oh yes, he saw her face, Rosamund's face; I gathered that it was utterly sweet, and utterly inexorable. He couldn't pass her.

So, he turned into his own room, backing, he says, so that he could keep looking at her. And when he stood on the threshold of his own door she wasn't there.

No, he wasn't frightened. He couldn't tell me what he felt; but he left his door open all night because he couldn't bear to shut it on her. And he made no other attempt to go in to Pauline; he was so convinced that the phantasm of Rosamund would come again and stop him.

I don't know what sort of excuse he made to Pauline the next morning. He said she was very stiff and sulky all day; and no wonder. He was still infatuated with her, and I don't think that the phantasm of Rosamund had put him off Pauline in the least. In fact, he persuaded himself that the thing was nothing but a hallucination, due, no doubt, to his excitement.

Anyhow, he didn't expect to see it at the door again the next night.

Yes. It was there. Only, this time, he said, it drew aside to let him pass. It smiled at him, as if it were saying, "Go in, if you must; you'll see what'll happen."

He had no sense that it had followed him into the room; he felt certain that, this time, it would let him be.

It was when he approached Pauline's bed, which had been Rosamund's bed, that she appeared again, standing between it and him, and stretching out her arms to keep him back.

All that Pauline could see was her bridegroom backing and backing, then standing there, fixed, and the look on his face. That in itself was enough to frighten her.

She said, "What's the matter with you, Edward?"

He didn't move.

"What are you standing there for? Why don't you come to bed?"

Then Marston seems to have lost his head and blurted it out:

"I can't. I can't."

"Can't what?" said Pauline from the bed.

"Can't sleep with you. She won't let me."

"She?"

"Rosamund. My wife. She's there."

"What on earth are you talking about?"

"She's there, I tell you. She won't let me. She's pushing me back."

He says Pauline must have thought he was drunk or something. Remember, she *saw* nothing but Edward, his face, and his mysterious attitude. He must have looked very drunk.

She sat up in bed, with her hard, black eyes blazing away at him, and told him to leave the room that minute. Which he did.

The next day she had it out with him. I gathered that she kept on talking about the "state" he was in.

"You came to my room, Edward, in a *disgraceful* state."

I suppose Marston said he was sorry; but he couldn't help it; he wasn't drunk. He stuck to it that Rosamund was there. He had seen her. And Pauline said, if he wasn't drunk then he must be mad, and he said meekly, "Perhaps I *am* mad."

That set her off, and she broke out in a fury. He was no more mad than she was; but he didn't care for her; he was making ridiculous excuses; shamming, to put her off. There was some other woman.

Marston asked her what on earth she supposed he'd married her for. Then she burst out crying and said she didn't know.

Then he seems to have made it up with Pauline. He managed to make her believe he wasn't lying, that he really had seen something, and between them they arrived at a rational explanation of the appearance. He had been overworking. Rosamund's phantasm was nothing but a hallucination of his exhausted brain.

This theory carried him on till bedtime. Then, he says, he began to wonder what would happen, what Rosamund's phantasm would do next. Each morning his passion for Pauline had come back again, increased by frustration, and it worked itself up crescendo, towards night. Supposing he *had* seen Rosamund. He might see her again. He had become suddenly subject to hallucinations. But as long as you *knew* you were hallucinated you were all right.

So, what they agreed to do that night was by way of precaution, in case the thing came again. It might even be sufficient in itself to prevent his seeing anything.

Instead of going in to Pauline he was to get into the room before she did, and she was to come to him there. That, they said, would break the spell. To make him feel even safer he meant to be in bed before Pauline came.

Well, he got into the room all right.

It was when he tried to get into bed that—he saw her (I mean Rosamund).

She was lying there, in his place next the window, her own place, lying in her immature child-like beauty and sleeping, the firm full bow of her mouth softened by sleep. She was perfect in every detail, the lashes of her shut eyelids golden on her white cheeks, the solid gold of her square fringe shining, and the great braided golden rope of her hair flung back on the pillow.

He knelt down by the bed and pressed his forehead into the bedclothes, close to her side. He declared he could feel her breathe.

He stayed there for the twenty minutes Pauline took to undress and come to him. He says the minutes stretched out like hours. Pauline found him still kneeling with his face pressed into the bedclothes. When he got up, he staggered.

She asked him what he was doing and why he wasn't in bed. And he said, "It's no use. I can't. I can't."

But somehow, he couldn't tell her that Rosamund was there. Rosamund was too sacred; he couldn't talk about her. He only said:

"You'd better sleep in my room tonight."

He was staring down at the place in the bed where he still saw Rosamund. Pauline couldn't have seen anything but the bedclothes, the sheet smoothed above an invisible breast, and the hollow in the pillow. She said she'd do nothing of the sort. She wasn't going to be frightened out of her own room. He could do as he liked.

He couldn't leave them there; he couldn't leave Pauline with Rosamund, and he couldn't leave Rosamund with Pauline. So, he sat up in a chair with his back turned to the bed. No. He didn't make any attempt to go back. He says he knew she was still lying there, guarding his place, which was her place. The odd thing is that he wasn't in the least disturbed or frightened or surprised. He took the whole thing as a matter of course. And presently he dozed off into a sleep.

A scream woke him and the sound of a violent body leaping out of the bed and thudding on to its feet. He switched on the light and saw the bedclothes flung back and Pauline standing on the floor with her mouth open.

He went to her and held her. She was cold to the touch and shaking with terror, and her jaws dropped as if she was palsied.

She said, "Edward, there's something in the bed."

He glanced again at the bed. It was empty.

"There isn't," he said. "Look."

He stripped the bed to the foot-rail, so that she could see.

"There *was* something."

"Do you see it."

"No. I felt it."

She told him. First something had come swinging, smack across her face. A thick, heavy rope of woman's hair. It had waked her. Then she had put out her hands and felt the body. A woman's body, soft and horrible; her fingers had sunk in the shallow breasts. Then she had screamed and jumped.

And she couldn't stay in the room. The room, she said, was "beastly."

She slept in Marston's room, in his small single bed, and he sat up with her all night, on a chair.

She believed now that he had really seen something, and she remembered that the library was beastly, too. Haunted by something. She supposed that was what she had felt. Very well. Two rooms in the house were haunted; their bedroom and the library. They would just have to avoid those two rooms. She had made up her mind, you see, that it was nothing but a case of an ordinary haunted house; the sort of thing you're always hearing about and never believe in till it happens to yourself. Marston didn't like to point out to her that the house hadn't been haunted till she came into it.

The following night, the fourth night, she was to sleep in the spare room on the top floor, next to the servants, and Marston in his own room.

But Marston didn't sleep. He kept on wondering whether he would or would not go up to Pauline's room. That made him horribly restless, and instead of undressing and going to bed, he sat up on a chair with a book. He wasn't nervous; but he had a queer feeling that something was going to happen, and that he must be ready for it, and that he'd better be dressed.

It must have been soon after midnight when he heard the door knob turning very slowly and softly.

The door opened behind him and Pauline came in, moving without a sound, and stood before him. It gave him a shock; for he had been thinking of Rosamund, and when he heard the door knob turn it was the phantasm of Rosamund that he expected to see coming in. He says, for the first minute, it was this appearance of Pauline that struck him as the uncanny and unnatural thing.

She had nothing, absolutely nothing on but a transparent white chiffony sort of dressing-gown. She was trying to undo it. He could see her hands shaking as her fingers fumbled with the fastenings.

He got up suddenly, and they just stood there before each other, saying nothing, staring at each other. He was fascinated by her, by the sheer glamour of her body, gleaming white through the thin stuff, and by the movement of her fingers. I think I've said she was a beautiful woman, and her beauty at that moment was overpowering.

And still he stared at her without saying anything. It sounds as if their silence lasted quite a long time, but in reality, it couldn't have been more than some fraction of a second.

Then she began. "Oh, Edward, for God's sake say something. Oughtn't I to have come?"

And she went on without waiting for an answer. "Are you thinking of *her*? Because, if—if you are, I'm not going to let her drive you away from me. . . . I'm not going to. . . . She'll keep on coming as long as we don't—Can't you see that this is the way to stop it. . .? When you take me in your arms."

She slipped off the loose sleeves of the chiffon thing and it fell to her feet. Marston says he heard a queer sound, something between a groan and a grunt, and was amazed to find that it came from himself.

He hadn't touched her yet—mind you, it went quicker than it takes to tell, it was still an affair of the fraction of a second—they were holding out their arms to each other, when the door opened again without a sound, and, without visible passage, the phantasm was there. It came incredibly fast, and thin at first, like a shaft of light sliding between them. It didn't do anything; there was no beating of hands, only, as it took on its full form, its perfect likeness of flesh and blood, it made its presence felt like a push, a force, driving them asunder.

Pauline hadn't seen it yet. She thought it was Marston who was beating her back. She cried out: "Oh, don't, don't push me away!" She stooped below the phantasm's guard and clung to his knees, writhing and crying. For a moment it was a struggle between her moving flesh and that still, supernatural being.

And in that moment Marston realised that he hated Pauline. She was fighting Rosamund with her gross flesh and blood, taking a mean advantage of her embodied state to beat down the heavenly, discarnate thing.

He called to her to let go.

"It's not I," he shouted. "Can't you *see* her?"

Then, suddenly, she saw, and let go, and dropped, crouching on the floor and trying to cover herself. This time she had given no cry.

The phantasm gave way; it moved slowly towards the door, and as it went it looked back over its shoulder at Marston, it trailed a hand, signalling to him to come.

He went out after it, hardly aware of Pauline's naked body that still writhed there, clutching at his feet as they passed, and drew itself after him, like a worm, like a beast, along the floor.

She must have got up at once and followed them out on to the landing; for, as he went down the stairs behind the phantasm, he could see Pauline's face, distorted with lust and terror, peering at them above the stairhead. She saw them descend the last flight, and cross the hall at the bottom and go into the library. The door shut behind them.

Something happened in there. Marston never told me precisely what it was, and I didn't ask him. Anyhow, that finished it.

The next day Pauline ran away to her own people. She couldn't stay in Marston's house because it was haunted by Rosamund, and he wouldn't leave it for the same reason.

And she never came back; for she was not only afraid of Rosamund, she was afraid of Marston. And if she *had* come it wouldn't have been any good. Marston was convinced that, as often as he attempted to get to Pauline, something would stop him. Pauline certainly felt that, if Rosamund were pushed to it, she might show herself in some still more sinister and terrifying form. She knew when she was beaten.

And there was more in it than that. I believe he tried to explain it to her; said he had married her on the assumption that Rosamund was dead, but that now he knew she was alive; she was, as he put it, "there." He tried to make her see that if he had Rosamund he couldn't have *her*. Rosamund's presence in the world annulled their contract.

You see I'm convinced that something *did* happen that night in the library. I say, he never told me precisely what it was, but he once let something out. We were discussing one of Pauline's love-affairs (after the separation she gave him endless grounds for divorce).

"Poor, Pauline," he said, "she thinks she's so passionate."

"Well," I said, "wasn't she?"

Then he burst out. "No. She doesn't know what passion is. 'None of you know. You haven't the faintest conception. You'd have to get rid of your bodies first. *I* didn't know until—"

He stopped himself. I think he was going to say, "until Rosamund came back and showed me." For he leaned forward and whispered: "It isn't a localised affair at all. . . . If you only knew—"

So, I don't think it was just faithfulness to a revived memory. I take it there had been, behind that shut door, some experience, some terrible and exquisite contact. More penetrating than sight or touch. More—more extensive: passion at all points of being.

Perhaps the supreme moment of it, the ecstasy, only came when her phantasm had disappeared.

He couldn't go back to Pauline after *that*.

If the Dead Knew

1

The voluntary swelled, it rose, it rushed to its climax.

The organist tossed back his head with a noble gesture, exalted; he rocked on his bench; his feet shuffled faster and faster, pedalling passionately.

The young girl who stood beside him drew in a deep, rushing breath; her heart swelled; her whole body listened, with hurried senses desiring the climax, the climax, the crash of sound. Her nerves shook as the organist rocked towards her; when he tossed back his head her chin lifted; she loved his playing hands, his rocking body, his superb, excited gesture.

Three times a week Wilfrid Hollyer went down to Lower Wyck, to give Effie Carroll a music lesson; three times a week Effie Carroll came up to Wyck on the Hill to listen to Hollyer's organ practice.

The climax had come. The voluntary fell from its height and died in a long cadence, thinned out, a trickling, trembling diminuendo. It was all over.

The young girl released her breath in a long, trembling sigh.

The organist rose and put out the organ lights. He took Effie by the arm and led her down the short aisles of the little country church and out on to the flagged path of the churchyard between the tombstones.

"Wilfrid," she said, "you're too good for Wyck. You ought to be playing in Gloucester Cathedral."

"I'm not good enough. Perhaps—if I'd been trained—"

"Why weren't you?"

"My mother couldn't afford it. Besides, I couldn't leave her. She hasn't anybody but me."

"I know. You're awfully fond of her, aren't you?"

"Yes," he said shortly.

They had passed down the turn of the street into the Market Square. There was a plot of grass laid down in the north-east corner. Two tall elms stood up on the grass, and behind the elms a small, ivy-covered house with mullioned windows, looking south.

"That's our house," Hollyer said. "Won't you come in and see her?"

They found her sitting by herself in the little cramped, green drawing-room. She was the most beautiful old lady; small, upright and perfect; slender, like a girl, in her grey silk blouse. She had a miniature oval face, pretty and white: a sharp chin, and a wide forehead under a pile of pure white hair. And sorrowful blue eyes, white-lidded, in two rings of mauve and bistre.

She couldn't be so very old, Effie thought. Not more than sixty.

Mrs. Hollyer rose, holding out a fragile hand.

Presently she said: "I wanted to see you; after all you've done for him."

"I? I haven't done anything."

"You've listened to his playing. He can't get anybody to do that for him in Wyck."

"They hear enough of me on Sundays."

"Then they haven't heard him. He plays much better on week-days, when he plays to me," said Effie.

"So, I can imagine," Mrs. Hollyer said.

"She thinks I'm better than I am," said Hollyer.

"Go on thinking it. That's the way to make him better." She was smiling at Effie as if she liked her.

All through tea-time and after they talked about Wilfrid's playing and Wilfrid and Wyck, and the people of Wyck, and how they knew nothing and cared nothing about Wilfrid's playing.

Twilight came, twilight of October. He was going to walk back with Effie down the hill to Lower Wyck.

As the house door closed behind them, he said: "Now you know why I'm nothing but an organist at Wyck."

"Wilfrid, she's the most beautiful thing I've seen yet—your mother. No wonder you can't leave her."

"It isn't that altogether. I mean we're tied here because we can't afford to leave; and because I've got this organ job. I should never have had it anywhere else." He paused. "And you know, I couldn't live on it—without mother. She's got the house."

Effie said nothing.

"So here I am. Thirty-five and still dependent on my mother."

"Oh, Wilfrid, what will you do when—when—"

"When my mother dies? That's the awful thing. I shall have enough then. There'll be the house and her income. I hate to think of it. I don't think of it-"

"You see," he went on, "when I was a kid, I was so seedy they didn't think I'd live. So, I was brought up to do nothing. Nothing but my playing. They gave me this job just to keep me quiet. And now I'm strong enough, but there's nothing else I can do."

He hung his head, frowning gloomily.

"You know why I'm telling you all this?"

"No. But I'm glad you've told me."

"It's because—because—if I had a decent income, Effie, I'd ask you to marry me. As it is, I can only hope that you won't ever care for me as I care for you."

"But I *do* care for you. You know I do."

"Would you have married me, Effie? Do you care as much as that?"

"You know I would. I will the minute you ask me."

"I shall never ask you."

"Why not? I can wait."

"My dear, for what?" He paused again. "I can't marry in my mother's life-time."

"Oh, Wilfrid—I didn't mean that. Your dear, beautiful mother. You know I didn't."

"Of course, darling, I know. But there it is."

He left her at the gate of the cottage where she lived with her father.

As he went back up the hill he meditated on his position. He was right to make it clear to her, now that she had begun to care for him. He would have told her long ago if he had known that she cared. Yesterday he didn't know it. But today there had been something, in her manner, in her voice, in the way she looked at him in the church after his playing, that had told him.

Poor little Effie. She would have nothing either, unless her father—and Effie's father was a robust man, not quite fifty.

Well—he mustn't think of it. And he mustn't let his mother think. He wondered whether he was too late, whether she had seen anything. He tried to slink past the drawing-room and up the stairs. But his mother had heard him come in. She called to him. He went to her, shame-faced, as if he had committed a sin.

Her large, gentle eyes looked at him, wondering. He could see them wondering.

"Wilfrid," she said suddenly, "do you care for that little girl?"

"What's the good of my caring? I can't marry her. I've just told her so."

"It's too late. She's in love with you. You should have told her before."

"How could I if she didn't care? You can't be fatuous."

"No—poor boy. Poor Effie."

"Mother—why couldn't I have been brought up to a profession?"

"You know why—you weren't strong enough. It was as much as I could do to keep you alive."

"I'm strong enough now."

"Only because I took such care of you. Only because you hadn't to go out and earn your own living. You'd have been dead before you were twenty if I hadn't kept you with me."

"It would have been better if you'd let me die."

"Don't say that, Wilfrid. What should I have done without you? What should I do without you now?"

"You mean if I married?"

"No, my dear. I'd be glad if you could marry. I don't want to keep you tied to me for ever. If you can get better work and better pay by going anywhere else, I shan't mind your leaving me."

"I shouldn't get anything. I'm not good enough. I shall never be worth more than fifty pounds a year anywhere. We can't live on that."

"If you could live on half my income, I'd give it you, but you couldn't."

"No. We'll just have to wait."

"I hope for your sake, my dear, it won't be too long."

"What do you mean, mother?"

"What did *you* mean?"

"Why, I meant we'd have to wait till I heard of something."

"You *might* have meant something else." She smiled.

"Oh, mother—*don't*."

"Why not?" she said cheerfully.

"You know—you know I couldn't bear it."

"You'll have to bear it someday—I'm an old woman."

"Well, I shall be an old man—by then."

He tossed it back to her, laughing, as he left her to wash his hands and brush his hair. He laughed, to shake off her pathos and to hide his own.

When he talked about waiting, he hadn't meant what she thought he meant. He was simply trying to dismiss a too serious situation with a reassuring levity. Waiting to hear of something? Was it likely he would ever hear of anything? Could he have made a more frivolous suggestion?

It was she who had faced it. She had made him see how hopeless their case was, his and Effie's. He saw it now, as he saw his own face in the glass, between two hair-brushes, a little drawn, even now, a little sallow and haggard. Not a young face.

He would be an old man—an old man before he could dream of marrying. His mother, after all, was only sixty, and she came of a long-lived family. Her apparent fragility was an illusion; she had never had a day's illness as long as he could remember. Nerves like whipcord, young arteries, and every organ sound. She would live ten—fifteen—twenty years longer, live to be eighty. He was thirty-five now, and Effie was twenty-five. Before they could marry, they would be fifty-five and forty-five; old, old; too old to feel, to care passionately. He had no right to ask Effie to wait twenty years for him.

He must give up thinking about her.

His mother was still in her chair by the drawing-room fire, waiting for him. She turned as he came to her, and held up her face to be kissed, like a child, he thought, or like a young wife waiting for her husband. She put her hands on his hair and stroked it. And he remembered the time when he used to say to her: "I shall never marry. You're all the wife I want, Mother."

And now it was as if he had been calculating on her death.

But he hadn't. He hadn't. You couldn't calculate on anything so far-off, so unlikely. He had done the only possible, the only decent thing. He had given Effie up.

2

The doctor had gone. Hollyer went back into his mother's room. She lay there, dozing, in the big white bed, propped high on the pillows. Through her mouth, piteously open, he could hear her short quick breath, struggling and gasping.

The illness had lasted nine days. Even now Hollyer hadn't got used to it. He still looked at the figure in the bed with the same stare of shocked incredulity. It was still incredible that his mother's influenza should have turned to pleurisy, that she should lie like that, utterly abandoned, the neat pile of her hair undone, and her face, with its open mouth, loose and infirm between the two white loops that hung askew, rumpled by the pillow. He knew in a vague way how it had happened. First his own attack of influenza, then his mother's. His had been pretty bad, but hers had been slight, so slight that it had not been recognised, and through it she had still nursed him. Then she had gone out too soon, in the raw January weather. And now the doctor came morning and evening; she had a trained nurse for the night, and Hollyer looked after her all day.

He had got used to the nurse. Her expensive presence proved to him that he had nothing to reproach himself with; he had done, as they said, everything that could be done.

He knew that the nurse and the doctor disagreed about the case. Nurse Eden declared that his mother would get over it. Dr. Ransome was convinced she wouldn't; she hadn't strength in her for another rally. Hollyer himself agreed with Nurse Eden. He couldn't believe that his mother would die. The thought of her death was unbearable, therefore he denied it, he put it from him. When he left her for the night he would come creeping back at midnight and dawn, to make sure that she was still there.

The little room was half filled by the big white bed. It seemed to him there was nothing in it but the white bed and his mother and Nurse Eden in her white uniform. She had looked in on her way downstairs to tea. Everything was cold and white. On the window panes the frost made a white pattern of moss and feathers. From his seat between the bed and the fire he could see Nurse Eden and her small, pure face brooding above the pillows as she shifted them with tender, competent hands.

"She'll be better in the morning," she said. "She always gets better in the night."

She did. Always she gained ground in the night under Nurse Eden and always she lost it in the daytime, getting worse and worse towards evening.

The afternoon wore on. At four o'clock old Martha, the servant, tapped at the door. Miss Carroll, she said, was downstairs and wanted to see him. Martha took his place at the bedside.

Every day Effie came to inquire, and every day she went away sad, as if it had been her own mother who was dying. This time she stayed, for the old doctor had stopped her in the Square and told her to get Hollyer out of his mother's room, if possible. "Talk to him. Take him off it Make him buck up."

She sat in his mother's chair behind the round tea-table and poured out his tea for him, and talked to him about his music and a book she had been reading. When he looked at her, at her sweet face, soft and clear with youth, at her hands moving with pretty gestures, his heart trembled. That was how it would be if Effie was his wife. They would sit there every day and she would pour out his tea for him. He would hear her feet running up and down the stairs.

When she got up to go, she said, "Whatever you do, Wilfrid, don't keep on thinking about it."

"I can't help thinking."

She put her hand on his sleeve and stroked it. At her touch he broke down.

"Oh, Effie—I cannot bear it. If she dies, I shall never forgive myself."

"Nonsense. Don't talk about her dying. Don't think about it."

She turned to him on the doorstep. "Just think how strong she is. I can't see her ill, somehow. I see her there, all the time, sitting upright in her chair, looking beautiful."

That was how *he* had once seen her, sitting there between the fire and the round tea-table, for years and years, as long as his own life lasted.

But now he saw Effie. Upstairs, in his mother's room, as he watched, he saw Effie. Effie—the sweet face, and the sweet hands moving. He heard Effie's voice in the rooms, Effie's feet on the stairs. That was how it would be if Effie was his wife.

That was how it would be if his mother died.

He would have an income of his own, and a house of his own; he would be his own master in his house.

If his mother died, Effie and he would sleep together. Perhaps in that bed, on those pillows.

He shut his eyes and covered his face with his hands, pressing in on his eyelids as if that way he could keep out the sight of Effie.

3

That evening the doctor came again. He left a little before nine o'clock, the hour when Nurse Eden would begin her night watch. He refused to hold out any hope. She was sinking fast.

As Hollyer turned from the front door he met Nurse Eden coming downstairs. She signed to him to follow her into the drawing-room, moving before him without a sound. She shut the door.

He was afraid of Nurse Eden; there was something—he didn't know what it was, but—there was something unbearable in her small, pure face; in the thrust of her chin tilted by the stiff cap-strings; in her brave, slender mouth, straightening itself against the droop of its compassion; and in the stillness of her dense, grey eyes. Her eyes made him feel uneasy, somehow, and unsafe. He was going to sit up with her tonight; but he would rather have shared his night-watch with old Martha.

"Well?" she said.

"He says this is the end."

"It may be," said Nurse Eden. "But it needn't."

"You've seen her."

"Yes."

"*Well—?*"

"She hasn't gone yet, Mr. Hollyer—She's on the edge. She's in that state when a breath would tip her one way or the other."

"A breath?"

"Yes, Mr. Hollyer. Or a thought."

"A thought?"

"A thought. If I had Mrs. Hollyer to myself, I believe I could bring her round even now."

"Oh, Nurse—"

"I *have* brought her round. Night after night I've brought her."

"What do you do?"

"I don't know what I do. But it works. Haven't you noticed she gets better in the night when I've had her; and that she slips back in the day?"

"Yes, I have."

"You see, Mr. Hollyer, Dr. Ransome's made up his mind. And when the doctor makes up his mind that the patient's going to die, ten to one the patient does die. It lowers their resistance. It isn't every one that would feel it; but your mother would."

"If," she went on, "I had her day *and* night, I might save her."

"You really think that?"

"I think there's a chance."

He didn't know whether he believed her or not. Dr. Ransome shrugged his shoulders and said Nurse Eden could try it if she liked. She had a wonderful way with her; but he wouldn't advise Hollyer to count on it. Nothing but a miracle, he said, could save his mother.

110

Hollyer didn't count on Nurse Eden's way. But he thought—something stronger than himself compelled him to think—that his mother would not die.

And each hour showed her slowly coming back. Under his eyes the miracle was being accomplished. At midnight her breathing and temperature and pulse were normal; and by noon of the next day even Ransome was convinced. He wouldn't swear to the miracle, but whatever Nurse Eden had or had not done, he believed Mrs. Hollyer would recover.

Hollyer not only believed it, but he was certain, as Nurse Eden was certain. She came to him, radiant with certainty, and told him that his mind could be at rest now.

But his mind was not at rest. It had only rested while he doubted, as if doubt absolved him from knowledge of some secret that he could not face. With the first moment of certainty, he was aware of it. It was given to him in physical sensations, a weight and pain about his heart that did not lie. In a flash he saw himself back in his old life of dependence and frustration. There would be no Effie sitting with him in the house, no Effie running up and down the stairs. He would not sleep with Effie in the big, white bed. They would grow old, wanting each other.

He tried to jerk his mouth into a smile, but it had stiffened. It opened, gasping, as his muffled heart-beats choked him.

He went upstairs to his mother's room. She was sitting up in bed, clear-eyed, almost alert, and she turned her face to him as he entered.

"I don't know how it is," she said, "I thought I was going, but there's something that won't let me go. It keeps on pulling me back and back." (Nurse Eden looked at him.) "Is it you, Wilfrid?"

He knelt down and buried his face in the bedclothes by her side. His sobs shook the mattress. The nurse took him by the arm; he got up and stared at her as if dazed and drunk with grief. She led him from the room.

"You're upsetting her," she said. "Don't come back till you've pulled yourself together."

When he went back his mother was sleeping calmly. Hollyer and the nurse withdrew from the bedside to the window and talked there in low voices.

"Did you hear what she said, Nurse?"

"Yes. We can get her through, between us, if we make up our minds she's to live. Think of what she was yesterday."

"But do you think we ought to? I don't want her brought back to suffer."

"She isn't going to suffer. There's no reason why she shouldn't be as well as ever. If you want her to live."

"Want her? Of course, I want her to live."

"I know you do. But you must get rid of your fear."

"My fear?"

"Your fear of her dying."

"Do you think my fear could—could make her?"

"I know it could. Make up your mind with me that she's going to get well."

"Supposing she wants to go? Supposing she's fighting against us all the time?"

"She isn't fighting. She hasn't any fight in her—— Now, while she's sleeping, is the time. You've only got to say to yourself 'She shall live. She's going to live.' There—you sit in that chair, make yourself quite comfortable, shut your eyes, and keep on saying it. Don't think of anything else."

He sat down. He said it over and over again: "She shall live. She's going to live. She shall live——" He tried to think of nothing else; but all the time he was aware of the dragging of his heart. He shut his eyes, but he couldn't get rid of the vision of Effie. Effie sitting in his mother's place. Effie sleeping beside him in the big bed.

"She *shall* live. She's going to live." The words meant nothing. Only the dragging weight at his heart had meaning. And it didn't lie.

He thought: If that's how I feel about it, I'd better keep my mind off her.

Then he was aware that he was tired, dead beat, too tired to think. And presently, sitting upright in the chair, he fell asleep.

He was waked by Nurse Eden's voice calling to him from the bed: "Mr. Hollyer! She's going!"

His mother lay in the nurse's arms, her head had fallen forward on her chest, her mouth was open; and through it there came a groaning, grating cry. Once, twice, three times; and she was gone.

After the funeral Hollyer went up into his mother's room. Nurse Eden was there, removing the signs of death. She had covered the bed with a white counterpane. She had opened the door and window wide, and a flood of clean cold air streamed through the room.

"Nurse," he said, "come here a minute."

She followed him into his bed-sitting room on the other side of the landing. Hollyer shut the door.

"You remember that night when my mother got better?"

"Indeed, I do."

"Do you still think you brought her back?"

"I do think it."

"Do you really believe that a thought—*a thought* could do that?"

"Yes."

"But it doesn't always work. It breaks down."

"Sometimes. That night she died I felt it wasn't working. I was up against a wall. I couldn't get through. But remember, before that, she was going when I brought her back."

"Could a thought—another thought—kill?"

"It depends. Perhaps, if it was a very strong thought. A wish."

Her queer eyes looked through him and beyond him, not seeing him, seeing some reality that was not he. He had gone to her for her truth and she had given it him. A wish, even a hidden wish, could kill. In the dark, secret places of the mind your thoughts ran loose beyond your knowing; they burrowed under the walls that shut off one self from another; they got through. It was as if his secret self had broken loose, and got through to his mother, and had killed her secretly, in the dark. His wish was a part of himself, but stronger than himself. The force behind it was indestructible, for it was a form of his desire for Effie; so that while he lived, he could not kill it.

It had been there all the time, cunningly disguised. It was there in his fear of Nurse Eden; it was there in that obstinate belief of his that his mother would live. His beliefs were always the expression of his fears. He had been afraid that his mother would not die. That was his fear. He saw it all clearly in the moment while Nurse Eden's voice went on.

"But it wasn't *that*, Mr. Hollyer," she was saying. "We were all wishing her to live— No. I think she was too far gone. She had got beyond us."

It was too late for Nurse Eden to go back on it. He knew. He was certain.

4

He knew, and if he were to keep on thinking about it— but he was afraid to think. You could go mad, thinking. The moment of his certainty remained in his memory; he knew where to find it if he chose to look that way. But he refused to look. Such things were better forgotten.

He told himself there was nothing in it. Nothing but Nurse Eden's hysteria and vanity. She wanted you to believe she was wonderful, that she could do things. She didn't really believe it herself. In her own last moment of honesty, she had confessed as much. He was a fool to have been taken in by her.

Meanwhile, three months after his mother's death, he had married Effie Carroll. Her father, who had held out against the engagement, surrendered suddenly on the day of the wedding, and made his daughter an allowance of fifty pounds a year. He said he didn't want to profit by her folly, and the fifty pounds were no more than the cost of her keep.

It was horrible to think they should owe their happiness to his mother's death; but as things had turned out they didn't owe it; they could have married even if she had lived. And as he had now no motive for wishing her dead, he almost forgot that he had ever wished it.

Not that Hollyer reproached himself; his tendency, when he thought it all over, was to reproach his mother. He had found out something about himself. Before he married, he had gone to Dr. Ransome to be overhauled, and Ransome had told him there was nothing much the matter with him; never was. And if the old pessimist said there wasn't much the matter, you might depend upon it there wasn't anything at all. Except, Ransome said, molly-coddling; and that wasn't Hollyer's fault.

"Whose was it, then?" Hollyer had asked. "My mother's?"

"No. Your dear mother, Hollyer, had no faults. But she made mistakes, as we all do."

"You mean, if I'd been allowed to live like other people I'd have been all right?"

"Well—you weren't a very robust infant; and later on, there *was* a slight risk. Personally, I'd have taken it. You must take some risks. But your mother was afraid. You were all she had. And I daresay she wasn't sorry to keep you with her."

"I see."

He saw it clearly. He had been sacrificed to his mother's selfishness. Nothing but that had doomed him to his humiliating dependence, his poverty, his intolerable celibacy. He found himself brooding over it, going back and back to it, with a certain gratification, as if it justified him.

His mind was appeased by this righteous resentment. When the remembrance of his mother's beauty and sweetness rushed at him and accused him, he turned from it to his brooding.

He had begun to talk, to say things about his mother. Put into spoken words his grievance seemed more real; it acquired validity.

He had felt so safe. His mother couldn't hear him. She would never know what he thought about her; he would have died rather than let her know. And he had only talked to Effie. Talking to his wife was no worse than thinking to himself. After all he had gone through, he felt he was entitled to that relief.

It was June, a hot, close evening before lamp-light; they were sitting together in the drawing-room, Effie in his mother's chair and he at his piano in the recess on the other side of the fireplace. And there was something that Effie said when he had stopped playing and had turned to her, smiling.

"Wilfrid—are you happy?"

"Of course, I'm happy."

"No, but—really?"

"Really. Absolutely. You make me happy."

"Do I? I'm so glad. You see, when I married you, I was afraid I couldn't. It was so hard to come after your mother."

He winced.

"How do you mean? You don't come 'after' her."

"I mean, after all she was to you. After all she did. Your life with her was so perfect."

"If it's any consolation to you, Effie, it wasn't."

"Wasn't?"

"No. Anything but."

"Oh, Wilfrid!"

He seemed to her to be uttering blasphemy.

"It's better you should know it. My dear mother didn't understand me in the least. My whole up-bringing was a ghastly blunder. If I'd been let live a decent life, like any other boy, like any other man, I might have been good for something. But she wouldn't let me. She pretended there was something the matter with me when there wasn't, so that she could keep me dependent on her."

"Wilfrid *dear*, it may have been a blunder and it may have been ghastly—"

"It was."

"But it was only her love for you."

"A very selfish sort of love, Effie."

"Oh *don't*," she cried. "Don't. She's *dead*, Wilfrid."

"I'm not likely to forget it."

"You talk as if you'd forgotten— If the dead knew—"

If the dead knew—

"If they knew," she said, "how we spoke about them, how we thought—"

If the dead knew—

If his mother had heard him; if she knew what he had been thinking; if she knew that he had wished her dead and that his wish had killed her—

If the dead knew—

"Happily, for us and them, they don't know," he said.

And he began playing again. He was aware that Effie had risen and was now seated at the writing-table. As he played, he had his back to the writing-table and the door.

The book on the piano ledge before him was Mendelssohn's *Lieder ohne Worte*, open as Effie had left it at Number Nine. He remembered that was the one his mother had loved so much. His fingers fell of their own accord into the prelude, into the melody, pressing out its thick, sweet, deliberate sadness. It wounded him, each note a separate stab, yet he went on, half-voluptuously enjoying the self-inflicted pain, trying to work it up and up into a supreme poignancy of sorrow, of regret.

As he stopped on the closing chord, he heard somewhere behind him a thick, sobbing sigh.

"Effie—"

He looked round. But Effie was not there. He could hear her footsteps in the room overhead. She had gone, then, before he had stopped playing, shutting the door without a sound. It must have been his imagination.

He played a few bars, then paused, listening. The sighing had begun again; it was close behind him.

He swung round sharply. There was nobody there. But the door, which had been shut a minute ago, stood wide open. A cold wind blew in, cutting through the hot, stagnant air. He got up and shut the door. The cold wind wrapped him in a belt, a swirl; he stood still in it for a moment, stiff with fear. When he crossed the room to the piano it was as if he moved breast high in deep, cold water.

Somewhere in the secret place of his mind a word struggled to form itself, to be born.

"Mother."

It came to him with a sense of appalling, supernatural horror. Horror that was there with him in the room like a presence.

"Mother."

The word had lost its meaning. It stood for nothing but that horror.

He tried to play again, but his fingers, slippery with sweat, dropped from the keyboard.

Something compelled him to turn round and look towards his mother's chair.

Then he saw her.

She stood between him and the chair, straight and thin, dressed in the clothes she had died in, the yellowish flannel nightgown and bed jacket.

The apparition maintained itself with difficulty. Already its hair had grown indistinct, a cap of white mist. Its face was an insubstantial framework for its mouth and eyes, and for the tears that fell in two shining tracks between. It was less a form than a visible emotion, an anguish.

Hollyer stood up and stared at it. Through the glasses of its tears, it gazed back at him with an intense, a terrible reproach and sorrow.

Then, slowly and stiffly, it began to recede from him, drawn back and back, without any movement of its feet, in an unearthly stillness, keeping up, to the last minute, its look of indestructible reproach.

And now it was a formless mass that drifted to the window and hung there a second, and passed, shrinking like a breath on the pane.

Hollyer, rigid, pouring out sweat, still stared at the place where it had stood. His heart-beats came together in a running tremor: it was as if all the blood in his body was gathered into his distended heart, dragging it down to meet his heaving belly.

Then he turned and went headlong towards the door, stumbling and lurching. He threw out his hands to clutch at a support and found himself in Effie's arms.

"Wilfrid—darling—what is it?"

"Nothing. I'm giddy. I—I think I'm going to be sick."

He broke from her and dragged himself upstairs and shut himself into his study. That night his old single bed was brought back and made up there. He was afraid to sleep in the room that had been his mother's.

He had run through all the physical sensations of his terror. What he. felt now was the sharp, abominable torture of the mind.

If the dead knew—

The dead *did* know. She had come back to tell him that she knew. She knew that he thought of her with unkindness. She had been there when he talked about her to Effie. She knew the thought he had hidden even from himself. She knew that she had died because, secretly, he had wished her dead.

That was the meaning of her look and of her tears.

No fleshly eyes could have expressed such an intensity of suffering, of unfathomable grief. He thought: the pain of a discarnate spirit might be infinitely sharper than any earthly pain. It might be inexhaustible. Who was to say that it was not?

Yet could it—could even an immortal suffering—be sharper than the anguish he felt now? If only he had known what he was doing to her— If he had known. If he had known—

But, he thought, we know nothing, and we care less. We say we believe in immortality, but we do not believe in it. We treat the dead as if they *were* dead, as if they were not there. If he had really believed that she was there, he would have died rather than say the things he had said to Effie. Nobody, he told himself, could have accused him of unkindness to his mother while she lived. He had really loved her up to the moment, the moment of supreme temptation, when he wanted Effie. He had not willed her to die.

He had been barely conscious of his wish. How, then, could he be held accountable? How could he have destroyed the thing whose essence was the hidden, unknown darkness? Yet, if men are accountable at all, he was accountable. There had been a moment when he was conscious of it. He could have destroyed it then. He should have faced it; he should have dragged it out into the light and fought it.

Instead, he had let it sink back into its darkness, to work there unseen.

And if he had really loved his mother, he would have wished, not willed her to live. He would have wanted her as he wanted her now.

For, now that it was too late, he did want her. His whole mind had changed. He no longer thought of her with resentment. He thought, with a passionate adoration and regret, of her beauty, her goodness, and her love for him. What if she *had* kept him with her? It had been, as Effie had said, because she loved him. How did he know that if she had let him go he would have been good for anything? What on earth could he have been but the third-rate organist he was?

He remembered the happiness he had had with her before he had loved Effie; her looks, her words, the thousand things she used to do to please him. The Mendelssohn she had given him. A certain sweet cake she made for him on his birthdays. And the touch of her hands, her kisses.

He thought of these things with an agony of longing. If only he could have her back; if only she would come to him again, that he might show her—

He asked himself: How much did Effie know? She must wonder why he had taken that sudden dislike to the drawing-room; why he insisted on sleeping in his study. She had never said anything.

A week had passed—they were sitting in the dining-room after supper, when she spoke.

"Wilfrid, why do you always want to sit here?"

"Because I hate the other room."

"You didn't use to. It's only since that day you were ill, the last time you were playing. Why do you hate it?"

"Well, if you want to know—you remember the beastly things I said about mother?"

"You didn't mean them."

"I did mean them—But it wasn't that. It was something you said."

"I?"

"Yes. You said 'If the dead knew—'"

"Well—?"

"Well—they do know—I'm certain my mother knew. Certain, as I'm certain I'm sitting here, that she heard."

"Oh, Wilfrid, what makes you think that?"

"I can't tell you what makes me think it-But—she was there."

"You only think it because you're feeling sorry. You must get over it. Go back into the room and play."

He shook his head and still sat there thinking. Effie did not speak again; she saw that she must let him think.

Presently he got up and went into the drawing-room, shutting the doors behind him.

The *Mendelssohn* was still on the piano ledge, open at Number Nine. He began to play it. But at the first bars of the melody he stopped, overwhelmed by an agony of regret. He slid down on his knees, with his arms on the edge of the piano and his head bowed on his arms.

His soul cried out in him with no sound.

"Mother—Mother—if only I had you back. If only you would come to me. Come—Come—"

And suddenly he felt her come. From far-off, from her place among the blessed, she came rushing, as if on wings. He heard nothing; he saw nothing; but with every nerve he felt the vibration of her approach, of her presence. She was close to him now, closer than hearing or sight or touch could bring her; her self to his self; her inmost essence was there.

The phantasm of a week ago was a faint, insignificant thing beside this supreme manifestation. No likeness of flesh and blood could give him such an assurance of reality, of contact.

For, more certain than any word of flesh and blood, her meaning flashed through him and thrilled.

She knew. She knew she had him again; she knew she would never lose him. He was her son. As she had once given him flesh of her flesh, so now, self to innermost self, she gave him her blessedness, her peace.

The Victim

Steven Acroyd, Mr. Greathead's chauffeur, was sulking in the garage.

Everybody was afraid of him. Everybody hated him except Mr. Greathead, his master, and Dorsy, his sweetheart.

And even Dorsy now, after yesterday!

Night had come. On one side the yard gates stood open to the black tunnel of the drive. On the other the high moor rose above the wall, immense, darker than the darkness. Steven's lantern in the open doorway of the garage and Dorsy's lamp in the kitchen window threw a blond twilight into the yard between. From where he sat, slantways on the step of the car, he could see, through the lighted window, the table with the lamp and Dorsy's sewing huddled up in a white heap as she left it just now, when she had jumped up and gone away. Because she was afraid of him.

She had gone straight to Mr. Greathead in his study, and Steven, sulking, had flung himself out into the yard.

He stared into the window, thinking, thinking. Everybody hated him. He could tell by the damned spiteful way they looked at him in the bar of the "King's Arms;" kind of sideways and slink-eyed, turning their dirty tails and shuffling out of his way.

He had said to Dorsy he'd like to know what he'd done. He'd just dropped in for his glass as usual; he'd looked round and said "Good-evening," civil, and the dirty tykes took no more notice of him than if he'd been a toad. Mrs. Oldishaw, Dorsy's aunt, *she* hated him, boiled-ham-face, swelling with spite, shoving his glass at the end of her arm, without speaking, as if he'd been a bloody cockroach.

All because of the thrashing he'd given young Ned Oldishaw. If she didn't want the cub's neck broken, she'd better keep him out of mischief. Young Ned knew what he'd get if he came meddling with *his* sweetheart.

It had happened yesterday afternoon, Sunday, when he had gone down with Dorsy to the "King's Arms" to see her aunt. They were sitting out on the wooden bench against the inn wall when young Ned began it. He could see him now with his arm round Dorsy's neck and his mouth gaping. And Dorsy laughing like a silly fool and the old woman snorting and shaking.

He could hear him. "She's my cousin if she is your sweetheart. You can't stop me kissing her." *Couldn't* he!

Why, what did they think? When he'd given up his good job at the Darlington Motor Works to come to Eastthwaite and black Mr. Greathead's boots, chop wood, carry coal and water for him, and drive his shabby second-hand car. Not that he cared what he did so long as he could live in the same house with Dorsy Oldishaw. It wasn't likely he'd sit like a bloody Moses, looking on, while Ned—

To be sure, he had half killed him. He could feel Ned's neck swelling and rising up under the pressure of his hands, his fingers. He had struck him first, flinging him back against the inn wall, then he had pinned him—till the men ran up and dragged him off.

And now they were all against him. Dorsy was against him. She had said she was afraid of him.

"Steven," she had said, "tha med 'a killed him."

"Well—p'r'aps next time he'll knaw better than to coom meddlin' with my lass."

"I'm not thy lass, ef tha canna keep thy hands off folks. I should be feared for my life of thee. Ned wurn't doing naw ''arm."

"Ef he doos it again, ef he cooms between thee and me, Dorsy, I shall do 'im in."

"Naw, tha maunna talk that road."

"It's Gawd's truth. Anybody that cooms between thee and me, loove, I shall do 'im in. Ef 'twas thy aunt, I should wring 'er neck, same as I wroong Ned's."

"And ef it was me, Steven?"

"Ef it wur thee, ef tha left me—Aw, doan't tha assk me, Dorsy."

"There—that's 'ow tha scares me."

"But tha' 'astna left me—'tes thy wedding claithes tha'rt making."

"Aye, 'tes my wedding claithes."

She had started fingering the white stuff, looking at it with her head on one side, smiling prettily. Then all of a sudden, she had flung

122

it down in a heap and burst out crying. When he tried to comfort her, she pushed him off and ran out of the room, to Mr. Greathead.

It must have been half an hour ago and she had not come back yet.

He got up and went through the yard gates into the dark drive. Turning there, he came to the house front and the lighted window of the study. Hidden behind a clump of yew he looked in.

Mr. Greathead had risen from his chair. He was a little old man, shrunk and pinched, with a bowed narrow back and slender neck under his grey hanks of hair.

Dorsy stood before him, facing Steven. The lamplight fell full on her. Her sweet flower-face was flushed. She had been crying.

Mr. Greathead spoke.

"Well, that's my advice," he said. "Think it over, Dorsy, before you do anything."

That night Dorsy packed her boxes, and the next day at noon, when Steven came in for his dinner, she had left the Lodge. She had gone back to her father's house in Garthdale.

She wrote to Steven saying that she had thought it over and found she daren't marry him. She was afraid of him. She would be too unhappy.

2

That was the old man, the old man. He had made her give him up. But for that, Dorsy would never have left him. She would never have thought of it herself. And she would never have got away if he had been there to stop her. It wasn't Ned. Ned was going to marry Nancy Peacock down at Morfe. Ned hadn't done any harm.

It was Mr. Greathead who had come between them. He hated Mr. Greathead.

His hate became a nausea of physical loathing that never ceased. Indoors he served Mr. Greathead as footman and valet, waiting on him at meals, bringing the hot water for his bath, helping him to dress and undress. So that he could never get away from him. When he came to call him in the morning, Steven's stomach heaved at the sight of the shrunken body under the bedclothes, the flushed, pinched face with its peaked, finicking nose upturned, the thin silver tuft of hair pricked up above the pillow's edge. Steven shivered with hate at the sound of the rattling, old man's cough, and the "*shoob-shoob*" of the feet shuffling along the flagged passages.

He had once had a feeling of tenderness for Mr. Greathead as the tie that bound him to Dorsy. He even brushed his coat and hat tenderly, as if he loved them. Once Mr. Greathead's small, close smile—the greyish bud of the lower lip pushed out, the upper lip lifted at the corners—and his kind, thin "Thank you, my lad," had made Steven smile back, glad to serve Dorsy's master. And Mr. Greathead would smile again and say, "It does me good to see your bright face, Steven." Now Steven's face writhed in a tight contortion to meet Mr. Greathead's kindliness, while his throat ran dry and his heart shook with hate.

At mealtimes from his place by the sideboard he would look on at Mr. Greathead eating, in a long contemplative disgust. He could have snatched the plate away from under the slow, fumbling hands that hovered and hesitated. He would catch words coming into his mind: "He ought to be dead. He ought to be dead." To think that this thing that ought to be dead, this old, shrivelled skin-bag of creaking bones should come between him and Dorsy, should have power to drive Dorsy from him.

One day when he was brushing Mr. Greathead's soft felt hat a paroxysm of hatred gripped him. He hated Mr. Greathead's hat. He took a stick and struck at it again and again; he threw it on the flags and stamped on it, clenching his teeth and drawing in his breath with a sharp hiss. He picked up the hat, looking round furtively, for fear lest Mr. Greathead or Dorsy's successor, Mrs. Blenkiron, should have seen him. He pinched and pulled it back into shape and brushed it carefully and hung it on the stand. He was ashamed, not of his violence, but of its futility.

Nobody but a damned fool, he said to himself, would have done that. He must have been mad.

It wasn't as if he didn't know what he was going to do. He had known ever since the day when Dorsy left him.

"I shan't be myself again till I've done him in," he thought.

He was only waiting till he had planned it out; till he was sure of every detail; till he was fit and cool. There must be no hesitation, no uncertainty at the last minute, above all, no blind, headlong violence. Nobody but a fool would kill in mad rage, and forget things, and be caught and swing for it. Yet that was what they all did. There was always something they hadn't thought of that gave them away.

Steven had thought of everything, even the date, even the weather.

Mr. Greathead was in the habit of going up to London to attend the debates of a learned Society he belonged to that held its meetings in May and November. He always travelled up by the five o'clock train, so that he might go to bed and rest as soon as he arrived. He always stayed for a week and gave his housekeeper a week's holiday. Steven chose a dark, threatening day in November, when Mr. Greathead was going up to his meeting and Mrs. Blenkiron had left Eastthwaite for Morfe by the early morning bus. So that there was nobody in the house but Mr. Greathead and Steven.

Eastthwaite Lodge stands alone, grey, hidden between the shoulder of the moor and the ash-trees of its drive. It is approached by a bridle-path across the moor, a turning off the road that runs from Eastthwaite in Rathdale to Shawe in Westleydale, about a mile from the village and a mile from Hardraw Pass. No tradesmen visited it. Mr. Greathead's letters and his newspaper were shot into a postbox that hung on the ash-tree at the turn.

The hot water laid on in the house was not hot enough for Mr. Greathead's bath, so that every morning, while Mr. Greathead shaved, Steven came to him with a can of boiling water.

Mr. Greathead, dressed in a mauve and grey striped sleeping-suit, stood shaving himself before the looking-glass that hung on the wall beside the great white bath. Steven waited with his hand on the cold tap, watching the bright curved rod of water falling with a thud and a splash.

In the white, stagnant light from the muffed windowpane the knife-blade flame of a small oil-stove flickered queerly. The oil sputtered and stank.

Suddenly the wind hissed in the water-pipes and cut off the glittering rod. To Steven it seemed the suspension of all movement. He would have to wait there till the water flowed again before he could begin. He tried not to look at Mr. Greathead and the lean wattles of his lifted throat. He fixed his eyes on the long crack in the soiled green distemper of the wall. His nerves were on edge with waiting for the water to flow again. The fumes of the oil-stove worked on them like a rank intoxicant. The soiled green wall gave him a sensation of physical sickness.

He picked up a towel and hung it over the back of a chair. Thus, he caught sight of his own face in the glass above Mr. Greathead's; it was livid against the soiled green wall. Steven stepped aside to avoid it.

"Don't you feel well, Steven?"

"No, sir." Steven picked up a small sponge and looked at it.

Mr. Greathead had laid down his razor and was wiping the lather from his chin. At that instant, with a gurgling, spluttering haste, the water leaped from the tap.

It was then that Steven made his sudden, quiet rush. He first gagged Mr. Greathead with the sponge, then pushed him back and back against the wall and pinned him there with both hands round his neck, as he had pinned Ned Oldishaw. He pressed in on Mr. Greathead's throat, strangling him.

Mr. Greathead's hands flapped in the air, trying feebly to beat Steven off; then his arms, pushed back by the heave and thrust of Steven's shoulders, dropped. Then Mr. Greathead's body sank, sliding along the wall, and fell to the floor, Steven still keeping his hold, mounting it, gripping it with his knees. His fingers tightened, pressing back the blood. Mr. Greathead's face swelled up; it changed horribly. There was a groaning and rattling sound in his throat. Steven pressed in till it had ceased.

Then he stripped himself to the waist. He stripped Mr. Greathead of his sleeping-suit and hung his naked body face downwards in the bath. He took the razor and cut the great arteries and veins in the neck. He pulled up the plug of the waste-pipe, and left the body to drain in the running water.

He left it all day and all night.

He had noticed that murderers swung just for want of attention to little things like that; messing up themselves and the whole place with blood; always forgetting something essential. He had no time to think of horrors. From the moment he had murdered Mr. Greathead his own neck was in danger; he was simply using all his brain and nerve to save his neck. He worked with the stern, cool hardness of a man going through with an unpleasant, necessary job. He had thought of everything.

He had even thought of the dairy.

It was built on to the back of the house under the shelter of the high moor. You entered it through the scullery, which cut it off from the yard. The window-panes had been removed and replaced by sheets of perforated zinc. A large corrugated glass sky-light lit it from the roof. Impossible either to see in or to approach it from the outside. It was fitted up with a long, black slate shelf, placed, for the convenience of butter-makers, at the height of an ordinary work-bench. Steven had his tools, a razor, a carving-knife, a chopper and a meat-saw, laid there ready, beside a great pile of cotton waste.

Early the next day he took Mr. Greathead's body out of the bath, wrapped a thick towel round the neck and head, carried it down to the dairy and stretched it out on the slab. And there he cut it up into seventeen pieces.

These he wrapped in several layers of newspaper, covering the face and the hands first, because, at the last moment, they frightened him. He sewed them up in two sacks and hid them in the cellar.

He burnt the towel and the cotton waste in the kitchen fire; he cleaned his tools thoroughly and put them back in their places; and he washed down the marble slab. There wasn't a spot on the floor except for one flagstone where the pink rinsing of the slab had splashed over. He scrubbed it for half an hour, still seeing the rusty edges of the splash long after he had scoured it out.

He then washed and dressed himself with care.

As it was wartime Steven could only work by day, for a light in the dairy roof would have attracted the attention of the police. He had murdered Mr. Greathead on a Tuesday; it was now three o'clock on Thursday afternoon. Exactly at ten minutes past four he had brought out the car, shut in close with its black hood and side curtains. He had packed Mr. Greathead's suitcase and placed it in the car with his umbrella, railway rug, and travelling cap. Also, in a bundle, the clothes that his victim would have gone to London in.

He stowed the body in the two sacks beside him on the front.

By Hardraw Pass, half-way between Eastthwaite and Shawe, there are three round pits, known as the Churns, hollowed out of the grey rock and said to be bottomless. Steven had thrown stones, big as a man's chest, down the largest pit, to see whether they would be caught on any ledge or boulder. They had dropped clean, without a sound.

It poured with rain, the rain that Steven had reckoned on. The Pass was dark under the clouds and deserted. Steven turned his car so that the headlights glared on the pit's mouth. Then he ripped open the sacks and threw down, one by one, the seventeen pieces of Mr. Greathead's body, and the sacks after them, and the clothes.

It was not enough to dispose of Mr. Greathead's dead body; he had to behave as though Mr. Greathead were alive. Mr. Greathead had disappeared and he had to account for his disappearance. He drove on to Shawe station to the five o'clock train, taking care to arrive close on its starting. A troop-train was due to depart a minute earlier. Steven, who had reckoned on the darkness and the rain, reckoned also on the hurry and confusion on the platform.

As he had foreseen, there were no porters in the station entry; nobody to notice whether Mr. Greathead was or was not in the car. He carried his things through on to the platform and gave the suitcase to an old man to label. He dashed into the booking-office and took Mr. Greathead's ticket, and then rushed along the platform as if he were following his master. He heard himself shouting to the guard, "Have you seen Mr. Greathead?" And the guard's answer, "Naw!" And his own inspired statement, "He must have taken his seat in the front, then." He ran to the front of the train, shouldering his way among the troops. The drawn blinds of the carriages favoured him.

Steven thrust the umbrella, the rug, and the travelling cap into an empty compartment, and slammed the door to. He tried to shout something through the open window; but his tongue was harsh and dry against the roof of his mouth, and no sound came. He stood, blocking the window, till the guard whistled. When the train moved, he ran alongside with his hand on the window-ledge, as though he were taking the last instructions of his master. A porter pulled him back.

"Quick work, that," said Steven.

Before he left the station, he wired to Mr. Greathead's London hotel, announcing the time of his arrival.

He felt nothing, nothing but the intense relief of a man who has saved himself by his own wits from a most horrible death. There were even moments, in the week that followed, when, so powerful was the illusion of his innocence, he could have believed that he had really seen Mr. Greathead off by the five o'clock train. Moments when he literally stood still in amazement before his own incredible impunity. Other moments when a sort of vanity uplifted him. He had committed a murder that for sheer audacity and cool brain work surpassed all murders celebrated in the history of crime. Unfortunately, the very perfection of his achievement doomed it to oblivion. He had left not a trace.

Not a trace.

Only when he woke in the night a doubt sickened him. There was the rusted ring of that splash on the dairy floor. He wondered, had he really washed it out clean. And he would get up and light a candle and go down to the dairy to make sure. He knew the exact place; bending over it with the candle, he could imagine that he still saw a faint outline.

Daylight reassured him. *He* knew the exact place, but nobody else knew. There was nothing to distinguish it from the natural stains in the flagstone. Nobody would guess. But he was glad when Mrs. Blenkiron came back again.

On the day that Mr. Greathead was to have come home by the

four o'clock train Steven drove into Shawe and bought a chicken for the master's dinner. He met the four o'clock train and expressed surprise that Mr. Greathead had not come by it. He said he would be sure to come by the seven. He ordered dinner for eight; Mrs. Blenkiron roasted the chicken, and Steven met the seven o'clock train. This time he showed uneasiness.

The next day he met all the trains and wired to Mr. Greathead's hotel for information. When the manager wired back that Mr. Greathead had not arrived, he wrote to his relatives and gave notice to the police.

Three weeks passed. The police and Mr. Greathead's relatives accepted Steven's statements, backed as they were by the evidence of the booking office clerk, the telegraph clerk, the guard, the porter who had labelled Mr. Greathead's luggage and the hotel manager who had received his telegram. Mr. Greathead's portrait was published in the illustrated papers with requests for any information which might lead to his discovery. Nothing happened, and presently he and his disappearance were forgotten. The nephew who came down to Eastthwaite to look into his affairs was satisfied.

His balance at his bank was low owing to the non-payment of various dividends, but the accounts and the contents of Mr. Greathead's cash-box and bureau were in order and Steven had put down every penny he had spent. The nephew paid Mrs. Blenkiron's wages and dismissed her and arranged with the chauffeur to stay on and take care of the house. And as Steven saw that this was the best way to escape suspicion, he stayed on.

Only in Westleydale and Rathdale excitement lingered. People wondered and speculated. Mr. Greathead had been robbed and murdered in the train (Steven said he had had money on him). He had lost his memory and wandered goodness knew where. He had thrown himself out of the railway carriage. Steven said Mr. Greathead wouldn't do *that*, but he shouldn't be surprised if he had lost his memory. He knew a man who forgot who he was and where he lived. Didn't know his own wife and children. Shell-shock. And lately Mr. Greathead's memory hadn't been what it was. Soon as he got it back, he'd turn up again. Steven wouldn't be surprised to see him walking in any day.

But on the whole people noticed that he didn't care to talk much about Mr. Greathead. They thought this showed very proper feeling. They were sorry for Steven. He had lost his master and he had lost Dorsy Oldishaw. And if he *did* half kill Ned Oldishaw, well, young

Ned had no business to go meddling with his sweetheart. Even Mrs. Oldishaw was sorry for him. And when Steven came into the bar of the King's Arms everybody said "Good evening, Steve," and made room for him by the fire.

<h2 style="text-align:center">3</h2>

Steven came and went now as if nothing had happened. He made a point of keeping the house as it would be kept if Mr. Greathead were alive. Mrs. Blenkiron, coming in once a fortnight to wash and clean, found the fire lit in Mr. Greathead's study and his slippers standing on end in the fender. Upstairs his bed was made, the clothes folded back, ready. This ritual guarded Steven not only from the suspicions of outsiders, but from his own knowledge. By behaving as though he believed that Mr. Greathead was still living he almost made himself believe it.

By refusing to let his mind dwell on the murder he came to forget it. His imagination saved him, playing the play that kept him sane, till the murder became vague to him and fantastic like a thing done in a dream. He had waked up and this was the reality; this round of care-taking, this look the house had of waiting for Mr. Greathead to come back to it. He had left off getting up in the night to examine the place on the dairy floor. He was no longer amazed at his impunity.

Then suddenly, when he really had forgotten, it ended. It was on a Saturday in January, about five o'clock. Steven had heard that Dorsy Oldishaw was back again, living at the "King's Arms" with her aunt. He had a mad, uncontrollable longing to see her again.

But it was not Dorsy that he saw.

His way from the Lodge kitchen into the drive was through the yard gates and along the flagged path under the study window. When he turned on to the flags, he saw it shuffling along before him. The lamplight from the window lit it up. He could see distinctly the little old man in the long, shabby black overcoat, with the grey woollen muffler round his neck hunched up above his collar, lifting the thin grey hair that stuck out under the slouch of the black hat.

In the first moment that he saw it Steven had no fear. He simply felt that the murder had not happened, that he really *had* dreamed it, and that this was Mr. Greathead come back, alive among the living. The phantasm was now standing at the door of the house, its hand on the doorknob as if about to enter.

But when Steven came up to the door it was not there.

He stood, fixed, staring at the space which had emptied itself so horribly. His heart heaved and staggered, snatching at his breath. And suddenly the memory of the murder rushed at him. He saw himself in the bathroom, shut in with his victim by the soiled green walls. He smelt the reek of the oil-stove; he heard the water running from the tap. He felt his feet springing forward, and his fingers pressing, tighter and tighter, on Mr. Greathead's throat. He saw Mr. Greathead's hands flapping helplessly, his terrified eyes, his face swelling and discoloured, changing horribly, and his body sinking to the floor.

He saw himself in the dairy, afterwards; he could hear the thudding, grinding, scraping noises of his tools. He saw himself on Hardraw Pass and the headlights glaring on the pit's mouth. And the fear and the horror he had not felt then came on him now.

He turned back; he bolted the yard gates and all the doors of the house, and shut himself up in the lighted kitchen. He took up his magazine, *The Autocar*, and forced himself to read it. Presently his terror left him. He said to himself it was nothing. Nothing but his fancy. He didn't suppose he'd ever see anything again.

Three days passed. On the third evening, Steven had lit the study lamp and was bolting the window when he saw it again.

It stood on the path outside, close against the window, looking in. He saw its face distinctly, the greyish, stuck-out bud of the under-lip, and the droop of the pinched nose. The small eyes peered at him, glittering. The whole figure had a glassy look between the darkness behind it and the pane. One moment it stood outside, looking in; and the next it was mixed up with the shimmering picture of the lighted room that hung there on the blackness of the trees. Mr. Greathead then showed as if reflected, standing with Steven in the room.

And now he was outside again, looking at him, looking at him through the pane.

Steven's stomach sank and dragged, making him feel sick. He pulled down the blind between him and Mr. Greathead, clamped the shutters to and drew the curtains over them. He locked and double-bolted the front door, all the doors, to keep Mr. Greathead out. But, once that night, as he lay in bed, he heard the "*shoob-shoob*" of feet shuffling along the flagged passages, up the stairs, and across the landing outside his door. The door handle rattled; but nothing came. He lay awake till morning, the sweat running off his skin, his heart plunging and quivering with terror.

When he got up, he saw a white, scared face in the looking-glass.

A face with a half-open mouth, ready to blab, to blurt out his secret; the face of an idiot. He was afraid to take that face into Eastthwaite or into Shawe. So, he shut himself up in the house, half-starved on his small stock of bread, bacon and groceries.

Two weeks passed; and then it came again in broad daylight.

It was Mrs. Blenkiron's morning. He had lit the fire in the study at noon and set up Mr. Greathead's slippers in the fender. When he rose from his stooping and turned round, he saw Mr. Greathead's phantasm standing on the hearthrug close in front of him. It was looking at him and smiling in a sort of mockery, as if amused at what Steven had been doing. It was solid and completely lifelike at first. Then, as Steven in his terror backed and backed away from it (he was afraid to turn and feel it there behind him), its feet became insubstantial. As if undermined, the whole structure sank and fell together on the floor, where it made a pool of some whitish glistening substance that mixed with the pattern of the carpet and sank through.

That was the most horrible thing it had done yet, and Steven's nerve broke under it. He went to Mrs. Blenkiron, whom he found scrubbing out the dairy.

She sighed as she wrung out the floor-cloth.

"Eh, these owd yeller stawnes, scroob as you will they'll navver look clean."

"Naw," he said. "Scroob and scroob, you'll navver get them clean."

She looked up at him.

"Eh, lad, what ails 'ee? Ye've got a faace like a wroong dishclout hanging ower t' sink."

"I've got the colic."

"Aye, an' naw woonder wi' the damp, and they misties, an' your awn bad cooking. Let me roon down t' 'King's Arms' and get you a drop of whisky."

"Naw, I'll gaw down mysen."

He knew now he was afraid to be left alone in the house. Down at the "King's Arms" Dorsy and Mrs. Oldishaw were sorry for him. By this time, he was really ill with fright. Dorsy and Mrs. Oldishaw said it was a chill. They made him lie down on the settle by the kitchen fire and put a rug over him, and gave him stiff hot grog to drink. He slept. And when he woke, he found Dorsy sitting beside him with her sewing.

He sat up and her hand was on his shoulder.

"Lay still, lad."

"I maun get oop and gaw."

"Nay, there's naw call for 'ee to gaw. Lay still and I'll make thee a coop o' tea."

He lay still.

Mrs. Oldishaw had made up a bed for him in her son's room, and they kept him there that night and till four o'clock the next day.

When he got up to go Dorsy put on her coat and hat.

"Is tha gawing out, Dorsy?"

"Aye. I canna let thee gaw and set there by thysen. I'm cooming oop to set with 'ee till night time."

She came up and they sat side by side in the Lodge kitchen by the fire as they used to sit when they were together there, holding each other's hands and not talking.

"Dorsy," he said at last, "what astha coom for? Astha coom to tall me tha'll navver speak to me again?"

"Nay. Tha knaws what I've coom for."

"To saay tha'll marry me?"

"Aye."

"I maunna marry thee, Dorsy. 'Twouldn' be right."

"Right? What dostha mean? 'Twouldn't be right for me to coom and set wi' thee this road ef I doan't marry thee."

"Nay. I darena'. Tha said tha was afraid of me, Dorsy. I doan't want 'ee to be afraid. Tha said tha'd be unhappy. I doan't want 'ee to be unhappy."

"That was lasst year. I'm not afraid of 'ee, now, Steve."

"Tha doan't knaw me, lass.'"

"Aye, I knaw thee. I knaw tha's sick and starved for want of me. Tha canna live wi'out thy awn lass to take care of 'ee."

She rose.

I maun gaw now. But I'll be oop tomorrow and the next day."

And tomorrow and the next day and the next, at dusk, the hour that Steven most dreaded, Dorsy came. She sat with him till long after the night had fallen.

Steven would have felt safe so long as she was with him, but for his fear that Mr. Greathead would appear to him while she was there and that she would see him. If Dorsy knew he was being haunted she might guess why. Or Mr. Greathead might take some horrible blood-dripping and dismembered shape that would show her how he had been murdered. It would be like him, dead, to come between them as he had come when he was living.

They were sitting at the round table by the fireside. The lamp was lit and Dorsy was bending over her sewing. Suddenly she looked up, her head on one side, listening. Far away inside the house, on the flagged passage from the front door, he could hear the "*shoob-shoob*" of the footsteps. He could almost believe that Dorsy shivered. And somehow, for some reason, this time he was not afraid.

"Steven," she said, "didsta 'ear anything?"

"Naw. Nobbut t' wind oonder t' roogs."

She looked at him; a long wondering look. Apparently, it satisfied her, for she answered: "Aye. Mebbe 'tes nobbut wind," and went on with her sewing.

He drew his chair nearer to her to protect her if it came. He could almost touch her where she sat.

The latch lifted. The door opened, and, his entrance and his passage unseen, Mr. Greathead stood before them.

The table hid the lower half of his form; but above it he was steady and solid in his terrible semblance of flesh and blood.

Steven looked at Dorsy. She was staring at the phantasm with an innocent, wondering stare that had no fear in it at all. Then she looked at Steven. An uneasy, frightened, searching look, as though to make sure whether he had seen it.

That was her fear—that *he* should see it, that *he* should be frightened, that *he* should be haunted.

He moved closer and put his hand on her shoulder. He thought, perhaps, she might shrink from him because she knew that it *was*, he who was haunted. But no, she put up her hand and held his, gazing up into his face and smiling.

Then, to his amazement, the phantasm smiled back at them; not with mockery, but with a strange and terrible sweetness. Its face lit up for one instant with a sudden, beautiful, shining light; then it was gone.

"Did tha see 'im, Steve?"

"Aye."

"Astha seen annything afore?"

"Aye, three times I've seen 'im."

"Is it that 'as scared thee?"

"'Oo tawled 'ee I was scared?"

"I knawed. Because nowt can 'appen to thee but I maun knaw it."

"What dostha think, Dorsy?"

"I think tha needna be scared, Steve. 'E's a kind ghawst. Whatever 'e is 'e doan't mean thee no 'arm. T' owd gentleman navver did when

134

he was alive."

"Didn' 'e? Didn' 'e? 'E served me the woorst turn 'e could when 'e coomed between thee and me."

"Whatever makes 'ee think that, lad?"

"I doan' think it. I *knaw*"

"Nay, loove, tha dostna."

"'E did. 'E did, I tell thee."

"Doan' tha say that," she cried. "Doan' tha say it, Stevey."

"Why shouldn't I?"

"Tha'll set folk talking that road."

"What do they knaw to talk about?"

"Ef they was to remember what tha said."

"And what did I say?"

"Why, that ef annybody was to coom between thee and me, tha'd do them in."

"I wasna thinking of *'im*. Gawd knaws I wasna."

"*They* doan't," she said.

"*Tha* knaws? Tha knaws I didna mean 'im?"

"Aye, *I* knaw, Steve."

"An', Dorsy, tha 'rn't afraid of me? Tha 'rn't afraid of me anny more?"

"Nay, lad. I loove thee too mooch. I shall navver be afraid of 'ee again. Would I coom to thee this road ef I was afraid?"

"Tha'll be afraid now."

"And what should I be afraid of?"

"Why—*'im*."

"*'Im?* I should be a deal more afraid to think of 'ee setting with 'im oop 'ere, by thysen. Wuntha coom down and sleep at aunt's?"

"That I wunna. But I shall set ''ee on t' road passt t' moor."

He went with her down the bridle-path and across the moor and along the main road that led through Eastthwaite. They parted at the turn where the lights of the village came in sight.

The moon had risen as Steven went back across the moor. The ash-tree at the bridle-path stood out clear, its hooked, bending branches black against the grey moor-grass. The shadows in the ruts laid stripes along the bridle-path, black on grey. The house was black-grey in the darkness of the drive. Only the lighted study window made a golden square in its long wall.

Before he could go up to bed, he would have to put out the study lamp. He was nervous; but he no longer felt the sickening and sweating terror of the first hauntings. Either he was getting used to it, or—something had happened to him.

He had closed the shutters and put out the lamp. His candle made a ring of light round the table in the middle of the room. He was about to take it up and go when he heard a thin voice calling his name: "Steven." He raised his head to listen. The thin thread of sound seemed to come from outside, a long way off, at the end of the bridlepath.

"Steven, Steven———"

This time he could have sworn the sound came from inside his head, like the hiss of air in his ears.

"Steven—"

He knew the voice now. It was behind him in the room. He turned, and saw the phantasm of Mr. Greathead sitting, as he used to sit, in the armchair by the fire. The form was dim in the dusk of the room outside the ring of candlelight. Steven's first movement was to snatch up the candlestick and hold it between him and the phantasm, hoping that the light would cause it to disappear. Instead of disappearing the figure became clear and solid, indistinguishable from a figure of flesh and blood dressed in black broadcloth and white linen. Its eyes had the shining transparency of blue crystal; they were fixed on Steven with a look of quiet, benevolent attention. Its small, narrow mouth was lifted at the corners, smiling.

It spoke.

"You needn't be afraid," it said.

The voice was natural now, quiet, measured, slightly quavering. Instead of frightening Steven it soothed and steadied him.

He put the candle on the table behind him and stood up before the phantasm, fascinated.

"*Why* are you afraid?" it asked.

Steven couldn't answer. He could only stare, held there by the shining, hypnotising eyes.

"You are afraid," it said, "because you think I'm what you call a ghost, a supernatural thing. You think I'm dead and that you killed me. You think you took a horrible revenge for a wrong you thought I did you. You think I've come back to frighten you, to revenge myself in my turn.

"And every one of those thoughts of yours, Steven, is wrong. I'm real, and my appearance is as natural and real as anything in this room—*more* natural and more real if you did but know. You didn't kill me, as you see; for here I am, as alive, more alive than you are. Your revenge consisted in removing me from a state which had become unbearable to a state more delightful than you can imagine. I don't mind telling you, Steven, that I was in serious financial difficulties (which, by the way, is a good thing for you, as it provides a plausible motive for my disappearance). So that, as far as revenge goes, the thing was a complete frost. You were my benefactor. Your methods were somewhat violent, and I admit you gave me some disagreeable moments before my actual deliverance; but as I was already developing rheumatoid arthritis there can be no doubt that in your hands my death was more merciful than if it had been left to Nature.

"As for the subsequent arrangements, I congratulate you, Steven, on your coolness and resource. I always said you were equal to any emergency, and that your brains would pull you safe through any scrape. You committed an appalling and dangerous crime, a crime of all things the most difficult to conceal, and you contrived so that it was not discovered and never will be discovered. And no doubt the details of this crime seemed to you horrible and revolting to the last degree; and the more horrible and the more revolting they were, the more you piqued yourself on your nerve in carrying the thing through without a hitch.

"I don't want to put you entirely out of conceit with your performance. It was very creditable for a beginner, very creditable indeed. But let me tell you, this idea of things being horrible and revolting is all illusion. The terms are purely relative to your limited perceptions.

"I'm speaking now to your intelligence—I don't mean that practical ingenuity which enabled you to dispose of me so neatly. When I say intelligence, I mean intelligence. All you did, then, was to redistribute matter. To our incorruptible sense matter never takes any of those offensive forms in which it so often appears to you. Nature has evolved all this horror and repulsion just to prevent people from making too many little experiments like yours. You mustn't imagine that these things have any eternal importance. Don't flatter yourself you've electrified the universe.

"For minds no longer attached to flesh and blood, that horrible butchery you were so proud of, Steven, is simply silly. No more terrifying than the spilling of red ink or the rearrangement of a jig-saw puzzle. I saw the whole business, and I can assure you I felt nothing but intense amusement. Your face, Steven, was so absurdly serious. You've no idea what you looked like with that chopper. I'd have appeared to you then and told you so, only I knew I should frighten you into fits.

"And there's another grand mistake, my lad—your thinking that I'm haunting you out of revenge, that I'm trying to frighten you . . . .
. . . . . My dear Steven, if I'd wanted to frighten you, I'd have appeared in a very different shape. I needn't remind you what shape I *might* have appeared in . . . . What do you suppose I've come for?"

"I don't know," said Steven in a husky whisper. "Tell me."

"I've come to forgive you. And to save you from the horror you *would* have felt sooner or later. And to stop your going on with your crime."

"You needn't," Steven said. "I'm not going on with it. I shall do no more murders."

"There you are again. Can't you understand that I'm not talking about your silly butcher's work? I'm talking about your *real* crime. Your real crime was hating me.

"And your very hate was a blunder, Steven. You hated me for something I hadn't done."

"Aye, what did you do? Tell me that."

"You thought I came between you and your sweetheart. That night when Dorsy spoke to me, you thought I told her to throw you over, didn't you?"

"Aye. And what did you tell her?"

"I told her to stick to you. It was you, Steven, who drove her away. You frightened the child. She said she was afraid for her life of you. Not because you half killed that poor boy, but because of the look on your face before you did it. The look of hate, Steven.

"I told her not to be afraid of you. I told her that if she threw you over you might go altogether to the devil; that she might even be responsible for some crime. I told her that if she married you and was faithful—*if she loved you*—I'd answer for it you'd never go wrong.

"She was too frightened to listen to me. Then I told her to think over what I'd said before she did anything. You heard me say that."

"Aye. That's what I heard you say. I didn' knaw. I didn' knaw. I thought you'd set her agen me."

"If you don't believe me, you can ask her, Steven."

"That's what she said t' other night. That you navver coom between her and me. Navver."

"Never," the phantasm said. "And you don't hate me now."

"Naw. Naw. I should navver 'a hated 'ee. I should navver 'a laid a finger on thee, ef I'd knawn."

"It's not your laying fingers on me, it's your hatred that matters. If

138

that's done with, the whole thing's done with."

Is it? Is it? Ef it was knawn, I should have to hang for it. Maunna I gie mysen oop? Tell me, maun I gie mysen oop?"

"You want me to decide that for you?"

"Aye. Doan't gaw," he said. "Doan't gaw."

It seemed to him that Mr. Greathead's phantasm was getting a little thin, as if it couldn't last more than an instant. He had never so longed for it to go, as he longed now for it to stay and help him.

"Well, Steven, any flesh-and-blood man would tell you to go and get hanged tomorrow; that it was no more than your plain duty. And I daresay there are some mean, vindictive spirits even in my world who would say the same, not because *they* think death important but because they know *you* do, and want to get even with you that way.

"It isn't *my* way. I consider this little affair is strictly between ourselves. There isn't a jury of flesh-and-blood men who would understand it. They all think death so important."

"What do you want me to do, then? Tell me and I'll do it! Tell me!"

He cried it out loud; for Mr. Greathead's phantasm was getting thinner and thinner; it dwindled and fluttered, like a light going down. Its voice came from somewhere away outside, from the other end of the bridle-path.

"Go on living," it said. "Marry Dorsy."

"I darena. She doan' knaw I killed 'ee."

"Oh, yes"—the eyes flickered up, gentle and ironic—"she does. She knew all the time."

And with that the phantasm went out.

The Finding of the Absolute

1

Mr. Spalding had gone out into the garden to find peace, and had not found it. He sat there, with hunched shoulders and bowed head, dejected in the spring sunshine.

Jerry, the black cat, invited him to play; he stood on his hind legs and danced, and bowed sideways, and waved his forelegs in the air like wings. At any other time, his behaviour would have enchanted Mr. Spalding, but now he couldn't even look at him; he was too miserable.

He had gone to bed miserable; he had passed a night of misery, and he had waked up more miserable than ever. He had been like that for three days and three nights straight on end, and no wonder. It wasn't only that his young wife Elizabeth had run away with Paul Jeffreson, the Imagist poet. Besides the frailty of Elizabeth, he had discovered a fatal flaw in his own system of metaphysics. His belief in Elizabeth was gone. So was his belief in the Absolute.

The two things had come at once, to crush him. And he had to own bitterly that they were not altogether unrelated. "If," Mr. Spalding said to himself, "I had served my wife as faithfully as I have served my God, she would not now have deserted me for Paul Jeffreson." He meant that if he had not been wrapped up in his system of metaphysics, Elizabeth might still have been wrapped up in him. He had nobody but himself to thank for her behaviour.

If she had run away with anybody else, since run she must, he might have forgiven her; he might have forgiven himself; but there could be nothing but misery in store for Elizabeth. Paul Jeffreson had genius, Mr. Spalding didn't deny it; immortal genius; but he had no morals; he drank; he drugged; in Mr. Spalding's decent phrase, he did everything he shouldn't do.

You would have thought this overwhelming disaster would have completely outweighed the other trouble. But no; Mr. Spalding had a balanced mind; he mourned with equal sorrow the loss of his wife and the loss of his Absolute. A flaw in a metaphysical system may seem to you a small thing; but you must bear in mind that, ever since he could think at all, Mr. Spalding had been devoured by a hunger and thirst after metaphysical truth. He had flung over the God he had been taught to believe in because, besides being an outrage to Mr. Spalding's moral sense, he wasn't metaphysical enough.

The poor man was always worrying about metaphysics; he wandered from system to system, seeking truth, seeking reality, seeking some supreme intellectual satisfaction that never came. He thought he had found it in his theory of Absolute Pantheism. But really, Spalding's Pantheism, anybody's Pantheism for that matter, couldn't, when you brought it down to bed-rock thinking, hold water for a minute. And the more Absolute he made it, the leakier it was.

For, consider, on Mr. Spalding's theory, there isn't any reality except the Absolute. Things are only real because they exist in It; because It is Them. Mr. Spalding conceived that his consciousness and Elizabeth's consciousness and Paul Jeffreson's consciousness existed somehow in the Absolute unchanged. For, if that inside existence changed them you would have to say that the ground of their present appearance lay somewhere outside the Absolute, which to Mr. Spalding was rank blasphemy. And if Elizabeth and Paul Jeffreson existed in the Absolute unchanged, then their adultery existed there unchanged. And an adultery within the Absolute outraged his moral sense as much as anything he had been told about God in his youth. The odd thing was that until Elizabeth had run away and committed it, he had never thought of that. The metaphysics of Pantheism had interested him much more than its ethics. And now he could think of nothing else.

And it wasn't only Elizabeth and her iniquity; there were all the intolerable people he had ever known. There was his Uncle Sims, a mean sneak if ever there was one; and his Aunt Emily, a silly fool; and his cousin, Tom Rumbold, an obscene idiot. And his uncle's mean sneakishness, and his aunt's silly folly, and his cousin's obscene idiocy would have to exist in the Absolute, too; and unchanged, mind you.

And the things you see and hear—A blue sky, now, would it be blue in the Sight of God, or just something inconceivable? And noises, music? For example, I am listening to Grand Opera, and you to the jazz band in your restaurant; but the God of Pantheism is listening to both, to all the noises in the universe at once. As if He had sat down on the piano. This idea shocked Mr. Spalding even more than the thought of Elizabeth's misconduct.

Time went on. Paul Jeffreson drank himself to death. Elizabeth, worn out with grief, died of pneumonia following influenza; and Mr. Spalding still went about worrying over his unadjustable metaphysics.

And at last, he, too, found himself dying.

And then he began to worry about other things. Things that had, as he put it, "happened" in his youth, before he knew Elizabeth, and one thing that had happened after she left him. He thought of them as just happening; happening *to* him rather than *through* him, against his will. In calm, philosophic moments he couldn't conceive how they had ever happened at all, how, for example, he could have endured Connie Larkins. The episodes had been brief, because in each case boredom and disgust had supervened to put asunder what Mr. Spalding owned should never have been joined. Brief, insignificant as they were, Mr. Spalding, in his dying state, was worried when he looked back on them. Supposing they were more significant than they had seemed? Supposing they had an eternal significance and entailed tremendous consequences in the afterlife? Supposing you were not just wiped out, that there really *was* an afterlife? Supposing that in that other world there was a hell?

Mr. Spalding could imagine no worse hell than the eternal repetition of such incidents; eternal repetition of boredom and disgust. Fancy going on with Connie Larkins for ever and ever, never being able to get away from her, doomed to repeat—And, if there *was* an Absolute, if there was reality, truth, never knowing it; being cut off from it forever—

"He that is filthy let him be filthy still."

That was hell, the continuance of the filthy state.

He wondered whether goodness was not, after all, *the* important thing; he wondered whether there really was a next world; with an extreme uneasiness he wondered what would happen to him in it.

He died wondering.

2

His first thought was: Well, here I am again. I've not been wiped out. His next, that he hadn't died at all. He had gone to sleep and was now dreaming. He was not in the least agitated, nor even surprised.

He found himself alone in an immense grey space, in which there was no distinguishable object but himself. He was aware of his body as occupying a portion of this space. For he had a body; a curious, tenuous, whitish body. The odd thing was that this empty space had a sort of solidity under him. He was lying on it, stretched out on it, adrift. It supported him with the buoyancy of deep water. And yet his body was part of it, netted in.

He was now aware of two figures approaching. They came and stood, like figures treading water, one on each side of him, and he saw that they were Elizabeth and Paul Jeffreson.

Then he concluded that he was really dead; dead like Elizabeth and Jeffreson, and (since they were there) that he was in hell.

Elizabeth was speaking, and her voice sounded sweet and very kind. All the same he knew he was in hell.

"It's all right," she said. "It's queer at first, but you'll get used to it. You don't mind our coming to meet you?"

Mr. Spalding said he'd no business to mind, no right to reproach her, since they were all in the same boat. They had, all three, deserved their punishment.

"Punishment?" (Jeffreson spoke). "Why, where does he think he is?"

"I'm in hell, aren't I? If—"

"If *we're* here. Is that it?"

"Well, Jeffreson, I don't want to rake up old unpleasantness, but after—after what happened, you'll forgive my saying so, but what else *can* I think?"

He heard Jeffreson laugh; a perfectly natural laugh.

"Will *you* tell him, Elizabeth, or shall I?"

"You'd better. He always respected your intelligence."

"Well, old chap, if you really want to know where you are, you're in heaven."

"You don't mean to say so?"

"Fact. I daresay you're wondering what we're doing here?"

"Well, Elizabeth—perhaps. But, frankly, Jeffreson, *you*—"

"Yes. How about me?"

"With your record I should have thought you'd even less business here than I have."

"Wouldn't you? I lived on unpaid bills. I drank. I drugged. There was nothing I didn't do. What do you suppose I got in on? You'll never guess."

"No. No. I give it up."

"My love of beauty. You wouldn't think it, but it seems that actually

144

counts here, in the eternal world."

"And Elizabeth, what did she get in on?"

"Her love of me."

"Then all I can say is," said Mr. Spalding, "Heaven must be a most immoral place."

"Oh, no. Your parochial morality doesn't hold good here, that's all. Why should it? It's entirely relative. Relative to a social system with limits in time and space. Relative to a certain biological configuration that ceased with our terrestrial organisms. Not absolute. Not eternal.

"But beauty—Beauty *is* eternal, is absolute. And I—I loved beauty more than credit, more than drink or drugs or women, more even than Elizabeth.

"And love is eternal. And Elizabeth loved me more than you, more than respectability, more than peace and comfort, and a happy life."

"That's all very well, Jeffreson; and Elizabeth may be all right. Mary Magdalene, you know, *Quia multum amavit*, and so forth. But if a blackguard like you can slip into heaven as easily as all that, where *are* our ethics?"

"Your ethics, my dear Spalding, are where they've always been, where you came from, not here. And if I *was* what they call a bad man, that's to say a bad terrestrial organism, I was a thundering good poet. You say I slipped in easily; do you suppose it's easy to be a poet? My dear fellow, it requires an inflexibility, a purity, a discipline of mind— of *mind*, remember—that you haven't any conception of. And surely *you* should be the last person in the world to regard mind as an inferior secondary affair. Anyhow, the consequence is that I've not only got into heaven, I've got into one of the best heavens, a heaven reserved exclusively for the very finest spirits."

"Then," said Mr. Spalding, "if we're in heaven, who's in hell?"

"Couldn't say for certain. But we shouldn't put it that way. We should say: Who's gone back to earth?"

"Well—am I likely to meet Uncle Sims, or Aunt Emily, or Tom Rumbold here? You remember them, Elizabeth?"

"Oh, yes, I remember. They'd be almost certain to be sent back. They couldn't stand eternal things. There's nothing eternal about meanness and stupidity and nastiness."

"What'll happen to them, do you suppose?"

"What should you say, Paul?"

"I should say they'd suffer damnably till they'd got some bigness and intelligence and decency knocked into them."

"It'll be a sell for Aunt Emily. She was brought up to believe that stupidity was no drawback to getting into heaven."

"Lots of people," said Jeffreson, "will be sold. Like my father, the Dean of Eastminster; he was cocksure he'd get in; but they won't let him. And why, do you suppose? Because the poor old boy couldn't see that my poems were beautiful.

"But even that wouldn't have dished him, if he'd had a passion for anybody; or if he'd cared two straws about metaphysical truth. Your truth, Spalding."

"Bless me, all our preconceived ideas seem to have been wrong."

"Yes. Even I wasn't prepared for that. By the way, that's what you got in on, your passion for truth. It's like my passion for beauty."

"But—aren't you distressed about your father, Jeffreson?"

"Oh, no. He'll get into some heaven or other someday. He'll find out that he cares for somebody, perhaps. Then he'll be all right— But don't you want to look about a bit?"

"I don't see very much to look at. It strikes me as a bit bare, your heaven."

"Oh, that's because you're only at the landing-state."

"The landing *what?*"

"State. What we used to call landing place. Times and spaces here, you know, are states. States of mind."

Mr. Spalding sat up, excited. "But—but that's what I always said they were. I and Kant."

"Well, you'd better talk to him about it."

"Talk to *him?* Shall I see Kant?"

"Look at him, Elizabeth. *Now* he's coming alive—Of course you'll see him when you get into your own place—state, I mean. You'd better get up and come along with me and Elizabeth. We'll show you round."

He rose, they steadied him, and he made his way between them through the grey immensity, over a half-seen yet perfectly solid tract of something that he thought of, absurdly, as condensed space. As yet there were no objects in sight but the figures of Elizabeth and Jeffreson; the half-seen, yet tangible floor he went on seemed to create itself out of nothing, under his feet, as the desire to walk arose in him. And as yet he had felt no interest or curiosity; but as he went on, he was aware of a desire to see things that became more and more urgent. He would see. He must see. He felt that before him and around him there were endless things to be seen. His mind strained forwards

146

towards vision.

And then, suddenly, he saw.

He saw a landscape more beautiful than anything he could have imagined. It was, Jeffreson informed him, very like the umbrella pine country between Florence and Siena. As they came out of it on a great, curving road they had their faces towards the celestial west. To the south the land fell away in great red cliffs to a shining, blue sea. Like, Jeffreson said, the Riviera, the Estérel. West and north the landscape rolled in green hill after green hill, pine-tufted, to a sweeping rampart of deep blue; such a rampart, such blue as Mr. Spalding had seen from the heights above Sidmouth, looking towards Dartmoor. Only this country had a grace, a harmony of line and colour that gave it an absolute beauty; and over it there lay a serene, unearthly radiance.

Before them, on a hill, was an exquisite little white, golden and rose-red town.

"You may or may not believe me," said Jeffreson, "but the beauty of all this is that I made it. I mean Elizabeth and I made it between us."

"You made it?"

"Made it."

"How?"

"By thinking of it. By wanting it. By imagining it."

"But—out of what?"

"I don't know and I don't much care. Our scientists here will tell you we made it out of the ultimate constituents of matter. Matter, unformed, only exists for us in its ultimate constituents. Something like electrons of electrons of electrons. Here we are all suspended in a web, immersed, if you like, in a sea, an air of this matter. It is utterly plastic to our imagination and our will. Imperceptible in its unformed state, it becomes visible and tangible as our minds get to work on it, and we can make out of it anything we want, including our own bodies. Only, so far as our imaginations are still under the dominion of our memories, so far will the things they create resemble the things we knew on earth.

"Thus, you will notice that while Elizabeth and I are much more beautiful than we were on earth" (he *had* noticed it), "because we desired to be more beautiful, we are still recognisable as Paul and Elizabeth because our imaginations are controlled by our memories. You are as you always were, only younger than when we knew you, because your imagination had nothing but memory to go on. Everything you create here will probably be a replica of something on earth you remember."

"But if I want something new, something beautiful that I haven't seen before, can't I have it?"

"Of course, you can have it. Only, just at first, until your own imagination develops, you'll have to come to me or Turner or Michael Angelo to make it for you."

"And will these things that you and Turner and Michael Angelo make for me be permanent?"

"Absolutely, unless we unmade them. And I don't think we should do that against your will. Anyhow, though we can destroy our own works we can't destroy each other's, that is to say, reduce them to their ultimate constituents. What's more, we shouldn't dream of trying."

"Why not?"

"Because old motives don't work here. Envy, greed, theft, robbery, murder, or any sort of destruction, are unknown. They can't happen. Nothing alters matter here but mind, and I can't will your body to come to pieces so long as you want it to keep together. You can't destroy it yourself as you can other things you make, because your need of it is greater than your need of other things.

"We can't thieve or rob for the same reason. Things that belong to us belong to our state of mind and can't be torn away from it, so that we couldn't remove anything from another person's state into our own. And if we could we shouldn't want to, because each of us can always have everything he wants. If I like your house or your landscape better than my own, I can make one for myself just like it. But we don't do this, because we're proud of our individualities here, and would rather have things different than the same——By the way, as you haven't got a house yet, let alone a landscape, you'd better share ours."

"That's very good of you," Mr. Spalding said. He was thinking of Oxford. Oxford. Quiet rooms in Balliol. He seemed to hesitate.

"If you're still sitting on that old grievance of yours, I tell you, once for all, Spalding, I'm not going to express any regret. I'm *not* sorry, I'm glad I took Elizabeth away from you. I made her more happy than unhappy even on earth. And please notice it's I who got her into heaven, not you. If she'd stayed with you and hated you, as she would have done, she couldn't have got in."

"I wasn't thinking of that," said Mr. Spalding. "I was only wondering where I could put my landscape."

"How do you mean—'put' it?"

"Place it—so as not to interfere with other people's landscapes."

"But how on earth could you interfere? You 'place' it, as you call it, in your own space and in your own time."

His own space, his own time—Mr. Spalding got more and more excited.

"But—how?"

"Oh, I can't tell you how. It simply happens."

"But I want to understand it. I—I *must* understand."

"You shouldn't put him off like that, Paul," Elizabeth said. "He always did want to understand things."

"But when I don't understand them myself—"

"You'd better take him to Kant, or Hegel."

"I should prefer Kant," said Mr. Spalding.

"Well, Kant then. You'll have to get into his state first."

"How do I do that?"

"It's very simple. You just think him up and ask him if you can come in."

Elizabeth explained. "Like ringing somebody up, you know, and asking if you can come and call."

"Supposing he won't let me."

"Trust him to say so. Of course, we mayn't get through. He may have *thought off*."

"You can think off, can you?"

"Yes, that's how you protect yourself. Otherwise, life here would be unbearable. Just keep quiet for a second, will you?"

There was an intense silence. Presently Jeffreson said: "Now you're through."

And Mr. Spalding found himself in a white-washed room, scantily furnished with three rows of bookshelves, a writing-table, a table set with mysterious instruments, and two chairs. A shaded lamp on the writing-table gave light. Mr. Spalding had left the umbrella pine country blazing with sunlight, but it seemed that Kant's time was somewhere about ten o'clock at night. The large window was bared to a dark-blue sky of stars.

A little, middle-aged man sat at the writing-table. He wore eighteenth-century clothes and a tie wig. The face that looked up at Mr. Spalding was lean and dried, the mouth tight, the eyes shining distantly with a deep, indrawn intelligence. Mr. Spalding understood that he was in the presence of Immanuel Kant.

"You thought me up?"

"Forgive me. I am James Spalding, a student of philosophy. I was

149

told that you might, perhaps, be willing to explain to me the—the very extraordinary conditions in which I find myself."

"May I ask, Mr. Spalding, if you have paid any particular attention to *my* philosophy?"

"I am one of your most devoted disciples, sir. I refuse to believe that philosophy has made any considerable advance since the Critique of Pure Reason."

"T-t-t. My successor, Hegel, made a very considerable advance. If you have neglected Hegel—"

"Pardon me, I have not. I was once Hegel's devoted disciple. An entrancing fantasy, the Triple Dialectic. But I came to see that yours, sir, was the safer and the saner system, and that the recurrent tendency of philosophy must be back to Kant."

"Better say Forward with him. If you are indeed my disciple, I do not think that conditions here should have struck you as extraordinary."

"They struck me as an extraordinary confirmation of your theory of space and time, sir."

"They are that. They are that. But they go far beyond anything I ever dreamed of. If was not in my scheme that the Will—to which, if you remember, I gave a purely ethical and pragmatical role—that the Will and the imagination of individuals, of you and me, Mr. Spalding, should create their own space and time, and their own objects in space and time. I did not anticipate this multiplicity of spaces and times. In my time there was only one space and one time for everybody.

"Still, it is a very remarkable confirmation, and you may imagine, Mr. Spalding, that I was gratified when I first came here to find everybody talking and thinking correctly about time and space. You will have noticed that here we say state, meaning state of consciousness, where we used to say place. In the same way we talk about states of time, meaning time as a state of consciousness. My present state, you will observe, is exactly ten minutes past ten by my clock, which is my consciousness. My consciousness registers time automatically. My own time, mind you, not other people's."

"But isn't that frightfully inconvenient? If your time isn't everybody else's time, how on earth—I mean how in heaven—do you keep your appointments? How do you co-ordinate?"

"We keep appointments, we co-ordinate, exactly as we used to do, by a purely arbitrary system. We measure time by space, by events, movements in space-time. Only, whereas under earthly conditions there was apparently one earth and one sun, one day and one night for everybody, here everybody has his own earth, his own sun and his own day and night. So, we are obliged to take an ideal earth and sun, an ideal day and night. Their revolutions are measured exactly as we measured them on earth, by the movements of hands on a dial marking minutes and hours.

"Only our public clocks have five hands marking the revolutions of weeks, months and years. That is our public standardised time, and all appointments are kept, all scientific calculations made by it. The only difference between heaven and earth is that here public space-time is regarded as it really is—an unreal, a purely arbitrary and artificial convention. We know, not as a result of philosophic or mathematical reasoning, but as part of our ordinary conscious experience, that there is no absolute space and no absolute time. I would say no *real* space and no real time, but that in heaven a state of consciousness carries its own reality with it as such; and the time state or the space state is as real as any other.

"Of course, without an arbitrary public space-time, a public clock, states of consciousness from individual to individual could never be co-ordinated. For example, you have come straight from Mr. Jeffreson's twelve-noon to my ten o'clock p.m. But the public clock, which you will see out there in the street—we are in Königsberg; I have no visual imagination and must rely entirely on memory for my scenery—the public clock, I say, marks time at a quarter to eight; and if I were asking Mr. Jeffreson to spend the evening with me, the hour would be fixed for us by public time at eight. But he would find himself in my time at ten.

"Now I want to point out to you, Mr. Spalding, that this way of regarding space and time is not so revolutionary as it may appear. I said, if you remember, that under terrestrial conditions there was apparently one earth and one sun, one day and night for everybody. But really, even then, everybody carried about with him his own private space and time, and his own private world in space and time. It was only, even then, by an arbitrary system of mathematical conventions, mostly geometrical, that all these private times and spaces were co-ordinated, so as to constitute one universe. Public clock time, based on the revolutions of bodies in a mathematically determined public space, was as conventional and relative an affair on earth as it is in heaven.

"Our private consciousnesses registered their own times automatically then as now, by the passage of internal events. If events passed quickly, our private time outran clock time; if they dragged, it was behindhand.

"Thus, in dream experience there are many more events to the second than in waking experience; and consciousness registers by the tick-tick of events, so that in a dream we may live through crowded hours and days in the fraction of time that coincides with the knock on the door that waked us. It is absurd to say that in this case we do not live in two different time-systems."

"Yes, and——" Mr. Spalding cried out excitedly—"Einstein has proved that motion in public space-time is a purely relative and arbitrary thing, and that the velocity, or time value, of a ray of light moving under different conditions is a constant; when on any theory of absolute time and absolute motion it should be a variant."

"That," said Kant, "is no more than I should have expected."

"You said, sir, that the only distinction between earthly and heavenly conditions is that this artificial character of standardised space-time is recognised in heaven and not on earth. I should have said that the most striking differences were, firstly, that in heaven our experience is created for us by our imagination and our will, whereas on earth it was, in your own word, sir, 'given.' Secondly that in heaven our states are not closed as they were on earth, but that anybody can enter anybody else's. It seems to me that these differences are so great as to surpass anything in our experience on earth."

"They are not so great," said Kant, "as all that. In dreaming you already had an experience of a world created by each person for himself in a space and time of his own; a world in which you transcended the conditions of ordinary space and time. In telepathy and clairvoyance, you had experience of entering other people's states."

"But," Mr. Spalding said, "on earth my consciousness was dependent on a world apparently outside it, arising presumably in God's consciousness, my body being the ostensible medium. Here, on the contrary, I have my world inside me, created by my consciousness, and my body is not so much a medium as an accessory after the fact."

"And what inference do you draw, Mr. Spalding?"

"Why, that on earth I was nearer God, more dependent on him than in heaven. I seem to have become my own God."

"Doesn't it strike you that in becoming more god-like you are actually nearer God? That in this power of your imagination to conceive, this freedom of your will to create your universe, God is cutting a clearer path for himself than through that constrained and obstructed consciousness you had on earth?"

"That's it. When I think of that appalling life of earth, the pain, sir, the horrible pain, the wickedness, the imbecility, the endless struggling through blood and filth, and being beaten, I can't help wondering how such things can exist in the Absolute, and why the Absolute shouldn't have put us—or as you would say, *thought* us into this heavenly state from the beginning."

"Do you suppose that any finite intelligence—any finite will could have been trusted, untrained, with the power we have here? Only wills disciplined by struggling against earth's evil, only intelligences braced by wrestling with earth's problems are fitted to create universes. You may remember my enthusiasm for the moral law, my Categorical Imperative? It is not diminished. The moral law still holds and always will hold on earth. But I see now it is not an end in itself, only the means to which this power, this freedom is the end.

"That is how and why pain and evil exist in the Absolute. It is obvious that they cannot exist in it as such, being purely relative to states of terrestrial organisms. That is why the comparatively free wills of terrestrial organisms are permitted to create pain and evil.

"When you talk of such things existing in the Absolute, unchanged and unabridged, you are talking nonsense. You are thinking of pain and evil in terms of one dimension of time and three dimensions of space, by which they are indefinitely multiplied."

"How do you mean—one dimension of time?"

"I mean time taken as linear extension, the pure succession of past, present and future. You think of pain and evil as indefinitely distributed in space and indefinitely repeated in time, whereas in the idea, which is their form of eternity, at their worst they are not many, but One."

"That doesn't make them less unbearable."

"I am not talking about that. I am talking about their significance for eternity, or in the Absolute, since you said that was what distressed you.

"You will see this for yourself if you will come with me into the state of three-dimensional time."

"What's that?" said Mr. Spalding, deeply intrigued.

"That," said the philosopher, "is time which is not linear succession, time which has turned on itself twice to take up the past and future into its present. For as the point is repeated to form the line, of space, so the instant is repeated to form the linear time of past, present, future. And as the one-dimensional line turns at right angles to itself to form the two-dimensional plane, so linear or one-dimensional time turns on itself to form two-dimensional or plane time, the past-present, or present- future. And as the plane turns on itself to form the cube, so past-present and present-future double back to meet each other and form cubic time, or past-present-future all together.

"This is the three-dimensional state of consciousness we shall have to think ourselves into."

"Do you mean to say that if we get into it, we shall have solved the riddle of the universe?"

"Hardly. The universe is a tremendous jig-saw puzzle. If God wanted to keep us amused to all eternity, he couldn't have hit on anything better. We shall not be able to stay very long, or to take in *all* past-present-future at once. But you will see enough to realise what cubic time is. You will begin with one small cubic section, which will gradually enlarge until you have taken in as much cubic time as you can hold together in one duration.

"Look out through that window. You see that cart coming down the street. It will have to pass Herr Schmidt's house opposite and the "Prussian Soldier," and that grocer's shop and the clock before it gets to the church.

"Now you'll see what'll happen."

3

What Mr. Spalding saw was the sudden stoppage of the cart, which now appeared as standing simultaneously at each station, Herr Schmidt's house, the inn, the grocery, the clock, the church and the side street up which it had not yet turned.

In this vision solid objects became transparent, so that he saw the side street through the intervening houses. In the same way, distributed in space as on a Mercator's projection, he saw all the subsequent stations of the cart, up to its arrival in a farmyard between a stable and a haystack. In the same duration of time, which was his present, he saw the townspeople moving in their houses, eating, smoking and going to bed, and the peasants in their farms and cottages, and the household of the Graf in his castle. These figures retained all their positions while the amazing experience lasted.

The scene widened. It became all Königsberg, and Königsberg became all Prussia, and Prussia all Europe. Mr. Spalding seemed to have eyes at the sides and back of his head. He saw time rising up round him as an immense cubic space. He was aware of the French Revolution, the Napoleonic wars, the Franco-Prussian war, the establishment of the French Republic, the Boer war, the death of Queen Victoria, the accession and death of King Edward VII., the accession of King George V., the Great War, the Russian and German Revolutions, the rise of the Irish Republic, the Indian Republic, the British Revolution, the British Republic, the conquest of Japan by America, and the federation of the United States of Europe and America, all going on at once.

The scene stretched and stretched, and still Mr. Spalding kept before him every item as it had first appeared. He was now aware of the vast periods of geologic time. On the past side he saw the mammoth and the caveman; on the future he saw the Atlantic flooding the North Sea and submerging the flats of Lincolnshire, Cambridgeshire, Norfolk, Suffolk, Essex, and Kent. He saw the giant tree-ferns; he saw the great Saurians trampling the marshlands and sea-beaches of the past. A flight of fearful *pterodactyls* darkened the air. And he saw the ice creep down and down from the poles to the vast temperate zone of Europe, America and Australasia; he saw men and animals driven before it to the belt of the equator.

And now he sank down deeper; he was swept into the stream that flowed, thudding and throbbing, through all live things; he felt it beat in and around him, jet after jet from the beating heart of God; he felt the rising of the sap in trees, the delight of animals at mating-time. He knew the joy that made Jerry, the black cat, dance on his hind legs and bow sideways and wave his forelegs like wings. The stars whirled past him with a noise like violin strings, and through it he heard the voice of Paul Jeffreson, singing a song. He was aware of an immense, all-pervading rapture pierced with stabs of pain. At the same time, he was drawn back on the ebb of life into a curious peace.

His stretch widened. He was present at the beginning and the end. He saw the earth flung off, an incandescent ball, from the wheeling sun. He saw it hang like a dead white moon in a sky strewn with the corpses of spent worlds. But to his surprise he saw no darkness. He learned that light is older than the suns; that they are born of it, not it of them. The whole universe stood up on end round him, doubling all its future back upon all its past.

He saw the vast planes of time intersecting each other, like the planes of a sphere, wheeling, turning in and out of each other. He saw other space and time systems rising up, toppling, enclosing and enclosed. And as a tiny inset in the immense scene, his own life from birth to the present moment, together with the events of his heavenly life to come. In this vision Elizabeth's adultery, which had once appeared so monstrous, so overpowering an event, was revealed as slender and insignificant.

And now the universe dissolved into the ultimate constituents of matter, electrons of electrons of electrons, an unseen web, intensely vibrating, stretched through all space and all time. He saw it sucked back into the space of space, the time of time, into the thought of God.

Mr. Spalding was drawn in with it. He passed from God's immanent to his transcendent life, into the Absolute. For one moment he thought that this was death; the next his whole being swelled and went on swelling in an unspeakable, an unthinkable bliss.

Joined with him, vibrating with him in one tremendous rapture, were the spirits of Elizabeth and Paul Jeffreson. He had now no memory of their adultery or of his own.

When he came out of his ecstasy, he was aware that God was spinning his thought again, stretching the web of matter through space and time.

He was going to make another jigsaw puzzle of a universe.

The Mahatma's Story

You remember the Grigley's *Mahatma*, that queer Bengali chap they brought back with them from Bombay? This is one of the tales he told them.

At one time he used to turn up for supper at the Grigleys' every Sunday, dressed in a very long black frock-coat, and a high waistcoat buttoned up to his chin like a clergyman's, and a great white turban wreathed round his head and flopping over one ear. He would arrange himself on Grigley's divan, with his face very meek and his backbone very stiff and his legs very sinuous and curly, like a cross between a blessed Buddha and a boa-constrictor sitting up on its coils. He told his stories in a little quiet, sing-song voice, smiling at the Grigleys all the time, as if they were very young and rather silly children. We would sit before him on the floor, staring at him, the Grigleys with solemn faces full of childlike wonder, and the rest of us rather critical and incredulous—enlightened Westerners, you know.

At first, we thought he was pulling all our legs, trying to see what we Westerners would swallow. But no, it was the Grigleys' wonder and our criticism and incredulity that amused him. The things he told us were to him so obvious and of their kind so elementary that he couldn't conceive how any reasonable being could regard them with interest, much less with wonder or suspicion.

I remember at the end of one of his most incredible yarns—about a man, I think, who could be in two places at once—Mrs. Grigley looked up with her little intense face and said,

"Anything—*anything* can happen in the East. The *East is wonderful!*"

She was going on like that, undeterred by the *Mahatma's* supple shrug, when George Higgins cut in. He would begin to believe, he said, when things like that began to happen in the West.

The *Mahatma* looked at him as if he had been a baby and smiled. "When the East comes to the West they do happen," he said.

It seems that about nine years ago the East came to the West in the person of a certain Rama Dass. He was proclaimed as a *Mahatma* by the members of a small occult society which lived on the wonder of him for a year or two. Then suddenly and violently it died of Rama Dass. He had caused a sort of scandal that no society, however occult, can be mixed up with and survive. But if the *Mahatma's* story is as true as he swore it was, Rama Dass must certainly have possessed powers.

To us the remarkable thing about him was, not his powers—the *Mahatma* had inured us to powers—but the light the whole queer story threw on certain mysterious events involving people whom we all knew. One of them indeed is so well known that I wouldn't give his name if it wasn't that he was under suspicion at the time, and the *Mahatma's* story clears him.

I mean Augustin Reeve.

You remember he disappeared? Well, we knew things had happened, very queer things, but none of us had ever understood how or why they happened, or how much queerer the real explanation was (if it *is* the real one). Who would have imagined that Augustin Reeve could ever have been mixed up with Rama Dass? But that, of course, was Varley's doing; his contacts were frequently unclean. Not that he had anything to do with the scandal; that was a story none of us were concerned with; I only mention it as proving the *Mahatma's* point, that the powers of Rama Dass were by no means spiritual. To him they were just the lowest, cheapest sort of magic.

The person who matters is, of course, Augustin Reeve. That's where the mystery comes in. He had everything to lose and nothing in the world to gain, unless you count Delia. Oh, well, I suppose she counted; talking of scandal, she seems to have been at the bottom of his disappearance. The point is—if it was only Delia—he could have had her without disappearing.

Here are the facts as they appeared to us at the time. Seven years ago, Reeve, as I say, vanished. So did Varley's wife, Delia. Muriel Reeve, Reeve's wife, stayed on at the house in Chelsea, which, by the way, was her house. She had the money. When you called there, you found Clement Varley in possession. Clement Varley, of all people in the world, who hadn't a decent coat to his back or an address he could own up to, nothing but his beautiful wife Delia, who kept him by sitting for Reeve and, it was said, by complacencies less innocent. Literally we didn't know where they went home at night. They used to receive us at a shabby little club they belonged to. And there he was, as I say, in possession. Oh—of everything: of Reeve's studio, of Muriel's car, of Reeve's servants (till they left), of Reeve's furniture, of Reeve's cellar—and of Muriel. He was quite off his head, suffering from delusions of greatness, imagining that he was a genius, that he had painted Reeve's pictures and that the whole place belonged to him and always had. He was wearing one of Reeve's suits.

And there was Muriel, behaving as if it was all true, humouring him in his madness—actually living with him. But for Muriel, we should simply have supposed that the Reeves had lent him the house while they went abroad somewhere. As it was, it looked like some infamous bargain between Reeve and Varley. That was the incredible thing—that Reeve could lend himself—that Muriel—the angelic Muriel—An inexplicable mystery.

But if you admit Rama Dass and his powers——

Reeve, mind you, had been gone about a year before we heard of him. Then somebody came on him in an opium den down in Limehouse. And it was after that that the stories began to get about. He had taken to drugging, to drink, to every vice you could think of. He did horrible things, things he had to hide for. It looked like it.

Then one day Delia turned up, very shabby, at Grigley's studio and gave him her address as a model. Somewhere in Limehouse. Grigley called there.

Reeve opened the door. He was frightfully shabby too, and very queer. He behaved as if he didn't know Grigley, had never met him and didn't want to meet him. He was very gentle and very polite about it, but firm. He didn't know Grigley. And Grigley had to go away.

Of course, as bluff it was pitiable, and it seemed to confirm all those stories.

And the mystery of it—if it had been Clement Varley you could have understood. He had the sort of corrupt beauty which would have lent itself. But Augustin Reeve, with *his* beauty, with his dignity and iron-grey serenity, you couldn't see him playing any part that wasn't noble. Augustin Reeve skulking in awful places to hide a vice, forgetting his old life and repudiating his old friends—it wasn't conceivable; if you don't believe in Rama Dass.

The next thing was the show of Reeve's Limehouse Scenes (superb masterpieces) at Varley's villainous little club. They sold. Everything he did sold. And we began to hope that he might return to us. Not a bit of it. When he'd made enough money, he went over to Paris with Delia, and, as you know, he never came back again.

We heard that Varley and Muriel had run across him there. And when Varley was next seen in Chelsea, he had Delia with him and Muriel was living again with Reeve in Paris.

Soon after that Varley went smash and disappeared. He couldn't make money and apparently, he had spent most of Muriel's. Anyhow he disappeared.

As for Reeve, he must have made pots and pots before he died.

Those were the facts, as far as we knew them. And I say, if you exclude Rama Dass, they are inexplicable.

We only realised him by an accident. We were dining with the Grigleys and the *Mahatma* was there. We'd been talking about poor Atkinson's death, and Grigley said,

"He would have been a fine man in finer circumstances. The poor devil hadn't a chance."

The *Mahatma* asked us what we called a chance, and I said, "Well, a decent income and a decent wife. A wife he could have lived *with* and an income he could have lived *on*."

Then the *Mahatma* said there were no such things as chances. There was nothing but the *Karma* that each man makes for himself. Then he told his queer story. I shan't attempt to tell it in his words. He had formed his style chiefly on the Bible, and at times he was startling. This is the gist of it.

****

First of all he said he knew a man who was always saying what we said, that he hadn't a chance. And he asked us if we'd ever heard of Clement Varley?

Of course, we'd heard of him, long before things had begun to happen. Muriel Reeve had taken him up and they were more or less looking after him, and Delia Varley was even then notorious. So was Clement in his way. He had once had a studio and he'd spoiled more canvases than he could afford to pay for, painting the abominations he called portraits. We wondered how on earth the Reeves could put up with the beast, he was so morose and lazy and discontented. I admit he hadn't much to be contented about. But the Reeves were extraordinarily good to him. He wasn't bad at copying and he might have made a decent living that way if he'd stuck to it.

Unfortunately, he thought he was a great painter, or at least that he would have been if, as he said, he'd had a chance. He didn't consider himself in the least responsible for his laziness and his vile temper and viler pictures. He believed these things were so because he hadn't an income or a decent place to live in, and because he was tied to a woman, he had left off caring about, who had left off caring about him.

The *Mahatma* was only interested in their case so far as Rama Dass came into it. Still, he told us things. He says the two spent most of their time tormenting each other. Delia would fly out at Clement because he didn't earn enough and because he didn't paint like Augustin Reeve. She said he'd no business to marry her when he couldn't keep her, and she'd remind him a dozen times a day that she was keeping *him*.

And Clement would shriek and call on God to witness that nobody could paint within half a mile of a woman like Delia; and that it was all very well for Reeve. *He* didn't depend on his painting for a living; *he* hadn't got to prostitute his genius; he'd had the sense to marry a woman with money, a woman of refinement, a woman who was a perfect angel. But he, Clement, hadn't had a chance.

And Delia would shriek back at him that it was all very well for Muriel. Augustin Reeve was a perfect angel too. But if Muriel had had to live cheek by jowl with a brute like Clement, she wondered what sort of angel she'd have been then. And she would keep on nagging at him to give up trying to paint and find work as a clerk in a bank or something.

Varley's case was complicated by his hideous jealousy of Reeve. And, of course, he fell in love with Muriel.

Those two women were as different as they could well be. Muriel was sombre and intense, black-haired and white, the blonde whiteness of honey. Delia's hair was like a heavy gold helmet clapped on to her head, and her skin was exquisite; cyclamen-white and pink. Her mouth and eyes glistened as though water ran over them. Her mouth was very red, redder than fair women's mouths generally are, and it had sulky corners. She was beautiful; but she had the temper of a she-devil. And Muriel really was a heavenly angel. You can't blame Varley for falling in love with her. And you can't blame Delia for falling in love with Reeve. Lots of women were in love with him. But that he should have become infatuated with Delia and Muriel with Varley, that's the uncanny thing; he wasn't that sort of man and she wasn't that sort of woman; besides they hadn't been married a year. This is where the *Mahatma's* tale comes in.

161

He said that one evening Varley and his wife brought Rama Dass to Reeve's studio. It would, of course, be Varley that brought him. He'd picked him up in some nasty East End den. And Rama Dass had begun talking, he supposed, about his powers. And then Varley had started grousing as usual, saying he hadn't had a chance, and that if he'd only had what he called Reeve's luck he'd have done something tremendous, and that it was all very well for Reeve, and so on.

If only they could change places——

Delia—it must have been Delia—looked at Rama Dass. And Rama Dass made queer Eastern faces at them—you can see him—and said, "Why not?" He could make them change places in five minutes if they liked. Only they must give him five minutes. And Reeve—it must have been Reeve—said he'd like to see Rama Dass try.

That wasn't a challenge that Rama Dass was likely to let pass. And you can hear the women joining in: "Oh do try, Mr. Rama Dass, *do* try." You see, Reeve and Muriel didn't believe that anything would happen. It was just their idea of a joke.

And Mr. Rama Dass tried. I've no doubt that was what he'd been brought there for. Varley and Delia were in deadly earnest.

He must have tried for all he was worth. He put them all four to sleep, laid out on Reeve's divan. Then he squatted down by each of them in turn and did some sort of incantation business, mumbling in their ears. And when they came up out of that horrible sleep, they *had* changed places.

That's to say, they had exchanged memories.

Varley found himself completely at home in Reeve's Chelsea house with Reeve's servants and Reeve's furniture and Reeve's bathroom—that must have been the strangest experience of all—and Reeve's wife. He remembered having painted Reeve's pictures. His possession of Reeve's memory entailed most of Reeve's habits, so that his reactions to his surroundings were correct.

You might have thought it would be a bit of a shock to Muriel, finding herself Varley's wife. But the ingenious Mr. Rama Dass had provided for that. His infamous magic poisoned her with Delia's first passion as well as Delia's memory.

In the same way he provided for Reeve's shock when he found himself with Delia. He had done the thing so well—whatever it was he did do—that Reeve drove off peaceably in a taxi-cab with Delia and Rama Dass, and settled down in Varley's rooms in Limehouse—those inconceivably squalid rooms—with every appearance of content. He couldn't remember anything else. His mind behaved exactly as if he had lived in Limehouse for years and years, and before that wherever it was that Varley had happened to be living, down to the room over the tobacconist's shop where he had been born.

Rama Dass had even provided for the case in which these transferred memories should clash. Say, Reeve with Varley's memory, or Muriel with Delia's, remembering each other's original circumstances. At all these points of contradiction Rama Dass had established complete forgetfulness, so that their memories dove-tailed very neatly and nothing destroyed the fourfold illusion. You'll say he couldn't have tampered with the memories of everybody concerned, all the people who had known Varley and Reeve; but this very exchange of circumstances lessened the chances of contact. Reeve had quite thoroughly disappeared from his circle and Varley from his; and if any of us did knock up against one of them, why, we were left with our unsolved mystery on our hands. And, naturally, Reeve's friends avoided Varley and Muriel.

I said it was Reeve who mattered most, but as Varley hadn't disappeared yet, whatever else he had done, Varley looms more considerably in this tale. We know, that's to say, the *Mahatma* seems to have known, more about Varley's behaviour than Reeve's. This because Rama Dass fairly haunted Varley, and the *Mahatma* was keeping an eye on Rama Dass.

What appears most evident is that Varley had got his chance. He had got *all* the things he had declared were necessary to him if he was to show what was in him. Money, leisure, the right surroundings, and the right woman.

But mark what happened.

When he found himself in Reeve's big studio, he remembered the very pattern of the carpet, he was familiar with the "Salamander" stove and the white-painted pipes of the radiators. Long years of comfort stretched behind him. He remembered with emotion the pictures on the walls and easels. As the *Mahatma* took care to point out, it was only their memories they had exchanged. They had kept their own bodies, and their own temperaments, and wills. After all, the powers of Rama Dass, though considerable, were not sufficient to cause them to exchange personalities completely. The self, as the *Mahatma* said, can neither be changed nor exchanged. It was beyond Rama Dass. And as Varley's temperament had always cried out for Persian carpets and voluptuous divans and anthracite stoves and woman's sympathy, it had nothing to say against these illusions of his memory. The presence of the pictures confirmed him in his belief that he was a great painter.

And yet, when at last he had every mortal thing he had ever wanted, when the very scene supported him and invited him to work, for months and months he seems to have simply given himself up to sloth; driving in Muriel's car, sprawling on Reeve's divans, making love to Reeve's wife; drinking much too much, and eating frightful quantities of rich food, till he grew so sleek and fat that his own mother wouldn't have known him. Not attempting to work. His bitterest complaint used to be that he couldn't paint because he hadn't enough money to pay for models; but now, when Reeve's best models turned up on his doormat every morning, he sent them away; and swore at them for coming, too.

In nine months, he hadn't done a stroke. He had always some excuse; he would say the light was bad, or he wasn't in the mood, or Muriel took up all the time he might have worked in. If she put her nose into the studio, he would swear at her for always hanging about; if she left him to himself, he complained that he was neglected and that he might as well never have married her, for all the good she was to him. And again, when the angel who, thanks to Rama Dass, must, have believed in him as she had believed in Augustin Reeve, when the angel tried encouraging him to paint again, he screamed out that he couldn't paint to order and she'd better mind her own business and not come meddling with his. He'd stamp about the studio and call upon God to tell him *how* he could do anything with a woman like that in the house.

And presently they began to hear about Augustin Reeve. First of all, Delia turned up, imploring Varley to let her sit for him. Then Reeve's pictures began to be shown here and there. And when Muriel praised them—she seems to have retained her judgment—he flew into a rage and swore at her. He said it was all very well for Reeve. *He* had the spur of poverty. He must paint or starve. But as for himself the life he lived was enough to kill all inspiration. He might as well be a grocer. Muriel's money was a drag on him; the house was a drag on him; what did he want with money and houses? Muriel was a drag on him. No artist ought to marry. And then his old cry: He hadn't had a chance.

At last, his jealousy of Reeve and that itch of his vanity which he mistook for inspiration, whipped him on to work again.

He must have expected to see, rising up magically under his hand, pictures like those of Augustin Reeve (his old manner) which fairly surrounded him in that house. You see, he thought, poor chap, he had painted them himself. But though he tried his level best to paint in Reeve's old manner he kept on turning out things that were too lamentably in his own. For he had kept his own body, and his body had kept to its own memory which was much deeper than his mind's memory, and it made his hand move in its old way. It couldn't have moved in any other way. And when he compared what it was doing with what he believed it to have done in the days before he married Muriel, he laid the whole blame of his impotence on her.

"See," he would shout, "what I was before I knew you and what I am now."

And he wished to God he had never married her. He said she had destroyed his soul.

When she reminded him that she had at least given him the sympathy and understanding he had wanted, he said he wanted nothing of the kind and that her business wasn't to understand him—he could understand himself—but to give him pleasure. He was beginning to hanker after Delia's unspiritual beauty.

This didn't seem to us to fit in with Rama Dass and his love-magic. But the *Mahatma* explained it. Rama Dass had only worked his love-magic on Reeve and Muriel who wouldn't have changed without it. And Varley's will and temperament were stronger than his memory. Memory, the *Mahatma* said, is only a record; it has no power but that which will and temperament put into it. And Rama Dass hadn't interfered with Varley's temperament and will.

He, Varley, seems to have heard that Reeve and Delia were in Paris; and it occurred to him that here was another chance he hadn't had. So, he went to Paris to see what it would do for him.

It did nothing but bring him into touch with Delia again. Meanwhile, whatever it was that Rama Dass had done to Reeve, the effect seems to have worn a bit thin under the friction of Delia's tongue. The *Mahatma* couldn't tell us much, he seems to have lost track of them after Paris; but I imagine things happened something like this: Reeve would be frightfully sorry for Muriel. The angel's sweetness would show up more beautifully than ever under Varley's treatment. And Muriel would be sorry for Augustin Reeve.

I daresay the sight of him was more powerful even than Rama Dass's beastly love-magic. And she worshipped his genius. He seemed greater than ever in his poverty. He *was* greater. Because he kept his own temperament and his own will he had been cheerful and contented even down in Limehouse, the *Mahatma* says. He trailed behind him the dark tissue of Varley's memory, but when he came to join his own piece on, he made it shining.

I ought to tell you that when he took over Varley's three rooms, he found any amount of canvases stacked against the wall. When he turned them round and looked at them, though he remembered himself as painting them he couldn't conceive how he had done anything so vile. And because he never kept his failures, he destroyed every one of those abominations so that of Varley's life nothing remained that could interfere with Reeve's knowledge of his greatness. After that he began painting in what we know as his second manner.

And because he had no money for models, he painted Delia over and over again; he painted himself; he painted the people of the house where he lodged; he went out into the streets and along the river and painted what he saw there. Within his range there was nothing paintable he didn't paint. He was a greater artist in the Limehouse days than he was before or since. He stuck to his work all the tighter because it was his only means of getting away from Delia.

And now in Paris, from being sorry for each other, he and Muriel went on to falling in love.

I believe *they* kept pretty straight. But Varley and Delia had no sort of self-control and they fairly gave themselves up to it. And as Muriel's money enabled him to keep her in considerable comfort, she was glad enough to live with him this time; and between them they spent what was left of Muriel's money. He seems to have sunk lower and lower, and to have painted more and more abominable pictures, till Clement Varley became another name for grotesque incompetence. These horrors didn't bring him in a cent, so that he was as poor as ever when he and Delia came back to London.

And then, suddenly, he disappeared, and was never heard of again.

We all know what became of Augustin Reeve. He died three years ago, more famous than he had ever been. As the *Mahatma* put it, "each was in the end brought back to that estate he had in the beginning. For a man's estate is what his self is."

And whenever he hears it said that somebody "hadn't a chance" he tells this tale of Rama Dass and Clement Varley.

He tells it in his quiet, sing-song voice, smiling almost maliciously at the absurdity of our wonder.

Well, I can understand that smile and that supple shrug of his. What beats me is his attitude to Reeve and Muriel. Nothing more horrible could well have happened to two innocent people. And he could have saved them. He could have stopped Rama Dass's little game if he'd liked, or what's the good of being a *Mahatma*? But he took it all as a matter of course or as the fitting punishment of their Western levity.

What's more, that smile suggests that the same thing might happen any day to any of us, if we persist in our scepticism. And the moral of it seems to be that if you can't despise Rama Dass like a *Mahatma*, you'd better fear him. In either case you'll keep out of his way.

Jones's Karma

1

The *Mahatma* was sitting on the divan in Grigley's studio, cross-legged, like a Buddha. He meditated.

I was playing Debussy on Grigley's piano. Yes, of course I asked the *Mahatma* whether he minded my playing the piano while he meditated, and he had replied that it was indifferent to him whether I played the piano or did not play the piano. But when I left off, he came up, pop, out of his meditation. And as he was always particularly bright at these moments of emergence, Grigley tackled him.

"You say the will is free, Guru. How do you reconcile that with your theory of *Karma*? You can't escape your *Karma*."

"You cannot escape it, Bikkhu," said the *Mahatma*; "but you made it for yourself in your last life and you were free to make it different."

"Not if your last life was made by the *Karma* of your life before."

"That also you made and the *Karma* before it."

"Oh, if you go back and back to the beginning——"

"If you go back and back to the beginning you start free."

"Still, it comes to this," I said: "if you could live your life again in the same circumstances, I take it you would do the same things. Nothing would be different. And you would not be free."

"You would be free," the *Mahatma* said, "to do the same things."

"But each thing would be predictable."

"Predictable, yes. But that is not your concern. It is not you who predict."

I persisted. "No; but the possibility of prediction would mean that I was doomed, not free."

"There you are again," said the *Mahatma*, "with your pairs of opposites. It would mean that you were doomed *and* free. You come to the crossroads. *I* know which turn you are going to take. You take it.

169

But you were free to take the other."

"Not if you knew, Guru."

"Why not? My knowledge has no hold on you. There is no path from my knowledge to your action, Bikkhu."

"Talk about living your life again," said Grigley, "who *would* live it, if they knew?"

"I would," I said, "if I were free to live it differently; if when the wrong turn came, I could take the right one."

"Then," said Grigley, with an air of saying something important, "it wouldn't be the same life."

"No. I stipulated for the power to live it differently."

I happened just then to think of two or three things I would very gladly have had different if I could.

Grigley's little wife heaved up a stifled sigh out of the sofa cushions. "If only one *could* live one's life again, on those terms," she said.

We all laughed, for Grigley's wife was a notoriously innocent and happy person.

"Why, what would you have different?" I said.

"Me, probably," said Grigley.

"Good thing it was impossible."

"It is not impossible," the *Mahatma* said. "Time is nothing. Or it is everything. You can go forward or you can return on the path of time. You have only to will it so in the moment of dying. For, as the wish formed at the moment before sleeping is powerful in the waking life of the next day, so the wish formed in the moment before dying is all-powerful in the next life. People do not know how important that moment is, so they do not will."

He had one of his fruitful pauses.

"There was a man who knew; for a *Mahatma* had told him. He came back to the same time-space, to the same womb. His name," said the *Mahatma*, "was Jones. I will tell you the story of Jones's *Karma*."

2

"The family of Jones was exceedingly particular about its *caste*. If it had lived in India, where the laws of *caste* are laid down precisely, so that mistakes are not possible, it would have been safe. But it lived in Europe, where there are no rigid laws, where the *castes* mix among themselves, and *caste* itself is a flexible thing, a thing of each man's interpretation, and each man is a law to himself in this thing.

"So that at every turn the family of Jones was liable to contamination.

"We of the faith of Buddha do not, as you know, believe in *caste*, and for us there is no such things as contamination from mixing. But for those who believe, these things are so; and he who is deceived by the illusion of contamination is contaminated.

"In the house next to Jones's house in the suburb of Putney there lived a little boy—Jones was about eleven years old at this time—a little boy whose *caste* was many degrees lower than the *caste* of the Joneses. Jones was brought up to believe that his *caste* was higher and holier than the *caste* of the families round about him and would be contaminated by mixing. It was even, they said, higher and holier than the *caste* of the other Joneses, for his family was distinguished by the name of Uppingham. Uppingham Jones.

"The Uppingham was not joined firmly on to the Jones with a stroke, as your custom is, for it was indeed but the second name of Jones's father: Albert Uppingham Jones; but it seemed to exalt these Joneses above all others. So much so that there was nobody in the suburb of Putney who was judged fit to be the companion of Jones. And thereby Jones suffered from an exceeding loneliness.

"And when he saw the little boy, whose name was Peter Hawkins, playing by himself in the next garden, a great longing came upon Jones either to go into the garden of the Hawkinses and play with him there, or else persuade him to come into his own garden. And Peter Hawkins had the same longing when he looked through the hedge and saw Jones looking in at him. So that nothing would appease him but that he must have Jones for his playmate.

"At the bottom of the gardens there was a gap in the hedge of which the two, by agreement, tearing down the bushes and parting them asunder, made so large an opening that each could creep through to the other. It was generally Jones who went through into Peter's garden, for Peter's garden had in it a swing and a summer-house and a pond with a row-boat; and Peter had there also a great store of European toys, steam engines, sailing ships, velocipedes, and the like costly things which Jones's parents could not be prevailed on to give him. All these things were now at his disposal through the generosity of Peter.

"I should tell you that these gardens of the Joneses and the Hawkinses were long and wide and ended each in a wild grass-place set about with many tall and thick bushes, so that the children playing there were concealed from the rest of the gardens and the houses. The swing, the summer-house, and the pond were likewise hidden.

And on the far side of the Hawkinses' garden there was a high wall and behind it a lane leading to a side-door in the Hawkinses' house. And there, Jones was led, secretly, by Peter into his house and played with him there in his playroom. And Peter's father and mother had compassion upon Jones because he was kept so close and strict in the solitude of his *caste*, and they rejoiced in his great friendship with Peter and helped him to keep it secret.

"This hidden communion lasted for three years. Then Jones was sent away to a public school; and three years later Peter followed him there. They had continued to meet, furtively, in the holidays, more by the desire of Peter than of Jones, for Peter loved Jones with a love that was greater than Jones's love for him.

"At this school—it is your strange English custom—Peter Hawkins was assigned to Jones in some sort as his servant; not because his *caste* was lower, for I am told that a great lord may be thus servant to a common boy, but because, being two years younger than Jones, he stood many degrees below him in the school.

"And because there were many patricians at this school the low *caste* of Peter became manifest to Jones, so that secretly in his heart he felt ashamed of his love for Peter and of Peter's love for him. Nevertheless, he did not break with Peter, but used their relation of servant and master as a cloak for his curious friendship.

"Indeed, he had no desire to break with Peter, for Peter had much money and was in many ways of great use to him over and above his appointed service. For example, Jones had much talent for the learning of languages, but he was but a poor mathematician, while Peter, who was backward in Greek and Latin, had much skill in numbers and in geometry. And when he rose rapidly in the school and was no longer the servant of Jones, he proved his great love by helping him with his mathematics, so much so that there was hardly a problem that Jones would have attempted to solve without him. Moreover, he had, with great courage, saved Jones's life when bathing.

"All these things Jones could bring forward as his excuse when he was mocked at by the young patricians for his attachment to a fellow of low *caste*. I am telling you all this that you may understand how many were the obligations that bound Jones to Peter and what reason he had to love him.

"Now, in Jones's class in school there was a certain young lord who had his seat not far from the suburb of Putney, and he had attached himself to Jones so firmly that when the time came for Jones to leave that school, he invited him most earnestly to visit him at his seat. At the same time, he pointed out to him that he would suffer much disadvantage if, at the outset of his career, he continued to be seen with such a one as Peter Hawkins. For Jones and the young lord were to finish their studies together at the university of Oxford, while Peter, in accordance with his *caste*, went down into the city to serve in the shop of his father Hawkins who was a draper.

"Jones understood that this was the turning of the ways, that the hour had struck when he must choose between Peter and the young lord.

"So, it happened that on one of your great national festivals, which you call cricket-matches, at a certain public place the name of which I have forgotten——"

"'Lord's?'"

"Yes, that is so," said the *Mahatma*, "the Place of the Lord. And Jones, on his way to the pavilion, with that great one who was his friend and with his friend's sister, a high lady in her own right, did to his horror observe Peter and his father and mother coming towards him with the palms of their hands extended and a loud salutation, your 'Hullo!' in which it was discernible that the initial letter was not sounded. And this, I understand is, in your country, one of the most grievous signs of a dishonourable birth. I speak according to the tradition and not as a Buddhist.

"And Jones, trembling with the shock of the encounter, turned his head somewhat to one side and made as though he had not seen the hands of the Hawkinses nor heard their salutation, and so passed them by.

"And it happened thus on more than one occasion when Jones met Peter while in the company of the lord and his sister. And from that time onward he ceased altogether from his former communication with Peter, as if he had not so much as known his name. And Peter, perceiving that he was repudiated, ceased altogether from communication with Jones.

"Thus, did Jones betray the friend to whom he owed so many and so great debts.

"That was the first turning of his roads.

"The next was when he had made, secretly, the acquaintance of a certain young girl who came many times to play ball" (he meant tennis) "in the garden of the Hawkinses.

"Her name was Sarah Bunning.

"And it so happened that many times the ball would fly over the hedge into the garden of Jones, and that Sarah Bunning would be sent to fetch it; for it was not possible for Peter to pass any more into Jones's place, because of the betrayal and his great and sore pride. And Jones would come out and aid her in her search. I think," said the *Mahatma* with a look of subtlety, "that in consequence of these meetings the ball was sent flying abroad more often than there was necessity, and that so dexterously as to lodge it in the thick places of the jungle which was at the bottom of the Jones's compound, where the search for it would take much time and keep those two long in each other's company.

"And when the season of this ball-play was over, Jones planned to meet the girl, secretly, one night after dark in a certain grove of birch trees on Putney Heath.

"And here appears Jones's freedom. For that evening he received a message from a friend asking him to dine with him at his club in Piccadilly at the very hour which he had appointed to meet Sarah Bunning. So that assuredly a choice of ways was given him. And Jones wavered, perceiving that here was his chance to escape, if he would, that great temptation. He went to the telephone that was set up in his father's house and summoned a hansom to take him into Piccadilly.

"But at the last moment the thought of Sarah Bunning so overcame him that he drove instead to about a stone's throw of the place of assignation; and having the conveyance there ready, he persuaded her to enter it and so took her to a certain hidden place that he knew of in Soho. And afterwards they met many times in that place.

"For the young girl was of an exceedingly fine and perfect beauty; but she had not the bearing nor yet the speech of Jones's *caste*; her *caste* indeed was lower even than that of the Hawkinses. So that, while Jones did excessively love her, he could not stoop from the noble state of Jones so far as to marry her. Nevertheless, he promised her that if she should find herself with child by him, he would marry her.

"But presently a time came when he thought to marry a high friend of that young lord for whom he betrayed Peter. And for that lady he betrayed Sarah Bunning.

"She died in childbirth in the hospital of Queen Charlotte which is set apart for women of low *caste*.

"And in the end the high lady refused, for reasons of *caste*, to marry Jones.

"Jones was so greatly smitten with grief for the loss of that lady, and with remorse for the death of Sarah Bunning that, though his disposition was by no mean warlike, he volunteered with your army in South Africa, where at that time you were fighting the Boers.

"And it was there that he came to the third turning.

"It was on the open *veld*. Jones and his comrade, a young captain whose name was George Denby, were flying on horseback from a Boer ambush, when Denby, who rose somewhat in front, had his horse shot under him, he himself being severely wounded in the groin so that he lay like a dead man with his foot held fast in his stirrup. He cried out to Jones with a great cry to help him. And Jones saw that he had but to dismount and cut away the stirrup leather and set him on his own horse in front of him, and with the start they had they might get away safe to the British lines. At that moment, while he yet planned the rescue, a bullet sounded past Jones's head, and another, and yet another; and his courage so forsook him that he put spurs into his horse and galloped away, leaving that young captain to die there on the *veld*.

"The thought of how he had betrayed his comrade was a punishment almost too great for Jones to bear. And many years after, being in India, he happened to meet one of my friends, the *Mahatma* who told me this story. They began talking, even as we were talking just now, about free will and destiny and the turning of the ways and whether a man would or would not live his life again. And Jones confessed to my friend that he had done three things in his life that he would gladly return and undo. He had betrayed the friend who trusted him; he had seduced his sweetheart; and he had deserted his captain on the field of battle.

"And the *Mahatma* told him, as I have told you, that if he would live his life again, he had only to will it so in the moment of dying. And if he would take the other turn, he had only to will it. So, when he came to die, Jones uttered the wish that he should come back and live his life again as it had been, and that when he came to those three turnings he should remember and each time take the right one.

"And he was brought back into that same space-time and into the same mother's womb. And from his birth-hour his life unrolled itself in every particular exactly as it had been before up to the first turning.

"Jones was crossing in front of the pavilion at—at———?"

"Lord's?"

"Lord's, with the young lord and his sister, and Peter and his father were coming towards him as before, with outstretched palms and saluting him loudly after their manner. And Jones remembered his former base betrayal, and instead of passing by and looking the other way, he came forward and grasped Peter by the hand and also his father and mother. And he reminded the young lord that he had known Peter beforetime at their school, and he presented him to the young lord's sister.

"And, except that his communion with Peter remained now unbroken, Jones's life went on as it had gone before up to the moment when the hansom came to his summons. But when he thought of Sarah Bunning, he remembered his second betrayal and her death in shameful childbirth, and, turning his back on the birch grove, he ordered the driver of the hansom to go furiously towards Piccadilly and to the club of his friend there.

"Now, men do not encounter lightly and to no purpose; and it happened that at that club Jones made acquaintance with a certain Colonel Rivers, and this had afterwards, as you shall see, a great working on his *Karma*.

"And so, when the nine months were up which had formerly unrolled the pregnancy and death of Sarah Bunning, and now brought instead her betrothal and marriage to Peter Hawkins, Jones volunteered with your army in Africa as before, yet not as flying from his shame, but in the quest of glory. And the ambush happened as before. But when Jones came upon the dead horse and his wounded comrade, George Denby, lying in that place on the *veld*, he remembered that third and last betrayal. And he dismounted and cut the stirrup strap that bound Denby to his horse, and lifted him up and set him on his own saddle, while the bullets sounded past him; and so, brought him alive and safe into the camp of the British.

"You would have thought that Jones had now worked out his *Karma* and accomplished his redemption. But no. In taking each time another turning he had started another chain of events, so that his life could not unroll itself altogether in the same pattern as before. Moreover, when he came back from South Africa, he was still but a young man, not thirty.

"And soon after his return from the war the lord his friend gave a banquet at your Criterion hall in honour of Jones's general, and Jones also was invited. Now, at this banquet there were many lords of *caste*, even more exalted than that of his friend. And as he went up the principal staircase between two of these very great ones, he saw Peter Hawkins, who stood above him on the landing looking down at him, having come there to see the general pass. And when he saw him, he came forward with his hand outstretched and with the same cry as before.

"Mark that on the last repetition of his *Karma* Jones's memory gave him warning and support; but he had made no provision for this third encounter. Occurring at another time and in a place where he least expected it, catching him thus unaware, it overcame him even as at the beginning, so that he turned his head aside and made as though he had not seen Peter. And when the very great ones, laughing, inquired who his friend was, he answered that he did not know the man, thus for the second time betraying him.

"Further, because of the slight change in his record which was set up in that moment when he had acknowledged Peter and renewed their communion, Jones had been compelled, unwillingly, to meet again that girl whose fascination he had run from. For she was now Peter Hawkins's wife. So that at an hour when, again, he was unprepared, he was caught a third time in the snare of her great beauty. And, taking occasion of Peter's absence for three months on business in the United States, he again tempted her so that she fell. And she bore a child that by all reckoning was manifestly not her husband's, and died, as she had died beforetime, at its birth.

"Thus, their *Karma* was repeated.

"You will remember that I told you how, on that evening when he had fled from the second temptation of Sarah Bunning, he had become acquainted with one Colonel Rivers. And so great was the friendship which thereafter sprang up between them that Jones went out to stay with Colonel Rivers at Jabalpur in Central India.

"Now, the regiment of George Denby, who was by this time major, was stationed at Jabalpur; and it happened that he had three days' leave from his service. And he asked Jones to come to him to a place about twenty miles upcountry near the jungle, where he had a bungalow and there was much *sambhar*. And when Jones arrived at the bungalow, he was told that cholera had broken out in the village and that the major had gone there to aid the police in isolating the sick people.

"And at this news the joints of Jones became as if they had been water, and he said to himself that truly he had come at an inconvenient season, and that the best thing he could do would be to depart instantly as he had come. But when he looked for the *tonga* that had brought him thither, it had departed. And at that moment the major arrived at the bungalow. He pressed Jones to stay, making light of the

177

cholera and saying that there were but two cases in all, and they had them so well in hand that the doctor who had come up from Jabalpur had returned there, and how there was more cholera in Jabalpur than there was in this village.

"And when the major had stripped and bathed himself and put on clean clothes that had not been near the cholera, they dined together; and in the cool of the evening they went up into the jungle to shoot *sambhar*, returning about ten at night.

"At midnight they went to bed.

"Towards morning Jones was wakened by a noise of groaning and of retching in the major's room. And it seemed to him that between the groaning and the retching he could hear his name called, although but faintly. He got up and went into the major's room and found him doubled up, with his knees drawn even to his chest, leaning his head out of bed and sore retching.

"And at that sight and that sound the bones of Jones became again as water, and his stomach sank towards the ground. And when he had given Denby a little brandy he made an excuse that he would go into Jabalpur and bring back a doctor.

"He dressed in great haste, and having summoned the major's *tonga*, he departed to Jabalpur. And there he found that the doctor he knew of had gone to a far place beyond the town. It was the same wherever he called, for the cholera was by this time raging, and all the doctors were scattered abroad. He left a message at the house of one and set his face to return, as he believed, to the bungalow; though at the thought of the cholera his flesh and his bones melted.

"And it may be that he would indeed have returned there but that as they passed the railway station, he saw the train standing ready to go to Bombay. It wanted but a minute to its starting. And at the sight of the train, Jones jumped out of the *tonga* and ran to it. In his haste to catch it—for it was now moving—he climbed into the nearest wagon which was full of natives flying from Jabalpur. There was cholera on that train.

"Jones died on it an hour before it reached Bombay."

3

"And you expect me to believe, Guru," said Grigley, "that that man's will was free."

"Most certainly, Bikkhu, it was free. No will but his own compelled him to betray Peter, and seduce Sarah, and leave Denby to die.

In these three deeds he had made his own *Karma*. And though his free will refused those deeds the second time, yet at the third time his *Karma* compelled him to their accomplishment."

"How do you make that out?"

"Because in dying he had willed only to undo the actual deeds done in one place and one time; not to resist the same temptation at all times and all places. And those final turning-points he neither remembered nor had foreseen, so that his *Karma* had power to repeat itself.

"You will observe," said the *Mahatma*, "the concatenations of Jones's *Karma*. If he had not overcome the temptation to desert his comrade, he would have been disgraced, and there would have been no reception in his honour, and he would not have betrayed Peter a second time. If he had not overcome the temptation to betray Peter, he would not have met Sarah again, and seduced her a second time. And if he had not overcome the temptation to seduce Sarah, he would not have met Colonel Rivers, and gone out to Jabalpur, and found Denby sick with cholera and deserted him a second time.

"Yet when you talk of free will and bondage you talk of the pairs of opposites. You are free and you are bound also. It is according. But so long as you affirm the reality of the pairs of opposites you are subject to illusion."

He paused.

"Notwithstanding, there is a path of perfect freedom. When it is indifferent to a man whether he is himself or not himself, whether he lives or dies, whether he catches the cholera or does not catch the cholera. Thus, he escapes from desiring and undesiring, from the pairs of opposites, and from the chain of happening and the round of births."

At this point Mrs. Grigley interrupted the *Mahatma* to tell us that dinner was getting cold. We went into the dining-room.

On the table there was the Grigleys' delicious dinner and there was a bowl of boiled rice for the *Mahatma*. To these Grigley pointed.

"Which is it to be, *Guru*? There's no compulsion."

The *Mahatma* spread out his brown palms. "Truly, there is no compulsion. For it is indifferent to me, Bikkhu, whether I eat my rice or your dinner."

He ate Grigley's dinner.

Heaven

1

Mr. Sessions had made up his mind. He would go. It would be a pity not to while he was in the neighbourhood; he might never have another chance. Nothing but the funeral would have brought him to Sutton now—his first cousin, and a Sessions, the last but one.

Why, he hadn't seen the place for thirty years; not since Rose Milton married; not since his mother died. And he was fifty-seven.

He knew how to get there. Out at the back of the house, through the apple orchard to the fir-wood. Along the bridle-path between the palings and the banked edge of the wood under the black eaves of the firs. At the end of the path the yellow high road would cut through the forest, and a hundred yards down it he would come to the "Old Green Dragon." He knew how it would look, with its red roofs crushed low over its windows, squatting there in the yellow bay of the road under the black-green crescent of the firs. He would see the tall sign, the green dragon on a white ground, standing out by the highway above the stone horse trough. He would see the bow window of the parlour, the small, greenish, bottle-end panes, the thin red curtains.

The bridle-path was the same, dark under the eaves of the fir-wood. It gave him the hallucination of his youth. He was five-and-twenty, going to see Rose Milton. She would be sitting in the bow window between the red curtains, with her crochet work in her hands, waiting for him, looking up the road. The inn garden ran back into the forest; there would be a little lawn there and the arbour of the weeping willow where Rose and Alice Milton had brought him his tea, the first time. The first time. When he stayed talking.

He remembered the second time, and the slight shock he had when he caught sight of Rose behind the bar; the little dreaming face suddenly alert, suddenly attentive. Her mouth had an adorable smile for the rough carters drinking their beer, a small, rounded smile, as if it were saying something. She didn't want to shame and hurt them by her refinement, her difference. He remembered her eyes when she saw him, shining; she hadn't thought he would come again. And Alice's face when she looked at him.

The two sisters were alike, except that Rose was dark and Alice was the taller and slenderer, and her face looked as if it had been made of some firmer and clearer stuff. Too firm; too clear. And she had grey eyes, light and wide, like—like gates thrown open. He could see them now, Alice's eyes.

He remembered, too, the uncanny things that happened on wet days in the red-curtained parlour, when Alice would be at her tricks, willing Rose to do things. She had only to look at her and say, "You're drinking raw whisky," and Rose's little face would crumple with disgust and she would pour away her tea into the slop bowl. She would make her think that Bunny the cat was a baby, so that she would rock him on her breast, hushing him to sleep. And he had seen Rose come out of the bar carrying a pint pot, guarding it from the draught with her curved hand. She had thought it was a lighted candle. But she only laughed when he asked her what she was doing; it was "that Alice" again, she said.

Sometimes he had wondered whether it was Alice who———. But no; it was himself. Or, rather, it was his mother. She wouldn't hear of his marrying Rose Milton. She wouldn't hear of his going to see her. Yet he had gone.

★★★★★★★★★★

He remembered all the times; the first time and the last. They were the only times he had ever taken his own way against his mother, escaping from the gloomy Highbury house, running down to Rose Milton on a Saturday. The only times he had deceived his mother, pretending he went to see his aunt and cousins. He had only that, his infatuation for Rose Milton, only those Saturday escapades to reproach himself with; and he had made up for them on Sundays, going with his mother to church, morning and evening, sitting with her and her Sunday friend, Mr. Minify, through the long afternoon, listening while she sang hymns to them in her thin, high voice, and accompanied herself on the American organ; taking her to sacred concerts in the Albert Hall.

And the evenings of all the other days; it seemed to him, looking back on his young life, that he had spent them all at home. He had been so determined to make up to her for his father's death; and before that, as long as he could remember, to make up for his father's life, for all that his father was and wasn't.

Had he really determined anything? Wasn't it she who had determined, she who had willed, while he followed, without resistance, her determination and her will?

Who could have resisted her? He could see her now, her beautiful face between the lace lappets of her cap, between the blonde bands of her hair, and that look when his father worried her, that look of resignation, of heavenly patience, sacred martyrdom. Why, he had loved her so much that he had hated Mr. Minify, poor old Minify who had got nothing; for all his Sunday devotion, nothing.

Then, last spring, his mother had gone down with him to Sutton. He couldn't stop her; how on earth could he have stopped her? Besides, he had wanted her to see Rose Milton.

And when she had seen her, he knew that he would have to choose between his mother and Rose. Between Rose and his mother. If he had the courage——

He put off going down to Sutton till he was certain that he had it; and when he went Rose was engaged to be married to George Pargeter.

It was Alice Milton who told him, walking with him in the wood.

"It's your own fault," she said. "You should have taken her when you could. . . . Even now, if you tried, you could take her."

"Oh, no. Oh, no."

"Why not?"

"I don't know. One doesn't."

"Ah—You haven't any will of your own. You never will have as long as your mother lives. Perhaps not even afterwards. She may be stronger afterwards."

"Don't say such terrible things."

"You're a coward. You can't bear thinking of terrible things."

"I can't bear thinking of mother's dying. You don't understand. I *love* her. I've been happy with her all my life."

"If you'd been unhappy, you'd have had more chance. But you aren't happy with her. You're only happy when you get away from her into a world of your own."

"Oh, I've a world of my own, have I, though I haven't a will of my own?"

"It isn't any good to you. You can't do anything in it. You can't get what you want. You want Rose and you can't have her because your mother doesn't mean you to, and you can't lift up your hand to take her."

He couldn't. He couldn't. Lifting up his hand to take anything was an effort beyond him.

He was not angry with Alice. He knew she was saying these things to him because she loved him. And there was something beautiful about her. But he didn't love her. He would never want to take her in his arms. He wondered whether anybody would, ever. Perhaps it was because he was afraid of her, because of those tricks she played with her sister.

"Alice, is it true you can make people do things?"

"Sometimes."

"No. But against their will. Could you make me?"

"Oh—your *will*!"

"Could you? Could you? Could you make me get up and come to you?" He meant, could you make me care for you against my will?

"Of course, I could."

"I hope you won't. I should loathe it."

"You needn't be afraid. I shan't *make* you do anything. I'd never do it. It's wicked. It's the wickedest thing you can do, to tamper with another person's will. . . . Unless I had to save you."

"Oh, don't," he said. "Don't save me."

He hadn't hated Alice at the time. Only afterwards, when he remembered the things she had said about his mother, he hated her.

He had come to the end of the path, to the high road. He wondered where Rose Milton—Rose Pargeter—and Alice were now.

The road was different. It had lost its bright yellow freshness. It was bleached and powdered by the March wind, broken into great pits and ruts by the hauling trollies, and at intervals up and down it the fir-wood had been cut back for a depth of twenty yards or so and marked out into building lots. Ahead of him he could still see the stone water trough; but the standard with the swinging sign was not there.

When he came to the bay of the road, the old white-washed, red-tiled inn was gone, and in its place stood a gaudy three-storied hotel, its upper half yellow brick, its lower half chocolate paint. The vast saloon doors at one corner were flanked by pillars of sham yellow marble, and above them an enormous gas globe hung out its triangular facets shining with cut stars. Above that the corner bore like a breastplate a carved placard advertising Truman and Hanbury's ales in gold letters on a green ground.

As he stared at this structure Mr. Sessions had a sense of desolation, of violent unreality. Over the door he read the name of George Pargeter, Rose's husband.

In the hotel they told him the old inn had been pulled down fifteen years ago, and that Mrs. Pargeter and her sister Alice were dead.

★★★★★★★★★★

Mr. Sessions drew himself closer into the corner of the third-class railway compartment. A shiver went over his skin like a trickle of ice-water. The March wind had got at him. He had taken a chill at the funeral.

From time to time, he fixed a sudden, nervous, inimical stare at his fellow-passenger. Huddled in the opposite corner, the young man showed an inflamed face and watery eyes above a dirty woollen muffler. A rattling, strangling sound in his throat broke into a gusty cough. He apologised to Mr. Sessions. He said he was suffering from a bad attack of influenza. But Mr. Sessions hadn't any pity for him. He thought: "He's no business to be travelling, infecting other people. It should be made a punishable offence."

He had always been afraid of infection; he had always been afraid of change; always afraid of death, because he conceived of it as entailing some prodigious effort to meet it. He wanted to go on living, to go on being cashier of the firm he had worked for since he was a boy. He felt safe in his round of duties that were habits, where he had no responsibility and was never called on to make a decision. And influenza this year was of a peculiarly virulent type.

Supposing he caught it?

Supposing it turned to pneumonia?

Supposing he——?

2

Glass. Glass. He was sure it must be glass. *Not* ice. It felt warm—well, distinctly warmish under your feet. He didn't know how long he had been gliding and sliding over the glass. There was no way of judging space by the time you took getting through it; no way of judging time by the space you got through. No measurements.

He had tried counting the crystal slabs of the pavement. But that wasn't any good. You couldn't count them. Mr. Sessions gathered that this must be a special sort of space; and the queer thing was that you got from point to point of it without passing through intermediate space.

He supposed it was because there was no friction. No friction. That would account for it. He supposed that time, the time you measured by, would be going on all the same over your head, and it would be very awkward, when you got to the place you were bound for, not knowing what time it was really.

It was this very singular behaviour of space and time that made Mr. Sessions think he must be dreaming. And the fact that the air all around him was buoyant like water.

Then something seemed to take hold of him under his armpits and lift him off his feet, so that he came, half floating, half treading water, into the great open Square of the City.

It was paved like the roadway with slabs of crystal; the wide houses round it were built of crystal, block upon block, with gold veins running through them, and cemented—no, welded together with gold. And in the middle of the Square, raised on crystal steps and facing Mr. Sessions, was a great crystal cross with a sun blazing away at the heart of it.

This was queerly familiar to him; and the sight of the cross gave him his first faint sense of uneasiness. He had a feeling that something, something unpleasant was going to happen. Then he saw his mother coming towards him slantways across the Square; he had the impression that she came out of one of the houses.

Young—young. And he remembered her as an old woman; but he knew it was his mother, mysteriously, irrefutably, as you know things in dreams. She was rather like her portrait in the wedding photograph they had at home in the drawing-room over the piano, dressed in her white wedding gown with a long white veil floating behind her; her face had the sharp, thin-lipped, dominant beauty that he knew; it had the look he knew of holy but complacent resignation, the self-satisfied—yes, he could see now it was a self-satisfied smile.

He was aware, disagreeably aware, that he was not glad to see his mother. The feeling he had was not pleasure, not pleasure at all; it was more like fear. He consoled himself by the reflection that he was only dreaming, and that you were not responsible for anything you felt in dreams. Not responsible. That was the best of dreaming; you were not responsible.

His mother's face with the sharp smile on it was tilted up to him to be kissed.

"I was afraid," she said, "you wouldn't know me in my crown."

He saw then that instead of a wedding wreath she wore a crown, a gold one, with stars standing up and twinkling all round it. It struck him that it was just like her to draw his attention to it first thing. He could see her coming into the dining-room at Highbury with her Prayer-book in her hand and a new hat on. He dropped at once into his old cajoling manner.

"I say—I say—it's what they call a martyr's crown" (just as he used to say it's what they call a boot-shaped hat), "isn't it?"

"Yes. A martyr's."

"Well, you couldn't wear anything more becoming."

"Oh—becoming! It's *suitable*, my dear; that's all I think about. . . . And so, you've come to me, Albert?"

She pressed his hand, and a thrill, stringent and not quite pleasant, shot up his arm.

"I knew you would."

"Yes. I seem to have come, somehow, from somewhere."

"You came," she said, "from the dark place, across the bridge over the great gulf."

"I don't remember any dark place or any gulf. I don't remember coming over any bridge. I just *came*."

"My dear Albert, you *couldn't* come any other way. Not in your unregenerate state. Didn't they explain?"

"Didn't who explain what?"

"The guides—the spiritual guides who brought you over?"

"I don't remember any guides. I don't know what you're talking about. What was there to explain?"

"The scheme of redemption. Don't imagine that you could have got over by yourself, in your own strength, on your own merits, that you had the *entrée*——"

"But I did, I tell you. I came sliding over the glass, for ages, by myself; there wasn't anybody with me. I came bang into the middle of all this."

"That was the cross," she said, "the cross. It drew you. It's a magnet. The sun in it's a magnet. The Magnet of the Universe."

He stood there, in the great open Square, blinking uncomfortably under the furious light that beat from the heart of the cross.

"It's too much for you," his mother said. "We'll go into the house."

He could see it was the principal house in the Square, distinguished from the others by its height and breadth and by a flight of crystal steps leading to a colonnade, all crystal and gold-veined, and yet curiously like the *façade* of St. Pancras Church. As he followed her through the massive gold doors, he had a sense of misgiving, of foreknowledge—or was it reminiscence? His mother had got him; she would hold him there behind the gold doors as she had held him in the shabby house at Highbury. He told himself that this wouldn't really happen. His mother was dead, and he would wake up presently and be free.

Meanwhile he took in the wonderful interior where every object shared the transparent hardness of the crystal walls. The couch they sat on might have been hewn from one block of clear emerald; the cross-legged chairs and tables had the fragile clearness of yellow topaz; the cabinet opposite glowed, a pigeon's-blood ruby; the flowers in the crystal bowl on the sapphire stand shook with the tremulous glitter of cut jewels.

At first, he thought he was in a hall of looking-glass blazing with electric light and reflected at each end in a long sequence of blaring halls. Then he saw that these vistas were not reflections; they were other rooms with other furniture, seen through and through as the light penetrated the transparent crystal. This would have surprised him if he hadn't known he was dreaming.

And from every surface there came a rapid, shimmering vibration, a dancing of innumerable points of light, so that the whole scene flashed and quivered like a cinema show.

And calmly, as if nothing in his surroundings called for remark, his mother was continuing their conversation. He heard himself saying with his old obedience, "If you think so, Mother, of course, it *is* so."

"Of course. Why, if I hadn't prayed and prayed and prayed for you, Albert, you wouldn't be here now."

"Quite so, but I can't think what *you're* doing here."

"I, Albert?"

"Yes, you." He thought of her dull, sober drawing-room at Highbury. "I can't make it out. It isn't like you somehow."

"What isn't like me?"

"All this splendiferousness—that ruby thing over there. What I mean is, it isn't your taste."

"No," said his mother, "it's God's taste."

"Well," Mr. Sessions said, "that beats me. It does, really."

He put his hand up to his head to screen off the vibrating light. His mother sat still and closed her eyes, and presently he was aware of a clouding and thickening in the transparency, like milk spreading through water, till the crystal turned to white chalcedony, the emerald to jade, the topaz to dull amber, the sapphire to lapis lazuli.

"Ah," said Mr. Sessions, "that's better. I couldn't have stood it much longer, that infernal glitter."

"Albert, will you please remember where you are?"

"That's just it," said Mr. Sessions. "*Where am I?*"

She looked at him with the old shocked, surprised expression he remembered.

"Oh, my dear," she said, "don't you know? You're in Heaven."

★★★★★★★★★★

"Then," said Mr. Sessions, "I'm not dreaming. I'm dead." He said it out loud, to himself. His mother had left him.

Somebody answered him. "You are what they *call* dead in the place you came from. Really, you are now in your eternal life." The voice was measured, slightly lyrical, and suave.

Somebody had come behind him into the room. He could see the figure of a man reflected in the crystal floor. It came forward and stood before him in an attitude that reminded him of something, the bent left arm stretched stiffly across his breast, the hand grasping a scroll. Somewhere, he had seen before the stiff, sharp folds of its white draperies, the sparse, tidy auburn beard, the sleek parted fall of the hair to the shoulders, the pale, meek face. Somewhere——

"I don't think," said Mr. Sessions, "I have had the pleasure——"

"You have. I met you on the bridge. I brought you over."

"Ah, so my mother says."

"My dear young man——"

"Not young. Not young," said Mr. Sessions.

"Very young in eternity. You'd better realise that anything your mother says is pretty certain to be true."

"I don't need to be told that, sir."

"You need to realise it."

"If I knew to whom I have the pleasure of speaking——"

"My name in time is Stanford Jones. It may be familiar to you."

It was, very familiar, but for the life of him he couldn't put an idea to it.

"Well, Mr. Jones——"

The stranger corrected him. "My eternal name is Aspirel."

"Mr. Aspirel, then." (He thought: What beastly affectation! Got up to look like Jesus Christ, too. Shocking bad taste, I call it.)

"Can I do anything for you?"

The stranger smiled with a sort of saccharine contempt. "You can

189

call me Aspirel, quite simply. Beyond that you can do nothing. On the contrary, it is I who must do everything for you."

"You have me, sir, at a disadvantage. I'm still no nearer know-ing——"

"Who and what I am and my business?"

"Precisely, if you would be so good."

"I am," said Aspirel, "Instructor-in-Chief for this district of Heaven. I am the Principal of the College of Spiritual Guides. And because of the very high position your mother holds here I have consented to undertake your education."

He sat down beside him on the emerald couch, and there was a pause in which Mr. Sessions observed the drooping eyelids of the principal, and the pinched mouth, furtive under its screen of auburn beard.

"You are interested in natural science," said Aspirel, making the statement without any note of interrogation.

Mr. Sessions replied that at one time when he was young, he had gone in for it, but, if he had ever known anything about it, he had forgotten all he knew.

"Just as well. You will have the less to unlearn. Our great difficulty with our students is that they are apt to remember too much. They have to be trained to forget. To let go all the theories, all the laws of natural science, all the great discoveries. What have your great discoveries revealed? Nothing. Ours have laid bare the secret of the universe."

When he had heard that Mr. Sessions felt a tingling revival of the intellectual curiosity which had once made him attend a course of lectures on geology at the London Polytechnic. He had even bought a second-hand copy of Haeckel's *History of Creation*, keeping it where his mother couldn't find it, in his office desk, and reading it in A.B.C. shops at his luncheon hour. He was pleased at the idea of enrolling himself as a by-student at the College of Spiritual Guides.

****

The operator had let go the handle of the Cosmological Machine. Aspirel's voice went on and on, solitary and immense, like the booming of a church organ, in the vast lecture hall of the College.

"You have now," he said, "seen how, by the use of a mechanism as simple as your office Dictaphone, you have had unrolled before you the drama of the cosmos, from the beginning of atomic motion, through the stupendous events of sidereal and geologic space, the blazing and cooling of the earth, the formation of igneous rocks, glacial rocks, through upheavals and subsidences, through the wonders of the carboniferous age, up and on to the evolution of the organic beings that we know.

"You have seemed to travel backwards through time; but in reality, you have not done so; for in our science the past is not past. You have simply been brought into touch with those vibrations through which the events of pre-organic time would have been made visible to a spectator, if spectator there had been. It is all," said Aspirel, becoming excited and waving his hands, "a question of vibrations, continuing through the air, through the ether, from universe to universe, through all space and all time, for ever and ever. You can catch those vibrations, as a tuning-fork catches sounds. Owing to their permanence the past is never really past.

"This," he ended up, "is part of the Great Secret that has been re-vealed to us——"

Great Secret——? Mr. Sessions thought. It all sounded vaguely reminiscent. At some time or other he had read something very like this in some book. All that about plant life, for example, he had read that in a book. A book with diagrams.

"But we have not yet," Aspirel went on, "so much as skirted the fringe of our revelation. That revelation which will lead us upwards and onwards to the knowledge and the vision of God. It is not till we come to the evolution of human forms that we approach its heart. This will be the subject of our next lecture."

If he could only remember the title of that book——

Everywhere he went in Heaven he was haunted by this sense of things already seen, already heard: the cloistered square of his mother's garden, set about with little shining trees; his mother's dining-room, austerely bare, with the long, narrow, cross-legged table at the top; her bedroom with its square bed; the windows and the roof of the great Conference Hall at the College, with the stalls of the Spiritual Guides each in a fretted niche. He remembered the fan work and the lace work, the traceries, the beaded points of the canopies. Gothic. Gothic style, that was; or was it Early English Perpendicular?

He would have liked to explore the City, to penetrate into the country beyond it, to play by himself with the Cosmological Machine. But no sooner had he started to do something by himself than his mother or Aspirel would pop out on him from behind some door or some pillar. And they would take him to a lecture by one of the Spiritual Guides, or to a Sacred Concert, or to the Bridge of the Passing, to watch the redeemed penitents as they came over from the Darkness to the Light.

This was his mother's favourite diversion, and it reminded Mr. Sessions of their autumn holidays at Dover when they went to the pier on rough days to see the seasick Channel passengers land. The penitents were very like the passengers, haggard and exhausted; frightened eyes in drawn, white faces, and a tendency to sink at the knees when the Guides grabbed them. Mr. Sessions wondered whether he had looked like that when he landed, and was told that he had, only much worse; it had been a job, Aspirel said, to get him along. The penitents, it seemed, were blinded by the light of Heaven just at first and didn't know what they were doing; they would fight like mad things, resisting the guides. And as he watched their struggles Mr. Sessions wondered why his mother had been so anxious that he should come into Heaven in that painful and ignominious way.

Every day he was beginning to find out some little thing about her he hadn't known before; for it seemed that this after-death state was one of singular clear-sightedness. And every day his uneasiness increased. The gorgeous gold and crystal architecture of Heaven could not disguise from him the fact, the disgusting fact, that he was being drawn again to something like his old life at Highbury, when his mother's will had frustrated him at every turn. All his life he had yearned, in his ineffectual way, for the society of people who had intellects, who could, as he put it, "talk about things." Here they never got away from their own quarter of the City. They never met anybody but the Spiritual Guides or the favoured students of the College.

His mother and Aspirel were trying to force him into intimacy with one of those whom Mr. Sessions recognised as old Dancy, the greengrocer and the verger of St. Jude's Church, Highbury. He remembered Dancy as a stupid and illiterate person to whom his mother paid a small pension that saved him from the disasters of his incompetence. In Heaven, as on earth, Dancy had a face of the purest imbecility, a cock eye, and a sloping smile that gashed his left cheek when he didn't understand what you said to him (he seldom did), and two exasperating phrases by which he safeguarded his idiocy: "Eggs is eggs," and "That's as it may be, Mr. Sessions."

And here he was in Heaven, an Operator in the College of the Guides. He turned the handle of the Cosmological Machine; he took most of the elementary classes, and Mr. Sessions found that he was expected to look up to Dancy as his spiritual superior. This was very irritating to Mr. Sessions.

He was beginning to wonder whether, at this rate, Heaven had anything new, anything wonderful to give him. The Sacred Concerts, for example. He had understood that Heaven was famous all the world over for its music, and there was something in *Revelation* about a New Song. Yet he could swear that this evening they were simply listening to the *Messiah*. There it went: "All we like sheep—All we like sheep——" bleating away; you couldn't possibly mistake it.

Yet his mother and Aspirel had been annoyed when he said it was the *Messiah*, and Aspirel had told him that it only seemed so to him because he was listening to heavenly music with earthly ears. And when he stuck to it, drawing their attention to the Handel full close, little Dancy had smiled his gash of a smile and spluttered, "That's as it may be. 'Eavenly music is 'eavenly music, 'andle or no 'andle, Mr. Sessions." The idiot was thinking of his blessed machine.

And that last lecture that wound up his course of Physical Science—the one on embryology. To be sure, Aspirel had told him to be prepared for a revelation which would transcend all that was known of embryology on earth; yet Mr. Sessions had his first decided shock of mistrust when Dancy (whose eternal name was Regius) turned the handle of the Cosmological Machine and Aspirel invited you to examine "the human germ-plasm in its earliest stage." You then saw, curled up in the form of a comma, microscopically small, a perfect human body with all its organs fully developed, the nervous system visible in the transparent flesh.

As Dancy-Regius went on turning the handle this form increased in size without altering its structure, remaining perfect through all the stages of its growth.

And suddenly Mr. Sessions remembered his Haeckel's *History of Creation*—those diagrams.

"But," he cried, "this isn't embryology. This is clean contrary to the laws of evolution."

"How—contrary?" said Aspirel. He looked more annoyed than ever. Dancy-Regius had disappeared; he had a class to take.

"Well, what I mean is, the embryo—in those early stages—doesn't look like that. We know perfectly well what it looks like. First, it's a uni—unicellular organism, then it's like a tadpole, then it's like a lizard, then it's like a fish, then it's like a series of gargoyles. Why, even when it's born it's like a monkey."

"To spiritual eyes," said Aspirel, "it's like none of these things. It is as we have shown you. Perfect from the very first."

"I don't believe it," said Mr. Sessions. "We're talking about Physical Science, aren't we?"

"Albert," said his mother, "do you set up your judgment against Aspirel's?"

"No. I set up the judgment of Darwin and Huxley and Herbert Spencer."

The two looked at each other and a smile passed. A smile of heavenly, yet slightly malicious, understanding.

"We will," said Aspirel, "refer you to their judgment."

They passed out of the lecture hall into one of the great classrooms, and down at the far end, in a form by themselves, the lowest form, which Dancy-Regius was teaching, they found them: Darwin and Huxley and Herbert Spencer. Mr. Sessions had seen their portraits, and he recognised them, Darwin by his bald head and snub nose and white beard, Huxley by his wide, truculent mouth and black side-whiskers, Herbert Spencer by the points of his collar and the great British Museum dome of his head, his long upper lip, and his resemblance to that nice old butler that the Taunton-Smiths had.

It was inconceivable, but there they were, sitting in a row before Dancy, the verger and the greengrocer, intoning the catechism. Dancy would shout at them: "Now, after me, Mr. Darwin. . . . After me, Mr. 'Uxley. . . . After me, Mr. Spencer——. And now, all together." And they would chant back at him:—

In six days——
In six days——
In six days, the Lord made heaven and earth,
The sea and all that in them is.

And when they saw Aspirel they rose and stood at attention.

It was Huxley who replied to his question whether Mr. Sessions was correct in his account of human evolution.

"Certainly not." He snapped his great, square jaws and glared at Mr. Sessions under his shaggy eyebrows. "Certainly not. If one of my demonstrators had made such a statement—so damnable and so ridiculous—he'd have been sent down from the University. In disgrace, sir."

"I like that," said Mr. Sessions, "when you said yourself——" But he couldn't remember exactly what Huxley *had* said. "I appeal to Mr. Darwin."

Darwin was dignified and cold, and, it struck Mr. Sessions, a little dazed.

"I agree with Mr. Huxley," he said.

"Well, then—to you, Mr. Spencer."

"I agree with Mr. Huxley and Mr. Darwin. *In toto.*"

As they stood up there Mr. Sessions noticed something about them unusual—uncanny.

"I can't think," he said, "what's happened to you. Or what you're doing here. In Dancy's class."

Huxley spoke. "What has happened to us, young man, is that our spiritual eyes have been opened by your mother and by our great master, Aspirel. We are here in the lowest form of his college owing to that sin of intellectual pride which made us so offensive to all right-thinking people when we were on earth. We are humble now, and it would become you, Mr. Sessions, to be humble too."

But he didn't look humble, not half so humble as Darwin and Herbert Spencer.

Then it seemed to Mr. Sessions a queer thing happened. He had turned to go out of the classroom, following his mother, when he looked back for a last view of the three. They were not there. No Darwin. No Huxley. No Herbert Spencer. Nothing but the empty form and the row of desks and Dancy wiping the chalk off the blackboard with a duster. How the dickens had they got away? The classroom had only one door.

"Well," said Aspirel, when they were on the other side of it, "you've got your answer. Are you satisfied?"

"No," said Mr. Sessions, "I am not. There's something queer about it. Something queer about the whole business."

Aspirel put his hand on his arm and held him so that they dropped behind his mother as she went on down the glassy corridor, her long white veil streaming behind her.

"You are not to say that," he said. "You are not to say it to your mother."

"It's true, then?"

"True? Yes. But the queerness is in your own eyes."

That was what he had found out about Aspirel. He would always wriggle out of it somehow. He always had his answer.

"Well, but—look here, Aspirel, on your own showing—take those first lectures: each turn of the machine represented thousands and thousands of years, didn't it?"

"It did."

"Then why, I ask you, do you allow that egregious Regius to make them say the world was created in six days?"

"Discipline. A necessary discipline to take down their intellectual pride. Full of it, they were, when they first came over."

"But the truth, Aspirel, the *truth*?"

"The truth, my dear friend, is there all right. In the symbol. When they're moved to the next form, they will attend my lectures on Symbol and Reality. The day of the Mosaic cosmology stands for aeons, for many aeons of the true. That," said Aspirel, "is one of our great revelations."

"Revelation? I seem to have heard something uncommonly like it before. On earth. I think *that* requires some explanation."

"It can be very easily explained," said Aspirel, "as false memory."

That was how he had you every time.

Mr. Sessions was getting sick of it. It was quite clear to him that Aspirel was hedging; that he wasn't honest; that under his tortuous and pretentious system of revelations there was something he was trying to conceal. Something—Mr. Sessions had a curious feeling that if only he could lay hands on it, he might escape.

That was what he wanted: to get away; to be safe from his mother and her power; to get away from the Sacred Concerts, from Aspirel and his eternal lectures. Aspirel bored him. All the Spiritual Guides bored him. His mother bored him. Heaven bored him, he wished he could say to extinction, but it was quite clear that he was inextinguishable; he was in for an immortality of boredom. If he didn't get away——. And how *was* he to get away? Some law of lateral gravitation kept him there. He could no more have got up and walked out of Heaven than he could have walked off the face of the earth.

He had set off one morning, half an hour before lecture time, for a stroll in the City. There was one thing he liked about it, those clear, shining, crystal streets; not a germ could lodge there. No danger of infection in Heaven.

Well—wasn't there? Wasn't there a spiritual infection? Wasn't his mind under the influence of the preposterous Aspirel, wasn't his mind becoming every day more and more contaminated with falsehood?

That morning he discovered that the Heavenly City was quite a small place, not larger than Sutton, if as large. He had come strolling to the ramparts, which in the form of a cloistered terrace enclosed it on every side. It seemed to be built up on a high platform, and through the arches of the cloisters you could see, framed, a country of green fields and tall pointed trees and blue streams and blue sky, a little formal and flat, flat and narrow like the landscape in a stained-glass window. He wondered how you could get to it; but when you leaned over the parapet you saw nothing, positively nothing, so immense was the height of the platform. Looking through the arches was like looking through a telescope, then. The landscapes must be hanging high up and isolated in space, an immense stretch, a bottomless pit of space between them and the City.

He was meditating on the impossible perspective, when he saw, coming towards him round the corner of the terrace, Aspirel.

"Oh, Lord, here he is again."

And in another minute the lecture had begun. Aspirel gave it then and there in the cloister.

"It is," he said, "a question of vibrations" (he was always repeating himself like that). "In our earthly state, vibrations, starting outside us and striking on our nerve-endings, gave rise to our consciousness of the world. In this, our heavenly state, vibrations, originating within us, give rise to the world of our consciousness. Our former bodies were transmitters, drawing the world of space in to us. Our present bodies are projectors, throwing our world out into space. As we were once spectators of a universe imposed on us from the outside by a superior power, we are now co-creators with God, imposing our universe from within upon inferior spirits.

"You have noticed that we can moderate the radiance and transparency of objects round us, external, that is to say, to our bodies. We do this by slowing down the rate of our own vibrations. . . ."

Where, oh where had he heard that before? He must have read it somewhere. His mind anticipated the next sentence.

"These psychic vibrations . . ."

Psychic vibrations. Ah, now he had it. He remembered. The round of the tapestry tablecloth; the lamplight glowing through the opaline shade—the dining-room at Highbury. He was sitting there reading. The book had a maroon cloth cover. He could see the capitals of the chapter headings, black on the white page: PSYCHIC VIBRATIONS. He could see the title of the book; gilt letters on the maroon ground: *The Science of Survival*, by Stanford Jones. That chap his mother was always talking about. "Read Stanford Jones's *Science of Survival*, Albert." He had read it. Stanford Jones was Aspirel's "name in time."

He heard himself saying, "Look here, Mr. Stanford Jones, this isn't any revelation. The whole time, the whole blessed time you've been at it you haven't told me one single blessed thing I didn't know. I've read *The Science of Survival*. Precious poor stuff it was, too."

★★★★★★★★★★

He was alone. Aspirel had gone away in a fit of temper. He had tried his favourite trick of mystification: "False memory." But he hadn't a word to say for himself when you confronted him with his own chapter headings. How a fellow like that—a conceited charlatan—should have contrived to get into Heaven, should be allowed to bamboozle people there as he had bamboozled them on earth——

"Good Heavens"——Mr. Sessions was aware that he was no longer alone. A little gentleman was coming towards him with the step, with the gesture, he remembered. "I'm blessed if that isn't old Minify."

Old Minify, looking incredibly younger and sprucer than he used to, yet like himself, with his head on one side, wistful and shrewd, as he used to come, every Sunday afternoon, into the drawing-room at Highbury, looking at you to see if you wanted him; never quite sure whether you did or didn't. Mr. Sessions had never been quite sure. Mr. Minify had been such a nuisance, with his futile, obstinate devotion to Mr. Sessions' mother.

He thought: "Just like him. Of course, after dangling round her there for twenty years he follows her up here."

Mr. Minify greeted him with his sidling, hesitating smile. "Well, Albert, this is very delightful surprise."

"Surprise?"

"I don't mean I'm surprised at your getting here. I mean I didn't know you'd come."

"I came three weeks ago."

"Bless me! Your mother didn't say a word."

"Now why," Mr. Sessions wondered, "why didn't she?" But she had always been mysterious and secretive with Minify, her poor frustrated lover, by way of showing her power. No doubt, even here she was keeping him on tenterhooks.

He stood there, as he used to, blinking and twinkling, his kind, eager mouth twitching nervously, not knowing how you were going to take him. And Mr. Sessions thought: "I wonder if he remembers what a little beast, I was to him."

They sat down on the parapet under one of the arches.

"How do you like it up here?" said Mr. Minify. He might be wistful, but he was shrewd. Mr. Sessions caught the thrust of his small lizard's eye glinting upwards.

"How do you?" he parried.

"Oh, I'm all right. I'm through with all the lectures; they let me potter about now as I please. But I suppose they've fairly roped you in?"

"They have. This is the first minute I've had to myself in three weeks, and I wouldn't have it now if I hadn't told that damned Aspirel what I thought of him."

"Oh, you told him, did you?"

"I did. . . . You say you've been to all the lectures—well, I put it to you, are you any the wiser? Did they tell you a single confounded thing you hadn't heard before?"

"Not a thing. But I didn't expect 'em to. I only went to please your dear mother."

"Well, to my mind the whole thing's a regular imposition."

"Did you get as far," said Mr. Minify, "as the vision of God?"

"No. He's always dangling it in front of you. He says the whole course is leading up to that. But you never get there."

"*I* did."

"Well——"

Mr. Minify lowered his voice. "Strictly between ourselves, there's nothing in it."

"Did you *see* anything?"

"Oh, yes, I *saw* it all right."

"What was it like?"

"Well, I don't know. It sparked about a lot, and the organ was play-ing 'Abide with me,' with variations all the time, but when it settled down it looked something like that picture that used to hang in the spare bedroom in your mother's house. God lolling about in the sky, and Jesus and the Virgin Mary and the dove coming down out of Heaven, all sort of hung up on a screen. It hurts your eyes a bit, but it doesn't last long."

"Yes. Just something you remembered. That's how they put you off. Put you off. I call it an infernal swindle."

"All right, only don't let your mother hear you."

"Mother—I suppose *she's* all right? I mean she isn't in it?"

"Oh, Lord, no. She's been got at—got at, I tell you, by that hum-bug Aspirel. Between you and me, Albert, I should like to wring the fellow's neck."

"Why don't you then?"

"Because she wouldn't *like* it. She wouldn't like *me* if I did it. You can't do these things."

"Perhaps not. Anyhow, if I'd known Heaven was like this, I'd have been damned if——"

Mr. Minify looked shrewder than ever, and not at all wistful.

"Oh—so you think you're in Heaven, do you?"

"Well—aren't I?"

"No. You're in your mother's heaven."

He seemed to be chuckling over it, as if it were a good joke. "And it's no use your saying you'd have been damned as long as she didn't mean you to be damned. . . . You know, of course, how you got here?"

"I *don't*. The whole thing beats me."

"She willed you over."

"She *said* she prayed."

"Praying or willing, it's the same thing. You came because you hadn't any will to set against hers. You were always a bit weak, Albert."

"I like that. How did *you* get here if she didn't will you?"

"She willed me right enough. She likes to have me hanging round her here just as she liked to have me on earth. It flatters her innocent vanity, gratifies her lust of power, and it makes her feel virtuous, resisting me. Just as it did on earth, dear woman. Heaven wouldn't *be* heaven for your mother, Albert, if she didn't have me to torment."

There had come to Mr. Minify, in his after-death state, the same formidable lucidity that had come to Mr. Sessions.

"You know all this, yet——"

"I know all this, yet—it makes no difference."

He went on.

"But you mustn't suppose I came *because* she willed me. I came because I wanted to; I'm staying because I want to. Heaven wouldn't be heaven for me without her to hanker after. It's *my* heaven, Albert. But it isn't yours."

"But Darwin, and Huxley, and Herbert Spencer, did she will *them* over?"

"Well—perhaps the less said about that the better."

"*Did* she?"

"Not as you think. The fact is, you know, when you see them, they're not really there. They're fakes—hallucinations of your dear mother's mind. Projected. You may have noticed how they disappeared when she went away."

An idea came to Mr. Sessions.

"I say—do you think by any chance that *we're* hallucinations?"

"Alas—no. *We* don't disappear."

Mr. Sessions meditated.

"Do you imagine," he said presently, "that she's got my father here too?"

"He was here a little while ago. She thought she ought to have him. And he was useful—she always liked to have him to play off against me. But he couldn't stand it, and he got away."

"How?"

"By his intense aversion——"

"Oh, if intense aversion does it——"

"*And* the free exercise of his will. As he used to."

"Minify—do you think if we tried, we could get away?"

"You forget. I don't want to."

"No, but me—me? Could I?"

"It would be your will against hers. Or, as they say here, your vibrations against hers. Hers and Aspirel's. You'd have to break through their universe. Break through all this. They've made it up between them out of their ideas. So, there isn't very much of it. Nothing beyond these ramparts—nothing but mirage—her memories of the stained-glass windows in St. Jude's Church."

That was it—those landscapes. He remembered.

"It's limited. But it's jolly hard."

Mr. Minify pricked up his ears, cocking his little head.

"I must leave you, Albert—I think I hear your dear mother coming. She won't like to see us together."

"Why not?"

"Because—I know too much."

He disappeared down the steps that led to the centre of the City.

With her measured tread, her self-conscious dignity, her everlasting complacent smile, his mother came to him. Above the white veil the stars twinkled, twinkled in her martyr's crown. She put her hand on his arm.

"My dear Albert," she said, "I want you to make it up with Aspirel. You mustn't allow a trifling misunderstanding to interfere with your eternal welfare. I don't know what's come over you. You didn't use to be like this, so full of pride and contradiction."

"It's because I see things clearer. I can't help seeing them."

"I can tell you, in your present state of mind, you've precious little chance of seeing anything. As for seeing God——"

"God? I shall never see Him. I shall never see reality. Never see truth." He let her have it. "Not here."

With that cry he broke loose from her.

★★★★★★★★★★

He hadn't meant to say it. He didn't want to shatter her illusions, to put her out of conceit with herself and her heaven. If only she had let him alone.

But, of course, he hadn't shattered it. As for putting her out of conceit, he told himself you couldn't do it. All round him her heaven stood firm, compact crystal, held together by her will, the heaven of her mind and Aspirel's. He could see now what it was made of, bits out of the Bible, the glassy, jewelled New Jerusalem, the stained-glass windows of St. Jude's, the sacred pictures she had loved. Why, he had it now—that dining-room, it was the room of Leonardo da Vinci's "Last Supper," and his mother's bedroom, of course, it was St. Ursula's. And the shining cross and the Bridge of the Passing and the penitents, all the redemptive ideas of her creed.

And Dancy-Regius—he remembered her old distrust of intellectual people, her hatred of freethinkers, of men like Darwin and Huxley and Herbert Spencer; you could see that her chief joy in heaven was their humiliation, their subjection to the verger-greengrocer.

The rest was Aspirel with his silly fancy science, his system of vibrations. Well, there had been something in it, since the two of them had managed to impose their universe. They would go on imposing it for ever and ever. He could see the whole length and depth of his damnation, to be shut up, to be shut out from truth, from reality, in the tight prison of their ideas, hallucinated, for ever and ever, with no power to escape, nothing, nothing but this discarnate lucidity of his that made him see through the illusion. Impossible to break through. As Minify had said, it was jolly hard. It would take a lot of breaking.

If only by some supreme effort of his will—but there, he had never had any will.

It was then that he saw Aspirel coming towards him down the steps of his mother's house. He had forgotten. There was another lecture at eleven.

And at the sight of Aspirel with his meek, conceited face, his gesture of obstinate, implacable pursuit, and at the thought of the lecture, of the sickening, enervating boredom of the lecture, something inside Mr. Sessions got up and said, "I will not stand it. I will not be bored."

And he was aware of something that was he and yet not he, greater than he, above and beyond him, invading his being from the outside, rising up in him in a clear jet, a soaring, thrusting column of pure will. Of resistance. Of rebellion.

It landed him clean outside Heaven.

3

He was going along the bridle-path, dark under the eaves of the fir-wood. He came to the high road, the bright, yellow track through the forest; the firs were set thick there; faint grey daylight stood like deep water between their red stems. Down the road he could see the sign swinging on the tall standard.

He came to the low, white-washed, red-roofed inn, set back humbly in the yellow bay of the road under the black crescent of the firs. He went through the passage between the parlour and the bar and out into the garden.

And there on the little lawn by the arbour of the weeping willow he found Alice Milton. She was waiting for him. He knew her by her clear, firm face and her grey eyes, wide like gates thrown open.

"It's Alice," she said.

"Alice——"

He had a sense of reality, of sheer invulnerable, indestructible reality, rising up out of some queer foregoing state of hallucination.

"Where am I, then?"

"In the garden of the 'Green Dragon.' Don't you remember?"

"But the 'Green Dragon' was pulled down fifteen years ago."

She smiled. "It wasn't. It can't be pulled down unless you pull it."

"But I was at Sutton the other day, before I—— It wasn't there, and they told me——"

"This isn't Sutton. It's Heaven. *Your* heaven."

"Then why are you in it?"

"Because it's my heaven too."

"Alice—did you make me come?"

"No; you came by your own will. And you were free to go where you wanted. You might have gone to Rose's heaven."

"Where is it, Rose's heaven?"

"In another sky. It looks like Brighton."

It would, Rose's heaven.

"But," she went on, "I made you get up and go away out of your mother's heaven. You couldn't have done *that* yourself."

That was it. That was it. He had felt the tug of her.

"You said—you said you never would——"

"Yes, never. Unless—unless—— You see I *had* to save you. I had to get you out. . . . But you did the rest yourself. You came here by yourself. You came because you always used to come here when you made an effort—got away from your mother—did what you wanted."

"Yes. But I always wanted Rose. And Rose isn't here."

She smiled at him. Her odd smile, clear and firm and unspeakably tender.

"Ah," she said, "can't you see?"

And suddenly he saw. He saw that if he hadn't gone to Rose's heaven it was because he no longer wanted Rose and Rose's beauty. He wanted Alice's beauty. He wanted Alice. Alice was truth. Alice was reality.

Her voice wrapped him like the peace of God.

"Can't you see," it said, "that my heaven's your heaven now?"

"I see. The place of my desire."

"No," she said, "the place of your will."

The Intercessor

They had told him he couldn't miss it. There wasn't another house near it for a good mile. He knew where the bridle-path from the hill road struck the lane in the Bottom. It was down there, with a clump of ash trees close up against the back of it, trying to hide it.

Garvin followed the path. It went straight over the slope of the fields, hemmed in by stone walls, low and loose piled, part of the enormous network of stone flung across the north country to the foot of the fells.

At the end of the last field, a wild plum tree stood half naked on a hillock and pointed at the house. All that Garvin could see was a bald gable end pitched among the ash trees. It was black grey, like ash bark drenched with rain.

It stood, he now saw, in a little orchard of dead trees, shut in from the fields by walls, low and loose piled. Coming to this place he had the distinct thrill of fascination, a sense of the presence of old things.

Garvin was by nature and profession a hunter of old things, of old houses, old churches, old ways and superstitions. He had had his nose in a hundred parish registers, sifting the dust of oblivion for a clue to some forgotten family. He was gifted with an implacable persistence in following up a trail, a terrible and untiring industry in minute research. His almost legal precision had served him well when he left an estate agent's office in Pall Mall to work for the Blackadders on their County History.

The Blackadder enterprise was so vast that Garvin in his operations was but a minute part of the machinery. But it fired him; it gave him scope. As an estate agent, selling land for building lots, Garvin had done violence to his genius. The dream of Garvin and his passion was for wild open stretches, everlastingly unbuilt on, for moors and fells, for all places that have kept the secret and the memory of the ancient earth. It was this queer, half-savage streak in the respectable Garvin that marked him as *the* man for the Craven country.

He had travelled through the district all summer, working up his notes at night in small humble hotels and wayside inns. But when it came to the actual writing of his section, Garvin had taken rooms in a village in Craven. He had insisted on two things only when he took them, that the house must be old and that there must be no children in it. That was in July. And before August other lodgers had come and had brought many children. Garvin was driven out. He said he *must* have a place to himself, and was told, fairly and squarely, in broad Yorkshire, that he couldn't have it; leastways, not in August. If he wasn't satisfied where he was, he could go to Falshaw's in the Bottom. Likely enough he'd have it to himself there as much as he wanted.

Garvin ignored the hint of perdition. He inquired placably if Falshaw's was an old place, and was told that it was "old enough." He asked also whether at Falshaw's there would be any children. No (this time it was palpable, the sidelong, sinister intention), there wouldn't be; leastways not in August nor yet September—if all went well with Falshaw's wife. Garvin judged that the state of Falshaw's wife had acted somehow as a deterrent to tourists. It had kept Falshaw's empty. That was good. Anyhow he thought he'd risk it.

It was early evening in the first week of August that he set out for the house in the Bottom.

It didn't strike him (for the approach was sideways through a little gate in the low wall), it didn't strike him all at once that the house was not "old enough." But it struck him very sharply as he entered and took in, slantways, its bare rectangular front. So far from being old enough (for Garvin) it was not old at all, if you went by years. He had given it about a hundred at sight, when he came upon its date graved above the lintel of its door: 1800, and the initials of its founder: E. F.

If you went by years—but this gaunt and naked thing had grown old before its years. It wore the look of calamity, of terrible and unforgetting and unforgotten age. What it did was to throw back its century into some tract of dark and savage time.

He stepped back a few paces to get a better look at it. The front door stood open; its flagged passage showed like a continuation of the orchard path. At one end its wall was broken halfway by the roof of a pent-house. A clump of elder bushes here were the only green and living things about the place. It stood before Garvin, dark and repellent in its nakedness, built from floor to roof of that bleak stone that abhors the sun, that blackens under rain. The light of the August evening was grey round it; the heat of the August day lived only in the rank smell of the elder bushes by the pent-house wall.

It seemed to Garvin that the soul of eighteen hundred hung about him in the smell of the elder bushes. He found it in the blurred gleam of the five windows, deep set and narrow, that looked out on the orchard of dead trees. Garvin's delicate sense of time was shaken under their poignant, impenetrable stare, so that the figures 1800 troubled him, stirred in him the innermost thrill of his passion for the past.

He knocked with his stick on the open door. The sounds struck short and hard. Nobody answered. Garvin took another look at the house. The wall-space to the left of the threshold was narrow and had but one window which he had passed as he entered. The long, two-windowed wall on the right bounded the house place. Garvin saw through the open door that this interior was diminished by two wooden partitions, one of which formed the passage, the other shut off the staircase at the back.

The door at the end of the passage was closed. So was the door on his left, leading into the small room he had passed. The door in the partition on his right stood ajar, so that when he knocked again, he heard the loud scraping of a chair on the stone floor. Somebody had got up and was probably listening there, but nobody came. He knocked again on the inner door imperiously.

This time he heard footsteps. They advanced heavily to the door and paused there. The door swung to with a click of the latch and the footsteps retreated. They trailed off somewhere into the depths of the house to the back. Somebody called out there to somebody else, "Onny! Onny!" and Garvin waited.

Some moments passed before the door at the end of the passage (the door into the backyard) opened, and a girl, whom he took to be Onny, came to him. She was a young girl, sturdy and full-blown in the body, florid and fair in the face; in all commonplace and a little coarse. She came heavily, with no sign of interest or of haste, but staring at Garvin with her thick grey eyes.

He asked if he could have rooms. Onny didn't know, she was sure.

Would she be good enough to find out?

She didn't know. He could find out himself. Ooncle was in the tool shed.

With more good will than her speech indicated she led the way to the shed under the elder bushes.

There was no one there. Onny now reckoned that Ooncle would be in the mist-house.

A gate in the wall behind the elder bushes opened into the mist-house yard. Falshaw was alone there, pitching dung from the cowshed. At the girl's call he came forward, leaning on his pitchfork. He was a big man, thick in the girth, and fair like his niece, and florid. Garvin reckoned his age at fifty or thereabouts. For in this body, built for power, the muscles had begun to slacken; it was sunken in its secret foundations. Garvin supposed that this was because of Falshaw's age. What baffled him was the contradiction between Falshaw's face and its expression. It was natural that Falshaw should grow old; but what had Falshaw done that his face, formed by nature in an hour of genial grossness, should have all its contours tortured to that look of irremediable gloom?

The gloom did not lift as the big man slouched nearer, and (contemptuous of the stranger's greeting) inquired what Garvin wanted. His manner intimated that whatever it was Garvin would probably have to want it.

As to whether Garvin could put up at Falshaw's, Falshaw, like his niece, didn't know, he was sure. It depended upon whether the missus could "put oop" with Garvin.

Garvin, suddenly remembering what he had heard about Falshaw's wife, protested that his requirements would be slight. Falshaw did not know about that either, he was sure; but he reckoned that Garvin would have to ask the missus. The missus was "oop there," in the house.

He was about to leave Garvin to deal with the situation when he seemed to think better of it, and to have decided that, after all, he would see him through. All this time he had clung to his pitchfork. He now planted it firmly in the earth to await his return. He seemed to leave it with reluctance and regret.

The girl Onny smiled as if she was pleased at the turn affairs were taking. Garvin thought he saw hope for himself in Onny's smile.

As they reached the door that had been shut against Garvin, Falshaw drew himself up and squared his shoulders with a tightening of all his muscles. He seemed to take the young man under his protection with an air of dogged courage in seeing him through. It struck Garvin then that Falshaw was afraid of his wife.

She sat in twilight and slant-wise from the doorway, so that she had her back both to them and to the light. The sound of the lifted latch had been answered by a loud and sudden scraping of her chair; it was like a shriek of fright. She rose as Garvin entered, and turned, as if she suffered the impulse of the pregnant woman to hide herself.

He approached her, uttering some such soft and inarticulate sound as he would have used to soothe a shy animal. As she swung heavily round and faced him, he saw that he was likely to be mistaken as to Mrs. Falshaw's impulses. Otherwise, he would have said that it was she who was afraid. But whatever her instinct was, fear or hostility, it already was submerged in the profound apathy of her gloom.

For the expression on Falshaw's face was a mere shadow fallen on it from his wife's face, where gloom and heaviness had entered into the substance of the flesh and the structure of the bone. Gloom was in the very fibre of her hair, a dull black, rusted.

It was Falshaw, with his air of protection, who put it to her whether it would be possible for them to take Garvin in.

"Ya knaw how *thot'll* end," said she significantly.

Things had happened, then, at Falshaw's. The gloom on Falshaw's face renewed Garvin's impression that Falshaw, perhaps on account of these things, was afraid of his wife. He looked from her to his niece Onny, who stood leaning awkwardly against the dresser and twisting and untwisting a corner of her apron. There was a queer, half frightened, half sullen look on her face. And Garvin received a further impression, that the things that had happened at Falshaw's were connected unpleasantly with Falshaw's niece. It might well be. The girl was coarse.

By way of establishing his own incorruptibly moral character, Garvin drew a portrait of himself as a respectable, intellectual, dry-as-dust alien to human interests and emotions, intolerant of the society of his kind. So much so that he was obliged to stipulate that wherever he lodged there must be no other lodgers, and no children.

"There'll be no other lodgers. You can depend on thot," said Falshaw.

"And—no children?"

The girl Onny stirred uneasily. Her face, florid a second ago, was white as Garvin looked at it. She hid her hands in her apron, turned on her heel abruptly, and left the room.

Then Garvin was sure that he knew. *That* was the trouble in the house. Falshaw's eyes followed his niece as she went out. There was some tenderness in the gross man, and plainly he was sorry for the girl. But his wife's face had tightened; it had grown even more forbidding than it had been. The woman, Garvin judged, had been hard on Onny. He could see Onny being ground under that nether millstone.

Of course, they would resent his touching on the sore point, but it happened to be the point on which Garvin himself was uneasy, and he really had to settle it. He approached it gently and with some confusion.

"I was told," he began, and hesitated.

"What were ya told?" said Falshaw.

"Why—that there weren't any."

"Speak oop. Ah doan' understond ya."

Garvin plunged. "I mean—any children. I say, you know, there aren't any, really, are there?" He plunged deeper. "I mean, of course, in the house." And deeper still. "I mean—at present."

"There's noa fear o' thot—here."

It was Falshaw's wife who spoke.

2

It was as if the heart of her gloom had suddenly found utterance. Silence followed it.

They had seated themselves round the deep, open hearth place, Garvin on the settle facing Mrs. Falshaw, and Falshaw in the middle facing his hearth. His attitude indicated that he was seeing Garvin through, not because he liked him or approved of him, but as a simple matter of justice between man and man.

He did not look at Garvin when he spoke to him. He had not looked straight at him since he had brought him into the house. He seemed unable to face another man fairly and squarely in the presence of his wife. That might be, Garvin supposed, either because he was afraid of her or because his consciousness of approaching fatherhood had made him shy.

Now, as his wife spoke, he turned on Garvin a dumb and poignant look that besought his pity and his comprehension. It was as if he had said, "You see what's wrong with her"; as if he was letting him into the secret of her malady, of the gloom that hung about them both. And Garvin understood that the unfortunate woman had fallen into some melancholy incidental to her state. She had got it into her head that the unborn thing had died within her or would die. A curse was on her. She would never be the mother of a living child.

She sat there, leaning forward, propping her weight with hands planted on her thighs, and staring at the hearth, a creature bowed and stupefied with her burden. Her husband leaned forward too, staring as she stared, moved to a like attitude by sympathy. He pushed out his loose lips from time to time, as if he said, "That's how it takes her. That's how it takes her."

Garvin's delicacy prompted him to inquire whether it would be inconvenient for Mrs. Falshaw to take him in.

At this innocent query Falshaw actually smiled. It was the most extraordinary smile. Without altering the expression of his face, it went quivering through his whole vast bulk, as if his body were invaded by a malign mirth. It became articulate.

"We woan't," said Falshaw, "put ourselves out for anybody."

Garvin took this as an intimation in the northern manner that he was to consider himself at home.

Falshaw now approached his wife so near as to reckon that they could let the yoong mon have the parlour and the back bedroom, and Mrs. Falshaw replied from the depths of her apathy that he, Falshaw, could do as he liked.

A brief inspection showed Garvin that his quarters, though small, were incomparably clean. He moved into them in the afternoon of the next day.

He was pleased with the cool stone-flagged parlour. Its narrow walls concentrated the light in a clear equable stream on his table under the window. He ranged his books on the top of the low cupboard that flanked the fireplace; and, if the room was still cold and strange to him, he had only to look at them to feel instantly at home. Nobody interfered with him.

It was his bedroom that made him realise that Falshaw had meant what he said. They weren't going to put themselves out for anybody, not they. Garvin's expert eye had measured the resources of the house, and he knew that he had got the worst bedroom in it. It was such a room as is only given to a servant even in houses like the Falshaws'. And nobody had turned out of it for him. With all its cleanness, it had the musty smell of long disuse. Garvin, however, preferred this smell to any kindred sign that might suggest recent habitation. Apart from its appearance and the smell, the room inspired him with a profound discomfort and distrust. He prowled about in it for half an hour, searching in vain for possible sources of this feeling.

So little did the Falshaws put themselves out that nobody came upstairs to tell the lodger that his tea was waiting for him in the parlour. He drank it lukewarm and stewed to an abominable blackness. A delicious scent of home-baked bread and hot girdle cakes came from the Falshaws' kitchen, while Garvin sniffed suspicion at a sour loaf and a slab of salt butter from the village shop. Bacon from the shop appeared at his supper, its rankness intensified by a savour of hot stew wafted through the doorway. He ventured to ask Onny if he couldn't have some of the new bread, he had smelt baking, and was told that they only baked once a week for themselves. The idea seemed to be that any food cooked by the Falshaws was sacred to the tribe. He wouldn't be allowed to eat it.

But Garvin was ready to endure any privation of mere appetite in the satisfaction of his passion for peace, and peace (he could feel it) was what he had found at Falshaw's.

Before going to bed he had assured himself that he had his side of the house entirely to himself. He found out that the girl Onny slept with Mrs. Falshaw in the large front room over the kitchen. He supposed that this arrangement was unavoidable if they wanted to keep the young minx out of harm's way. As for Falshaw, he was lodged in a commodious chamber next his wife's, covering both the parlour and the passage. Garvin's room was certainly not commodious. The roof of the house, low and short on the front of it, long and steep-pitched on the back, dwarfed Garvin's room to the proportions of a garret. The space on this side of the house was further taken up by a landing, lighted through a small pane in the slope of the roof.

The doors of the three rooms opened on to the landing. There was also, at the top of a short stair, a fourth door, opposite Garvin's. This door was locked (Garvin in his fastidious curiosity had tried it). But the wall, flanking the well of the staircase, reassured him. There could be no width behind it for anything bigger than a box-room. Garvin was certain of his peace.

Oh, certain. At evening an almost unnatural stillness had fallen on the place. It was in the house, in the orchard, and in the yard down there under the ash trees. It deepened with each hour of the night. He was almost oppressed with his sense of it as he lay in bed, waiting for the sleep which he knew would be shy of visiting him in his strange quarters.

He would have had a better chance—as far as sleeping went—if there *had* been some noise about; some noise, that was to say, outside his own body. For in the silence Garvin's body, with all its pulses, had become a centre of intolerable clamour.

Garvin's body grew quiet. He was deliciously, delicately aware of the approach of sleep, of sleep entering his veins, of sleep and silence and oblivion flooding his brain, his heart, submerging him, or just submerging, when, with a terrible, vain resistance and resentment, he found himself being drawn out of it.

What amazed him as he came up was the slenderness of the thread that drew him, a sound so fragile, so thin that he was almost unaware of it as sound. His resentment flamed to indignation as the thing became audible and recognisable, distinctly recognisable, as the crying of a child.

It came from one of the upper rooms: it was hardly a crying, a sobbing, a whimpering rather, muffled by closed doors. The wonder was how it could have waked him; the sound was so distant, so smothered, so inarticulate.

It went on for a long time, and Garvin could not say whether it ceased or whether he slept through it. He knew he did sleep.

3

In the morning he was aware that, as the victim of their deception, he was more interesting to the Falshaws than he had been overnight. Returning from a stroll before breakfast, he found Mrs. Falshaw standing in the door of the house and watching him. She slunk away at his approach and shut the kitchen door between them. Falshaw, encountered in the passage, eyed him steadily with suspicion that turned at close quarters to defiance; as much as to say that, if Garvin was up to anything, he, Falshaw, was ready for him.

Garvin would have dealt with Falshaw then and there but for the presence of the girl Onny, who was stationed in the doorway of the parlour, watching also. She lingered in her waiting on him, and he discerned in her queer eyes a vague animal terror, half spiritualised by an unspoken, an unspeakable appeal. It was borne in on him that her change of attitude was somehow connected with the disturbance of the night. He gathered from it that if her fear could have spoken it would have besought him to spare her, to say nothing.

His annoyance was accompanied by an inward shrug of cynical comprehension. Nothing more likely, said Garvin in his shrewdness, than that Onny should have borne a child, and that her child should be a shame and a burden to the Falshaws. They couldn't have resented it more than he did; but he meant to wait and see the extent of the nuisance before he made his protest.

All day the inviolate stillness of his solitude was a reproach to the resentment that he felt. The child was kept quiet, smuggled away somewhere out of sight.

But that night and the next night he heard it. And no wonder. He had found that its crying came from the small garret facing his, where apparently it was locked in and left to sleep alone.

It had its trick of waking at the same hour. The crying would begin about eleven and go on till past midnight. There was no petulance in it and no anger; it had all the qualities of a young child's cry, except the carnal dissonances and violences. The grief it uttered was too profound and too persistent, and, as it were, too pure; it knew none of the hot-blooded throes, the strangulated pauses, the lacerating resurgences of passion. At times it was shrill, unbroken, irremediable; at times it was no more than a sad sobbing and whimpering, stifled, Garvin gathered, under the bedclothes. He lay and listened to it till he knew all its changes and inflections, its languors and wearinesses, its piteous *crescendos* and amazements, as of a creature malignly re-created, born again to its mysterious, immitigable suffering.

As he never slept until it had ceased, Garvin was qualified to witness to the Falshaws' abominable neglect. Nobody came near the poor little wretch to comfort it. It was probably frightened there, all by itself. The mere sound of the crying wouldn't have kept him awake but for his pity for the helpless thing that made it. In the daytime he found himself thinking about it. He couldn't get away from the thought of it. He worried over it. He had the horrible idea that the child suffered on his account; that the Falshaws kept it locked up in the garret in the daytime that it might be out of the lodger's way. As this theory was inconsistent with their allowing it to keep the lodger awake at night, he could only suppose that the Falshaws were as indifferent to its suffering as to his. They had more than one devil in their blood. Likely enough, it was the devil of Puritanism that made the man and woman cruel to the child of Onny's sin.

But the girl herself?

He had the very worst opinion of the girl Onny. He was convinced that Onny, and not Mrs. Falshaw, was the mother of the child. Not that he was inclined to think hardly of the girl for having it. What he couldn't stand was her behaviour to it now that she had had it. There was nothing very intimately revealing in Onny's heavy, full-blown face; but Garvin had judged her gross. He saw her now sinning grossly, for the sin's sake, without any grace of tenderness. She was the kind predestined to go wrong. She lacked the intelligence that might have kept her straight. He could see her going to meet her sin half way, slowly, without any beating of the heart, finding the way by some dull instinct older than her soul.

He was obliged to admit that the poor thing had at any rate let *him* alone. Probably her instinct sufficed to tell her that he was not her prey. But he had gathered that she was responsible for the Falshaws' unwillingness to take him in; and it was plain enough that they kept a sharp look-out on her. He knew their habits now. He knew, for instance, that Falshaw accompanied his niece on any errand undertaken after dark. Indoors they wouldn't trust her out of their sight a minute on his side of the house. Now he came to think of it, he had never once seen her there in the hours of dusk and dark; he had never found her alone in his room at any hour. Mrs. Falshaw was always hovering somewhere near; her forbidding eye was for ever on the poor girl as she swept and scoured.

This austerity of the Falshaws had its inconveniences for Garvin. He didn't expect a tidy room at bed time, or hot water, or sheets invitingly turned down. But nobody seemed to think of closing the window when the evening mists came on and settled on his bed, or when the rain beat in and made it damp.

He determined to deal with Onny.

He dealt with her on the morning after his third bad night.

"Look here," he said; "why don't you keep that child quiet?"

Her gross colour fled. And yet she faced him.

"You've heard her, sir?"

"Of course, I've heard her."

Her thick eyes stared at him. They were curiously without shame.

"You don't look as if you had," she said.

That and her stare staggered him. Before he could answer her, she had given utterance to a still more amazing thing.

"You needn't go," she said. "She won't hurt you."

With that she left him.

4

That night, his fourth, Garvin found that his nerves were growing so increasingly, so frightfully sensitive to sound that the crying seemed to come from the threshold of his door, from his bedside, from his pillow. It got from his nerves into his dreams, and he woke with the sense of a child's body pressed to his body, the palms of its hands upon his breast, its face hidden against his side, and the vibration of its sobbing above his heart. The thing passed, with a fainter, shivering, vanishing vibration which he felt as somehow external to himself.

He sat up, wide awake, and listened. The crying had ceased. His nerves were all right again.

He supposed he'd have (as Falshaw would have said) to put up with it. He could, after all, reckon on six or seven hours' good sleep, and in the daytime the poor little thing was quiet enough in all conscience. He couldn't very well resent it.

And yet he did resent it. He resented the cruelty of it. So much so that he spoke about it to Mackinnon, the doctor, whose acquaintance he had made when he was lodging up in the village. Mackinnon had called at the house in the Bottom to see how Mrs. Falshaw was getting on. Garvin lay in wait for him and asked him if he couldn't do something. He, Garvin, couldn't stand it.

The doctor was a little Highlander, red haired, fiery, and shrewd. He looked shrewdly at Garvin and told him that if he couldn't stand *that* his nerves must be in an awful state. And he took him off with him in his motor on a long round that swept the district.

That evening, Garvin, drowsed with the wind of speed, refused the solicitations of the County History and went to bed before ten.

He was in the act of undressing when he heard the child cry.

The sobbing whimper was no longer stifled under bedclothes; it sounded distinctly from the open landing. Garvin unlatched his door and looked out.

At this hour of the newly risen moon there was light on the landing like a grey day. He saw a girl child standing on the garret stair. It had on a short nightgown that showed its naked feet. It was clinging to the rail with one hand.

Its face was so small, so shrunken and so bleached, that at first its actual features were indistinct to him. What *was* distinct, appallingly distinct, was the look it had; a look not to be imagined or defined, and thinkable only as a cry, an agony, made visible.

The child stood there long enough to fix on him its look. At the same time, it seemed so withdrawn in the secret of its suffering as to be unaware of him.

It descended the stair, went close past him, and crossed the landing to the women's room.

Now on these hot August nights the door was left half open, leaving a wide passage way into the room. Garvin could see it. He looked for the child to go in where its mother lay. Instead of going in it stood there motionless as if it kept watch.

Then all at once it began crying, crying and beating on the open door with its tenuous hands, beating and pushing as against a door closed and locked.

It was then that Garvin knew.

The creature gave up its efforts at last and turned from the door sobbing. Garvin could not see its face now, for it had raised its arms and held them across its forehead with the backs of the hands pressed against its weeping eyes. Thus blinded, it made its way across the landing towards Garvin's door, and passed by him, still unaware, into his room.

He went in and shut to the door. The child was standing by the foot of the bed as if it watched somebody who slept there. It stayed, watching, while Garvin undressed and got into bed. Then—Garvin was not frightened nor even surprised at what happened then; he seemed to have expected it—the little creature climbed up the bedside and crept in beside him. He felt, flesh to flesh, its body pressed to his body, the palms of its hands upon his breast, and its face hidden against his side.

5

He knew now what he was in for; he knew what was the matter with the house; he knew its secret, the source of what, so far as *he* went, he could only call its fascination. For he could swear to his own state of mind—he was *not* afraid.

On one point only he was uncertain. He did not yet know whether he were alone or not in his experience, whether the Falshaws knew what he knew, and whether it was the things that they knew, that they had heard and seen, their experiences, which accounted for their abiding gloom. Neither they nor anybody else had told him precisely what he would be in for if he insisted on staying at Falshaw's; but there had been (he remembered now) a rather sinister inflection laid on certain words that had been said to him.

They came back to him now. He could have very little doubt that the place had a sinister reputation, and that the Falshaws knew it. He had not understood it at the time, because his mind had been so misled by Falshaw's bodily grossness that it could only form a gross conception of the trouble of the house, of the things that, as they had intimated to him, had happened there. Poor Garvin profoundly repented the infamy of some of his suspicions, those relating to the girl Onny.

He found on the morning of his experience that Falshaw's attitude, like his own, had changed somewhat overnight. The gross man was still suspicious (like Garvin), but there was more solicitude than hostility in his suspicion. He watched Garvin as if he thought he were going to be ill, as if he knew and were on the look-out for the symptoms of his malady.

Ill or not (he certainly felt all right), Garvin was an object of even greater interest to his friend Mackinnon. The doctor called that evening with the evident intention of cheering him up. Garvin felt that Mackinnon was on the look-out for something, too. They talked about the County History and Garvin's part in it, which Mackinnon plainly regarded as conferring lustre upon Garvin. Incidentally he put him in the way of much valuable information, for the doctor knew something (sometimes he knew a great deal) about each house and its family within thirty miles round.

In the pauses of the conversation, they could hear Falshaw talking to his wife. The two were sitting up late, and he seemed to be arguing with her.

It was eleven o'clock before Mackinnon went. The clank of the gate behind him was instantly followed by the sound of Mrs. Falshaw's chair scraping on the stone flags of the kitchen and by Falshaw's fist knocking upon Garvin's door.

He was almost respectful as he stood looming before Garvin's writing-table.

"Mr. Garvin," he began, "ah've soommat to saay to you. If you doan't loike what you've found you'd better goa. There's noa call for you to give th' ouse a bod naame. There's too mooch been saaid. Ah'm dommed if ah'll put oop with it."

"I know the worst," said Garvin quietly, "and *I* can put up with it. How do you know what your next lodger'll do—or say?"

Falshaw's huge bulk seemed to sway there as he placed his balled fists on the table for support. He was silent.

"Mr. Falshaw, I don't know how much you know, or what—but if it happens to be what I know———"

"Ah doan't saay as 'tisn't. What ah saay is that there's noa call for you to stomach it. You can goa."

"I don't want to go. Why should I?"

"You doan't?" He peered at him.

"Of course not."

"Then, sir" (it was the first time that Falshaw had called him "sir"), "you bean't afeard?"

"No more, Mr. Falshaw, than you are yourself."

"Ah've noa cause to be afeard. Ah knaw nothing."

A tremor passed through him as from some centre stirred by utterance. His face quivered. Its brute heaviness was redeemed for a moment by some inscrutable pathos. It was impossible to say whether Falshaw deplored his ignorance or repudiated knowledge.

On the whole, Garvin inclined to think that he *was* alone in his experience.

6

Three days passed. Night after night Garvin witnessed the same supernatural event.

His senses were now so perfectly adjusted to his experience that he no longer thought of it as supernatural. What struck him as marvellous was the change it worked in the Falshaws now that they knew he had it. He was evidently set apart, consecrated by his experience. He had become for them an object of extraordinary respect—he would almost have said of affection. Whereas they had once disregarded his wishes and treated his little likings and dislikings with an almost insolent contempt, now, everything that he had ever asked for, that he had ever wanted without asking for, was remembered and provided.

The fresh home-made bread that he had coveted appeared daily at his table; his meals had a savour and variety which he would have judged beyond the scope of Mrs. Falshaw's art. He could hardly suppose that they did it for the sake of gain; for, poor as they were, they had taken him in under protest and had made no effort to keep him until now.

This change from hostility to the extreme of friendliness dated from the evening when he had declared to Falshaw that he felt no fear.

The statement (he had to own it) required qualification. It was true enough that he felt no fear of the primal, the complete manifestation. That, having all the colours and appearances of flesh and blood, had the value, the assurance, almost the inevitability of a natural thing. It had parted with its horror from the moment when he perceived that it was responsive to his pity and accessible to his succour.

But Garvin, reviewing his experiences, distinguished between the perfect and the imperfect. Beyond the primal haunting, round and about the central figure, the completed vision, he was conscious of a borderland of fear into which he had not yet entered.

219

It was chiefly present to him as a disagreeable feeling that he had about his bedroom—a feeling which little Garvin, as he valued his own manliness, sternly refused to attend to. Still, it was there. But for that sense he had, he would have preferred his garret to the long eastern chambers looking on the orchard of dead trees. The branches that hung before his window were alive. At sunset the light ran through their leaves, kindling them to a divine translucent green. And yet he loathed it.

The room had, clearly, some profound significance for the child, since it was always compelled to come there. But the significance was something that Garvin didn't care to explore; he felt it to be part of the peculiar, foggy unpleasantness of the borderland.

It was strange that, while he knew no terror of the perfect apparition, the bedfellow, his fear of the borderland was growing on him. His feeling was that if the things that were *there* became visible, they would be more than he could endure.

There were degrees in the clearness of the primal manifestation; degrees which, as he made it out, corresponded to the intensity of the emotion, the suffering behind it. The child's form gathered and lost substance. At times it was of an extreme tenuity, suggesting nothing tangible. At times it had, not only the colour, but the pressure of flesh and blood. At time its face, its hands, and little naked feet had the peculiar livid whiteness of white skin seen under water. Its feet along the floor were like feet moving through water.

He saw it now by day as well as night. It would pass him in the passage, on the stairs. It lay in wait for him at his door or at its own. He had an idea that it spent hours playing in the backyard under the ash trees. Once when he looked out of his window, he could have sworn that he saw it hanging over the great stone water tank that stood there at the corner of the wall. He had never once seen it in his sitting-room, and what went on in the Falshaw's kitchen he could not say.

Thrice he saw it in the garden, coming towards him from the backyard to a corner under the orchard wall. As it passed under the trees, he could see the grass growing through its feet. It carried in its hand a little cup of water which it emptied there in the corner. It was busy and absorbed, very earnestly and seriously bent upon this act. He noticed that always, out of doors, the appearance was imperfect, but he discerned dimly that, out of doors, it had a happy look.

He examined the corner that it visited. A long flat-faced stone stood upright in the wall there; below it, hidden by the grass, he found a small plot marked out with stones.

A child's garden ruined beyond remembrance. There were gaps in its borders where the stones had been upheaved or buried. In the middle, trampled and beaten into the earth, he came upon the fragments of a broken cup.

It was thus that he began to construct the child's history. He had found that its more complete manifestations occurred indoors, on the landing and after dark, and that they culminated in bodily contact, the pressure of its form—the bedfellow's—against his own. And so he argued that outside, in the open air, it had been happy. It was within the house that the suffering which was its life had come to pass; the suffering was somehow connected with the closing of Mrs. Falshaw's door; it was habitually intenser at night time, and it had its unspeakable climax, its agony, in Garvin's room.

On all these points he was certain with an absolute and immutable certainty. What baffled him was their date. Things had happened. He had more than a sense, an intolerable sense, of their happening. But *when* had they happened? To which one of the four generations that the house had known?

He thought he could tell if he could only get into the room where, as far as he could make it out, the whole thing started, the garret opposite his own with the stair before its door. It was the child's room and was bound to contain some sign or trace of the child. He must contrive to get in somehow.

He found a pretext. The parlour was still lumbered with the packing-cases his books had travelled in (Garvin had bruised his shins over them more than once). He approached Falshaw and asked him if he might not store the packing-cases in that boxroom that they had upstairs. He supposed it was a boxroom.

Falshaw hesitated. His gloom deepened. Presently, with some visible perturbation, he replied. Mr. Garvin might do as he liked. He would give him the key of the room. Mr. Garvin would be so good as to put the packing-cases in the space behind the door, without—Falshaw's trouble grew on him—disarranging anything.

He carried the cases upstairs and left them on the landing after giving Garvin the key of the room. It was evident that nothing would induce him to go in there himself.

Garvin's heart beat thickly as he entered. The room—he could see at a glance—was not used as a boxroom. It was not used now for anything at all. It was a long garret, narrowed excessively by the sloping roof, and bare of all furniture but a chest of drawers and a washstand near the window, and, drawn to the far end of the room against the wall, two objects, each covered with a white sheet.

Garvin drew back the sheets. Thrust away, hidden out of sight, shrouded like the dead, were a child's little chair and a child's cot. He could see the slender hollow in the mattress where its body had lain.

He raised the edge of the coarse blue and white counterpane. The pillow beneath was not soiled, neither was it freshly clean. There was a small round patch, slightly discoloured, slightly dented, by the pressure of a child's head.

For a moment that brought the thing horribly near to him.

He felt the hollows with his hand and found that they were hard. His reason told him that it must have taken more than one generation to make them so. He was, therefore, no surer of his date. The room had given him an uncomfortable sensation, and that was all.

That evening, setting out for his walk, he met Falshaw in the path coming over the brow of the hill. They exchanged a greeting and some remarks about the weather. There was a wind on the hill, and Falshaw advised Garvin not to go far. It was beating up, he said, for rain.

Garvin turned and walked back with him towards the lane. A sudden impulse seized him to make Falshaw talk. They stopped at the rise where the naked plum tree pointed to the house in the Bottom.

"That's not an old house for these parts, Falshaw. How long have you had it?"

"Ever since ah can remember. Ma faather had it before me, and 'is faather before 'im agen."

"Four generations, then?"

"Three, sir." He added, "There'll be four soon enough if all goas well."

It was his first open reference to his wife's state.

"Why shouldn't all go well?"

"Thot's what I tell the missus. But ah can't move 'er. She's got it into 'er 'ead thot thick," said Falshaw gloomily.

Garvin murmured something vaguely consoling; and all the time his mind was running on his date. He must make Falshaw give it to him.

"You see, Mr. Garvin, she's bin, you may say, in a dark state ever since——"

He stopped. Speech was painful and difficult to him.

"Ever since?" For a moment Garvin felt that Falshaw might be giving him the date.

But if Falshaw had hovered on the verge of a confidence he now drew back. All he said was, "It's more soomtimes than ah can put oop with."

He meditated.

"And t' doctor, e cooms to cheer 'er oop, but 'e can't *do* nowt."

"What does he think?" asked Garvin, recalled to sympathy by the man's misery.

"Think? 'E doan't think. 'E saays it's natch'ral to 'er condition. But—ah doan't remember——"

He stopped again, and fell into the gloom that Garvin recognised as the shadow of his wife's dark state.

"It's a bod job, Mr. Garvin, it's a bod job."

"I wonder," said Garvin, "if I ought to stay much longer. She may be doing too much. Honestly, hadn't I better go?"

Falshaw shook his head.

"Doan't you think thot, sir; doan't you think thot."

"I can't bear," Garvin went on, "to be giving trouble at a time like this."

"Trooble? You call *thot* trooble?"

"Well——"

"You'll bring trooble, Mr. Garvin, if you goa."

"I don't understand."

"And ah doan't understond it neither. But—if you *con* stop, Mr. Garvin, doan't you goa. Doan't you goa."

He paused.

"If she sees you con stond it, maybe she'll mak' out thot things can't be so bod."

Things? It was vague; but when it came to the point, to Garvin's point, Falshaw *was* vague. Garvin felt that they were on the verge again. He was determined to find out how much Falshaw knew, or how much he didn't know. He would tackle him there and then. He would tackle him suddenly and straight.

"Things can't be so bad if I can stand them?" he questioned. "And how bad do you think they are yourself, Falshaw?"

"Ah doan't think. And ah—*knaw* nobbut what ah I've heard. What you've heard." (He glossed it further.) "What folks saay."

"And these things—that they say, how long have they been said?"

Falshaw winced. "Ah doan't knaw."

There was no doubt that Falshaw repudiated any personal knowledge of the things; but then, Garvin reflected, he might be lying. He pressed it home.

"Before your time?"

"Noa. Not afore *ma* time. Thot couldn't be."

He said it simply and uncontrollably, as if it had been wrung from him, not by Garvin but by the pressure of some suffering of his own. He was profoundly unaware of having given Garvin what he wanted.

"You know *that!*" said Garvin, who was for the moment insensible to pity in the excitement of following his trail.

Falshaw rallied. "Ah knaw nothing, ah tell you, but what ah've heard. Nothing but what *you've* heard, Mr. Garvin."

They had come to the stone stile that led into the lane. They stood there facing each other.

"It's not what I've heard," said Garvin. "It's what I've seen."

At that Falshaw turned from him and bowed himself upon the stone wall.

7

Up till that moment Garvin had barely hinted at the nature of his experiences. He was aware that his previous intimations had given Falshaw some uncomfortable emotions; but he was not prepared for the violence of the passion with which his final revelation was received.

He couldn't leave the man there in his agony; neither could he touch him nor speak to him. A certain awe restrained him in the presence of a feeling so tremendous and inscrutable.

It was Falshaw who recovered first, pulling his huge bulk together and steadying himself to speak. It was as if under it all he had not forgotten the consideration due to Garvin, who had become so inexplicably the witness and partaker of his tragedy.

"Mr. Garvin," he said. "Ah think ah knaw what you may have seen. And ah tell you you've noa call to be afeard. It woan't harm you."

It was what Onny had told him.

"I know," he said, "it won't harm me."

"It wouldn't," Falshaw went on. "There's a soort o' pity in they things."

He paused, feeling for his words.

"They knaw; and they doan't coom to those that are afeard of 'em. They doan't coom so as to be seen."

He paused again, meditating, and fell back upon his phrase. "It's the pity in them."

He climbed the stone stile and went slowly towards his house.

Garvin turned and walked again to the brow of the hill. There he stopped and looked back. Above the stone wall of the orchard, in the corner of the child's garden, he saw Falshaw standing, with his head bowed to his breast.

He said to himself then that he might have known. The child's garden under the orchard grass—that belonged clearly to the Falshaws' time. Why—as grass grows—within fifteen, within ten years it would have been buried, grassed over, without a stone to show that it had ever been. It belonged, not to Falshaw's father's generation, nor yet to Falshaw's but to the generation that his wife bore in her womb.

8

The wild plum tree on the hill rocked in the south-west wind, and pointed, gesticulated at the house.

Garvin's gaze followed the network of stone walls flung over the country. He had a sense of the foregoneness of the things he saw. He saw that network as a system of lines that, wherever you picked it up and followed it, led in some predestined way to the house as its secret and its centre. You couldn't get away from the house.

It was in an effort to get away from it that he walked on towards the fells.

The wind, as Falshaw had warned him, was beating up for rain. The south-west was black with rain. He could see it scudding up over the shoulder of the fell.

Halfway he turned and was blown home before the storm, leaning backwards, supporting himself on the wind. A mile from the Bottom the rain caught him and soaked him through.

Falshaw and Onny stood at the door of the house, watching for him. They were troubled at his drenching. He changed, and threw his dripping clothes down over the stairhead to be dried in the kitchen. He knew that neither Falshaw nor Onny had the nerve to go to his room to fetch them. He was glad to get out of it himself.

Mrs. Falshaw had kept his supper hot for him by the kitchen hearth. She proposed that he should sit and eat it there while the fire was being lit in the parlour. He had owned to a chilliness.

She had set the lamp on the supper table, and sat in the ring of twilight with darkness behind her. Portions of her face and body thus appeared superficially illuminated, while the bulk of her became part of the darkness. Garvin was deeply aware of her face and of her eyes, which were fixed on him with an intolerable hunger. The face was sombre and sallow; it was hewn with a hard, unrounded heaviness, unlike her husband's. It would have been deadly hard but for the fugitive, hunted look that gave it a sort of painful life in deadness. Whether she sat or stood she was a creature overtaken, fixed in her fear, with no possibility of escape.

There were moments when he thought that she was about to speak, to ask him what he had seen. He felt somehow that she knew. She knew he had seen something. Whatever Mackinnon thought, he, Garvin, knew, and her husband knew, that she suffered no bodily ailment. What weighed on her was her sense of the supernatural, and her fear of it and of its inscrutable work on her, penetrating her flesh and striking the child that was to be born.

It had been already brought home to him that his value, his fascination for her lay in his shared sense of it. That was the secret that they kept between them.

It was terrible to have to sit in that tongue-tied communion, and eat, bearing his own knowledge and her sense of it. He was glad when it was over and he was safe in the parlour, a place which he felt to be immune from these influences.

Onny was in there, on her knees by the hearth, trying to coax the fire to draw up the damp chimney. His impulse urged him to talk to Onny as he had talked to Falshaw. He was at that stage when he had to talk to somebody; and he wanted to know how much Onny knew.

"Onny," he said, "my bed's damp; why didn't you go up and shut the window?" He knew why.

She rose and stood before him, awkwardly wiping her hands on her rough apron.

"Because I'm afeard, sir."

He looked at Onny. She was coarsely made as to the body, but to his purified perception there seemed to flow from her an almost radiant innocence and probity.

"What are you afraid of?"

She glanced aside miserably.

"You knaw what."

"Yes, I know. But you told me yourself it wouldn't hurt me."

"Hurt you? Little Affy——"

It had a name then, but he hadn't caught it.

"Little——?

"Little Affy."

"Effy," he murmured.

"Yes, sir. Little Affy never 'urt anyone in her life."

He said it over to himself. It touched him even more than Falshaw's "There's a sort of pity in they things." It brought the child nearer to him, poignantly near, in tender flesh and blood. He felt the sting of an intolerable evocation.

It was not yet complete.

"Who *was* little Effy?"

The girl's eyelids flickered and reddened and filled with tears.

"I mustn't talk about her, sir."

"Why not?"

"I promised Ooncle."

"It doesn't matter, does it, as long as I'm not afraid?"

"You're *not* afraid, sir" (she whispered it), "to sleep with her?"

"No, Onny, I'm not afraid."

The girl said "Goodnight" as if she had said "God bless you," and left him to his thought.

Whatever Onny had or hadn't seen, she *knew*.

He could not doubt that he was alone in his complete experience, yet he would have said that if ever there was a man and a woman and a girl that were haunted, it was Falshaw and his wife and the girl Onny. He could only suppose that their haunting was vague and imperfect. They lived on the edge of the borderland of fear, discovering nothing clearly, yet knowing all. Onny, at any rate, knew the worst.

For he always put it to himself that it *was* the worst, even while he felt in his flesh the horror of the borderland, his own borderland, beyond.

It was on him that night, though he tried to fortify himself by reiterating that he knew the worst, and that if his nerves could stand that they could stand anything. He was not afraid (as Onny had suggested) to sleep as he had slept; he was not afraid of his bedfellow. He was afraid of his bedroom and of his bed, of the white sheets and the coarse quilt, of the whole twilight bulk of it, waiting for him in the corner by the window wall.

His sense of terror had defined itself as a sense of evil surpassing the fear of the supernatural. It was borne in on him that some iniquitous thing had had its place in this house and in this room.

He lay awake there, listening to the sounds of the night; to the wind sweeping the ash boughs along the roof above his window; to

227

the drip of the rain in the stone trough beneath. The sounds of the night comforted him; and before long his brain became fogged with a grey stupor. But the stupor was like a veil spread over some backward, bottomless pit of fear. Tenuous itself, intangible, it yet held him, perilously it held him, breaking, delaying, lengthening out, moment by moment, his imminent descent.

The air in the close garret oppressed him to suffocation. He got up and opened the window. The wind and the rain had passed, the ash trees were still; a clear light, grey as water, filled the room. Things showed in it solid and distinct. Something seemed to shift in Garvin's brain with the sudden shifting of his body, and, as he stood there, he was aware of something happening before him.

He couldn't say what it was that happened. He only knew that it was bound to happen; it had been foreshadowed by his fear. He knew what that sudden shifting in his brain meant. He had simply gone over the borderland of fear and was in the gripping centre.

There were two there, a man and a woman. He did not discern them as ordinary supernatural presences; the terror they evoked surpassed all fear of the intangible. Of one thing he was certain. The man was Falshaw. He could swear to that. The woman he had with him was a woman whom Garvin had never seen. He couldn't say what it was he saw, but he knew that it was evil. He couldn't say whether he really saw it, or whether he apprehended it by some supreme sense more living and more horrible than sight.

It was monstrous, unintelligible; it lay outside the order of his experience. He seemed, in this shifting of his brain, to have parted with his experience, to have become a creature of vague memory and appalling possibilities of fear. He had told the truth when he had said that he was not afraid.

Until this moment he had never known what fear was. The feeling was unspeakable. Its force, its vividness was such as could be possible only to a mind that came virgin to horror.

The whole thing lasted for a second or so. When it passed and the two with it, Garvin turned and saw the child, in its nightgown and with its naked feet, standing in the middle of the room and staring at the bed as he had stared. The fear on its face was more terrible to Garvin than his own fear. If it *was* his own.

He turned sick and knew nothing. He supposed he must have fainted.

9

The next day Garvin said to himself that he would see Mackinnon. His nerves had gone to pieces for the time being, and he would have to get Mackinnon to patch them up. He found himself clinging to the thought of Mackinnon.

He spent the morning and afternoon out of doors, as far from Falshaw's as his legs would carry him; and in the evening he went to see Mackinnon.

The doctor was out, and Garvin waited. He hadn't the pluck to go back to Falshaw's without seeing Mackinnon.

By the time Mackinnon appeared (late for dinner) Garvin knew that he hadn't really come there to consult him. He had come to talk to him, and to make him tell what he knew about the Falshaws. He couldn't think why on earth he hadn't done it before; but he supposed Mackinnon must have put him off by the stupid things he had said about his nerves. He didn't mean to be put off to night, and he wasn't going to talk about his nerves.

Neither was Mackinnon. He only looked at Garvin and said it was odd, his being there; for he had just gone round to Falshaw's to see Garvin and bring him back to dine.

They dined alone together (Mackinnon was a bachelor); but it was afterwards in his den, over the cigarettes and whisky, that they talked.

"I say," said Garvin, who began it, "do you know anything about those Falshaws?"

"Oh, as much as I know about most people," said Mackinnon.

"Do you know what's the matter with them!"

"Would you expect me to own it if I didn't?"

"You know as well as I do that there's something wrong with them."

"There's something wrong with Mrs. Falshaw. Melancholy. They get it. She's had it ever since."

"Ever since what? That's what I want to know."

Mackinnon shrugged. "Ever since she began to be———"

"You think *that* accounts for it?"

"Presumably."

"Well—but how about Falshaw? And how about the girl Onny? And if it comes to that—how about *me*?"

"You? I suppose you've been hearing some queer stories. There *are* queer stories."

"I haven't heard one of them," said Garvin.

29

"Are you quite sure?"

"Positive."

"What *have* you heard, then?"

"I told you the other day."

"Yes," said Mackinnon; "that's one of the stories."

"How do you account for them?"

"The stories?"

"Yes."

"The facts account for the stories right enough."

"You mean they've been fabricated after the fact?"

"That's what happens."

"You forget," said Garvin, "that I haven't heard the stories and that I don't yet know the facts."

"I can give you them if you want them. They're quite as queer as the stories, and more interesting, because more human."

"I think," said Garvin, "you'd better hear *my* story first."

"Haven't I heard it?"

"Not my latest. Do you want it?"

"Well, I'd like to see if it's different from other people's. You know they all say they've *heard* things."

"Do they say they've seen them?"

"No. None of them seems to have gone as far as that."

"Well, I've gone as far as that—farther."

He told Mackinnon as casually as he could what he had seen.

Mackinnon was inclined to be impatient. "Yes, yes—a child that cries—in a nightgown—of course. But can you describe her? Can you give me any details?"

"She was very small; she had short hair—bleached—and pale eyes. The flesh under her eyes was sunken. Two little pits—just here. Her face was sallow white and drawn a little, by her nostrils——"

"Queer," murmured Mackinnon, "very queer."

Garvin went on till Mackinnon interrupted him again.

"Beating on the door? Which door?"

"The door of Mrs. Falshaw's room."

"All right. Go on."

Garvin went on, to the scene in the orchard. "And I've seen it hanging over that stone tank at the back."

"Good God!" said Mackinnon softly.

Garvin came to his last experience.

"There," he said, "I own I'm a bit vague."

"You're certain you saw a man and a woman?"

"Yes. And I'm certain that the man was Falshaw. But the woman I know nothing about. It wasn't Mrs. Falshaw."

"No," said Mackinnon thoughtfully. "Can you describe her?"

"I couldn't see her very well. I think she was big and young and——" He stopped. "I don't know. That part of it's beastly." He recovered and went on.

"And the beastliest thing about it is that I didn't understand it, Mackinnon, I didn't understand it—and, frankly, I was in an awful funk."

Mackinnon stared. "You didn't understand it?"

"I'm only talking about what I felt at the time. I'm explaining what made it so horrible. I seemed to have parted with my power of understanding—a whole tract of knowledge—clean gone——"

Mackinnon was silent.

"What room were you in?" he asked presently.

"The small room at the back."

"I know." The doctor shifted his position as if he were trying to shake off something.

"Well," he said, "that yarn of yours would be queer enough if you knew the facts. As it is, I don't mind telling you that it's the queerest yarn I've heard yet."

"Can *you* account for it?"

"My dear Garvin, you can't live up here, in this country and with these people, and still go about accounting for things. If you're a wise man you accept them."

"You accept my statements, then?"

"I have to. They square with the facts. Did you say anything to the Falshaws?"

"A little—to him—and Onny. I can't tell how much they know. They wouldn't say."

"Onny wouldn't?"

"She let out that the child's name was Effy; and then she told me she'd promised Falshaw not to talk about her."

"She isn't allowed to talk about her—because she—*knows*. She didn't tell you that Effy was the Falshaws' child?"

"No."

"She was. Their only child. She died three years ago."

"How?"

"Drowned. In the stone tank under your window."

"She fell in," said Garvin dreamily.

"She fell in. There was nobody about. She must have had some sort of fit, or she could have got out all right."

"Who found her?"

"The woman you saw."

Garvin winced.

"The Falshaws were severely censured at the inquest. You see, the child oughtn't to have been left alone. She'd had one fit about a month before and they knew it."

"And before that?"

"Can't say. Nobody knew. They weren't likely to know. The child was left by herself night and day."

"I see. That's what's the matter with them."

"No doubt it's what's given Sarah Falshaw this idea of hers that the baby will be born dead. Shouldn't wonder if it was. Good thing, too, when you think how she made the other one suffer."

Mackinnon's fire broke out. "Women like that oughtn't to bear children. But they do. They always will do."

"She wants it to live?"

"I can't tell you what she wants—now."

"She didn't want—the other one?"

"Oh, she wanted her well enough. But she wanted something else more. And she had to want. She'd been all right to the child until she found that out; and then she couldn't bear the sight of it."

"She wanted another man, I suppose?"

"Not a bit of it. She wanted her own husband. It isn't a pretty story to tell, Garvin."

10

All the same he told it.

"I'd say she was like an animal, only animals don't carry the thing to the point of insanity. And animals—most of them, at any rate—aren't cruel to their young."

"What did she do to it?"

"She did nothing. That was it. She used to say it was Falshaw's fault that she didn't care for it. Everything, you see, was Falshaw's fault. But she behaved as if it was the child's fault that Falshaw didn't want her. You'd have said she had a grudge against it. Things certainly got worse after it came. But she'd led him a life before that. Lord, what a life a woman *can* lead a man when she wants him more than he wants her

232

and he lets her know it.

"They'd been all right at first. You wouldn't think it, but Sarah was a fine-looking woman when he married her—one of those hard, black and white women who turn yellow when they worry. And Sarah was the sort that worried. She worried the life out of Falshaw. He was a big, strong, full-blooded fellow with a lot of exuberant young animality about him, and look at him now; what aged man do you suppose he is? Fifty, wouldn't you? Well, if you'll believe it, he's only thirty-eight. That's Sarah.

"He was twenty-three when he married her, and Sarah may have been a bit older. And they'd been married five years before the child came. He wasn't a bad sort, Falshaw, and he rubbed along with Sarah and her tongue and her temper for three years or so. He used to say she didn't mean it, and she couldn't help it, and she'd be all right when there was a youngster or two about. I suppose he thought all women were like that when they hadn't any children. The worst of it was she knew he thought it, and it riled her.

"Many a man would have tried to knock it out of her with a stout ash stick, but Falshaw wasn't that sort. He chuckled and grinned at her and reckoned secretly on the baby. And there's something exquisitely irritating, to a woman of Sarah's temperament, in a man who chuckles and grins and reckons on a baby that doesn't come. And long before it came, she'd tired him out and he took up with another woman, a bad lot.

"That was a temporary lapse. Falshaw's heart wasn't in it. And, though I don't suppose Sarah forgave him, she got over it. But she never got over Rhoda Webster.

"Rhoda was a servant girl at the White Hart Inn. I don't blame Falshaw, mind you. When I think what his life was, I'm glad he had that one bright spot of immorality to look back upon. He'd got into the way of going off to the White Hart—a good two miles—to get out of the range of his wife's tongue, and Rhoda wasn't by any means a bad girl—then. She was neither good nor bad; she was just natural, without a bit of art to help her one way or the other. Anyhow, there was so little harm in the girl—then—or in Falshaw for that matter, that nothing happened till he had her in his house after Sarah's child was born.

"Sarah was laid up for months—that's how it took her—and the man was at his wits' end. Rhoda got restless and left her place and was always in and out of Falshaw's house, looking after Falshaw. She'd walk the two miles from the village and back, just to cook his dinner and see him eat it. And when Sarah got about again, she wasn't fit for much and she had to mind the baby. So Falshaw kept on having the girl about the house. He said he had to have someone.

"That went on for months and months. It looked innocent enough; but Sarah began to suspect things. They had a row about it. Sarah said the girl was to go, and Falshaw said she was to stay, and if Sarah didn't like it she could lump it.

"It ended in the girl staying altogether. She slept in the house. Then Sarah found them out. And this time it broke her nerve. If she'd been a woman of any spirit, she'd have left him. But she wasn't that sort. The feeling she had for Falshaw wouldn't let her leave him. She had to stay. She wasn't going to leave him to the other woman, and the other woman wasn't going to leave him to her. So, there they were all three, shut up in that house, Falshaw carrying on with Rhoda behind his wife's back, and his wife stalking them, and seeing everything and pretending half the time she didn't see. And Rhoda, if you please, amiable, imperturbable, scouring and scrubbing, and behaving as if it didn't matter to her whether Falshaw carried on with her or not. She always had that air of not knowing what Sarah saw to worry about.

"At first I believe Falshaw made a great point of not leaving Sarah. But one night he never came near her. And then Sarah turned. The next night was a wet one, and she waited till Rhoda was in the backyard or somewhere, and she locked her out. Up till then Falshaw had chuckled and grinned and gone his own way, reckoning on the child that had come to keep things straight. He excused himself for everything by saying Sarah'd got the child.

"But when he came home that night, and found Rhoda standing on the front doorstep in the rain, he went for Sarah there and then and told her that if she did anything more to the girl he'd go out of the house—he and Rhoda—and leave her, as he put it, for good and all. He was sick of her. It was her own doing. She'd driven him to it. It had got to be, and she'd have to 'put oop with it.' Can't you hear him saying it? He hammered it in. She'd got the child. He'd given her the child; and it ought to be enough for her.

"Up till then she might have had some hope of getting him back, but when he began to talk about the child, she knew it was the end. And she blamed the child for it. If the child hadn't been born Falshaw's girl would never have got her foot into the house. If the child hadn't been born, she'd have had her strength, she could have turned the girl out and made her stay out. If the child hadn't been born, she'd have kept her good looks and had a hold on Falshaw.

"Which," said Mackinnon, "was all perfectly true."

"How old was the child then?" Garvin asked.

"Let me think. It must have been about three."

"It was older than that when *I* saw it," said Garvin.

"Up till then it hadn't suffered," said Mackinnon. "Sarah had been quite decent to it. But when she realised that she'd got it instead of her husband she couldn't bear it near her.

"The first thing she did was to turn it out of the bed where it used to sleep with her. They say she couldn't stand the touch of its body against hers. You see that was how she took it. You may think I'm unjust to the woman—Heaven knows she suffered—but if you'd seen her with that child and how *it* suffered—I've seen passion, animal passion, of unpleasanter kinds than you can imagine, and I've seen some very ugly results of its frustration; but that woman showed me the ugliest thing on God's earth—the hard, savage kind that avenges its frustration on its own offspring. If she couldn't have Falshaw with her she wouldn't have the child. That was her attitude.

"When it was older, she turned it out of her room—that long room in the front. It had to sleep by itself in some place at the back——"

"I know," said Garvin.

"Not that Sarah was actively or deliberately cruel. It was well fed and all that. But it loved its mother—and it knew. My God—how she *could!* I've seen the child making love to that woman—making love, Garvin, with its little face and its funny voice and its fingers—stroking her; and if she didn't push it away, she'd sit and take no notice of it. But it went on.

"I've seen that; and I've seen Rhoda kiss it and give it things when its mother wasn't looking. Rhoda was always good to it. But it would go from Rhoda to its mother any day.

"That was when it was little. She'd suckled it, you see, before she took a grudge against it.

"At last, she took to locking her door against it. Once Rhoda found it beating on the door and crying the house down, and she took it into her own bed.

"Rhoda slept in the servant's room, the room you have now.

"All this came out at the inquest, mind you, when Rhoda gave evidence. Lots of things came out. It seems that when Falshaw was annoyed with his wife or she with Falshaw, she vented her annoyance on the child. She found out that was the way to hurt him. For instance,

Falshaw had dug a little garden for it at the bottom of the orchard. And it made the child happy. She used to go running backwards and forwards from the stone tank to the garden, watering it from the little cup that Rhoda gave her. Rhoda and Falshaw used to play with her there.

"One day Mrs. Falshaw found them at it. And she took the cup from the child and broke it to pieces in a fury, and stamped on the garden till she'd destroyed it. Just because Falshaw made it. Rhoda took the child into the house so that it mightn't see what its mother was doing. She got that in at the inquest too. But she shielded Falshaw so well, and made the case so black against his wife, that it was considered to damage her evidence.

"And here's where you come in. When the child couldn't get into its mother's room it used to go across to Rhoda's, and creep into her bed and cuddle up to her for warmth. It was always cold. It fretted, you see, and though it was well fed its food didn't do it any good. I was always being called in. Once I spoke my mind to Sarah Falshaw, and she told me I didn't know what I was talking about.

"Then, one night, it went into Rhoda's room and found Falshaw there.

"And I'm inclined to think, Garvin, that you saw what it saw. For Falshaw turned round and cursed it. Heaven knows how much it understood. Falshaw may have frightened it. Anyhow it had some kind of fit—the first, I believe, it ever did have.

"After that it was afraid of Falshaw and of Rhoda, though it had been very fond of both of them. Oddly enough, it never was afraid of its mother. Account for *that* if you can."

"What happened," said Garvin, who didn't attempt to account for it, "when Effy died?"

"Falshaw sent Rhoda away, wouldn't have anything more to do with her. His wife blamed them both for the child's death, and Falshaw blamed himself. It sobered him. He's been a good husband to that woman ever since.

"It's queer, Garvin—but in one way it hasn't changed him. He still reckons on the child, the child that Mrs. Falshaw insists will be born dead. It may be. But it's far more probable——"

"What is?"

"That Sarah Falshaw will go off her head. That," said Mackinnon, "is what *I'm* waiting for."

They were silent a long time till Garvin spoke.

"But, Mackinnon, what do you make of it? Of my seeing these

things? It's a series of hallucinations, if you like. But a series, and it all tallies. On your own showing it all tallies."

"It does."

"What I can't get at is *why* it tallies—what makes me see?"

Mackinnon brooded, while Garvin excitedly went on.

"Is it, do you suppose, suggestion? Or some influence given off by these people—by their evil consciences?"

"Or," said Mackinnon gravely—"their evil."

11

It was morning. Garvin was sitting in the field under the plum tree, staring at the house in the Bottom, the house that seemed to stand always in the twilight, to gather upon its walls a perpetual dusk.

It knew no sun, only degrees of twilight, dark and clear. Yesterday under a grey sky it had been drenched in gloom. Today, when the south was golden white with the sun, when the hot air quivered like water over the grass tops in the field, the house stood as if withdrawn into its own grey, sub-lucid evening, intolerably secret, intolerably remote.

And now he knew its secret. "Their evil" saturating the very walls, leaking through and penetrating those other walls, the bounds of Garvin's personality, starting in him a whole train of experience not his own.

Their evil. It had been for Mackinnon an immense admission. It went beyond all accepted theories of suggestion; and considering what Mackinnon's information was compared with his, Garvin couldn't see that he could very well have gone further. The doctor had watched the outside of events, whereas he, Garvin, had been taken into the invisible places, into the mystic heart of suffering. He knew the un-named, unnameable secret of pity and fear.

These things had become the substance of his innermost self.

His knowledge, overlaid by his own adult experience, had been a little tangled and obscure; Mackinnon's revelations had served to make it orderly, clear, complete. From that tale, half savage, half sordid, from that tragedy of the Falshaws, from that confusion of sombre lusts, and unclean, carnal miseries, there emerged the figure of the child Effy, tender, luminous, spiritual, unspeakably lovable and pure.

He knew now what had happened to him. He had been made the vehicle of that spirit; he had been possessed, divinely coerced by Effy. What he had seen he had seen with Effy's eyes, with Effy's awful in-nocence and terror. He had slipped the intangible bonds, to become one (Heaven knew how) with that slender, fragile being, broken by the invasion of a knowledge out of all proportion to its understanding. For Effy's vision of evil had been thus immense and horrible because it had been so obscure, so unintelligible. He could not doubt that he had shared to some extent the child's malady.

But all that had been only for a moment. What really possessed him and remained with him was Effy's passion. Effy's passion (for the mother who had not loved her) was *the* supernatural thing, the possessing, pursuing, unappeasably crying thing that haunted the Falshaws' house. Effy's passion was indestructible. It was set free of time and of mortality. He could not detach Effy from her passion and think of her as in a place apart. Where it was, there, she was also.

As far as Garvin could make out from his experience, the place of the blessed or of the unblessed was not by any means a place apart. There were no bounds and partitions between flesh and spirit, the visible and invisible. He had seen Effy's spirit as flesh.

He asked himself why he had seen it? Why he and not any of the Falshaws of whose flesh she was? Falshaw and Onny had given him a hint. He saw Effy because he was not afraid to see her. Fear was the great blinder and divider. Falshaw could see that.

But hadn't Falshaw, in his moment of inspiration, seen further? Wasn't it Effy's pity that had spared them? She hadn't hurt them—she had never hurt anyone in her life. She hadn't pressed them hard.

Under Effy's pressure, her continual pursuing of him, Garvin's "Why?" had come to mean "For what reason? To what end?"

Mackinnon's story had enlightened him. He was the intercessor between Effy's passion and the Falshaws' fear.

Effy's suffering had endured with her indestructible, unappeasable passion. It was through him, Garvin, that her passion clamoured for satisfaction and her suffering for rest.

She had come back (so he made it out) to recover the love that had been withheld from her. She pursued them all; but if her father and Onny were afraid of her, her mother was mortally afraid. And it was her mother that she wanted to get at. She could only get at her mother through Garvin who had no fear.

It was clear to Garvin that Mrs. Falshaw divined what purpose he had been put to. Her fear divined it. And how, he now asked himself, was he, the intercessor, going to break down her fear? Plainly she, like her husband, was relying on Effy's pity to protect her from the vision of Effy. It was a sort of moral support to her; and morally the woman was already so shattered and undermined that to break any prop might bring down the whole structure. Mackinnon had warned him of that. And there was her state to be considered. He had been at Falshaw's now for nearly a month. It wanted but seven weeks of her time. But it was borne in upon Garvin that if he waited till *afterwards* it would be too late—for Effy.

If he was responsible for Mrs. Falshaw, how about his responsibility to Effy? That—seeing the incredible relation in which he stood to her—was unmistakable; it was supreme. And couldn't he, who knew her, rely upon Effy too?

He watched his opportunity for three days. Then, on the evening of the third day, the last of August, the thing was taken out of his hands. Mrs. Falshaw sent for him of her own accord.

She was sitting in her chair in the kitchen and excused herself from rising as he entered. There was nothing unusual in her appearance—nothing, as far as he could see, premonitory. What he did notice was the unabated fear in her eyes as she fixed them on him. She was holding something hidden in her lap.

A chair had been placed for Garvin close beside her.

"Mr. Garvin," she said, "d'ye knaw it'll be a month tomorrow you've been here? I didn't look for ya to stop soa long."

"Why shouldn't I? You've been very good to me."

"Good to ya? Who wouldn' be good to ya? You're a good man, Mr. Garvin, else you'd a been afeard to stop. You'd 'ave tuk and roon like the rest of 'em."

She brooded. Garvin sought for words to break the intolerable silence, and found none.

"Ah can't blaame 'em. Ah'm afeard myself."

"There's no need. It's not a thing to be afraid of. It's a thing to pity, Mrs. Falshaw—and to love. Such a little thing."

She looked at him. Her obscure soul was at his feet. Up till now she had not known the extent and substance of his knowledge; but now she knew. It was not only that she respected him as one who had seen the thing she feared and had not feared it. She yearned to him; she longed for touch with him, as if through him she reached, unterrified, the divine, disastrous vision.

"It's true what they saay?" she said. "You've heard it?"

"I've seen it."

"Tell me what you've seen?" she whispered.

He told her in a few words. He saw her body stiffen as she braced

239

herself to hear him. She heard him in silence until he began witness-
ing to Effy's form, her face, her features; then she gave a low moan of
assent. "Thot's her. Thot's Affy."

She now uncovered the thing she had held hidden in her lap. "Was
it like thot?" she said. "Would you knaw 'er from thot picture?" She
gave it him. It was a photograph of a much younger child than Effy
as he had seen her.

He hesitated. "Yes. Just. She's a little older than this and thinner—
ever so much thinner."

"Thot's Affy at three year old. She was seven when she died. She'd
be ten year old today. Today's 'er birthday."

Garvin got on with his tale as far as the child's coming to his bed.
He told how he had received the little thing and had warmed it at his
side. Hitherto Mrs. Falshaw had sat rigid and constrained, as if she held
herself back from realisation of the thing she feared; but at that touch
she trembled and broke down.

"You let 'er stay?" she cried. "You didn't send 'er away? You let little Affy stay with you?"

She drew back again and paused.

"She comes to you in 'er little night-shift?"

"Yes."

He wondered why she should ask him that and in that accent of
fear made vehement.

"Thot's how ah'm *afeard* of seeing 'er."

She leaned forward to him.

"There's times, Mr. Garvin, when ah'm scairt for ma life o' seeing
'er, anyway. And when the fear taks hold o' me, it strikes through, as if
it wud kill the child. And so 'twill, so 't wull. 'Tisn' likely as ah should
bear a living child. Ah'm not fit to 'ave un."

"Don't think of it," said Garvin.

"Thinking doan't mak' no difference. I doan't care," she cried savagely, "if 'tis killed."

"Don't say that, Mrs. Falshaw. Think of your husband."

That was not judicious of Garvin, as he saw. It stirred Mrs. Falshaw's
devil from its sleep.

"Falshaw!" She spat his name out. "'E thinks child-bearing's the
only cure for all a woman's suffering."

"He has suffered, too," said Garvin.

She softened. "'E's sot on it," she said. "'E saays if there's a child
about the plaace, there'll be an end of the trooble. But I tall 'im if

240

Affy's here, and she knaws, and she sees me takken oop with another child, 'twill be worse trooble for 'er then than 'tis now."

"You know what her trouble was and is."

She said nothing.

"And you know that at this moment, in this room, there's nothing between you and Effy but your fear."

"My little Affy! 'Tis more than that. If ah weren't afeard ah should see 'er, ah knaw. But if ah were a good woman ah shouldn't be afeard."

As she said it Garvin felt a light breath on the back of his neck. He turned and saw the child standing behind his chair. It slid past his shoulder and he saw it now in the open space between him and the hearth-stone, facing Mrs. Falshaw. It advanced, solicitous, adventurous. It put out its hand and, with a touch that must have fallen light as thistle-down, it stroked its mother's face.

Mrs. Falshaw shrank slightly and put up her hands to ward it off, and the child slid back again. Garvin cried out. "Don't send her away—don't, for God's sake, send her away."

Mrs. Falshaw and Effy seemed both unconscious of this cry.

He saw the child approach again fearlessly. It smiled, as with an unearthly pity and comprehension (he could not tell whether Effy had learnt this sad wisdom on earth, or in the place of the blessed). The look was superhuman. Urged by the persistence of its passion, the child hovered for a moment, divinely coercing, divinely caressing; its touch fell now on its mother's hair, now on her cheek, now on her lips, and lingered there.

And then the woman writhed and flung herself backwards in her chair away from it. Her face was convulsed with a hideous agony of fear. Then, even to Garvin's sight, Effy vanished.

That night Mrs. Falshaw was delivered of a dead child.

12

That was at midnight.

An hour before, Garvin had been roused out of his bed by Falshaw knocking at his door. He flung on his clothes and went to fetch Mackinnon.

The doctor was up till dawn with Mrs. Falshaw. When he looked in again at noon of the next day, he found the woman doing well. Her body, he said, was as strong as any horse.

He took Garvin away with him and put him up at his own house. It was better both for him and the Falshaws that he should be out of

241

the way. Garvin was worrying. He held himself responsible for the event. Having been assured four times that Mrs. Falshaw's body was out of danger, he insisted on his fear as to her mind. Mackinnon had said himself that she would go off her head. Did Mackinnon think now that that was at all likely?

The doctor was cautious. He wouldn't swear to Mrs. Falshaw's mind. It might be better, or it might be worse. So far there had been no disturbing symptoms. She had behaved just like any other woman. She had asked for the dead baby, and Falshaw had fetched it and put it in her arms. Mackinnon had left her looking at it. There was no distress. On the contrary, she was placid and curiously appeased. The mere act of child-bearing, Mackinnon declared, was sometimes enough to set a woman straight who had been queer before it. And Mrs. Falshaw had been decidedly queer.

Mackinnon was now steeped in the physical aspects of the case; and when Garvin dwelt morbidly on his own possible share in it, he became almost grossly derisive and refused to listen to any other view. He was fantastically fertile in suggesting things that Garvin might just as well suppose. But when Garvin began to tell him about the latest appearance of the child, he was angry and got up and left him. There was a real child in the village, he said, whom he had to attend to.

That was about nine o'clock in the evening. Garvin had settled himself comfortably in Mackinnon's study with a book, when he was told that Mr. Falshaw was outside and wanted to see him. It wasn't the doctor, it was Mr. Garvin, the maid was sure of it, that he had said he must see.

Garvin went to Falshaw. He was standing in the door of the doctor's house. The lamplight on his face showed it fallen and undone. He held, half-hidden under his arm, an oblong thing covered with a black cloth.

His wife, he said, wanted to see Garvin. She was in an awful way. They could do nothing with her. She kept on calling for Mr. Garvin. They couldn't get the child away from her to bury it (he glanced at the thing he held under his arm).

Garvin left a message for Mackinnon and went out with Falshaw.

The short cut from the village was a mile and a half by the lane through the Bottom. As they trudged through the dark, Falshaw, between fits of silence, took up his tale. He'd been up to the village to fetch the coffin. The child was to be buried in the morning soon after daybreak. And the trouble was that its mother wouldn't hear of the burying. She'd got the child in the bed with her and she wouldn't let it go. They'd taken it from her when she was asleep, and laid it on the cot in the back room, and the nurse, she'd dressed it pretty. They were at their supper, and the nurse was out of the wife's room but five minutes when Sarah she'd up and she'd got, somehow stealthy, into the back room and taken the child. And she turned mad-like when they tried to take it from her.

"An' what she saays is, Mr. Garvin, that you knaw all about it."

The high village road dropped to the lane. A mile off a solitary light shone in the Bottom. Coming from the village, they approached the house from the back, and Garvin saw that the light came from the long garret, Effy's garret, where the dead child had been laid.

Falshaw put the coffin in there and took Garvin to his wife's room. Mrs. Falshaw lay in a big bed facing the door. A candle burned on the table beside her. A nurse sat at the head of the bed and Onny at the foot. Mrs. Falshaw lay slant-wise on her left side with her back turned to them. The candle-light fell full on her and left the watchers in shadow.

Falshaw took Garvin by the arm and led him to the bedside. They stood there without speaking, made dumb by what they saw.

The bedclothes were turned back a little on this side, and in the uncovered space the dead child, wrapped in a flannel, lay cradled in its mother's left arm. With her left hand she held it tight against her side, with her right she supported her own sagging breast and pressed the nipple to its shut mouth.

Her face, thinned and smoothed, refined beyond Garvin's recognition, brooded over the dead face, in the stillness, the stupefaction, of desire accomplished.

"It's Affy. It's little Affy," she said. "She's afeard to suck."

"Thot's how she keeps on," said Falshaw.

"She's afeard o' me. She's afeard of her mother. You speak to 'er, Mr. Garvin, and tell her not to be afeard."

Garvin bent over the body, and she whispered fiercely, "You tell 'em it's little Affy, sir."

"Let me look," said Garvin.

Mrs. Falshaw closed her eyes. As Garvin laid his hand on the dead child, she drew back a little. Her breast dropped from its dead lips.

"Now," he heard Falshaw muttering at his elbow. And some innermost voice in him replied, "Not yet."

"There's Affy now. Standing by the doorway."

Garvin saw her.

It was Onny who had spoken.

She rose, fascinated; and Falshaw turned. They stood motionless, gazing at Effy as she came. Their lips were parted slightly. It was evident that they felt no fear. They were charmed, rather, as at the approach of some wonderful, shining thing. (The nurse sat on, stolidly unconscious.)

"She's gone," said Onny.

She had passed out of their momentary vision. Her business was not with them.

She came—Garvin saw her—no longer solicitous, adventurous, but with a soft and terrible swiftness, an irresistible urgency.

As Garvin stooped suddenly and lifted the dead child from the bed, he saw Effy slide through his hands into its place. In Mrs. Falshaw's eyes there was neither fear nor any discernment of the substitution; yet she saw as he saw. She saw with sanity. Her arms pressed the impalpable creature, as it were flesh to flesh; and Garvin knew that Effy's passion was appeased.

EPILOGUE

A year later Garvin was on Dartmoor, working up Stone Circles for the County History. A letter from Mackinnon reached him there. It came as an answer to his wonder.

"There's a man in your trade living at Falshaw's. He doesn't see or hear things; and he's there for nerves too. They tell me nothing *has* been seen or heard since you left.

"Mrs. Falshaw often talks about you. I saw her the other day, and she desired, almost with tears, to be remembered to you. The point she insists on is that you are a good man. I'm inclined to think, Garvin, that you knew more about that woman than I ever did. She is, I ought to tell you, absolutely sane—has been ever since that night.

"There's a little thing that may interest you. In Mrs. Falshaw's room—you remember it?—they've got a picture, an enlarged photograph of the child Effy, framed and hung on the wall. Under it there's a shelf with her things—a cup she used to drink out of—some tin animals—a doll. They suggest votive offerings on an altar of the dead. What does it mean? Just remembrance? Or—some idea of propitiation?

"You ought to know."

He did.

The Villa Désirée

1

He had arranged it all for her. She was to stay a week in Cannes with her aunt, and then to go on to Roquebrune by herself, and he was to follow her there. She, Mildred Eve, supposed he could follow her anywhere, since they were engaged now.

There had been difficulties, but Louis Carson had got over all of them by lending her the Villa Désirée. She would be all right there, he said. The caretakers, Narcisse and Armandine, would look after her; Armandine was an excellent cook; and she wouldn't be five hundred yards from her friends, the Derings. It was so like him to think of it, to plan it all out for her. And when he came down? Oh, when he came down he would go to the Cap Martin Hotel, of course.

He understood everything without any tiresome explaining. She couldn't afford the hotels at Cap Martin and Monte Carlo; and though the Derings had asked her to stay with them, she really couldn't dump herself down on them like that, almost in the middle of their honeymoon.

Their honeymoon—She could have bitten her tongue out for saying it, for not remembering. It was awful of her to go talking to Louis Carson about honeymoons, after the appalling tragedy of *his*.

There were things she hadn't been told, that she hadn't liked to ask: Where it had happened. And how. And how long ago. She only knew it was on his wedding night, that he had gone in to the poor little girl of a bride and found her dead there, in the bed.

They said she had died in a sort of a fit.

You had only to look at him to see that something terrible had happened to him some time. You saw it when his face was doing nothing: a dark, agonised look that made it strange to her while it lasted. It was more than suffering; it was almost as if he could be

245

cruel, only he never was, he never could be. *People* were cruel, if you liked; they said it put them off. Mildred could see what they meant. It might have put *her* off, perhaps, if she hadn't known what he had gone through. But the first time she had met him he had been pointed out to her as the man to whom just that appalling thing had happened. So far from putting her off that was what had drawn her to him from the beginning, made her pity him first, then love him. Their engagement had come quick, in the third week of their acquaintance.

When she asked herself, "After all, what do I know about him," she had her answer, "I know that." She felt that already she had entered into a mystical union with him through compassion. She *liked* the strangeness that kept other people away and left him to her altogether. He was more her own that way.

There was (Mildred Eve didn't deny it) his personal magic, the fascination of his almost abnormal beauty. His black, white and blue. The intensely blue eyes under the straight black bars of the eyebrows, the perfect, pure, white face suddenly masked by the black moustache and small, black, pointed beard. And the rich, vivid smile he had for her, the lighting up of the blue, the flash of white teeth in the black mask.

He had smiled then at her embarrassment as the awful words leaped out at him. He had taken it from her and turned the sharp edge of it.

"It would never do," he had said, "to spoil the *honeymoon*. You'd much better have my villa. Someday, quite soon, it'll be yours, too. You know I like anticipating things."

That was always the excuse he made for his generosities. He had said it again when he engaged her seat in the *train de luxe* from Paris and wouldn't let her pay for it. (She had wanted to travel third class.) He was only anticipating, he said.

He was seeing her off now at the big Gare d'Lyons, standing on the platform with a great sheaf of blush roses in his arms. She, on the high step of the railway carriage, stood above him, swaying in the open doorway. His face was on a level with her feet; they gleamed white through the fine black stockings. Suddenly he thrust his face forwards and kissed her feet. As the train moved, he ran beside it and tossed the roses into her lap.

And she sat in the hurrying train, holding the great sheaf of blush roses in her lap, and smiling at them as she dreamed. She was in the Riviera Express; the Riviera Express. Next week she would be in Roquebrune, at the Villa Désirée. She read the three letters woven into the edges of the grey cloth cushions: *P. L. M.: Paris-Lyons-Mediter-*

ranée—Paris-Lyons-Mediterranée, over and over again. They sang themselves to the rhythm of the wheels; they wove their pattern into her dream. Every now and then, when the other passengers weren't looking, she lifted the roses to her face and kissed them.

She hardly knew how she dragged herself through the long dull week with her aunt at Cannes.

And now it was over and she was by herself at Roquebrune.

The steep narrow lane went past the Derings' house and up the face of the hill. It led up into a little olive wood, and above the wood she saw the garden terraces. The sunlight beat in and out of their golden yellow walls. Tier above tier, the blazing terraces rose, holding up their rows of spindle-stemmed lemon and orange trees. On the topmost terrace the Villa Désirée stood white and hushed between two palms, two tall poles each topped by a head of dark green curving, sharp-pointed blades. A grey scrub of olive-trees straggled up the hill behind it and on each side.

Rolf and Martha Dering waited for her with Narcisse and Armandine on the steps of the verandah.

"Why on earth didn't you come to us?" they said.

"I didn't want to spoil your honeymoon."

"Honeymoon, what rot! We've got over that silliness. Anyhow, it's our third week of it." They were detached and cool in their happiness.

She went in with them, led by Narcisse and Armandine. The caretakers, subservient to Mildred Eve and visibly inimical to the Derings, left them together in the *salon*. It was very bright and French and fragile and worn; all faded grey and old, greenish gilt; the gilt chairs and settees carved like picture frames round the gilded cane. The hot light beat in through the long windows open to the terrace, drawing up a faint powdery smell from the old floor.

Rolf Dering stared at the room, sniffing, with fine nostrils in a sort of bleak disgust.

"You'd much better have come to us," he said.

"Oh, but, it's charming."

"Do you *think* so?" Martha said. She was looking at her intently.

Mildred saw that they expected her to feel something, she wasn't sure what, something that they felt. They were subtle and fastidious.

"It does look a little queer and—unlived in," she said, straining for the precise impression.

"I should say," said Martha, "it had been too much lived in, if you ask me."

247

"Oh, no. That's only dust you smell. I think, perhaps, the windows haven't been open very long."

She resented this criticism of Louis' villa.

Armandine appeared at the doorway. Her little slant, Chinesy eyes were screwed up and smiling. She wanted to know if *Madame* wouldn't like to go up and look at her room.

"We'll all go up and look at it," said Rolf.

They followed Armandine up the steep, slender, curling staircase. A closed door faced them on the landing. Armandine opened it and the hot golden light streamed out to them again.

The room was all golden white; it was like a great white tank filled with water where things shimmered, submerged in the stream; the white-painted chairs and dressing-table, the high white-painted bed, the pink and white striped ottoman at its foot; all vivid and still, yet quivering in the stillness, with the hot throb, throb, of the light.

"*Voilà*, Madame," said Armandine.

They didn't answer. They stood, fixed in the room, held by the stillness, staring, all three of them, at the high white bed that rose up, enormous, with its piled mattresses and pillows, the long white counterpane hanging straight and steep, like a curtain, to the floor.

Rolf turned to Armandine.

"Why have you given *Madame* this room?"

Armandine shrugged her fat shoulders. Her small, Chinesy eyes blinked at him, slanting, inimical.

"*Monsieur's* orders, *Monsieur*. It is the best room in the house. It was *Madame's* room."

"I know. That's *why*——"

"But no, *Monsieur*. Nobody would dislike to sleep in *Madame's* room. The poor little thing, she was so pretty, so sweet, so young, *Monsieur*. Surely *Madame* will not dislike the room."

"Who *was*—Madame?"

"But, *Monsieur's* wife, *Madame*, Madame Carson. Poor *Monsieur*, it was so sad——"

"Rolf," said Mildred, "did he bring her here—on their honeymoon?"

"Yes."

"Yes, *Madame*. She died here. It was so sad——. Is there anything I can do for *Madame?*"

"No, thank you, Armandine."

"Then I will get ready the tea."

She turned again in the doorway, crooning in her thick, Provençal voice. "*Madame* does not dislike her room?"

"No, Armandine. No. It's a beautiful room."

The door closed on Armandine. Martha opened it again to see whether she were listening on the landing. Then she broke out.

"Mildred—you know you loathe it. It's beastly. The whole place is beastly."

"You can't stay in it," said Rolf.

"Why not? Do you mean, because of *Madame?*"

Martha and Rolf were looking at each other, as if they were both asking what they should say. They said nothing.

"Oh, her poor little ghost won't hurt me, if that's what you mean."

"Nonsense," Martha said. "Of course, it isn't."

"What is it, then?"

"It's so beastly lonely, Mildred," said Rolf.

"Not with Narcisse and Armandine."

"Well, I wouldn't sleep a night in the place," Martha said, "if there wasn't any other on the Riviera. I don't like the look of it."

Mildred went to the open lattice, turning her back on the high, rather frightening bed. Down there, below the terraces, she saw the grey flicker of the olive woods and, beyond them, the sea. Martha was wrong. The place was beautiful; it was adorable. She wasn't going to be afraid of poor little *Madame*. Louis had loved her. He loved the place. That was why he had lent it her.

She turned. Rolf had gone down again. She was alone with Martha. Martha was saying something.

"Mildred—where's Mr. Carson?"

"In Paris. Why?"

"I thought he was coming here."

"So he is, later on."

"To the villa?"

"No. Of course not. To Cap Martin." She laughed. "So *that's* what you've been thinking of, is it?"

She could understand her friend's fear of haunted houses, but not these previsions of impropriety.

Martha looked shy and ashamed.

"Yes," she said. "I suppose so."

"How horrid of you. You might have trusted me."

"I do trust you." Martha held her a moment with her clear, loving eyes. "Are you sure you can trust *him?*"

"Trust him? Do *you* trust Rolf?"

"Ah—if it was like that, Mildred——"

"It *is* like that."

"You're really not afraid?"

"What is there to be afraid of? Poor little *Madame?*"

"I didn't mean *Madame.* I meant *Monsieur.*"

"Oh—wait till you've seen him."

"Is he *very* beautiful?"

"Yes. But it isn't *that*, Martha. I can't tell you what it is."

They went downstairs, hand in hand, in the streaming light. Rolf waited for them on the verandah. They were taking Mildred back to dine with them.

"Won't you let me tell Armandine you're stopping the night?" he said.

"No, I won't. I don't want Armandine to think I'm frightened."

She meant she didn't want Louis to think she was frightened. Besides, she was not frightened.

"Well, if you find you don't like it, you must come to us," he said.

And they showed her the little spare room next to theirs, with its camp-bed made up, the bedclothes turned back, all ready for her, any time of the night, in case she changed her mind. The front door was on the latch.

"You've only to open it and creep in here and be safe," Rolf said.

2

Armandine—subservient and no longer inimical, now that the Derings were not there—Armandine had put the candle and matches on the night-table and the bell which, she said, would summon her if *Madame* wanted anything in the night. And she had left her.

As the door closed softly behind Armandine, Mildred drew in her breath with a light gasp. Her face in the looking-glass, between the tall light candles, showed its mouth half open, and she was aware that her heart shook slightly in its beating. She was angry with the face in the glass with its foolish mouth gaping. She said to herself, is it possible I'm frightened? It was not possible. Rolf and Martha had made her walk too fast up the hill, that was all. Her heart always did that when she walked too fast up hill, and she supposed that her mouth always gaped when it did it.

She clenched her teeth and let her heart choke her till it stopped shaking.

She was quiet now. But the test would come when she had blown out the candles and had to cross the room in the dark to the bed.

The flame bent backwards before the light puff, she gave, and righted itself. She blew harder, twice, with a sense of spinning out the time. The flame writhed and went out. She extinguished the other candle at one breath. The red point of the wick pricked the darkness for a second and died. At the far end of the room the high bed glimmered.

She could feel her mouth set in a hard grin of defiance as she went to it, slowly, too proud to be frightened. And then suddenly, half way, she thought about *Madame*.

The awful thing was climbing into that high funereal bed that *Madame* had died in. Your back felt so undefended. But once she was safe between the bedclothes it would be all right. It would be all right so long as she didn't think about *Madame*. Very well, then, she wouldn't think about her. You could frighten yourself into anything by thinking.

Deliberately, by an intense effort of her will, she turned the sad image of *Madame* out of her mind and found herself thinking about Louis Carson.

This was Louis' house, the place he used to come to when he wanted to be happy. She made out that he had sent her there because he wanted to be happy in it again. She was there to drive away the unhappiness, the memory of poor little *Madame*. Or, perhaps, because the place was sacred to him; because they were both so sacred, she and the young dead bride who hadn't been his wife. Perhaps he didn't think about her as dead at all; he didn't want her to be driven away. He had the faithfulness for which death doesn't exist. She wouldn't have loved him if he hadn't been faithful. You could be faithful and yet marry again.

She was convinced that whatever she was there for, it was for some beautiful reason. Anything that Louis did, anything he thought or felt or wanted, would be beautiful. She thought of Louis standing on the platform in the Paris station, his beautiful face looking up at her; its sudden darting forward to kiss her feet. She drifted again into her happy, hypnotising dream and was fast asleep before midnight.

She woke with a sense of intolerable compulsion, as if she were being dragged violently up out of her sleep. The room was grey in the twilight of the unrisen moon.

And she was not alone.

251

She knew that there was something there. Something frightful and obscene. The greyness was frightful and obscene. It shut her in, it was the enclosing shell of the horror.

The thing that had waked her was there with her in the room.

For she knew she was awake. Apart from her supernatural certainty, one physical sense, detached from the horror, was alert. It heard the ticking of the clock on the chimney-piece, the hard, sharp shirring of the palm-leaves outside, as the wind rubbed their knife-blades together. These sounds were witnesses to the dreadful fact that she was awake, and that whatever was going to happen now was real. At the first sight of the greyness she had shut her eyes again, afraid to look into the room, because she was certain that what she would see there was real. But she had no more power over her eyelids than she had had over her sleep. They opened under the same intolerable compulsion. And the supernatural thing forced itself now on her sight.

It stood a little in front of her by the bedside. From the breasts downwards its body was unfinished, rudimentary, not quite born. The grey shell was still pregnant with its loathsome shapelessness. But the face—the face was perfect in absolute horror. And it was Louis Carson's face.

Between the black bars of the eyebrows and the black pointed beard she saw it, drawn back, distorted in an obscene agony, corrupt and malignant. The face and the body, flesh and yet not flesh, they were the essence made manifest of untold, unearthly abominations.

It came on to her, bending over her, peering at her, so close that the piled mattresses now hid the lower half of its body. And the frightful thing about it was that it was blind, parted from all controlling and absolving clarity, flesh and yet not flesh. It looked for her without seeing her; and she knew that unless she could save herself that instant it would find what it looked for. Even now, behind the barrier of the piled-up mattresses, the unfinished form defined and completed itself; it shook with the agitation of its birth.

Her heart staggered and stopped in her breast. Her breast was clamped down on to her backbone. She struggled to keep alive and conscious. If she were to die or faint that appalling presence there would have its way with her. All her will surged up against it. She dragged herself straight up in the bed suddenly and spoke to it.

"Louis! What are you doing there?"

At her cry it went, without moving; sucked, back into the greyness that had borne it.

She thought: "It'll come back. Even if I don't see it, I shall know it's in the room."

She knew what she would do. She would get up and go to the Derings. She longed for the open air, for Rolf and Martha, for the strong earth under her feet.

She lit the candle on the night-table and got up. She still felt that It was there and that standing up on the floor she was more vulnerable, more exposed to it. Her terror was too extreme for her to stay and dress herself. She thrust her bare feet into her shoes; slipped her travelling coat over her nightgown and went downstairs and out through the house door, sliding back the bolts without a sound. She remembered that Rolf had left a lantern for her in the verandah, in case she should want it—as if they had known.

She lit the lantern and made her way down the villa garden, stumbling from terrace to terrace, through the olive wood and the steep lane to the Derings' house. Far down the hill she could see a light in the window of the spare room. The house door was on the latch. She went through and on into the lamp-lit room that waited for her.

She knew again what she would do. She would go away before Louis Carson could come to her. She would go away tomorrow. Rolf and Martha would bring her things down from the villa, he would take her away into Italy in his car. She would get away from Louis Carson for ever. She would get away up through Italy.

3

Rolf had come back from the villa with her things. He had brought her a letter. It had been sent up that morning from Cap Martin.

It was from Louis Carson.

My darling Mildred:
You see I couldn't wait a fortnight without seeing you. I *had* to come. I'm here at the Cap Martin Hotel.
I'll be with you sometime between half-past ten and eleven——

Below, at the bottom of the lane, Rolf's car waited. It was half-past ten. If they went now, they would meet Carson coming up the lane. They must wait till he had passed the house and gone up through the olive wood.

Martha had brought hot coffee and rolls. They sat down at the other side of the table and looked at her with kind, anxious eyes as she turned sideways, watching the lane.

"Rolf," she said suddenly, "do you know anything about Louis Carson?"

She could see them looking at each other.

"Nothing. Only the things the people here say."

"What sort of things?"

"Don't tell her, Rolf."

"Yes. He *must* tell me. I've got to know."

She had no feeling left but horror, horror that nothing could intensify.

"There's not much. Except that he was always having women with him up there. Not particularly nice women. He seems," Rolf said, "to have been rather an appalling beast."

"Must have been," said Martha, "to have brought his poor little wife there, after——"

"Rolf, what did Mrs. Carson die of?"

"Don't ask *me*," he said.

But Martha answered. "She died of fright. She saw something. I told you the place was beastly."

Rolf shrugged his shoulders.

"Why, you said you felt it yourself. We both felt it."

"Because we knew about the beastly things, he did there."

"She didn't know. I tell you, she saw something."

Mildred turned her white face to them.

"I saw it too."

"You?"

"What? What did you see?"

"Him. Louis Carson."

"He must be dead, then, if you saw his ghost."

"The ghosts of poor dead people don't kill you. It was what he *is*. All that beastliness in a face. A face."

She could hear them draw in their breath short and sharp. "Where?"

"There. In that room. Close by the bed. Looking for me. I saw what *she* saw."

She could see them frown now, incredulous, forcing themselves to disbelieve. She could hear them talking, their voices beating off the horror.

"Oh, but she couldn't. He wasn't there."

"He heard her scream first."

"Yes. He was in the other room, you know."

"*It* wasn't. He can't keep it back."

"Keep it back?"

"No. He was waiting to go to her."

Her voice was dull and heavy with realisation. She felt herself struggling, helpless, against their stolidity, their unbelief.

"Look at that," she said. She pushed Carson's letter across to them.

"He was waiting to go to her," she repeated. "And—last night—he was waiting to come to me."

They stared at her, stupefied.

"Oh, can't you *see*?" she cried. "It didn't wait. It got there before him."

LEONAUR

ALSO FROM LEONAUR
AVAILABLE IN SOFTCOVER OR HARDCOVER WITH DUST JACKET

THE COMPLETE FOUR JUST MEN: VOLUME 2 *by Edgar Wallace*—*The Law of the Four Just Men* & *The Three Just Men*—disillusioned with a world where the wicked and the abusers of power perpetually go unpunished, the Just Men set about to rectify matters according to their own standards, and retribution is dispensed on swift and deadly wings.

THE COMPLETE RAFFLES: 1 *by E. W. Hornung*—*The Amateur Cracksman* & *The Black Mask*—By turns urbane gentleman about town and accomplished cricketer, life is just too ordinary for Raffles and that sets him on a series of adventures that have long been treasured as a real antidote to the 'white knights' who are the usual heroes of the crime fiction of this period.

THE COMPLETE RAFFLES: 2 *by E. W. Hornung*—*A Thief in the Night* & *Mr Justice Raffles*—By turns urbane gentleman about town and accomplished cricketer, life is just too ordinary for Raffles and that sets him on a series of adventures that have long been treasured as a real antidote to the 'white knights' who are the usual heroes of the crime fiction of this period.

THE COLLECTED SUPERNATURAL AND WEIRD FICTION OF WILKIE COLLINS: VOLUME 1 *by Wilkie Collins*—Contains one novel 'The Haunted Hotel', one novella 'Mad Monkton', three novelettes 'Mr Percy and the Prophet', 'The Biter Bit' and 'The Dead Alive' and eight short stories to chill the blood.

THE COLLECTED SUPERNATURAL AND WEIRD FICTION OF WILKIE COLLINS: VOLUME 2 *by Wilkie Collins*—Contains one novel 'The Two Destinies', three novellas 'The Frozen deep', 'Sister Rose' and 'The Yellow Mask' and two short stories to chill the blood.

THE COLLECTED SUPERNATURAL AND WEIRD FICTION OF WILKIE COLLINS: VOLUME 3 *by Wilkie Collins*—Contains one novel 'Dead Secret,' two novelettes 'Mrs Zant and the Ghost' and 'The Nun's Story of Gabriel's Marriage' and five short stories to chill the blood.

FUNNY BONES *selected by Dorothy Scarborough*—An Anthology of Humorous Ghost Stories.

MONTEZUMA'S CASTLE AND OTHER WEIRD TALES *by Charles B. Cory*—Cory has written a superb collection of eighteen ghostly and weird stories to chill and thrill the avid enthusiast of supernatural fiction.

SUPERNATURAL BUCHAN *by John Buchan*—Stories of Ancient Spirits, Uncanny Places & Strange Creatures.

LEONAUR

ALSO FROM LEONAUR
AVAILABLE IN SOFTCOVER OR HARDCOVER WITH DUST JACKET

THE FIRST BOOK OF AYESHA *by H. Rider Haggard*—Contains *She & Ayesha: the Return of She.*

THE SECOND BOOK OF AYESHA *by H. Rider Haggard*—Contains *She and Allan & Wisdom's Daughter.*

QUATERMAIN: THE COMPLETE ADVENTURES—1 *by H. Rider Haggard*—Contains *King Solomon's Mines & Allan Quatermain.*

QUATERMAIN: THE COMPLETE ADVENTURES—2 *by H. Rider Haggard*—Contains *Allan's Wife, Maiwa's Revenge & Marie.*

QUATERMAIN: THE COMPLETE ADVENTURES—3 *by H. Rider Haggard*—Contains *Child of Storm & Allan and the Holy Flower.*

QUATERMAIN: THE COMPLETE ADVENTURES—4 *by H. Rider Haggard*—Contains *Finished & The Ivory Child.*

QUATERMAIN: THE COMPLETE ADVENTURES—5 *by H. Rider Haggard*—Contains *The Ancient Allan & She and Allan.*

QUATERMAIN: THE COMPLETE ADVENTURES—6 *by H. Rider Haggard*—Contains *Heu-Heu or, the Monster & The Treasure of the Lake.*

QUATERMAIN: THE COMPLETE ADVENTURES—7 *by H. Rider Haggard*—Contains *Allan and the Ice Gods, Four Short Adventures & Nada the Lily.*

TROS OF SAMOTHRACE 1: WOLVES OF THE TIBER *by Talbot Mundy*—55 B.C.--an adventurer set during the Roman invasion of Britain.

TROS OF SAMOTHRACE 2: DRAGONS OF THE NORTH *by Talbot Mundy*—55 B.C. —Caesar plots, Britons war among themselves and the Vikings are coming.

TROS OF SAMOTHRACE 3: SERPENT OF THE WAVES *by Talbot Mundy*—55 B.C.--Caesar is poised to invade Britain—only a grand strategy can foil him!.

TROS OF SAMOTHRACE 4: CITY OF THE EAGLES *by Talbot Mundy*—54 B.C.—Rome—Tros treads in the streets of his sworn enemies!.

TROS OF SAMOTHRACE 5: CLEOPATRA *by Talbot Mundy*—Tros and the Roman Empire turn to the Egypt of the Pharaohs.

TROS OF SAMOTHRACE 6: THE PURPLE PIRATE *by Talbot Mundy*—The epic saga of the ancient world—Tros of Samothrace—draws to a conclusion in this sixth—and final—volume.